HIS PRECIOUS JEWEL

"Make sure you come back for me, Matt," Jade said softly, reaching up to run her palm across his jawline. "Just make sure you do."

A look of wonder spread across his face. "I'll do that, Jade," he said huskily. His eyes caressed her lips, seeming to trace the contour, and her pulse began to pound with excitement as she wondered how it would feel to have his mouth against hers. A long heart-stopping silence hung between them as he lifted her hand and placed a soft kiss against her palm. Jade felt trembly inside when he looked at her again. "Nothing could keep me from coming back for you, Jade," he said, his voice low and rough. "Nothing."

She shivered despite the heat. She'd never felt this way before. Even now her heart hammered inside her chest as though she'd been running. What was happening to her? she wondered.

Releasing her hand, he stepped away from her. "I'll be back for you, Jade Carrington. Just you be here when I come."

ROMANCE FROM JANELLE TAYLOR

ANYTHING FOR LOVE   (0-8217-4992-7, $5.99)

DESTINY MINE   (0-8217-5185-9, $5.99)

CHASE THE WIND   (0-8217-4740-1, $5.99)

MIDNIGHT SECRETS   (0-8217-5280-4, $5.99)

MOONBEAMS AND MAGIC   (0-8217-0184-4, $5.99)

SWEET SAVAGE HEART   (0-8217-5276-6, $5.99)

JADE

Betty Brooks

Zebra Books
Kensington Publishing Corp.

http://www.zebrabooks.com

ZEBRA BOOKS are published by

Kensington Publishing Corp.
850 Third Avenue
New York, NY 10022

First Printing: May, 1997
10 9 8 7 6 5 4 3 2 1

Printed in the United States of America

Chapter One

Charleston, South Carolina
1763

Sunlight blanketed the cobblestone streets of the city. Only a few people walked the wooden sidewalks, but those were dressed in their finest.

Matthew Hunter felt the stares of the passing people as he and Badger strode toward the docks. He knew his buckskin clothing was out of place, knew he looked like a mountain man come to the big city.

A couple approached, he with a brocaded waistcoat and ruffled shirt peeping from beneath his jacket and she in a blue, form-fitting sacque dress.

"Dammit, Matt!" Badger grumbled as the pair passed by, "you shoulda killed the weasel right where he stood." His leathery skin pulled into a deep frown.

The woman's skin paled and Matthew offered her a smile of apology.

"Calm down, Badger," he warned. When the couple was out of earshot range, he went on. "You know killing him was out of the question, unless I wanted to put my own neck in the hangman's noose. Anyway, LeCroix's just a tool. The one we want is the woman behind him. She's got the brains and the money both. If we stop her, we stop the Frenchman."

The frown on the old-timer's face deepened. "How you plannin' on stoppin' her?"

"By keeping her away from LeCroix," Matt replied, pausing before the raised platform where slaves were bought and sold.

"And just how you gonna do that?" The words were barely out of his mouth before comprehension widened Badger's eyes. "Well, I'll be a ring-tailed cat! If that ain't one of the most stupid ideas you ever had, then I—"

Ignoring his friend's sputtering, Matt swept a look over the dock on their right, noting the many masted wooden sailing ships that were vital to the city of Charleston. Those ships carried the raw riches found in the Colonies to England—copper, iron, coal, cotton, rice and indigo—and brought finished goods in return.

"Dammit, Matt, you ain't payin' a lick of attention to what I'm sayin' here."

"If you can think of a better way to stop LeCroix," Matt said mildly, "then I'm open to suggestions."

His roving gaze turned back to the Market on their left, taking in the crowd that had gathered around the raised platform. Soon the auction would begin and he would be able to set his plans into motion.

"I can't think of a goldarned thing," Badger admitted, "except maybe to kill the both of 'em. And like you done said, we'd get no thanks for doin' the job. Besides that, I ain't never killed a woman before. Reckon the idea of it ain't too appealin'."

Sighing heavily, he said, "Guess your way is the onliest one. But you mark my words, Matt, she's gonna be trouble."

"I'm used to trouble," Matt said shortly.

"Yeah," Badger agreed. "Reckon you are. Well, what're you gonna do with her after you got her?"

Matt smiled a noncommittal smile. "I'll do exactly what I said I would: stop the flow of weapons to the Indians. If I don't, eventually it'll be more than trappers like us who'll suffer the consequences."

"Yeah," Badger said, pulling a plug of tobacco from his pocket and biting off a hefty chaw. After working it around in his mouth, he lodged it in his jaw and said, "Them settlers have been warned often enough about moving west of the Alleghenies. You'd think some of 'em'd have enough sense to stay away."

"A musket loader tends to give a man a false sense of security," Matt said.

The crowd was growing larger. A heavy, overdressed woman jostled Matt's shoulder, glared at him haughtily, then turned to whisper to the man beside her.

Chuckling at the woman's rudeness, Matt told Badger, "If not for the likes of LeCroix, maybe a musket loader would be enough."

"Trouble is," Badger grumbled, "nobody'll believe us when we tell 'em about that double-dealin' Frenchman. He's got 'em all fooled."

Henri LeCroix held an enviable position, married to Scioto's daughter. He could move freely through the entire Wyandotte territory as well as that held by tribes friendly with the Wyandottes.

"I guess it takes one varmint to know another'n." Badger worked up a spit and let it fly toward the ground. A portly man stepped back and eyed him with distaste.

"Have you heard the new commander at Fort Kent is LeCroix's half-brother?" Matt asked.

The old man narrowed his eyes. "No. An' that ain't good news neither. You think he's in on LeCroix's plans?"

"I doubt it," Matt said. "But him bein' Pettigrew's kin certainly makes it easier for LeCroix to come and go as he pleases . . . on both sides of the Alleghenies."

The old man suddenly tensed. "Speak of the goldarned devil . . ."

Matt's silver-gray eyes focused with seeming indifference on the man who had caught his companion's attention. As thick as the crowd had become, it was still easy to spot LeCroix: the Frenchman stood a head taller than most of the other men.

Henri LeCroix's gaze was pinned on a woman with midnight-dark hair hanging down to her waist. She stood slightly apart from the group of indentured slaves who waited to be sold to the highest bidder. She was speaking earnestly to a hefty man beside her.

Matt tensed, guessing her identity at once.

"I'm frightened, Paddy," Jade whispered, moving closer to the one person in the world she could call friend.

From the first day they'd met—shortly after boarding ship—Patrick Fitzhugh had made it his business to look after her.

"Aye, lassie," the pickpocket soothed. "I know the worryin' is fair drivin' you insane, but you have no need o' the worry. Things have a way o' workin' out for wee angels like yourself." He patted her hand. "Dinna let the good folks see you frettin' over what canna be changed, lass. When it comes your time to climb them steps, do it with dignity. You dinna have need for shame, lass, so hold your head up real proud-like. Look over the heads o' them folks an' let 'em know you're somebody. And dinna worry, lass. It'll all work out in the end.''

Don't worry, he'd said, but, how could she *not* worry when she was about to be sold at auction to the highest bidder? Oh, God! What terrible fate awaited her in the next fifteen years?

Trying to control her fear, she pushed back a strand of perspiration-dampened hair. The Market was stifling hot and even the slight breeze brought no relief from the awful heat. "I wish we could stay together, Paddy," she said with quavering voice. "Do you think we could? Perhaps if we spoke to the auctioneer, he would—''

"Nay, lass," Patty said gruffly. "It canna be. The man wouldna listen to the likes of us. Askin' would only cause us trouble in the end.''

A stirring nearby caught her attention and Jade saw the auctioneer mounting the raised block. Despite the intense heat, an icy chill slithered down her spine. She realized the auction was about to begin, and her frightened gaze skittered across the crowd, searching for a kindly face among the men who had gathered to bid for people with no more feeling than if they were bidding on a commodity.

Suddenly, her attention was caught, and held, by a tall man clad in fringed buckskin. His imposing presence seemed to cast everyone around him in shadow. Even from this distance, Jade felt the impact of his almost overwhelming presence.

"Look at that, lass," Paddy muttered. "The tall man . . . the one in buckskins . . . he has the look of a mountain man. And he seems a mite took by you." He gripped her forearm tightly. "Smile at him, lass," Paddy urged. "Do it quick before he looks away.''

"Why?" she whispered, wondering if Paddy had lost his senses.

"Because it's fair certain a mountain man won't be running no fancy houses."

Fear was born anew as Paddy vocalized Jade's deepest anxiety . . . that she would wind up in a whorehouse, prey to the desire of every man who passed through the door. It spread its icy chill throughout her body until even her lips refused to cooperate as she tried to pull them into a smile.

Jade had never before experienced such fright. Not even when the press-gang searching for a crew had attacked her, nor when she'd been tried for killing one of their members as she attempted to save herself from rape, or even when she'd received the sentence of fifteen years as an indentured slave in the Colonies.

"Fitzhugh!" the auctioneer suddenly shouted. "You're first. Get up here and let these folks have a good look at you!"

"Take heart, lass," Paddy whispered swiftly, "and dinna ever lose hope . . . whatever comes to you." His shoulders were bowed as he climbed the steps to the raised auction block with all the vitality of a man climbing the steps to the gallows. But, as he reached the platform, he threw his shoulders back and lifted his head proudly. And if his feet moved a trifle slow as he crossed the platform to stand beside the auctioneer, no one really noticed. No one, that is, except Jade.

"Well, folks," the auctioneer began. "We've got a fine-looking bunch of slaves for the lot of you today. Every one of 'em is strong and healthy. Not one of 'em took ill on the ship. Like this one, for instance." He jabbed his thumb at Fitzhugh. "He's a man still in his prime. A fine, strong one with wide shoulders."

"And a wide stomach, too!" called a loud voice from the crowd. "I'll bet it takes a good bait of meat to feed that one."

"Suck in that stomach, Fitzhugh!" the auctioneer hissed.

Bile welled up in Jade's throat, merging with the fear that was already lodged there as she watched the indignity forced on her friend. Soon, it would be her time. She would stand where Paddy did now and would be compelled to face that same shameful abuse.

"Now, who'll be the first lucky man to bid on him?" the auctioneer asked. "Which one of you wants to start? Do I hear twenty pounds?"

Although there was a slight stirring in the crowd, no voice called out to confirm such a bid.

"Come now, gentlemen," the auctioneer cajoled. "Surely you can see his potential. Surely one of you needs a man such as this."

"Pardonnez-moi, monsieur," a loud voice rang out. "I am in a great hurry. Perhaps you would not mind putting the *jeune fille* on the block first."

"The what?" the auctioneer asked. "Speak English, man. We're on English soil here."

"The young girl," a man near the platform said. "The Frenchie wants the girl put on the auction block." There was no need to specify which girl; Jade was the only one there. All the other women to be auctioned were much older than she.

Jade looked out over the crowd, searching for, and finding, the man who had spoken. He was dressed in brown, his fine clothing giving the appearance of affluence, but his attire did nothing to hide the sharp angles of his face, or the cruelty that lay just below the surface.

"She'll go up next," the auctioneer promised. "Right now there's other business at hand. I have no bid yet for the man. You could speed up the process by placing the first bid.''

"Non!" the Frenchman said harshly. "And it would be in your best interests not to keep me waiting, Monsieur. I am long overdue at the governor's mansion now.''

Whether it was the mention of the governor or whether the auctioneer just had no mind to be delayed by arguing the point, Jade couldn't know. Whatever the reason, he gave Paddy a slight shove, pushing him to the back of the platform. Then he motioned Jade forward.

The time she dreaded had come. Her heart thudded with apprehension as she looked over the crowd of people. The buckskin-clad man was still there, unmoving, stoic. His shoulders were broad, his chest wide, his arms knotted with muscle. The obvious strength of him reached out to her, seeming to offer sanctuary.

Would he buy her? she wondered. Was he even the slightest bit interested in doing so?

With her gaze fastened on him, Jade stretched her lips wide, hoping to form some semblance of a smile. If only she could attract his attention, could make him want to bid on her. Her ploy didn't appear to work, though, for the buckskin-clad man looked away from her, focusing his attention on his companion, a wiry old man who was dressed in the same manner as himself. The tall man's lips moved as though he were speaking to the old man.

Despair clutched at her as the auctioneer snarled, "Get up here, Jade!''

As she climbed the steps to the auction block, she had to force one foot in front of the other. Her hands were trembling when she reached the auctioneer and she clenched them tightly, welcoming the resulting pain as her nails dug into her palms.

"Smile at the crowd or feel the lash of my whip!" the auctioneer snapped, his eyes piercing her with an angry glare. Then, looking out over the throng of people, he began his spiel. "Here she is, folks. Just look at her. Ain't she a jewel? See how long her hair is. Feels like pure silk." He picked up a heavy hank of her hair and allowed it to slide through his fingers. Jade barely controlled a shudder of distaste. "This girl's a beauty right enough," the auctioneer continued. "But that's just a bonus. Her back is strong. She'd have no trouble carrying heavy loads, yet she's young enough to serve a man for years. Now what am I bid for this likely-lookin' wench?"

Although Jade wanted to hang her head in shame, she forced herself to do otherwise, taking Paddy's advice and looking above the crowd, focusing her mind, as well as her gaze, on one of the ships as the auctioneer continued to praise her many virtues.

But suddenly, she could no longer ignore her circumstances, for the auctioneer pulled at the back of her brown sacque dress, flattening it against her breasts and hips. "Look at her, folks," he commanded the crowd. "You won't be seein' the likes of 'er on this platform again." Lowering his voice so it wouldn't carry beyond the auction block, he hissed, "Smile, dammit! Look happy."

Look happy? When she was being offered like a platter of sweetmeats to every man there? Jade decided the auctioneer must be insane.

"Rounded in all the right places," the man continued, pulling the dress tighter against her body. "Not too skinny and not too plump. She'd be a credit to any man's household."

Jade felt a flush of shame creeping up her neck, and wished that her fair skin didn't so readily betray her emotions. She lowered her head for a moment, and her eyes met those of Patrick Fitzhugh. He shook his graying head sorrowfully, reminding her of his last words of advice.

Immediately, she jerked her head up again, glaring resentfully across the crowd of people. Her eyes met those of the tall man in buckskin again and, in desperation, she forced her lips into a wide smile.

The auctioneer, having obviously done everything he could think of to ensure a good sale, said, "Now who'll start the bidding folks? Who'll give me twenty pounds for this comely wench?"

"Here, monsieur," the Frenchman shouted, raising his hand to signal his bid.

"I got twenty pounds, folks," the auctioneer said. "Who'll make it thirty? Thirty is a piddling amount for such a comely-looking wench as this one."

"Thirty pounds!" Another man, dressed in gray and wearing a powdered wig, lifted his hand to the auctioneer.

"Thirty pounds," the auctioneer said triumphantly. "The bid stands at thirty—"

"Thirty-one!" interrupted the Frenchman.

"Thirty-one!" the auctioneer shouted. "The bid stands at thirty-one pounds. How about thirty-five? Anyone out there bid thirty-five pounds?"

"Thirty-two!" the man in gray said.

"Fifty!" shouted the Frenchman.

Apprehension settled over Jade and tension roiled in her stomach, forcing bile into her throat again. The Frenchman was obviously determined to have her, and it seemed likely that he would outbid any others.

"Fifty pounds!" the auctioneer called. "The Frenchie just made a bid of fifty pounds. Anybody want to make it sixty?"

There was no answer. Apparently the man in gray had dropped out of the bidding. It seemed Jade's fate was sealed.

"Sixty once!" the auctioneer shouted. "Sixty twice. Sold to the man in—"

"One hundred pounds!" a voice rang out.

Jade's heart gave a lurch of hope. Who had made the bid? Not the Frenchman, for he wouldn't have raised his own bid. A quick glance at him found him glaring at the tall, buckskin-clad man.

Hope sprang to life within her breast.

"One hundred pounds!" The auctioneer's voice was almost gleeful. "The bid stands at one hundred pounds. Do I hear another bid? Does anyone want to make it one hundred and twenty-five pounds?"

The Frenchman was silent for a long moment, then, when Jade hoped he might have given up, he said, "One hundred twenty-five pounds!"

Her spirits took a downward plunge. The Frenchman seemed determined to have her, whatever it took.

"Two hundred pounds!" the buckskin-clad man responded.

Jade held herself so tightly, her entire body trembled. The bid now stood at two hundred pounds. Was the Frenchman willing to pay more than that for her? His face was tight, his eyes narrowed.

"How about it, Frenchie?" the auctioneer asked. "Any more bids?"

"Je vais finis!" The Frenchman spun on his heels and strode angrily away.

"Two hundred pounds!" the auctioneer shouted in a satisfied voice. "The bid now stands at two hundred pounds. Anybody else wanta make a bid on the wench?" The crowd remained silent, almost hushed, staring at the man who had placed such a bid. "Two hundred once, two hundred twice!" the auctioneer shouted. "Sold to the gentleman in buckskins! Now, if you'll just step around to the clerk, he'll take your money and give you the papers on her.''

Jade saw Paddy moving to the back of the crowd of indentured slaves. The auctioneer's eyes fell on a couple whose hands were clutched together, their heads downcast. "Get on up here," he growled, motioning them forward, already beginning his spiel, rattling on about their merits as household servants.

"That wasna so bad as you thought it would be, was it, lass?" Paddy asked, his fingers winding around Jade's forearm. "That smile of yours musta done it. Dinna you see the way the Frenchman looked before he left? He give your new owner the evil eye."

Your new owner. Jade shrank from the words even as she knew they were true. She was no longer a free woman. But then, she reminded herself, she hadn't been since that fateful night when she'd been forced to take another man's life.

Suddenly, Paddy looked past her, his gaze focusing on a point somewhere behind and above her head.

Spinning on her heels, Jade turned to face the man in buckskin.

"Are you ready to go?" His deep voice and probing gaze combined were enough to send shivers trembling down the length of her spine.

Would it do any good to say no? Jade wondered.

But she wasn't given the chance. Without waiting for an answer, he introduced himself. "I'm Matthew Hunter. The auctioneer said your name was Jewel, but he failed to provide a last name."

"Not Jewel," she said huskily. "My name is Jade. Jade Carrington." She wondered if she should offer her hand, then decided against it.

"Jade?" he questioned brusquely, his gray eyes narrowing sharply. "I thought—" He broke off suddenly, then said, "Never mind. I was obviously mistaken. Where are your things? Your possessions," he explained at her questioning look.

"I have none."

"No clothing?"

"Oh, yes! I have clothes." Of course she had clothing. Everyone had clothing, didn't they? She realized her face must be showing her embarrassment as she hurried to where she'd left the small bundle that contained her one change of clothing. Snatching up her belongings, she turned to face him again. "Here they are," she said.

"That's all you have?"

She could do nothing but nod her head.

"Well, come on then." He curled his fingers around her forearm and urged her through the crowd.

They were joined by an older man whose leathery skin showed the ravages of time and weather, then Jade found herself propelled along at a brisk pace until they'd cleared the crowd milling around the auction block. Only then did Matthew Hunter release her.

Realizing it wasn't likely she'd ever see Paddy again, Jade sent one fleeting look behind her and found him watching from the raised platform.

Swallowing the knot of pain lodged in her throat, she lifted her hand and gave a slight wave, waiting until Paddy returned the gesture. Then, feeling as though she'd lost her last friend—as she most certainly had—Jade faced forward again, hurrying after the man who now owned her.

Despite her abject misery, Jade couldn't help being fascinated by the town of Charleston. She wondered about the people who lived in the tall, thin, delicately tinted houses with high walls and intricate iron gates that allowed glimpses of flower gardens beyond.

She wondered about their destination when they passed an eatery from which came such a tantalizing aroma of roasting coffee and pralines that Jade's mouth began to water. If only she were there under different circumstances, she thought. If only she could enter that place and be seated at one of those little round cloth-covered tables and order whatever she pleased.

But she could not. Nor was she likely to be invited to eat with her owner. Or was it "owners?" They had told her nothing yet. Perhaps both men had bought her.

They passed a mercantile shop, which displayed in its window dresses and fabric and buttons and threads and shoes and lamps and guns and knives, all spread out for the passersby to view.

Jade wished the circumstances had been different. What fun she'd be having at this moment had she not come to this land a bond slave. If that had been so, then she'd not be standing here, gazing longingly at the sea-green dress displayed in the window. Instead, she'd be inside, asking the price and possibly making a purchase. But there was no use dreaming of such things. She *was* a bond slave, would be for fifteen years.

"Jade!"

The voice recalled her to the present and she hurried forward, toward the men who stood waiting impatiently for her to catch up to them.

They passed several more stores, each of them set farther and farther apart. It was then Jade realized they were nearing the edge of town. Why? she wondered. Were they leaving Charleston?

She was worrying that possibility over in her mind when they reached a building that stood apart from the others. Matt pushed open a wide door and motioned her inside.

Her nostrils twitched at the pungent scent of hay and she realized the building was a stable.

She stepped inside and, immediately, hard fingers circled her wrist, jerking her into the shadows.

Chapter Two

"Let her go, LeCroix," Matt commanded quietly.

Fear gripped Jade with its wintry fingers as the man called LeCroix pushed her behind him and said, "Stay there, *ma chérie.*" Then he turned to face Matt Hunter. "Mademoiselle Jewel is mine, *mon ami.* If you value your life, you will leave us alone."

"I am not your friend, LeCroix. Nor will I ever be," Matt Hunter said evenly. "Now stand aside and let us pass."

Jade caught a sudden movement in her peripheral vision and realized in that moment that LeCroix was not alone. She saw Matt's gaze slide past the Frenchman and knew he must be aware others had joined them.

As though they knew the element of surprise was no longer theirs, the two men strode forward, leaving the shadows and taking up positions a step behind LeCroix.

Jade's heart beat rapidly, her pulse thundering in her ears. The fear now slithered down her spine. *God! This can't be happening!* she silently cried.

The Frenchman's face was a dark mask, his cold gaze fixed on the tall, buckskin-clad man who faced him.

"You are outnumbered, Monsieur Hunter!" he snarled, his body bent forward ever so slightly, his very stance posing a threat. "You should not have interfered in my business. But I am a reasonable man. I will allow you to leave without injury. But you must do so now—before I change my mind!"

Would Matt Hunter leave her? Jade wondered, sending a terrified look at him. It was then she saw the glitter in his gray eyes, saw the slight grin that curled the corners of his mouth.

Confusion spread through her, mingling with her fear. Why would Matthew Hunter feel a sense of satisfaction about being waylaid by LeCroix and his henchmen? It didn't make sense. Could she have misread the mountain man?

"You had your chance to buy her, LeCroix," Matt said evenly. "But you backed away from that chance. Why? Was the price too high for your taste? Well, too bad. Now she's mine." His voice dropped an octave. "You lose, LeCroix," he said softly. "Now get the hell out of my way before you get hurt."

Jade could feel the tension in the air. It hung in the heavy silence like an early-morning fog. Surely Matt Hunter didn't intend to take on all three men. He couldn't win against such odds.

Badger! she suddenly remembered. Where was he?

She looked quickly toward the wide door . . . just as the old man stepped through the opening.

Nobody seemed to notice the old-timer join them. Not LeCroix, nor either of his two henchmen. Nor did Matthew Hunter notice, but then, he was concentrating all of his attention on the Frenchman and his companions. Matt gave every appearance of having forgotten Jade's existence, which was hardly surprising considering he'd hardly looked at her since he'd received the papers of ownership.

Why had he bought her? she wondered. Although he appeared ready to fight for possession of her, she sensed she was of little interest to him. Why then had he been willing to pay such a high price for her?

"I intend to have her!" LeCroix's words jerked her thoughts back to the present.

"Then you should have continued to bid on her," Matt said evenly.

"I am not a foolish man, monsieur," LeCroix said. "I realized at once that you were prepared to pay any price to keep me from having her. That is the reason I chose to stop bidding. After all, why should I pay more than is necessary for her." He opened his hand, showing Matt the gold pieces laying on his palm. "There it is, Monsieur Hunter. Two hundred pounds! Every cent you paid for her. Take it and leave us alone."

"Go to hell!" Matt said calmly.

"Do not say you were not warned." LeCroix turned to the man on his left. "Look after Mademoiselle, Toby. Monsieur Hunter is ours, Slade!"

Jade was aware of Badger moving in on LeCroix as Toby reached for her.

Move! Jade silently screamed at her frozen limbs. They did, and she hurled herself toward Matt, sliding quickly behind the solid strength of him, hoping he would stop the man who followed her.

Matt reacted as though she had uttered a cry for help. Swinging out a booted heel, he tripped Toby, sending him sprawling headlong on the hard, straw-littered floor.

Matt smiled then, and it wasn't a nice smile.

The other fellow, Slade, had been slower to attack, but he did so now, moving in on Matt who was broader of shoulders and longer of arm. Matt swung his left hand and hit his opponent hard across the lower face with the back of his clenched fist, a humiliating blow.

Slade staggered and went down, striking the ground with a hard thud that scattered hay dust into the air. His face was red with fury and shame as he lumbered to his feet again, dabbing bright flakes of blood from a split lip. With a rumbling growl, he rounded on Matt again.

Jade watched them intently, completely forgetting the danger Toby presented until she felt hard fingers curling around her wrist. She rounded on him then, struggling to free herself as he dragged her through the wide stable doors.

"No!" she cried, looking back at Matt. But he was too busy to notice her predicament. He dodged a blow from Slade's fist and struck the man several blows with his balled-up fist.

The sound of the blows were followed by grunts of pain.

Oh, God! Toby was intent on dragging her away from the others! "Let me go!" Jade cried, twisting her arm frantically, trying in vain to free herself from Toby's strong grip. "Mr. Hunter! Matt!"

The words had barely been uttered when Matthew dealt his opponent a blow that sent him crashing to the ground. When he spun around and sent a vicious kick upward, his boot connected with Toby's elbow. Howling with pain, the man released Jade to cradle his injured arm.

Matt turned to face LeCroix. "Your henchmen seem to have failed you, monsieur. Now it's just you and me." Matt smiled widely, showing even, white teeth. "You want the girl? Then come and get her."

"*Non, monsieur.* I would not give you the satisfaction," LeCroix sneered.

"I'll have to admit it would be satisfying."

"We will meet again, Monsieur Hunter," LeCroix spat. "Perhaps then, there will be a different ending. Meanwhile, take care of Mademoiselle Jewel. And, see that she is kept safe."

Matthew's smile grew wider. "She'll be as safe with me as she would've been with you," he said softly. "And just as untouched. You can depend on that fact, LeCroix. Take my word for it."

Jade's attention was focused on the two men—Matthew, unperturbed by the fight, and LeCroix, whose face was dark with fury. She was totally unaware of the presence of anyone else until, suddenly, a large hand clamped over her mouth and yanked her off her feet, mashing her against a large male body and pinning her arms against her sides.

Toby!

It *had* to be Toby. Somehow, he had managed to work his way around behind her.

Jade's frightened gaze skittered over the group before her. No. It couldn't be Toby. Nor Slade, either. They were part of the group standing in a circle that was completed by Badger, Matthew, and LeCroix.

All of the men seemed unaware of her plight . . . except for LeCroix, whose dark eyes glittered strangely as he flicked a glance toward her captor before returning his gaze to the large, buckskin-clad man who stood before him.

No! her mind screamed. She couldn't allow herself to be abducted.

"Ummmphh, ummmphh!" Jade tried her best to get Matthew's attention as she was carried toward a nearby building, but LeCroix, seeming to guess her intent, reacted immediately.

"The woman is mine, Hunter!" he shouted, his voice effectively covering the desperate offerings she made. "I will never give her up. And if you continue to stand in my way, then you will come to regret . . ."

Although LeCroix continued to spew out his diatribe in

an extremely loud voice, his words had no meaning for Jade, whose thundering heart pounded so fearfully that it drowned out every other sound around her.

Fighting desperately to free herself, Jade lashed out with her feet and connected with a shin bone. Her tormentor uttered a groan that was quickly stifled.

"Stop fighting if you don't want your pretty neck slit from ear to ear!" Although the threat was made in a low voice, it was no less intimidating.

Immediately, Jade ceased her struggles, allowing herself to go limp, knowing LeCroix's henchman would be slowed down if he were carrying deadweight.

"Hey!" shouted a male voice from somewhere behind them. "What's going on here? What're you doin' to that girl?"

"She's an escaped bond slave," Jade's captor growled.

"That true, girl?" the man asked, striding forward into Jade's line of vision.

She tried to shake her head, to tell him her captor wasn't speaking the truth, but his hand tightened around her mouth, effectively stopping any movement at all. The newcomer, becoming aware of her predicament, demanded that she be allowed to speak.

Reluctantly, her captor released her mouth. "Henri LeCroix's the man you're lookin' for, girl," he whispered hoarsely. "Not Hunter. That's the reason he set this up. Now get rid of this nosy busybody. Tell him you're a bond slave."

Was he crazy? she wondered. What made him think she wanted to be with LeCroix? Jade tried to estimate the strength of the man who confronted them. Even if she could convince him to help her, it was obvious that he would come out the loser if the two men fought.

Although Matthew and Badger were some distance away

from them, she judged them her only hope. She opened her mouth and screamed as loud as she could.

The ear-splitting sound startled both men, and it was a moment before her captor reacted. Then he struck her hard across the face.

The blow sent Jade's senses reeling and she felt herself flying through the air. Her body slammed against the far wall and Jade slid slowly down to the ground.

Darkness swirled around her like a heavy fog, clouding her vision, threatening to overcome her senses, but she fought against it, realizing she dare not succumb. A shout from somewhere nearby penetrated through ears that were still ringing from the vicious blow she had received and she was vaguely aware of boots thudding against the hard ground. She shook her head, trying to clear her vision, to bring it into focus. A heavy face bent toward her and she sensed heavy hands reaching down, intent on capturing her again.

No! God, no!

The sound of heavy boots coming closer brought memory, sharp as a knife and harsh as the snarl of a savage wolf, sweeping over her, and for a moment Jade thought she might faint.

Other boots had sounded that way, pounding against the ground in a place far away. London. The press-gang.

The memory of that time was so powerful, so intense, that her throat tightened with dread and her breath came in harsh rasps. God, no! It was happening all over again.

Summoning every ounce of strength she possessed, she twisted away from her attacker and rolled aside. Then, leaping to her feet, she fled, racing across the ground and into the street beyond, underneath vine-covered archways and past tall, thin houses.

A voice behind her called loudly, but nothing halted her flight. Jade ran around a corner and darted into the street, away from a fear that she found herself unable to control.

Her flight was mindless, panic-stricken, desperate with the need to escape, to find a sanctuary where she could rest and hide. She ran along narrow streets, past carriages, doorways, gaping people. There was nothing she recognized, nothing she was familiar with.

She ran until her legs would no longer carry her, until the fire in her chest threatened to consume her. Then, breathless, pain-wracked, exhausted, she came to a halt beside a brick wall in a corner of a twisted street.

Leaning her head against the cool stonework, Jade dragged deep breaths of air down into her tortured lungs, trying all the while to force rubbery legs to hold her weight while she hung there precariously, against the brick wall.

Time passed. Moments . . . perhaps eons . . . she didn't know. But slowly, her breathing eased and some of her strength began to return.

She lifted her head then, wiping the sweat from her brow, and with a shock that froze her body, became aware of someone watching her. For a second she could do nothing; she closed her eyes, denying the presence of another human being, feeling herself begin to tremble again.

"You have nothing to fear from me," a gruff voice said.

She snapped open her eyes. Matthew Hunter stood before her. She swallowed hard, moving her lips to form a word, but the sound would not come.

Slowly, as though gentling a startled mare, he stepped forward and circled her shoulders with his arms, pulling her against him. Jade was aware of an overpowering sense of relief. Her fear dissolved as though it had never been, because, strangely, she believed him; there was nothing to fear from Matthew Hunter. Somehow, he would protect her from the evils of the world.

No matter that he had only bought her to spite LeCroix,

the man who was obviously his bitter enemy. No. Never mind that.

Even as she told herself it didn't matter, she remembered the way Matthew had looked at Henri LeCroix.

There was hatred and anger between the two men, and strange though it seemed, it had something to do with her.

Chapter Three

Matt told himself he was a fool to comfort the woman who controlled the Frenchman, LeCroix. But he had been swayed by pity when he found her cowering against the wall like a rabbit that had been chased by wolves until it could go no farther.

Like that small creature, Jade quivered with fear, seeming to wait for that final moment when the hunter would leap forward and make its kill.

"There's no need to be afraid," he muttered, stroking her silky hair.

As though responding to his words, her body began to relax ever so slightly and she burrowed closer against him.

God, she looked so innocent, so damn young! How could she possibly be the brains behind LeCroix? he wondered.

But she must be, he reminded himself. She could be no other. Why else would LeCroix want her so badly that he would even try to steal her when his attempts to buy her had proven unsuccessful?

Matt could smell the perfume of her hair, could feel the shape of her breasts through his buckskin shirt.

Damnation! he cursed inwardly, realizing his lower body was reacting to the girl in his arms. He fought for control, silently chastising himself for even harboring such feelings.

The woman is evil! he told himself.

Evil? a silent voice asked. *How can such an innocent be evil?*

But she wasn't innocent, his mind argued silently. She couldn't be an innocent, even though she gave the appearance of one. Matt knew, from the conversation he'd overheard between LeCroix and his henchmen at the tavern, that Jade had been the mistress of the Duke of Wellingford.

Since when did you start believing Henri LeCroix's words, the inner voice demanded. *The man's a proven liar. He rarely speaks the truth.*

He would have had no reason to lie to his own cohorts, Matt's mind argued. *LeCroix had no idea I was listening, so he must have spoken the truth.*

Matt pulled back slightly from the girl and studied her bent head coldly.

Indeed, it was true. The woman did have the look of innocence. Her face was that of a winsome angel. And her hair . . . it was so long, so soft and silky, like a dark velvet sky at midnight. His gaze swept the length of it and he guessed it must be almost three feet long.

Why did she leave it hanging loose? he wondered irritably. It should be confined in some way, then perhaps she wouldn't appear so . . . so . . . angelic. Yes, he decided. There was no other word that described her appearance so well.

Her large eyes were still closed, fringed by long, silky lashes that brushed her unnaturally pale skin.

Suddenly, as he watched, her lashes swept up and she stared at him with those impossibly green eyes.

As her fear slowly receded and her trembling body ceased its quivering, Jade became intent on thanking the man who offered her comfort. Her lips were forming a smile when her eyes met his. Then she sucked in a sharp breath, her smile dying on her lips before it was ever completed.

Why did he stare at her in such a manner? His silver-gray eyes reminded her of ice on a frozen pond. They were so cold . . . so distant . . . so full of dislike.

Jade stepped back awkwardly, putting some distance between herself and the man who looked at her as though she were something that had crept from beneath a rock.

What had happened to the man who had behaved so kindly only moments ago, the man who had held her close and spoke so soothingly to her?

Perhaps he was angry because she had run away from him. After all, he'd paid good money for her. Were she in his place, she most certainly would be angered. In fact, she would probably be furious.

Yes, she silently decided. *That must be the reason behind that look in his eyes.*

She swallowed around the thickness in her throat and said, "Mister Hunter, please allow me to explain my reasons for—"

The sound of booted feet against cobblestones sent a new surge of fear through her and she spun around, her gaze seeking the man who hurried so quickly toward them.

It was Badger.

"Found 'er, did you," he said, his words more a statement than a question. His faded gaze swept over Jade, taking in her disheveled appearance before narrowing on Matthew Hunter again. "What do you think, Matt?" he asked gruffly. "Think we done outstayed our welcome in Charleston?"

Matt's lips quirked into a quick grin. "It looks like we have."

"Reckon so, reckon so."

Jade waited expectantly for one of them to make the first move toward leaving, but, surprisingly, both men remained where they were.

Matt seemed relaxed but alert, his wary gaze searching the area for any sign of trouble, while Badger reached inside a pocket for the chaw of tobacco that seemed necessary to his well-being.

Biting off a sizable hunk, the old man jammed the plug of tobacco in his pocket again. Still, they remained where they were while Badger worked up a good spit, then let it fly.

The tobacco struck the cobblestone sidewalk several feet away, leaving a yellowish-brown stain that slowly spread in a widening circle.

As though they had only been waiting for that moment to leave, the two men turned to retrace their journey without a word to Jade. There was really no need for words, though, since Matt's fingers had snaked around her wrist, capturing her as securely as a rope would have done.

"Reckon that Frenchie is busy tryin' to think up more trouble?" Badger inquired.

"Ambush is more his style," Matt replied shortly. "He'll most likely wait until we leave town before he shows his hand again."

A frown creased Badger's forehead, scoring the grooves deeper there. "Maybe I better forget about trappin' for a while an' ride along with you. No tellin' how many two-legged coyotes LeCroix'll have with him next time the two of you tangle."

"No need." Matt's fingers tightened around Jade's wrist as though he suspected her of trying to break free from his grip.

"Reckon I'll ride along anyhow," Badger said. "At least for today. Chances are he won't wait long to make his move."

"Suit yourself."

"M-Mister H-Hunter," Jade stuttered, her breath coming in rapid gasps as she trotted along beside him, forced to do so by the long strides that carried them along at such a swift pace.

He looked around at her with surprise, as though he had actually forgotten she was there. His eyebrows lifted inquiringly, but his pace never slowed.

"C-could you slow down a bit?" she gasped. "I-I'm having trouble k-keeping up."

"Why didn't you say we were going too fast?" he asked roughly, slowing his pace immediately.

"Guess you didn't give 'er a chance," the old man remarked, his gaze sweeping over Jade momentarily before moving back to his tall friend again. "Sure gonna slow you down, boy, havin' to drag a little bit of thing like her aroun' with you."

"I'll manage," Matt said shortly. "It's not like she's going to have to walk."

The two men fell silent, each seeming totally occupied with his own thoughts as they continued the journey back to the stable.

They passed the eatery again, and, as before, Jade's nose twitched, teased by the tantalizing aroma that permeated the air around the establishment.

They passed the mercantile shop that displayed the sea-green gown with cunning bows, and then the length between the buildings increased and they were approaching the stable again.

Jade felt a curious reluctance to enter the building again, but she had no recourse except to do so, for Matthew Hunter continued to pull her along with him.

They stopped just inside the door, and, as Jade's eyes adjusted to the dim light, she saw an old man, his back bent with years of hard labor, forking hay into the horse stalls.

The old man looked up as they entered. His grip tightened on the pitchfork while the lines in his forehead deepened. "I didn't have no part in what happened here before, Mister Hunter," he said, his voice quavering slightly. "I didn't know what the Frenchie was about or I woulda warned you. He just come in here bold as you please and ordered me to get out. Said I was to leave if I put any value on my life." His voice dropped lower, became sad. "Happens that I do value life. More'n I thought I did. Guess a man's never quite ready to die, no matter how many years he's already lived."

Matt brushed the old man's explanation aside as though it were of no consequence. "No harm done," he said. "I don't hold you responsible for LeCroix's actions."

"I got the horses saddled and waiting," the man said, relief evident in his voice as well as his expression. He seemed to stand a little taller, his back not quite so bent, his shoulders not so weighted. "All three of 'em. Just like you told me. They're right over there." He pointed toward the back of the stables where the shadows were deepest.

Matt narrowed his gaze on the old man, seeming to find some fault with his actions, and Jade felt a quick jab of fear. She probed the shadows where the old man said he'd left the saddled horses. She saw the horses, and she saw something else—the vague outline of a door set into the wall. It was most likely a room used for tack, but she was aware that it could also harbor a man who might intend ambush.

"Matt," she said hesitantly, intent on warning him. "There's a door over there. Do you think—"

"Be quiet!" he commanded, his fingers tightening around her wrist, his gaze never leaving the old man. "Bring the horses over here!"

"Sure thing!" the man said fearfully. "Ain't nothing to cause you alarm, Mister Hunter. They ain't nobody in here but me."

The old man hurried toward the three horses and untied the reins of the nearest one and urged the animal toward Matt, who in turn handed them over to Badger. The man mounted quickly. Matt waited until he held both the other horses' reins in his hand, then motioned for Jade to mount one of the horses. Having had little occasion to ride in the past, and no experience at all in riding a saddle such as the one she was faced with, she found mounting the horse difficult.

On her third clumsy try, Matt snorted with exasperation, circled her waist and lifted her onto the animal.

Jade settled into the saddle and attempted to arrange her skirts in such a way they would cover as much of her limbs as was possible.

"Let's ride," Matt said shortly, having mounted his own steed quickly.

Moments later, the three of them left the town of Charleston behind them.

Henri LeCroix, realizing he'd need reinforcements if he had any hope of gaining his benefactress's release, made the long journey to his trading post. He traveled hard, arriving there after five days of hard riding.

It was late and the moon rode high in the sky, partially covered by dark, heavy, rain-filled clouds that made the night oppressively dark.

Somehow, that state suited the Frenchman, for his mood was as black as the night. How could he have let Hunter, who had been his enemy since they had first chanced to meet over four years ago, get the better of him especially now, when it had been so important to his future?

They would meet again, he told himself, and next time, Hunter would be the loser. And when that day came, Matthew Hunter would pay dearly for that last encounter. He would pay with his life.

Dismounting easily despite the hours he'd been in the saddle, LeCroix looped the reins around the hitching post and mounted the steps. Pushing open the door, he found himself facing the one man who was able to send fear shivering through his body.

Scioto!

As chief of one of the many bands that made up the Wyandotte tribe, Scioto was a powerful man. Not one to be taken lightly. But that was not the reason for LeCroix's fear. No. His fear came from another source. From the night he'd witnessed Scioto's particular brand of justice toward those he considered his enemies. His nostrils twitched and he imagined he could smell burning flesh.

Nervously, LeCroix looked at the woman who stood beside Scioto, and he forced a smile.

"Juaheela," he exclaimed, moving forward to embrace the Indian woman before turning to face her father. "I offer you thanks for bringing my wife to see me, Scioto," he said, framing his words in such a way to remind the chief of their close relationship.

"Why have you not been to our village?" Scioto demanded harshly.

"I was waiting until I had something to bring you," LeCroix said, releasing the Indian woman and giving her father his full attention.

"You promised my people weapons," Scioto said sharply. "Yet you have not brought them. Our tomahawks are no good against the musket loaders of the white-eyes."

"I brought you weapons two moons ago," LeCroix said uneasily, using the Indian way of marking time.

"I could count the numbers you brought on both my hands," the chief said disdainfully. "You promised there would be more."

"There will be. But such arrangements take time, *n'est-ce pas?*" His mind whirled frantically as he tried to think of a way to pacify the chief. He looked at Juaheela, appealing to her for help.

Damn her! he silently cursed. Why did she stand there so silently, her face impassive as though what was occurring had nothing to do with her. She had done little to help him in this situation, had not interceded for him in any way. And after all he'd done for her, too!

Granted, she was a beautiful woman and he'd felt a great desire for her when they'd first met, but he wouldn't have married her if she hadn't been Scioto's daughter. He had done so because of her position in the tribe. He'd believed that position would guarantee him a passport to all the Indian tribes west of the Alleghenies. And it had worked. He could travel anywhere in that region without fear of harm—as long as he remained friendly with Scioto. But, since the first day he'd delivered weapons to his father-in-law, the Indian's demands had grown by leaps and bounds.

According to Scioto, the shipments never contained

enough weapons. And the chief refused to listen to explanations.

Lately his tone had become threatening, and LeCroix's fear of the man had increased. His only hope of salvation was Juaheela. But she rarely intervened between her father and her husband.

A stirring in the darkened shadows made him aware of others in the room. Probably warriors who had accompanied the chief on his mission.

Feeling the danger closing around him, LeCroix searched for an explanation that would satisfy the Wyandotte chief, fearing if he did not repair the damage quickly, Scioto might very well decide to end their association with the business end of a tomahawk.

"The weapons would surely have been in your hands long before now, *mon ami*," he said quickly, "but the woman in England who supplied the weapons has been taken prisoner by the white-eyes."

"The white-eyes know of our plans?" Scioto asked sharply, his stance becoming even more threatening than before.

"Non!" the Frenchman hastened to assure him. "She was imprisoned for another reason. She killed a man in England, and for that she was sentenced to slavery."

"You promised me weapons," Scioto said, obviously not caring about the reason they were not forthcoming. He seemed only to see that a promise had been made and broken. It was up to the Frenchman to keep that promise, regardless of circumstances.

"Oui! And you will have them. You have my word on it. The woman was sold at auction. I have but to steal her away from the man who bought her and we are back in business again."

This time his smile came easier. "Be patient, *mon ami.*

You will have your weapons. And soon, too. I give you my promise on that.''

The Frenchman knew he must do everything possible to keep that promise, for if he did not, even Juaheela would have a hard time sparing him from the torture stake. And even the thought of such an end sent terror streaking through him.

There was no way he would face death in that manner, he grimly told himself.

Non! He would sacrifice anything and anyone to escape that horrible fate.

A full day's ride to the north, Pontiac, chief of the Ottawa tribe, sat alone in his lakeshore wigwam, staring at the flames leaping and dancing in his firepit while his mind tried to deal with the news brought by Running Bear, news that contained a new threat for his People.

Although he had seen fifty summers, he was healthy and vigorous and bore the appearance of a much younger man. He was extremely grateful for that at the moment, because, after much thought, Pontiac had finally decided what must be done.

It would cost many lives, but nevertheless, it must be done. There was no other choice, not if his people wanted to remain free of British rule.

Rising to his feet, he left his wigwam to inform the council of the decision that had been made in Paris, of the terms for a peace agreement between Spain, France, and England. The agreement completely discounted his people and their needs.

"The white-eyes will soon learn of their mistake," Pontiac muttered bitterly. "And they will suffer greatly for it. My People will no longer allow themselves to be ignored, nor will they allow themselves to be pushed off their own land.''

Pontiac quickened his steps, intent on telling others of the new threat looming over them and presenting his solution to the problem.

Chapter Four

Fear held Jade in its grip, tightening her stomach in a coiled knot, as she raced down the cobblestone streets of London. Even as she fled, she had no idea why she ran, only knew she was afraid.

Then, suddenly, she heard it! The loud thudding of booted feet against cobblestones that echoed through the dark night.

She screamed, then screamed again. Not a sound passed her frozen lips, but inside she railed. Not again! Please, God, help me! Don't make me go through it all again!

Thud, thud, thud, sounded the booted feet, nearer this time. Again, she opened her mouth in a silent wail.

But her fate seemed inevitable.

Don't let them catch you. Run, run! *her mind shrieked. Her feet seemed paralyzed, frozen, unable to react to her silent command. Was there to be no escape from her savage destiny?*

Suddenly, she heard a shout. God, no! She had been seen!

Look! *a voice cried.* A woman!

The voice sounded so near, so near! She must flee! God, why wouldn't her legs move?

She threw a hurried look toward the sound of voices, probing the shadowed darkness.

Suddenly, as she had known they would, several men stepped out of a thick fog and stopped beneath a streetlamp. Her breath caught in her throat. There were so many of them, so many.

What could she possibly do against so many? Her legs felt as if they were bound by invisible chains.

She looked down, saw the fog swirling around her, circling her, holding her prisoner until the pressgang reached her.

No!

Her mouth opened and she screamed out her horror, but again, no sound emerged.

Then it was too late. Hands reached out, capturing her in a cruel grip and throwing her to the ground.

Fight them! *her mind ordered.* Save yourself!

Amazing though it seemed, the fog that had bound her limbs slipped away and she fought valiantly, using tooth and nail in every conceivable way, struggling against the soldiers . . . against the king's men, continuing the desperate battle even though she knew her efforts would prove futile.

She realized suddenly she had no recourse. There was nothing left to do except what she had already done so many times before.

Jade felt the slight weight of the soldier's knife pressing against her side, felt his hands grip the fabric of her dress and rip the bodice away. Her mind screeched a denial as her breasts were exposed to his lustful eyes, but she knew how to stop him. Yes, now she knew.

She reached for his knife, her fingers wrapping around it and gripping hard.

No! *her mind screamed again in denial.* Don't do it!

Jade ignored the warning, knowing there was nothing else she could do. She slid the sharp blade from its sheath, and, opening her mouth, she shouted out her fear and rage.

"Noooooooooooo!"

The sound of her own cry awakened Jade and she fought wildly to free herself, not only from her dreams but also from the hands that held her in a fierce grip.

"Let me go!" Her voice was shrill, her eyes wide with terror. "Don't hurt me! Please don't hurt me!"

"Stop it!" a harsh voice commanded. "You're all right, Jade. It was only a dream. Nobody's going to hurt you now!"

The deep voice penetrated her fear and she stopped fighting, trying to focus on the face that appeared to float above her. Matthew Hunter's face. His expression was grim.

"The soldiers," she gasped, her heart still jolting with remembered terror. "The soldiers were all around me. I couldn't get away from them. It was all going to happen again. All over again."

"It was only a dream," he repeated. "A nightmare. But you're awake now. There are no soldiers here, Jade. Nobody but us."

"Oh, God, Matt." She leaned into his strength. "It was terrible." Despite her efforts at control, she began to sob bitterly, her breath coming in quick, jerky gasps. "Why can't I forget?" Even now, the ghost of her dream remained. "Why does it keep coming back to me? Must I continue to live that moment over and over again? I just can't stand it! Every time I close my eyes I see the blood! All that blood, pumping around the knifeblade, spilling out across the cobblestones. Oh, God! Will it never end?"

"What's goin' on?" a gruff voice asked from somewhere nearby.

"Jade had a nightmare," Matt told the old-timer who had made his bed beneath the shelter of a willow tree. "Go back to sleep, Badger."

Shifting his attention to Jade again, Matt slid his arms around her shivering body, pulling her close against him.

"There's nothing to worry about now," he soothed gently. "It was only a nightmare. There was never any real danger."

"Yes," she whispered, tucking her head beneath his chin. "It *was* only a nightmare. But it was so real, Matt. So damn real. If only I could forget that time."

"Do you really deserve to forget?" he asked quietly, and something in his voice made her pull away and look up at him.

Although his face was shadowed, she sensed that same quality about him she'd felt once before. Dislike? Or was it really *hatred*. Again, she wondered why he should feel that way about her. Especially when she, herself, felt unaccountably drawn to him.

Vaguely, she was aware of the fresh scent of pine that filled the forest, surrounding them with its pungent perfume. She pressed closer against his strength, and his arms tightened around her slender form, drawing her closer to him. His head lowered slightly until his lips were only inches above her own.

Then, suddenly, with a snort of disgust, he flung her from him and moved away. "Go to sleep," he ordered sharply, stretching himself out on his bedroll. "It'll be light soon and we've got a long journey ahead of us tomorrow." Turning on his back, he dismissed her completely.

Jade lay stiffly on her bedroll, unable to fall asleep again. But it wasn't fear of the nightmare that made her wakeful. Not this time. This time it was Matt.

Why had he bought her? she wondered. He had made it more than obvious during the five days they'd been traveling together that he had no use for her. Unable to find an answer, Jade tried to relax her tense muscles. Only Matt knew the answer to her question, and for some reason, he chose to remain silent on the subject.

* * *

Why had he been so foolish as to buy her? Matt wondered. Surely, if he'd set his mind to it, he could have found another way to stop LeCroix from his nefarious dealings.

Matt had been careful to avoid any kind of conversation with her since they'd began their journey. Indeed, had even tried to ignore her presence. But that had been impossible. Although she had seemed content with the arrangement, he was aware of her at all times.

How could he be otherwise when she was so damn beautiful and the wilderness was conspicuously absent of feminine beauty?

Damn her nightmare! Because of it, Matt had found himself comforting her once more as he'd done in Charleston. But no more, he silently vowed. Whatever nightmares she suffered she had brought on herself. She deserved no consideration from him and she damned well wouldn't receive it, either. With that silent vow locked firmly in his mind, he closed his eyes and courted sleep.

Scioto sat with the other chiefs who had been invited to hear Pontiac speak and listened intently to what the man had to say.

In a compelling voice Pontiac spoke of the English soldiers. "Even now, our fate at their hands has already been decided." He paused, turning his eyes upon the chief who represented the Chippewa tribe, then upon the one who represented the Potawatomi tribe, then meeting Scioto's eyes before moving on to the next chief in the circle until he was sure he had claimed the attention of every chief and warrior who had been sent to represent their tribe at this council.

"Word has arrived that the English will not be leaving our territory, but they will remain on the St. Lawrence and the Great lakes. And ..." he spread both arms wide as though to encompass every man there, "they were given the whole country east of the Mississippi including the Floridas!"

"No," Black Buffalo thundered. "This cannot be! They cannot take our lands from us. We were not meant to live under English rule."

"No!" Pontiac agreed forcefully. "We were *not* meant to live that way." He rose to his fullest height and glared over their heads as though he were seeing into the distance. "The decision was made without our knowledge or consent and we will not honor such an agreement."

"Why were we not consulted?" the man on Scioto's left muttered. "Such a thing is not right."

"No!" thundered Pontiac. "It is not right. But according to the English, we have no rights!"

"It is our land!" shouted Scioto, enraged at the perfidy of the men who had signed such an agreement. "The choice of who lives on it should be ours."

"But we are dependent on the white-eyes for trade goods," said the man on Scioto's right. "A steel ax is much better than one made of stone, and stewing venison in an iron kettle is more sensible than putting it in a wicker basket with heated stones. And what about the white man's weapons? We need rifles. Our bows and arrows leave us at a disadvantage in battle."

"All that is true," Pontiac declared. "But those weapons are harder to get since the proclamation forbidding the sale of rifles to our People. Yet still, we find those who think to profit by providing us with weapons."

"But not in a great enough supply that we might use them to overcome the British," Scioto said. "Even my own supplier—my daughter's husband—has been unable to acquire more weapons for me. How can we overcome the British without the use of their weapons?"

"By sheer numbers," Pontiac replied quietly. "If all the Indian nations rise up against the British and attack the forts before more men can be brought in to protect them, then they can be vanquished."

"If we attack one fort, then troops will be sent in from another," Scioto said.

"Not if all the forts are attacked at one time," Pontiac said.

"All the forts?" muttered a man.

"Is it possible?" asked another.

"How could we do this?" said still another.

"Listen and I will tell you how," Pontiac said, then proceeded to tell them what he had in mind.

Jade awakened slowly, her body still aching with weariness from yesterday's unaccustomed ride. Opening her eyes, she looked up at the canopy of green overhead.

Snap!

The sound jerked her head around and she saw Matt entering the clearing from a path that led to the stream, wiping his hands on a small towel.

When he saw she was awake, he said, "Get a move on, Jade. Time's wasting. We should've already left here."

"I'm sorry I overslept." She pushed herself to her elbows. "I don't want to be a burden to you." She uttered a groan as she struggled to her feet, wondering if her stiff legs would support her. Finding they did, she sent a flickering glance around the clearing. Not noticing Badger, she asked Matt where he had gone.

"He's a trapper, Jade," Matt said. "He's gone home to run his trapline. "We ride alone from here."

She felt a surprising sense of loss when she realized the

old man would not be traveling with them. "Where are we going?"

"Upriver to Fort Pitt."

"Fort Pitt?"

"Yes," he said, "formerly known as Fort Duquesne until the British took it over. It's built on the fork of the Ohio, where the Allegheny and Monongahela rivers meet." He threw her a hard, probing look. "The walls are thick enough to protect its occupants from Indian arrows . . . and musket balls."

"I didn't know the Indians had rifles. I heard it was against the law to sell weapons to them."

"You heard right," he said bitterly. "It's been that way since '59. But it seems some folks are too greedy to abide by that law."

His bitterness silenced her.

Shaking the leaves from her dress, she gathered up the towel Matt had hung across a flowering bush. "Just give me a few minutes to wash." She headed for the willows growing beside the stream, knowing they were thick enough to afford privacy. "I'll be quick as a wink."

"All right," he agreed. "But Jade . . . if you've a mind to run away from me, then you'd best think again. You've got no place to run to out here."

"Why would I want to run away?" she asked, her dark lashes blinking in confusion. "Even in Charleston I had no place to go. I'm a stranger in your country, Matt." When he remained silent, she said, "Matt, would you answer a question for me?"

"Maybe."

"Why did you buy me?"

His look was inscrutable. "To keep LeCroix from getting you."

"Why should you care what happens to me?"

"Not to you, Jade. It's not you I care about." The words

stabbed into her with the sharpness of a knife. "It's all the innocent people you and LeCroix are hurting that concern me."

"I don't understand," she said huskily.

"Oh, come on, Jade! Don't bother to lie to me. I *know* what you and LeCroix have been up to."

"I haven't the slightest idea what you're talking about!" she snapped, anger rising quickly in her, driving away the pain. "If you think I've done something, then for God's sake, tell me what it is."

"Oh, I'll tell you," Matt growled. "It might even surprise you how much I know. You see, I know you've been supplying the money to buy the weapons LeCroix has been selling the indians."

"What? That's ridiculous! I haven't any money to supply anyone for anything!"

"Don't lie to me! I heard the story from LeCroix's own lips!"

"Then he was lying," she said fiercely. "He's a stranger to me. A despicable stranger! I never met him until he accosted us in Charleston."

"I realize that," he admitted. "But you were still supplying him with money you stole from your lover, the duke."

"I never had a lover," she snapped, her eyes flashing out her anger. "Not a duke, nor a prince, nor even a commoner. I don't know where you got such an idea, but you have the wrong woman!"

"Then how did you wind up a bond slave, Jade, and sentenced to fifteen years of slavery? And what about your own nightmares? They give you away? You were terrified last night. You talked about blood, and soldiers. Why? Because you killed the duke."

"I killed a man, yes. But not a duke. The man I killed was a soldier; one of the king's men . . . a man with the press-gang who kept the king's ships supplied with men."

He was silent for a long moment while he considered her words. "I might be inclined to believe you if LeCroix hadn't been so eager to own you. Explain away that, if you can!"

"I can't," she said wearily, tired of trying to defend herself against this man. "Maybe . . . You said LeCroix had never met the woman who was financing him. Perhaps he made the same mistake you did."

His gaze narrowed, traveling her features as he considered her words. "You must be the woman," he said slowly.

"Why must I be?"

"Because you were the only woman on the ship who even remotely resembled the description LeCroix was given."

Her lips thinned. "I can't explain that, Matt. But I am not involved with the Frenchman, nor do I know anything of his schemes. Maybe the woman he was looking for wasn't on that ship. There could've been some delay in sending her here. Whatever the reason, you must believe that I would never do such a thing. I'm here solely because I tried to protect myself from rape. My actions would not have been condemned had my attacker not been one of the king's own men."

He gripped her chin roughly and held her eyes with his probing gaze. "If you are speaking the truth, then the woman who financed LeCroix is still out there somewhere. He might still contact her."

"I am speaking the truth, Matt. I swear on my life. You must believe me."

He was silent for a long moment. Then, "I find myself wanting to believe you, Jade." He frowned suddenly. "I just remembered something. At the tavern, when they spoke of the woman they called her Jewel. Not Jade."

Relief flowed through her. "There you have it then. It was a case of mistaken identity. Pure and simple."

"Not so simple," he denied. "LeCroix made a grave

mistake, and when he realizes it, he'll start looking for his benefactress. And somehow, we must keep him from connecting with her.''

Chapter Five

The sun was peeping over the horizon when Jade mounted the horse she'd been given. She stifled a groan of pain as she settled into the saddle, feeling the leather rub against her sore inner thighs.

How long would it take her flesh to toughen enough to allow her to ride in comfort? she wondered.

As if he sensed her discomfort, Matt frowned at the skirt that was bunched up around her knees, exposing her calves and ankles to his view. "You need riding clothes," he said. "Don't you have something else to wear in that bundle of yours?"

"Nothing of that sort." Her jailers had only allowed her to bring one pitiful dress and a change of underclothing.

"Then we'll have to do something about it soon as we reach the fort."

He seemed distracted, his gaze lingering overlong on her exposed flesh before moving higher to meet her eyes.

A flush of embarrassment crept up her neck to stain her cheeks and she looked quickly away from him.

"Breeches would be better!" he said abruptly. "That is, if you're planning on doing much riding." He mounted his horse with effortless ease.

"How much I ride is for you to say," she said shortly, recalling too clearly her lowly position in life. "I will be in no position to make my own plans for another fifteen years."

He frowned at her. "Fifteen years is a long time to belong to someone else."

"Perhaps," she said. "But the alternative was death by hanging."

"Not much of a choice, was it, Jade?" Was his voice softer, she wondered, or was it only her imagination that made it appear so?

Jade was still wondering when Matt urged his horse forward and her mount jolted along behind.

Faint streaks of pink brightened the crest of the mountain when Scioto and his warriors reached the cabin in the clearing.

The logs still wore their coat of bark, for the man who'd built the cabin only a short time before had been intent on erecting the dwelling as quickly as possible.

The shutters that covered the windows were still fastened. A grave mistake, Scioto thought scornfully, as it allowed the warriors to reach the cabin without its occupants becoming aware of their presence.

The shedding of these white-eyes' blood would be almost too easy, but perhaps it would satisfy his warrior's hot blood for a short time. Perhaps even until the Frenchman could supply them with more weapons.

He crept closer.

* * *

Inside the cabin, Jedediah Collins swallowed the last of his coffee, grunted with satisfaction, and thumped his pewter mug down on the table. "You're a mighty good cook, Sarah, my love." He grinned across his empty plate at the woman he had married only three months ago. "That sow belly was done to a turn, and a man couldn't ask for fluffier biscuits, nor creamier tastin' gravy, neither. The Lord was smilin' down on me when the two of us stood before that preacher."

"Go on with you, Jedediah." Her voice was stern, yet her brown eyes twinkled with humor. "You're just tryin' to butter me up so's I'll use them dried peaches we got saved for winter."

"Now, Sarah," he cajoled. "There ain't nary a need to save them peaches. Before winter sets in we'll have us a bushel of 'em, and you know how my mouth has been waterin' at the thought of peach pie."

"Well, it can just keep on waterin'," she said firmly. "My ma gave me them peaches to use for a special occasion, an' that's what they'll be used for!"

Her lips tilted at the corners and her cheeks had a slight rosy flush when she added in a soft voice, "It was in my mind to use 'em when we celebrate our first wedding anniversary."

He rolled his eyes, enjoying the sight of her, yet pretending exasperation. "You don't expect me to wait a whole year before I get that peach pie, do you? Sarah, that'd be downright cruel!"

Sarah laughed, the sound reminding Jed of the bell chimes on his mother's old clock. He loved the sound of her laughter. It was a cinch Sarah'd had little enough to laugh about in the past.

But that was over now. Her mother, whose failing health

had claimed Sarah's young years, had died last summer after a long, lingering illness. Her death was too much for Sarah's father and he had followed his wife soon after.

Sarah was thirty years old now, not a young woman by any means, but Jedediah thanked the Lord daily for allowing him to find her.

She was strong, his Sarah. And she was healthy. She would be a good helpmate for a farmer such as himself. And she was still young enough to bear children. Thank God for that, for he would need strong sons in the years to come. And Sarah would make a mighty fine mother for them. He'd seen the way she was with other people's children, knew she wanted some of her own, but had thought it would never happen.

But it would. Jed would make certain of that. It was his intention to provide Sarah with every comfort he was capable of giving her. He loved her more than life itself.

Yes, they would have a good life together. He had settled on the best land hereabouts, land with rich soil that would sustain crops, and there were none to challenge his right of ownership.

It was good he had not listened to those who spoke against settling west of the Alleghenies. And there had been many voices warning him of dangers.

But they had been wrong. There had been signs of Indians, but none had yet offered any trouble. And if they did so now, well, he had his trusty musket loader to fend them off. Arrows were no good against his rifle.

He scraped back his chair and straightened himself. "Wish I could stay here and pass the day with you, Sarah," he said regretfully. "But I've already laid about long enough. I need to get the plow moving if I mean to get the seed in the ground on time." He moved over and gave her a swift peck on the cheek, a habit that he had begun

when they were first married and one that he had no
intention of breaking.

She smiled up at him. "Be careful, Jed," she said, words
that were her usual good-bye. "I don't want you getting
in trouble way out there in the fields where I can't hear
if you need me."

"I can take care of myself," he said, warmed by her love.
"Don't work too hard today, Sarah. I don't want you to
be tired when the time comes for bed. I got other things
than sleeping on my mind."

"Jed!" she exclaimed, swatting at him with her dish
towel, pretending indignation where there was none.
"How can you think of such things so early in the
morning?"

"Lordy, woman," he laughed. "Such things are never
far from my thoughts when you're around me."

"Get on with you," she scolded. "Else you'll never get
that plowing done. And Jed," she added, "I'll have hot
water waiting for you. In case you want a bath as soon as
you come in."

His grin stretched across his entire face as he opened
the door, and it was still there when the arrow struck him
in the chest.

"Jed!" Sarah's terrified scream was the last thing he
heard before he fell.

By midmorning, Jade's legs felt raw, and her gown was
perspiration-dampened across her back and under her
arms.

Matt pulled up before a pine thicket where saplings grew
so close together there was no way the horses could pass
through. He scanned the dense forest ahead, as if searching for another route.

Jade brushed a hand across her forehead, wiping away

beads of sweat. "Do you think we could rest for a moment?" she asked, unwilling to complain, yet finding no reason not to ask the question since they were no longer moving.

"Yes, of course," he said. "I should've thought of it myself." He dismounted easily and turned to help her from her mount.

It was a good thing he did, because, once on the ground, her knees refused to lock in place and her legs buckled beneath her weight. His hold tightened immediately and he lowered her to a sitting position on a fallen log.

"Rest a while." He fetched his waterbag from his saddle. "Here."

She accepted the bag and drank deeply from it, then wiped her mouth with the back of her hand. "Thank you. I was really thirsty."

"Why didn't you say so?" he asked, frowning at her.

She shrugged her shoulders. "I didn't want to be a bother."

"You're a strange girl, Jade," he said, squatting back on his heels. "And you present me with a problem."

She said nothing, her throat drying in fear of what he might say.

"What am I going to do with you?"

It was as bad as she thought. "I don't know," she said huskily. "Whatever you do is your decision. You bought me, therefore, you own me."

He was silent for a long, heart-stopping moment, then, "Tell me something about yourself, Jade."

She swallowed deeply. "What do you want to know?"

"Did you leave a family in England?"

"No. I'm completely alone." Realizing her choice of words made it sound as though she were asking for sympathy, she hurried to add, "My parents have been gone for many years. They were both killed in a carriage accident when I was quite young and I was taken in by my godfather who was on in years." Her lips twitched slightly at the thought of Sir Julian. "Papa Julian had a hard time dealing with a young girl. He was a bachelor, you see, and unused to small children." Her thoughts turned inward as she remembered long evenings spent in the sitting room while her godfather read to her from leather-bound books.

"Do you remember your mother and father?" Matt asked softly.

"Oh, yes!" Her eyes flashed with memories. "Father was a sea captain who met my mother in the West Indies."

"That explains your exotic looks," he said.

"I look very much like my mother, except for my eyes. I have my father's green eyes."

Feeling moisture dampen those eyes, Jade quickly lowered her lashes, unwilling for Matt to see how thoughts of her parents affected her. After all, she had accepted their deaths long ago.

But what would have happened, she wondered, if that carriage accident had never occurred. Things would've been so different then. If her parents had remained alive, she wouldn't have been working in the dress shop, wouldn't have been working anywhere, for her father had been a shrewd businessman.

When her father died, there'd been plenty of funds for her support. But Papa Julian had made some bad investments and the funds had disappeared. Not only the funds left by her parents, but the funds from his own accounts. In the end, that was what killed him, the knowledge that he'd lost not only his own fortune, but hers as well.

"What are you thinking about?" Matt asked, jerking her back to the present.

"Nothing important." She met his gaze. "Nothing important at all."

For a moment she thought he might pursue it, but then,

he rose to his feet and looked beyond the pine thicket at the distant mountains that rose high in the sky beyond the forest. "We'll have to backtrack," he said gruffly. "It's a certainty we can't go through this way."

"I'm ready whenever you are," she said, unwilling to cause him further delay.

He offered her the water and, uncertain when they would stop again, she gratefully accepted.

After he'd tilted the container against his own mouth, he attached it to his saddlebag again. Then they mounted the horses and backtracked for about ten minutes until they came to a narrow deer trail that had been worn down by countless hooves. It cut straight up the hillside through choking brush.

Urging his mount up the trail, Matt led the way up the hill, leaving nothing for Jade to do except cling to the saddle as her horse followed along behind.

Upon reaching the top of the hill, Jade pulled her mount up beside Matt's. He had paused there to study the thickly wooded area before them.

"Will we be able to get through?" She couldn't see an opening wide enough to allow the horses to pass.

"The deer trail continues on," Matt replied abruptly, his gaze probing the area before them. "I imagine it leads to water."

"Is something wrong, Matt?"

"Do you smell anything?"

She sniffed the air around them. "There's the scent of roses around us. From that bush, I guess." She nodded toward the wild rosebush. "But there's something else too, isn't there. I'm not sure what it—"

"Smoke," Matt said shortly.

"A campfire?"

"Maybe."

"Are there any settlers around here?" she asked, considering another possibility.

"Yeah. Somewheres about. Jedediah Collins built his cabin in a little valley on this hill. But I'm not sure just where it is."

"Then that's why we're smelling smoke," she said eagerly. "It's coming from their cabin. I don't suppose we could stop there." It was more a statement than a question.

"Yeah," he grunted. "We'll stop there. But we'll go quietly from here on. Just in case."

"In case of what, Matt?"

"In case there's trouble."

He urged his mount onward.

They were headed the right way, she knew, because as they went along, the acrid smell of smoke became even stronger. Even so, she was unprepared for what she saw when she broke from the forest into a small, sun-dappled glade.

Jedediah Collins had found a perfect place to build his cabin . . . at least it had seemed perfect. But something had gone wrong, for the cabin had caught fire. Now it was nothing but rubble. Nothing remained standing except the stone fireplace, and it was partially crumbled from the heat of the destruction.

"Stay close by!" Matt ordered sharply, remaining on his mount as he went closer to investigate.

They were almost upon the woman before they saw her—or what was left of her. She lay on her back, her arms flung wide, her mouth ajar, and one sightless eye staring upward into the blazing afternoon sun. The top of her head was a bloody mess where her scalp had been cut away.

Nausea rushed to Jade's throat. "Oh, God!" she cried, swallowing back the bile. "Who would do such a thing?"

"Indians!" He sent a swift look at her. "Stay beside me, Jade."

"I'm going to be sick."

"For God's sake!" he snapped, sending her a heated glance. "Get hold of yourself and stay on that horse!"

Anger dried up the bile and sent it back where it belonged. It lodged in her stomach and tightened there. Her knuckles whitened as her fingers gripped the reins. But even through her anger, she saw the sense in his words. She must not leave his protection. Not for a moment. Not when the Indians who had done such a horrible thing might still be lurking nearby.

Moments later, Matt found the man. His scalp had been taken in the same manner as the woman's. But he had probably come to an easier end because a single arrow pierced his chest and death would have been instantaneous.

After finding the man, Matt dismounted and dragged the two bodies toward the forest. Then he began to pile brush over them.

"What are you doing?" Jade asked uneasily.

"I'm covering them to hinder the scavengers that'll be after them."

"I'll help you," she said, grasping the saddle horn, intent on dismounting.

"No!" he said shortly, pinning her with his sharp gaze. "Stay on that horse, Jade. Don't even think of getting down."

"Why?"

"You'll have a better chance of getting away if the Indians are still around."

Jade stayed where she was, her gaze flickering uneasily around them, searching for any sign of movement in the shadows, afraid that, at any given moment, Indians would swarm from the forest and overcome them.

When Matt was finished with his grisly chore, he mounted his horse and turned back the way he had come.

"Are we returning to Charleston?" she asked hopefully.

"No. We're going to Fort Sheldon. They need to know about this attack."

"Is it a long way there?"

"Long enough, but barring trouble, we'll be there in three days."

Barring trouble, he'd said. And Jade knew what kind of trouble he was talking about. She sent a prayer winging to the heavens that the trouble he was referring to would not occur.

God! What kind of future lay ahead of her in such a savage environment? She would be doing well if she survived a year in this wilderness. Fifteen of them was unthinkable.

But she had been given no choice in the matter. She was unable to escape this savage destiny.

Chapter Six

They rode hard that day, stopping only when Matt thought it was necessary to rest the horses. Jade sent a hopeful glance toward Matt when the sun began to sink low on the western horizon, but he showed no sign of even slowing down.

Heaving a tired sigh, Jade wiped away the sweat beading her forehead and tightened her grip on the pommel, the memory of the devastation wrought by the murderous Indians keeping her silent. After all, she told herself, what did it matter that she was tired, or that her inner thighs were being rubbed raw by constant friction? She had more to lose than a little hide. Her very life could be at stake.

The sun finally disappeared below the horizon and the shadows deepened until night was upon them. Still they rode on, with nothing but the pale moonlight to light their way, traveling through dense forest that, Jade imagined, hid many dangers—including the savage Indians who had slain Jed Collins and his wife.

Jade swallowed back the bile that rose abruptly at the thought, and she swayed in the saddle. It was at that moment that Matt chanced to look across at her. He pulled up his mount.

"We'll stop here and rest a while," he said gruffly.

"Is it safe?" she asked fearfully, watching him dismount.

"It's safer than riding on when you're in a state of exhaustion," he replied, reaching up to lift her from the horse.

Jade gasped as the raw skin of her left leg scraped across the pommel. She bit her lip to keep from crying out with pain.

"What's wrong?"

"Nothing really," she said quickly. "My skin is a little sore from rubbing against the saddle." Her legs were shaky and her knees almost buckled when Matt released her abruptly.

"We'll have to get you some breeches to wear the first chance we get," he said.

He left her to see to the horses' needs and Jade lay back against the long grass to rest. They had stopped beside a shallow stream and Matt hobbled the horses near enough that they could water whenever they wanted. The long grass growing beside it would provide ample grazing for the night.

Jade's body relaxed slowly as she listened to the frogs croaking along the bank and the chuckling sound the water made as it followed the narrow bed of rocks on its way downstream.

It was such a peaceful sound, she thought, flexing her neck and shoulder muscles. She closed her eyes against the pale moonlight. So relaxing . . .

"Jade!" The voice was commanding, penetrating her sleep, demanding her attention. "Come on, Jade, wake up. We have to leave now!"

Coming fully awake, Jade realized it was Matt who was speaking to her. She uttered a groan and muttered, "Can't we rest here, Matt?"

"We already have." The voice was wry. "In fact, we've rested the whole night."

The whole night! Jade's eyes jerked open and she stared up at Matt, who was watching her with a peculiar intensity.

"Oh, God!" she said, "It doesn't feel like I slept so long, Matt. I thought I'd only just fallen asleep." She pushed aside the blanket covering her and felt the chill of the morning air. She shivered as goosebumps broke out on her flesh. "It's cold this morning."

She looked around, noticing the horses were saddled and waiting. "You've already put your bedroll away," she observed in surprise. "You should've awakened me earlier."

"You needed the sleep," he said, turning away and reaching for the leather bag that contained their meager supplies. "Besides, I didn't use my bedroll."

"You didn't? Matt! You shouldn't have stayed up all night. You needed to rest, too."

"I didn't stay up," he said. "Here." He handed her a piece of dried meat. "Chew on that. It's all the breakfast we have time for."

She took it from him, but instead of eating it, she watched him closely. There was something about what he'd said that gnawed at her mind. "You slept without a blanket?" she asked.

"No. I shared yours."

Her eyes widened slightly and her lips opened to utter protest, then quickly closed again. After all, what good would it do to object now. The thing was already done. Never mind that it wasn't the least bit proper. It had happened, and truth to tell, she hadn't suffered one whit because of it. Anyway, who was to know except the two of them.

"No objections?" he asked softly.

Jade felt the heat rising from her neck to stain her cheeks and cursed inwardly. Why did she have to blush so easily?

"It might make you feel better to know that I didn't plan it that way," he said softly. "But you fell asleep on the ground and I was afraid you would be cold sleeping alone."

"T-that was v-very thoughtful," she stuttered, feeling her blush deepen.

Biting off a large chunk of dried venison, she turned her attention to her meal, hoping he would drop the subject completely. And he did. Moments later, they continued their journey.

They reached Fort Sheldon three days after they'd found the burnt-out cabin and its unfortunate owners. It stood in the middle of a wide clearing, rising high above them— a wooden fortress with fifteen-foot walls that nothing could scale. And planted securely on a platform inside those walls stood a sentry wearing a red coat with gold braid. He watched them approach, his rifle unslung, held at the ready, just in case they proved to be enemies of the Crown.

Then, when they were close enough to hear, he called out, "Who goes there?"

"Matthew Hunter," Matt identified himself. "Put that musketloader away before you shoot yourself with it, Shorty, and open the gates for us."

A loud guffaw sounded, and immediately, the sentry's body assumed a more relaxed position. "Matt, you ornery coyote! I thought them redskins mighta lifted your hair before now, but I see you're still wearing it."

He looked down at the ground on his side of the fence and yelled, "Open the gates, Private! Matthew Hunter's out there!"

A loud grating of wood sliding against wood came from inside, and then the gates swung open to allow them entrance. Matt urged his mount into the fort, and Jade's horse followed suit as it had done from the beginning. They rode across the parade ground and stopped before a low building.

Dismounting, Matt wrapped his reins around the hitching post and reached to help Jade down. When she was standing beside him, he said, "Wait here for me. This won't take long."

She watched him disappear into the building, then turned to survey her surroundings.

Although it was early, several people could be seen exiting and entering the many buildings that were built in the shape of an L along two walls of the fort. The shortest length of the L, where she was standing, had a sign above the door proclaiming it to be the post commander's office. It was through that door Matt had disappeared.

Several businesses made up the longest portion of the L, with the fort laundry being the nearest one to Jade. Although there was no sign above the door to make that clear, the heavyset woman leaving the building carried an armload of freshly laundered sheets.

Jade's gaze wandered past the woman to dwell on the sutler's store, then moved past it, touching on the building beyond. But as quickly as she'd dismissed the sutler's store, her mind demanded that she give the store more attention. Feeling completely puzzled, she looked at it again and saw the portly man just exiting the store. There was something familiar about him, she realized, something—

No! She sucked in a sharp breath. It couldn't be. She must be mistaken. It couldn't be Patrick! Not out here in the middle of nowhere! But even as her mind denied that fact, the man looked her way and stopped as though he'd been struck by lightning.

His mouth moved, but no sound emerged.

God, it was him! Paddy Fitzhugh!

He took a step toward her, then stopped, remaining in disbelief.

"Paddy!" she cried aloud, running toward him.

"Jade?" His voice reached her. "Is that you, lass?"

Her eyes filled with tears of happiness as she flung herself at him and threw her arms around his neck. "I can't believe it, Paddy! I thought I'd never see you again! What are you doing here in this wilderness?"

He hugged her against him. "It's a miracle, lass," he said gruffly. "Who'd ever thought we'd see each other again!" His laugh was shaky and he patted her head awkwardly, then drew back to look at her face.

"What are you doing here?" she asked again.

"There's a simple enough explanation," he replied. "The man who bought me, Caleb Albright, runs the sutler's store here. And let me tell you, lass, it's a cushy job I have. Better'n I ever expected. I thought I'd prob'ly be bought by one of those big landowners around Charleston. Figured I might be set to working in the fields, and if that'd happened, then I don't guess I'd of been long for this world." His expression became solemn. "The good Lord was with me that day at the auction, lass, and he was smilin' down for sure."

"I'm happy for you, Paddy," she said, trying to push the memory of the burnt-out cabin from her mind. But she could not. That memory made her wonder if Paddy had really been so lucky.

He studied her serious expression, then spoke again. "Here I am rattling on about meself without givin' you a chance to get a word in edgewise." When she looked away from him, he cupped her chin and forced her to meet his eyes. "How about you, lassie? That's a real serious look you have on your face. Do you want to tell old Fitzhugh what put it there?''

Did she? Jade wondered. Paddy seemed so happy that she hated to interfere with that happiness. But he had a right to know about the danger he faced. ''We—Matthew Hunter and I—came here for a reason, Paddy. He's with the fort commander now, telling him all about it.''

''And what is Matthew Hunter tellin' Colonel Atchison, lass?''

''Yesterday, we found a burnt-out cabin. Nothing was left standing except the fireplace. And we found the people who had lived there—Jed and Mary Collins. They were dead, killed by the Indians who populate this area.'' The picture in her mind was as clear as the moment she'd first seen them, sprawled in death. ''They'd only been married a short time, Paddy,'' she whispered. ''Just a little while.'' She swallowed around the bile rising in her throat. ''It was awful, just awful.''

He patted her head awkwardly. ''This is a wild, savage land we've been brought to, lassie.''

''Yes,'' she said, her voice still husky with emotion. ''It is that.''

''Does your man think we're in danger here?'' Paddy asked.

Her man. Although Jade knew Paddy had only used the words because he'd forgotten Matt's name, she found herself liking the sound. She considered the relationship they implied. What would it be like to really be Matt Hunter's woman? she wondered.

Realizing Paddy waited for an answer to his question, she said, ''I honestly don't know. But he was in a hurry to get here and warn the fort of the possibility of an Indian uprising.''

''I guess we'll be learnin' soon enough,'' Paddy said thoughtfully. ''If the good Colonel Atchison believes there's danger lurking about, he'll surely send word to the settlers to take refuge inside the fort walls."

She studied the fifteen-foot walls. "It seems safe enough here. The Indians certainly can't climb over the walls."

"That's one consolation, lass. We're well protected here. They won't get into this place." He glanced at the sutler's store, then motioned her toward a bench nearby. "Set yourself down, lass. Nobody's missed me yet, so we might as well talk a while. Do you like your man? Is he good to you? Tell me everything that's been happening since you left the auction last week."

"Last week?" she questioned. "Has it really only been a week, Paddy?"

"Yes, lass," he said gruffly, patting her hand and trying to read her expression. "It really has. But from the sound of it, you've had a lot of hours crammed into those days." His gaze narrowed on her face again. "You haven't told me about your man, lass. What sort of man is he? Is he kind?"

"Kind? I don't know. I guess I hadn't thought of him like that."

"He's not been treating you badly, has he?" The words were spoken hopefully.

"No, not badly." She thought about the way Matt had confronted her when she'd had the nightmare. "I guess you would call him kind, Paddy. At least at times." The memory of the nightmare caused her to shiver slightly. "I had the dream again, Paddy."

The old man patted her hand. "I'm sorry, lass. I hoped that would end when we reached this new land."

"I guess not."

"Do you want to talk about it?"

"I don't know. They're still as bad as they ever were. And they come as often. I think maybe—"

"Jade!" Matt's sharp voice startled her, jerking her head around to find him standing only a few feet away.

"Matt." She stood quickly. "I didn't hear you come out."

"Obviously," he said coldly, eyeing Paddy with obvious dislike.

"This is my friend, Patrick Fitzhugh," she explained quickly. "I met him on the ship while we were crossing. The man who runs the sutler's store bought him at the auction."

She could see the tenseness drain away from Matt's big frame. He extended his hand toward Fitzhugh. "Irish?" he questioned, raising a dark brow.

"Irish and Scot," Fitzhugh corrected. He accepted Matt's hand with a hearty shake.

"Good to meet you," Matt said gruffly.

"Same here," the older man said.

"I'm afraid we have no time to talk right now," Matt said politely. "But I'm sure you'll be able to visit with Jade later on. As for me, I'll be leaving the fort within the hour."

"That soon?" said Jade. "I had hoped we'd have time for a bath first."

"You won't be going with me, Jade," he said abruptly.

"What do you mean?" she asked swiftly. "Why won't I be going?"

Instead of answering her question, he looked at Paddy. "Perhaps you'll have time for Jade occasionally. She'll be staying with the smithy for a while."

"That I will, sir. That I will."

"Come along, Jade," Matt urged, gripping her arm and tugging her with him.

"Where are we going?" she asked. "And what did you mean? Are you really leaving me here?"

"We're going to see a friend of mine," he told her. He left her second question unanswered.

Unable to do otherwise, Jade followed him across the parade ground, where soldiers wearing uniforms of red decorated with gold were assembling. When they reached the board sidewalk again, they were near the weaver's quarters. The door was open there and she could hear the sound of women's voices coming from within. The door next to that was closed and there was no sign to show what the building held.

Jade continued to follow Matt until they reached the last building. It was obviously the blacksmith's shop; she could hear the clang of iron on anvil coming from within.

Matt urged her through the door.

The only occupant was a large, dark-haired man dressed simply in homespun cloth. He wore a vest over his white shirt, and his dark breeches were buttoned at the knee over white stockings that covered his muscular legs. As she watched, he bent over to grasp the foreleg of a brown mare. The horseshoe in his left hand made his intent obvious.

"Silas!" Matt exclaimed. "It's been a coon's age since I saw you. How's Mary Lou and the kids?"

"Matt! You son-of-a-ringtailed-baboon!" The big man strode over to grip Matt's hand enthusiastically. "How in hell are you?" Sending a glance toward Jade, he said, " 'Scuse me, miss, but I ain't seen this ornery so-and-so for nigh on a year now."

"Has it really been that long?" Matt asked.

"Sure as shootin' has," the other replied. "And Mary Lou is gonna whale the tar outta you for keepin' away so long." After another look at Jade, he said, "Don't tell me you went and got hitched up, Matt."

"No such thing," Matt denied quickly. "This is Jade Carrington, Silas. And she's the main reason I stopped in. I need a favor."

"You name it, son."

"I have an errand to run for Colonel Atchison. I don't know how long it'll take me and it wouldn't be a good trip for a woman. I wondered if you could—"

"Say no more," Silas Brown interrupted. "We'd be powerful glad to have her with us. Come up to the house and say hello to Mary Lou."

"Of course. But I can't stay long. My errand is of the utmost urgency. I'll tell you about it later."

They went to the small cabin located nearby. At Silas's shout, a young woman with dark glossy hair peeping from beneath the white lace of her cap hurried from a back room. "Saints alive," she cried. "What's all the—" Spying her husband's companions, she broke off, then, "Matthew Hunter! I can't believe it's you!" She ran across the room to give him a hug. Then, drawing back, she scolded, "Where have you been? Surely not so busy you'd forget old friends?" Her gaze slid past him to Jade. "And who's this?" she demanded, hands on hips. "Matt! Have you gone and got married before I had time to look over the intended bride?"

Jade found herself blushing hotly and wondered why these people were so intent on taking her for Matthew Hunter's wife.

"Now, Mary Lou," Matt said gruffly. "You're jumpin' to the same conclusion Silas did. Can't the two of you think about anything but getting me hitched?"

"Not much else," she admitted with a smile. "So you're not married and I still have a chance to attend your wedding?"

"No, I'm not married, and no, you have no chance to attend my wedding because I fully intend to remain a bachelor the rest of my days."

"Now that we've got that settled to *your* satisfaction," Mary Lou said, turning her attention to Jade, "maybe you'd enlighten me to the identity of the young lady you brought to meet me, if not to get my approval.''

''He needs a safe place for her to stay for a few days,'' Silas said, providing the explanation before Matt could open his mouth. ''So he brought her to us.''

''As you should have,'' Mary Lou said, smiling a welcome at Jade as Matt introduced her.

''I hate to say it, dear,'' the woman told Jade, ''but you look as though Matt's been dragging you through the brush. I expect you could do with a rest.''

Matt laughed. ''You hit the nail on the head, Mary Lou,'' he said. ''She *has* been drug through the brush. Go on along with her, Jade. She'll take good care of you.''

Jade's eyes met his in a long look. Was he leaving without telling her where he was going? His mission must be extremely dangerous, which meant there was a good chance he would never return from it. ''Matt,'' she said, unable to allow the silence to continue, to allow him to leave without some sort of explanation. ''What is happening? What did the colonel—''

''Later,'' he said abruptly. ''Go with Mary Lou and freshen up. I need time to talk with Silas.''

''You won't leave while I'm gone?''

''No.'' His eyes darkened slightly. ''Be assured of that. I won't leave without seeing you again.''

Realizing she must be satisfied with that, Jade followed Mary Lou into a back room.

After Matt had apprised Silas of Jade's situation, he said, ''She'll have to be kept close by, Silas. I know LeCroix well enough to know he hasn't given up yet. Unless he's discovered his mistake. And the only way he could have done that was if he found the woman who's been financing him.''

"You seem mighty certain Jade is telling the truth, Matt," Silas said roughly.

"I'd bet my life on it."

"Well, that's exactly what you're doing. And not just your life. You're gamblin' the lives of the settlers as well."

"I know. I know. But there's something about her, Silas . . . something that tells me she couldn't be involved in anything like that."

"Maybe you just want to believe it," the smithy remarked slowly. "She's a mighty handsome woman, Matt. Has the look of an innocent angel about her."

"Yes," Matt agreed softly. "She does that."

"She couldn't be all that innocent, man. If she was, then she wouldn't be in the position she's in. She wouldn't be a bond slave." The big man held his friend's eyes. "Think on that, Matt. She musta done something bad for the court to have given her that sentence. Did you ask her about that?"

"Yeah, I did."

"And you were satisfied with her answer?"

Matt nodded his head. "She killed a man who was trying to ravish her."

"They don't condemn women for such as that."

"They do if the man you killed happened to be one of the king's men."

Silas expelled a heavy sigh. "Damned if I don't feel like a lousy skunk. Her explanation is a good one. Good enough to be true."

"That's what I thought, too." Matt strode across the room and looked out the window at the soldiers on parade. "How often does LeCroix come here?" he asked.

" 'Bout as often as you do. Haven't seen him for almost a year now. Fact is, he's got no reason to come here. Buys all his goods at Fort Kent. Leastways the goods he don't have sent directly from England."

"He might have a reason to come now, though," Matt said slowly. "Now that Jade is here."

"He don't know she's here, does he?" Silas asked.

"Not yet," Matt admitted. "But he has ways of learning."

"Well, don't worry about it. I'll keep an eye out for trouble. And you do the same, Matt. Watch yourself and leave Jade for me to look after. If LeCroix does come here, he'll have me to answer to. And if that ain't enough, there's plenty more help available from folks who don't particularly see eye to eye with the Frenchie. Don't worry about her none, just watch your own back. You'll be in that wilderness alone, and if you come across LeCroix it's a sure bet he won't be alone, that he'll have some of his sidekicks with him. Might even have some of those Wyandotte bucks as well. It's a cinch you better keep your eyes open." Silas stood. "How are you fixed for supplies?"

"Not too good."

"Mary Lou!" Silas called.

When she stuck her head in the doorway, he said, "Matt needs some supplies put together for . . ." He looked at Matt and asked, "How long, Matt?"

"Maybe a week."

"Pack a week's supply, Mary Lou. And make 'em as light as you can, because he'll be walkin' a good part of the time."

Matt smiled grimly. Silas was right. The quickest way to Fort Lawrence was upriver, and a horse would be more trouble than it was worth through that wilderness.

Mary Lou set to packing the items she thought Matt would need, putting in some extra things just in case it took him longer. When she was finished, she said, "I guess neither of you are gonna tell me what this is all about?"

"You guessed right," her husband said. "Nobody's gonna tell you."

"Hummph!" she said. "Then if you've no further use for me, I'll see if Jade needs help."

When Jade had finished her bath and changed into her only other garment, she joined the men in the other room. She was relieved to see that Matt was still there.

He studied her freshly scrubbed cheeks with dark, glittering eyes. "Why don't you come walk with me." He took her hand in his. "I have something to tell you."

They left the cabin together and found a place under the shade of a tall oak, the only tree growing inside the fort.

"Colonel Atchison needs someone to warn Fort Lawrence of a possible Indian uprising," he said.

"And you volunteered to go? Why, Matt? Why you?" She gestured toward the soldiers on the parade grounds. "There are plenty of others he could send."

"None with my knowledge of the forest."

"I guess nothing I say will change your mind, will it?" Before he could answer, she hurried on, "How long will you be gone?"

"As long as it takes." His fingers tightened around hers. "You'll be safe here."

"But *you* won't be. You could run into the Indians who killed those settlers."

"I can handle myself." He slipped a hand through her hair to the back of her neck, and she shivered beneath his touch. His expression was intense. "Be careful, Jade. There's rumors of a traitor inside the fort. There's a possibility he's linked with LeCroix."

"What if you don't come back?" she whispered around an obstruction in her throat.

Mistaking her words for worry about her own future, he said, "Silas will take care of you. I'm leaving your papers with him. If something unforeseen happens . . . if I don't come back, then he'll give them to you. You'll be a free woman then, and you can do whatever pleases you."

The knowledge that if he didn't return, he would surely be dead gnawed at her. "Take care of yourself, Matt," she said softly.

He nodded abruptly. "I'll do that, Jade," he said. A long silence hung between them, and then he spoke again. "Watch yourself, Jade." His voice was low and rough. "LeCroix might come around."

The thought that LeCroix might still come after her sent a shiver of fear through Jade. Surely though, she chided herself, he had learned of his mistake by now.

As though sensing her reaction, Matt said, "You're well protected here, Jade. Silas and Mary Lou will be watching after you. And there are enough soldiers here to guard the fort. The Indians won't dare attack here." He squeezed her hand gently. "You'll be just fine."

"I know," she said.

Releasing her hand, he stepped away from her. "I'll come back soon as I've warned Fort Lawrence. Then we'll decide what's to be done about you."

She forced a smile. "I'll be here."

She watched him stride toward the gates. And as he passed the sutler's store a man stepped out to watch him leave. Then he turned to look at Jade and she felt the color leave her face.

It was Toby, the man who had helped the Frenchman in Charleston.

Her gaze flickered to Matt who was already through the open gate. Should she call him back, let him know of the other man's presence?

No, she decided. His mission was too important to be

delayed. Her gaze went to Toby again, and when she realized she had his full attention she spun around with fear spreading through her and fled the place, intent on reaching the cabin where Matt had assured her she would be safe until he returned.

Chapter Seven

Tobias Wade made haste to reach Henri LeCroix's trading post to apprise him of the situation. Dark had settled across the land before he finally reached his destination. Entering the trading post, he found LeCroix sitting at a small table, nursing a glass of whiskey.

LeCroix listened in silence to what Toby had to say, then asked, "You are sure of your facts, monsieur?" His voice held a hard edge.

"As sure as I'm standing here," Toby said grimly. "She's there all right. I saw her with my own two eyes. And she saw me. Soon's she did, she took off at a run for the smithy's house. I asked around a bit but nobody knew nothing about her. Most knew Hunter had brought a woman to the fort, but that's about all they knew. Didn't know who she was nor why they were there."

"And what did they find out from you, *mon ami?*" the Frenchman asked.

"Nothing, LeCroix," Toby said hurriedly. "I didn't allow

as I knew anything about neither of 'em. I wouldn't, boss.
I allus said your bus'ness ain't none of mine less'n you
make it so."

"Very good, Monsieur Tobias," the Frenchman said,
giving his grudging approval of Toby's actions. "So long
as you keep that attitude we will do well together." He
looked over at the man behind the bar. "Bring another
glass, monsieur. My friend has worked up a thirst."

He waited until Tobias Wade emptied his glass, then
said, "You will return with me to Fort Sheldon, *mon ami.*
When we arrive, I will find an opportunity to see the girl
alone . . . to speak with her and explain exactly who I am.
If anyone seeks to interrupt our conversation or interfere
in any manner you will intercede."

"How far do you want me to . . . intercede?" Toby asked.

"I leave it to you to do whatever is necessary, Monsieur
Tobias," LeCroix said.

Jade bent over the big, black cast-iron pot and poked
her stick into the boiling water, using it to lift a white shirt
in order to see if the dirt had been boiled out of the fabric.

Although her judgment might be faulty since she was
inexperienced at laundering, Jade thought the garment
appeared reasonably clean. She dropped the shirt into the
bucket left near her and fished out another garment with
her stick.

Slowly, piece by piece, she emptied the boiling pot and
carried the clothing to the two remaining tubs. Dumping
them into one, she washed each piece separately, scrubbing
the fabric against the rub board before placing it into the
rinse tub.

When the last piece was done, she hung the clothing
out on a line strung between two posts. She was hanging

the last piece up to dry when a voice made her aware of another presence. She looked around . . . and stiffened.

It was the Frenchman, Henri LeCroix.

"Bonjour, ma chérie," he said.

"What are you doing here?" she demanded.

"Why else would I come except for you?" he asked. "Did you not expect me, *ma chérie?*"

"No. I did not expect you. Exactly what do you want with me?"

He laughed lightly and moved closer to her. Immediately, she stepped back, moving nearer to the cabin. "Stay away from me," she warned.

"Come, *ma chérie.* What is this little game you play? Surely you know there is no time for such things. We have many things to plan together, my little Jewel."

"I'm nobody's little Jewel. My name is *Jade.* Miss Carrington to you. And I'll thank you to remember that in the future."

He shrugged his shoulders. "As you wish, *mon coeur.*"

"I am not your heart, either," she said fiercely. "Kindly remember *that* in the future." She took another step toward the cabin, but he moved quickly, blocking her way. "Get out of my way right now," she commanded in a low, fierce tone, "else I will have no recourse except to call on Mr. Brown for help in removing you."

He stood where he was, his dark eyes flickering as he watched her. "You puzzle me, mademoiselle," he said slowly. "If I were to believe your words, they would wound me deeply. Surely you are ready to leave this place . . . to get on with our business. Even now, the Indians grow impatient with the delay. We must act quickly and I have already exhausted the funds you advanced. There is need for more now."

"I haven't the faintest notion what you're talking

about," she said stonily. "Now please allow me to pass before I scream my head off."

"*Non!*" he said, his mouth tightening grimly. "There is no need for that, mademoiselle. I will leave you for now. But we will meet again. You can be sure of that. We will most certainly meet again."

Without another word, he turned and stalked away from her. Shivering with fear, Jade hurried inside the cabin to help Mary Lou with the noon meal.

Jade stayed inside the cabin most of the day. It was late that evening when Mary Lou had taken some freshly made lemonade to her husband that Jade heard a knock on the door. Ever aware of the presence of LeCroix, Jade looked out the window and spied a soldier standing there.

Wondering if the man brought news of Matt, Jade opened the door to him. "Yes?"

"Note for you, ma'am." The soldier extended a folded piece of paper.

Jade squinted at the paper in the dwindling light. There were only a few words written there but they were all she needed. "Meet me at the stream near the edge of the forest as soon as you receive this," the paper read. It was signed simply, "Matt."

Why would Matt want her to meet him outside the fort? she wondered. Suddenly, she remembered the words he'd spoken just before he left her. *Be careful, Jade. There's rumors of a traitor inside the fort. There's a possibility he's linked with LeCroix.*

Realizing that she dare not delay, and knowing that she'd need an excuse for leaving the fort, she snatched up a basket and hurried to the gate, requesting permission from the guard to be allowed outside.

"It's getting close to dark, ma'am," he told her. "It ain't safe out there after the sun goes down."

"I won't be that long," she said. "I'm only going to the

stream near the forest." She nodded at the basket hung over her arm. "There's watercress growing there. I thought it would make a nice addition for the supper table."

"I wouldn't mind having some of that myself, ma'am. But I'd feel a mite easier if you'd take somebody out there with you."

She offered him a quick smile, then lowered her lashes flirtatiously. "I promise I won't be gone but a few minutes."

"All right then. But hurry. Otherwise, both Silas and Matthew Hunter are likely to have my hide."

He swung the gate open a crack and allowed her to slide through. "Hurry now."

Without hesitation, she rushed across the clearing toward the forest.

Matt knelt behind an elderberry bush, watching quietly as the warriors walked by. He had already encountered several of these small bands during his journey to Fort Lawrence, but he had not expected one so close to the walls of the fort.

Something was definitely happening, Matthew told himself, but whether or not it was Scioto, preparing for an all-out war against the whites who dared invade his land, Matt could not say.

He waited until the Indians had long faded into the shadows of the forest, then rose from his hiding place and continued on his way.

What could have happened? Jade wondered as she made her way across the clearing toward the nearby forest. What could be so bad that Matt found himself unable to enter the fort where his friends were . . . where she was?

His obvious need for secrecy sent a surge of fear across Jade that was so strong, it was almost smothering in its intensity.

Had she guessed right? Was the suspected traitor his reason for such secrecy? Could it possibly have something to do with Henri LeCroix's visit to the fort? It didn't make sense, because the Frenchman had claimed to come for her. He could have been lying about his reasons for coming, but if so, then why had he left the fort after their encounter?

The whole matter was very confusing to Jade, but she contented herself with the knowledge that she would be with Matt momentarily, and all would be explained to her.

At the edge of the forest, she paused for one last look at the fort and felt relief to find the young guard at his post, watching her from afar. She told herself she would keep her promise and take him some watercress from the stream.

The shadows were deep in the forest and the silence descended around her. It was an unnatural silence, she decided. There was no sound to be heard save the sighing of the wind through the trees.

"Matt?" she said, feeling a slight uneasiness at the continued silence. "Are you there, Matt?"

A rustle sounded in the bushes to her left and she turned to search the shadows. "Matt? Why don't you say something?"

"He cannot say anything, *ma chérie,* simply because he is not here."

"You!" she spun toward the voice.

When the Frenchman stepped into view, she glared at him. "What have you done with Matthew Hunter?"

"Done with him? *Chérie,* I have not laid eyes on Monsieur Hunter since we met in Charleston."

"Then why isn't he here?"

"Why would you think he was here?"

"He sent me a note."

"Non, mademoiselle. Monsieur Hunter did not send you the note. I did."

She should've known the moment LeCroix appeared that Matt was not responsible for the note. She had forgotten Matt's admonishment to be wary of the Frenchman. And she had walked into the trap he had set for her.

As he strode toward her, she backed quickly away. "Stay away from me, LeCroix. If you come any closer I'll scream my lungs out and—"

"Scream if you wish, *ma chérie.* It will do you no good. The soldiers at the fort cannot hear you."

Realizing that he was right, Jade turned to flee. But as she did, a large figure stepped from the shadows to block her way.

"Planned on going somewhere?" Toby reached out to capture her wrist in fingers of steel.

"Turn me loose!" she hissed, wrenching her arm, trying to pull herself free.

"You will only hurt yourself by resisting, mademoiselle," LeCroix told her. "You might as well resign yourself to coming with us."

"Never!" she spat.

"Very well," he said. "You leave me no choice. Tobias . . ." He gestured to Jade's wrists. "It seems we must keep her under guard until she learns how foolish she has been."

Despite her efforts to resist, Toby tied Jade's wrists behind her back, then propelled her through the woods to where a horse waited. He lifted her onto its back then mounted behind her, holding her unnecessarily close. They rode in a northwesterly direction putting distance between themselves and any hope of rescue that Jade might have had.

With each lengthening mile, Jade slumped a little lower in the saddle, fearful of not only her own fate but that of Matthew Hunter as well.

Chapter Eight

Upon reaching Fort Lawrence, Matt went straight to General Macklin's office.

"Well, I'll be damned if it isn't Matthew Hunter!" the general exclaimed, setting aside the papers he had been perusing. Keeping the desk between them, he extended his hand.

Matt gave the general's hand a hearty shake, then after seating himself in the one spare chair, wasted no time explaining his reasons for coming. General Macklin listened without interruption, then said, "I don't know for sure, Matt, but I think you're reading too much into the situation. It could've been a few wild bucks with a grievance who killed those people and burnt their cabin."

"You could be right," Matt said, "but I don't think so. There's too damn many warriors stirring through the forest to make me rest easy. And then, there's the rumors about the peace agreement settled on in Paris. If they're true, then the Indians are likely to be a trifle upset about it."

The general smiled grimly. "Which rumor have you heard? There've been several circulated around lately. The latest one has the Crown pulling our soldiers out and leaving the land west of the Alleghenies to the damned Spanish." He gave a loud guffaw. "Now, why in hell would anybody believe that one. After all we went through to get the damn place, we're not just going to hand it over to the Spaniards."

"The rumor I'm talking about is the one that has Spain and France relinquishing all rights east of the Mississippi."

"Well, that one you heard right, Matt. It's true."

"The Indians aren't gonna like it when they hear the news."

"Blister the Indians!" General Macklin said explosively. "They're no longer to be considered in the matter."

"I'm sure they know that. It worries me what they'll do about it."

"There's little they can do, Matt. Their weapons are primitive, not equal to a long rifle. I'm sure we've nothing to worry about. Those warriors you're concerned with are probably just hunting parties."

"Might be," Matt agreed. "But again, I don't think so. Neither did Colonel Atchison. There's been too many incidents where the Indians have attacked when they chanced to come across a lone white man."

"Isolated incidents," General Macklin said. "Nothing to worry about. Scioto and his Wyandotte bucks cause a few problems now and then. But as I said, they're just isolated incidents."

"Scioto could prove to be trouble in a big way."

"I guess. It won't hurt to keep a wary eye on him," the general said. Then, curling his lips in a smile, he said, "Now that you've delivered your message, how about sharing a meal with me?"

Although Matt was incredibly hungry, he knew dinner

at the general's house would be a long, drawn-out affair.
"Maybe next time," he said. "I've been on the trail so
long I'm not fit for man or beast. Right now, all I want is
a quick supper and a good long sleep."

"I'll hold you to the 'next time' part," General Macklin
said. "And Matt, thanks for coming. I'll send word to the
settlers to keep their eyes open for any sign of trouble."

Matt nodded, then quickly left the office and made his
way to the mess hall where he filled his empty belly.

An hour later, he sank onto a cot at the back of the
livery stable, content with the knowledge that he was safe
within the walls of the fort. It was the last time he'd be
able to sleep with any ease until he reached Fort Sheridan,
for in the forest, he knew he must keep a watchful eye lest
he wake to find his scalp missing.

He curled up, pulled a blanket over him, and in
moments he was fast asleep.

It was still dark when Jade awakened. Opening her eyes,
she stared around at the unfamiliar surroundings. A
moment later, she remembered her circumstances and
how she'd come to be there.

LeCroix had taken her captive and brought her to his
trading post. Now she was in an upstairs bedroom.

Pushing aside the covers, Jade slid from the bed, crossed
the floor to the window and stared outside. It was the first
light before dawn and the area surrounding the trading
post was still thick with dark shadows. Those shadows, she
mused, would cover her flight if she could make her way
to the ground.

Obviously, however, she could not. There was nothing
outside the window to aid her, and if she tried to jump
she would only break her neck.

Crossing to the door, Jade tried the knob. As she'd suspected, it was locked. She could do nothing but wait until someone decided to let her out.

Back at the window, she again stared outside, wondering where Matt was and if he was safe. She knew she must leave the trading post, that she must find her way back to the fort before Matt returned.

She'd been a fool for going outside the fort, for leaving the protection of its walls. But she had been tricked by the note the Frenchman had sent by the young soldier.

The soldier!

Jade had forgotten about him. Had he known the note was sent by LeCroix? Was he one of the Frenchman's accomplices, or merely a messenger who had no idea of the man's intention?

What about the young sentry who stood guard duty at the gate? Was he, too, an accomplice? If not, then what had been his reaction when she failed to return as she'd promised?

Had there been a hue and cry raised? Were the soldiers even now combing the forest in search of her? Surely they were, for it must have been obvious that she'd been taken against her will. Or was it? When the sentry was questioned, he would have told them she'd left of her own accord, wouldn't he?

A grating sounded just outside the door, as though a key had been inserted in the lock. Then, as she watched, the knob began to turn. She caught her breath, her heart hammering with fright, her gaze glued to the door.

Suddenly, it swung open and she saw LeCroix standing in the narrow cone of yellow light thrown out by the oil lamp he held in his hand.

"Bonjour, mademoiselle," he said, his voice seeming to drip with honey. "I trust you slept well."

"I did not! With good reason, monsieur. It's not every

day I find myself abducted and carried off to some godforsaken place in the wilderness."

"Je vous fais mille excuses," he said, his voice pained. "Such a thing would not have been necessary if you had agreed to come with me. *N'est-ce pas?"*

She ignored his apology, knowing he didn't mean it. "Why have you brought me here, Monsieur LeCroix?"

"My apologies if you were inconvenienced, mademoiselle. I had not intended to use force, but your unwillingness to come made it necessary. Why, *ma chérie?* Is it your wish that our business association come to an end, mademoiselle."

Jade's lips tightened. LeCroix must be referring to the purchase and sale of weapons. It was obvious that, like Matt Hunter, LeCroix had mistaken her for another woman. But if she denied that identity, if she convinced him he was wrong, then what would he do?

Feeling certain he wouldn't release her, if only to keep her from telling others of her abduction, she tried to think of another way out.

Trailing a shaky hand across her forehead, she uttered a sigh. "Must we speak of business now, Monsieur LeCroix?" Maybe that would do it. She allowed a pleading note to enter her voice. "I am fatigued from the long ride here, and I have had nothing to eat since yesterday morning."

Something indefinable flickered in his dark gaze and his lips curved into a smile. "Again, I must apologize, *ma chérie.* But I have not been completely lax in my duties. Even as we speak, our meal is being prepared for us." He held out his arm to her. "Allow me to escort you to the dining table."

"Your manners are very pretty, Monsieur LeCroix," she said, forcing a smile to her numb lips. "I'm afraid I hadn't expected to find a man such as yourself in this wilderness."

She forced herself to curve her fingers around his arm, controlling the shiver she felt as she did.

"Call me Henri, *s'il vous plaît,*" he said, his voice as smooth as warm butter.

"Should business partners be so informal?" she asked, arching a brow and sending him a sultry look.

Careful, an inner voice cautioned. *Don't overdo it lest he become suspicious.*

"It is my hope that we become much more than business partners, *ma chérie.*"

Never! she thought. Outwardly, she smiled enigmatically as though she could be entertaining such thoughts herself.

He escorted her downstairs. They sat at the table together while a rough-looking individual served them, then crossed the room and stepped behind a long, wooden bar. Taking a bottle from beneath the counter, he returned to the table and filled their glasses.

"This wine comes from the finest vineyards in France," LeCroix said, lifting his glass and studying the pale liquid inside. "It is very expensive, but I have a great weakness for it."

Since it was obvious he was waiting for her to taste it, Jade lifted her glass and breathed in the aroma. "A good year," she said, taking a sip of the bubbly liquid.

Obviously pleased, he turned his attention to his meal. When they had both finished eating, LeCroix laid his hand over hers to get her attention. "We must speak together soon about our business, *ma chérie.*"

Inside, Jade shrank from his touch, but she managed to present a composed front. "I thought we agreed to leave it a while, Henri." She used his given name in the hopes that she'd distract him from his purpose. It didn't work.

"You do still have access to the duke's funds, do you not, *ma chérie?*" His gaze was dark, probing.

"Of course. The funds have been left in a safe place."

She lowered her eyelashes to escape his penetrating gaze. "But I have been through so much, Henri . . . the prison, the guards . . . they were always watching me, seeming to be waiting until there was no one about to . . ."

She shivered, unable to finish. Her fear was real. She remembered well the weeks she'd spent in prison, knowing if she were ever left alone with one particular guard—a man she had known only as Stanley—that her efforts to protect herself would be useless. She would most certainly have been ravished.

But, thanks to the sergeant of the guards—an elderly man who'd told her he had a daughter her age—she had never been left alone with him. The sergeant had taken pity on her and made sure Stanley was never assigned to her wing of the dungeon. That hadn't kept him from coming by each day and tormenting her with the promise that one night she would wake to find herself alone with him.

"Prison is not a very nice place," Henri muttered. "But you are no longer there, *ma chérie*. You are free now. And we must continue our operations. I have a man waiting at this very moment. He is ready to travel to England to purchase more weapons. But I must have the funds for buying them before he can leave."

"Just give me a little time," she hedged.

"A little more, perhaps, but we must act soon, *ma chérie*. The Indians need the weapons. And if they do not get them, then they will take their anger out on me."

"Why do they need them so soon?"

"I am told they are planning a grand attack on all the forts west of the Alleghenies," he explained. "Scioto is not happy the weapons have been delayed, for he has told Pontiac, the chief of the Ottawas, that they will be forthcoming. He has given his word, and I have given mine. If

the weapons are not obtained soon, they will be very angry
. . . and so will I, *ma chérie*. So will I.''

Jade shivered inwardly at the threat in his voice. But if
she had any say in the matter, Scioto and Pontiac would
never have the weapons.

Realizing the man was still watching her closely, she tried
to cloak her reaction. She must hide her hatred of LeCroix,
must keep him from knowing she was not the woman he
thought she was.

Suddenly, the door was flung open and an Indian woman
entered the room. Her black eyes flashed as she saw the two
of them together, but otherwise, she showed no emotion.

"What are you doing here, Juaheela?" LeCroix
demanded, rising stiffly to his feet and pinning the woman
with a heated gaze.

"My husband's home is my home." Her voice was defi-
ant. "Where he is, then so will I be."

"Go back to your village," he ordered.

"No!" She held his gaze for a long moment before
sending a dark look toward Jade. "Why is another woman
seated at my table?"

"This is none of your business!" he snapped. "Return
to your people and leave me alone."

"I will go only when you are ready to go with me," she
declared.

"You are to obey me, Juaheela! This is not your concern."

"It is my concern whenever my husband looks at another
woman in such a manner," she replied. "Juaheela is no
child to be ordered about. Juaheela is a woman . . . the
daughter of a chief." Her lips curled in a smile, but it
was not a happy smile. "Scioto will be displeased to hear
LeCroix has replaced his wife with another woman."

"That is not true," LeCroix said hotly, striding toward

her and taking her by the forearm. "You have misunderstood, *ma chérie.*"

It was easy for Jade to see that LeCroix was intimidated by the other woman's words. That fact set her thinking. Perhaps if she appealed to Juaheela, the Indian woman would make him release her.

"Come, *ma chérie,*" LeCroix coaxed, taking his wife by the forearm. "We will speak of this together." He led her toward the winding staircase. "I can explain everything." He mounted the stairs, then glanced back at Jade with a dark frown before he addressed the man behind the bar. "See Jade to her room, Hal," he said abruptly. "And . . . you know what to do."

She found out the meaning of those words when Hal shoved her inside her room and locked the door. It seemed she was still not to be trusted.

Left to herself, Jade wandered over to the window and stared out into the nearby forest. If only she could see Matt striding into the clearing, she thought.

Surely he would come for her when he learned she was missing.

But how would he know where she was? she wondered silently. No one had seen her taken. He would have no way of knowing she was with LeCroix, therefore he could not rescue her.

She had only herself to depend upon. She must do whatever was necessary to free herself.

Juaheela listened to LeCroix's explanation, never commenting once while he told her exactly why he must keep the white woman with him. She could tell by his eyes that what he said was the truth. But she could also see something else. When he spoke the white woman's name, there was a different look there. Something he did not wish her to see. Something he might even be unaware of himself. But Juaheela was aware of it and knew there was something else between them. And she would not allow it.

The white girl could not remain at the trading post. Not if she could help it. Her love for the Frenchman was genuine and she would have no peace in her life if she were to lose him. She did not care about land and possessions. Her only care was for the man who stood before her, the man she was in danger of losing if she didn't act quickly.

"So you see why you must give me time, *ma chérie*," LeCroix said softly, smoothing a hand over her midnight-dark hair. "It is only about your people I am thinking. And the only reason I have the woman here now."

Henri LeCroix's dark eyes were soft as he bent to kiss her lips softly. Then, pulling away, he said, "The woman is only a business partner, *mon coeur*. Nothing more. She means less than nothing to me, yet she is the only one who can help us. Without her funds we can never acquire the weapons needed by your father and Pontiac."

Juaheela wrapped her arms around his neck and pressed her lips against his in a deep kiss. This man was hers, and she would keep him whatever it took.

"Do you think I could ever love another woman?" he muttered softly against her lips. "You are my wife, *ma chérie*. You are the woman I have chosen to spend my life with. You must remember that. We are promised to each other until the day we die, and you must believe that I will always honor that promise."

Juaheela smiled up at him. Yes. He would honor the promise he'd made to her. But he might need help in doing so.

She had every intention of providing him with that help.

Chapter Nine

The knowledge that he was being followed sliced through Matt with the keenness of a well-sharpened blade. Although he'd seen no one, and heard nothing, he knew that he was not imagining it.

The fine hairs at the base of his neck were sounding an alarm, standing straight out as though they might have been yanked upward by a strong hand.

Matt carefully controlled his features to remain unexpressive, and his pace never slackened or increased. There was nothing about him to reveal his awareness of the unseen presence that chose to remain hidden from him.

Matt had no idea who—or what—followed him. It could be an Indian, or it could be a wild beast. But whoever—or whatever—it was, the stalker followed without a sound.

The thumping that resounded in his ears was not his stalker; it was his own heart, pumping blood through his veins.

Matt cursed inwardly. How the devil was he supposed

to hear anyone, or anything, when his own body betrayed him so easily?

Even as he asked himself the question, he heard a loud snap coming from the bushes on the right.

Reacting to the sound, he reached for his knife, sliding it from its sheath and turning, with blade in hand, to face his stalker.

"Don't be so quick to use that knife, son!" a voice exclaimed, coming from behind the trunk of a lodgepole pine. The voice was quickly followed by a head wearing a coonskin cap.

"Badger!" Matt exclaimed, uttering a quick oath. "Damn! I knew I was being followed, but I had no notion it was you."

"And I knew the minute you knew," the old man grunted, stepping into view. "Been following you for nigh on to three miles now." He worked up a spit and let it fly toward the nearest bush. "You're gettin' mighty careless, boy," Badger went on. "It ain't like you a'tall. You been hightailin' it through these woods like you was the onliest one around. It's thinkin' like that what gets a man's hair lifted."

The old man settled himself on a nearby log that had fallen across the trail and Matt hunkered down in a frog squat nearby.

"So you've seen them, too." Matt's words were more a statement then a question.

"Dang right I seen 'em. An' it scared the bejeesus outta me, too, 'cause I 'spect them Injuns didn't go to all that trouble—paintin' themselves up like that—for no celebration."

"My thoughts exactly," Matt said grimly. "And I don't believe, like some others do, that they're just a few bucks out sowing their wild oats, either. Not since finding Jed and his wife, both of 'em dead, laying beside their burnt-out cabin.''

"No!" the old man exclaimed. "Not Jedediah Collins! And you say they kilt his wife, too?"

"Yeah."

"Well, gosh and be damned!" Badger said angrily. "I was at Jedediah's weddin'. He married him a mighty handsome woman." He fell silent for a long moment, as though he were remembering that event, then, "Damned if it don't look like a mess of trouble is headin' our way, Matt."

"It would seem so."

The old-timer pulled a powderhorn from his belt and held it out to Matt. "You recognize this?"

Matt frowned at the item, looking for something that might identify it. The bottom had a distinct curve, that seemed familiar. But where had he seen it? His gaze slid across the powderhorn again, then stopped. Two small letters had been carved into the horn—the letters *T* and *F*. "Titus Forbes," he muttered. "Where did you get it, Badger?"

"Took it off an Injun that jumped me a couple o' days ago." The lines in his forehead deepened. "Ol' Titus wouldn't of give it up easy, Matt."

"Maybe he just lost it."

"They's blood on it." Badger turned the powderhorn to reveal a brownish stain.

Matt's heart sank. Titus would never have voluntarily parted with the powderhorn, nor would he have likely lost it. And the dried blood gave little hope that he was alive.

"Things are going to get rougher here, Badger," Matt said. "If a man had any sense, he'd get himself across the Alleghenies and stay there until whatever's gonna happen is over."

"Yeah," Badger agreed, reaching in his pocket for the chaw of tobbaco and biting off a hefty plug. "That'd be the thing to do if a man had good sense. Trouble is, I never had much. Leastways, that's what my pap always told me. No sense a'tall.'' He sent a hard glare at Matt. "But you, now. You got a good head on your shoulders. Man like you could make a good living t'other side of the mountain. Man like you could settle down and raise himself a passel of kids.''

"Yeah," Matt agreed. "You're probably right. I could do all them things. Trouble is, I'd keep wondering what was happening over here. Guess the only way to have any peace of mind is to stay in the middle of it.''

"Maybe," Badger said. "But it's sure likely to be a mess.'' The old man's features sharpened slightly. "What'n hell happened to the little gal you bought at the auction? LeCroix don't have her, does he?''

"Nope. I left her with Silas at Fort Sheldon.''

"You reckon she'll give him any trouble?''

Matt pulled a daisy from the patch growing at his feet and idly twirled the flower between his thumb and forefinger. "She denied all knowledge of LeCroix and his business.'' Matt went on to explain Jade's circumstances.

"An' you believed her? Why's that?''

"A gut feeling," Matt muttered.

"I reckon I had that same feelin', Matt. But a feelin' ain't no kinda proof. No proof a'tall. It'd prob'ly pay a man to keep a close eye on 'er until he was certain of his facts. LeCroix mighta been mistook about who she was when he went after her, but there's always the chance he was right. And them feelings we got in our guts might just be hunger.''

"I've told myself the same thing, Badger, over and over again. And, whatever I believe, I made sure Silas knew the facts. He's keeping her under his eye, and he won't let LeCroix within hollering distance.''

"Good. It pays to be careful. An' let me tell you, Matt.

I'd be mighty disappointed if that little lady turned out to be the Frenchie's partner. Mighty disappointed."

"You and me both." Matt felt a curious ache in his chest at the mere thought. But it couldn't be so, he told himself. Jade had to be telling the truth. She had to be.

"Where you headed now?" Badger asked gruffly.

"Back to Fort Sheldon," Matt replied. "I've already been to Fort Lawrence to apprise them of the situation. Trouble is, General Macklin doesn't think there's any cause for concern."

"He'll change his mind soon enough, I reckon." The old man frowned. "He's usually a sensible enough person. Hope he's gonna take some precautions."

"He said he'd send word to the settlers, but he couldn't guarantee they'd be willing to come inside the fort."

"Some of them settlers is mighty stubborn," Badger said.

"Let's hope they use some sense this time," Matt said grimly. "If they don't, and war breaks out, then their families may pay the price." His studied the old man, noticing the fatigue that lined his features. "You look worn out, Badger. Why don't you come to Fort Sheldon with me?"

"Naw," Badger said. "I reckon not. I got me some traps set over yonder aways. An' if they's anything caught in 'em, it'll need takin' out afore the fur's spoilt."

"Better spoiled fur than a lifted scalp," Matt said. But he knew from past experience that the other man couldn't be swayed from his decision. "You keep a sharp eye out, Badger. Those Wyandotte bucks aren't above setting a trap of their own in the hopes of catching an old mountain man like yourself. And if you happened to fall in that trap, they wouldn't treat their catch the same way you would."

"What's that supposed to mean?"

"You make sure your catch is dead before you skin it. The Wyandotte don't."

Badger laughed sharply, without humor. "I been trappin' these hills for nigh on to fifty years now. You don't need to go warnin' me none. It's you that's got me worried, boy."

"Why's that?"

"If a man don't pay more attention when he's bein' followed, he's likely to wind up on the wrong end of a roasting stick."

With those warnings duly delivered, the two men went their separate ways.

Pontiac was pleased the meeting had gone so well. None there had objected to his plans, yet none except himself knew the full scope of his intentions . . . not even his most trusted associates. Only he could have devised such a plan, and only he could carry the thing out to completion. It was his eloquence that had swayed the council, his mind that had devised the plan, and none could dispute his right to lead them.

He liked the plan. Pontiac, war chief of the Ottawa, leading thousands of warriors against their enemies.

His lips curved in a smile. Soon, everyone would know his name, would know it was Pontiac who was responsible for driving the hated British from their lands. Only a man such as himself could organize and control the combined operations of so many separate nations.

Yes, only Pontiac could have accomplished so much. Soon even the British would know his name and be awed by his power.

Fort Detroit would be the first to feel his might.

Pontiac imagined how Major Henry Gladwin would feel when he woke up one morning and realized thousands of warriors were outside the gates of Fort Detroit. They would attack and . . .

But no, Pontiac thought, his dark brows pulling into a frown. Perhaps that was not the way it would be. Granted, he would like nothing better than to wage an all-out attack and take the fort by surprise. But perhaps there was a better way to go about it, a way that would not take so many Indian lives.

The fort at Detroit, which the English had inherited from the French, was a considerable structure, with walls the height of four men riding atop each's shoulders. He'd been inside that fort and knew there was almost a hundred houses inside, in addition to barracks and storehouses. Its walls extended all the way to the riverbank where there was a water gate to aid the unloading of trade goods and supplies.

The fort's major weakness was having been built on a slope rising from the shore, making it easy for anyone across the river to see most of the interior, and yet it remained the strongest English garrison west of Pittsburgh.

Perhaps, Pontiac decided, it would be best if he devised a different plan, one that would enable him to enter the fort while the enemy remained unaware of his attentions.

Yes, he mused, if he could enter the fort accompanied by a hundred warriors, then he could rid himself of Major Gladwin and his aides. Without their leaders to guide them, the white man would surely fall beneath Pontiac's might and he would return, triumphant, followed by every warrior who had gone into battle prepared to give their life.

It was a good plan. But it would take more thought on his part. He would leave nothing to chance, not when there were so many lives at stake.

But soon, he promised himself. Soon, Detroit would feel his strength, would feel the strength of all the combined Indian nations.

When that time came, the fort would burn, and it would continue burning until there was nothing left but ashes.

And there would be none to tell what had happened, either, for Pontiac meant to leave no survivors. Only in that manner could he teach the hateful British a much-needed lesson.

And after Fort Detroit had burned to the ground, Pontiac could turn his attention to Fort Pitt. After that, Fort Niagara, and while he was conquering those, others of his people could take the weaker forts until nothing was left of the people who had dared intrude on the land west of the Alleghenies.

Chapter Ten

Jewel Crawford stood among the bond slaves waiting to be sold at auction, but unlike those around her, she felt no trepidation about the future. Instead, she was confident that all would go as she'd planned.

A confident smile curved her lips as she scanned the crowd gathered around the Market.

Which one was he? she wondered. Which man was the Frenchman, LeCroix? She eyed each one in turn, searching every face for one that might reveal an intense need to purchase one particular woman. But, as hard as she looked, she could not identify him.

No matter, she told herself. He was definitely a gambler—only a gamester would enter a partnership like theirs—and as such, he would be good at keeping his feelings hidden from prying eyes. But he *was* there, she knew. LeCroix would never allow her to slip through his fingers. No, he would need the funds she provided to continue their business.

Her smile deepened. LeCroix was waiting out there in that crowd of people, more than eager to acquire her, eager as well to continue the business that had been interrupted when she'd found it necessary to shoot the Duke of Wellingford.

Poor Percy. Poor, dear Percy. He should have left well enough alone. He certainly hadn't needed the things she had taken from him. But she had. The gold and jewels had been used to supply LeCroix with funds so that he could purchase weapons to use as trade. If Percy had minded his own business, had kept his nose out of things that didn't concern him, then he would still be alive now and Jewel wouldn't have been sent to the Colonies.

But never mind. Perhaps Lady Luck had finally interfered in her life. After all, wouldn't she be able to better supervise her business from here? And that meant her goal—to be the richest, most sought-after woman in England—would be reached that much sooner.

According to the judge, Lady Luck had already favored her. Poor dear Percy's nephews had wanted to see her hang. But the duke's younger brother had interceded. Even so, Jewel felt no gratitude toward him.

"Fool!" she muttered, her lip thinning with contempt.

Percy's brother, Malcolm, had delayed her journey to the Colonies. He'd thought to recover the family jewels she'd stolen by keeping her in England a while, by making empty promises that she knew he would never keep—not with his brother's blood on her hands.

But his efforts to break her were to no avail. She would be stupid to divulge the whereabouts of her funds, and she couldn't tell them about the jewels. How could she when the man she'd sold them to was a stranger, a man from another country.

When he'd found he couldn't sway her with empty promises, Malcolm had resorted to threats. He would see her hang, he'd shouted. But she knew his threats were as empty as the promises that had preceded them. Only so long as she lived could Malcolm hope that someday he could recover his family's jewels.

He was wrong, though. She would never weaken. She'd had no fear of the Colonies, yet she'd kept that fact secret, lest they made her remain in London.

Her plan had worked even better than expected.

She was here now, and before long, she would finally meet the man who would be responsible for setting her free again.

The old soldier stumbled forward, blood streaming down one side of his face from the many cuts that marred his head. Staggering, he wondered how much farther he could travel before his wounds sent him sprawling against the ground.

He knew, without a doubt, that he'd never make it to Fort Sheldon. It was too far and his wounds were too severe. Still, he might be able to reach Abner Grant's place.

A red haze marred his vision and he blinked rapidly, wondering if he was on the verge of losing consciousness.

When he felt a wet stickiness moving slowly down his right cheek, he rubbed his hand across it and peered down at the blood he'd removed from his skin.

"Just a little blood is all," he muttered. "Them red devils ain't got me licked yet, an' they ain't gonna. Abe's place is just over the rise ahead and I'm gonna make it there. I gotta do it. Gotta warn the forts about Scioto, tell the soldiers what he's about or he'll massacre ever last one of 'em."

He stumbled onward.

* * *

Matt's spirits were high when he reached Fort Sheldon. He'd done everything he could for the moment. Now he would put the worry aside and leave it until something actually happened . . . if it did. Time enough then to confront whatever was brewing.

Now, though, he was eager to see Jade, as eager as a boy feeling the bloom of first love.

But if he went first to Silas's house, he would make a fool of himself. It would be better if he reported to the colonel first. Maybe—

"Hello, Mr Hunter," said a young soldier who'd approached on silent feet. "If you're lookin' for the colonel, he's over at the sutler's store."

"Thanks," Matt said gruffly, angry at himself for having come to a dead stop in the middle of the parade ground. Anyone watching him would think he'd lost his senses. As he probably had.

That thought decided him. Matt headed for the sutler's store. He'd chat with the colonel for a while, would take his time before ambling over to Silas's cabin.

He mounted the boardwalk and pushed open the door of the store. The colonel sat at a table, a bottle and glass placed on the table before him. Matt was surprised. The colonel hadn't struck him as a serious drinker, but perhaps he'd been wrong.

"Mind if I join you?" Matt asked, striding swiftly to Colonel Atchison's table.

"Not a whit. Pull up a chair and set yourself down, Matt," the colonel invited. "You can even share my bottle of whiskey." His gaze swept across the room and stopped on the portly man behind the bar. "Bring us another glass, Fitzhugh."

With an abrupt nod of his head, Patrick Fitzhugh reached for a glass from the shelf behind the bar and brought it to the table. "It's mighty glad I am to see you again, Mister Hunter," he said, setting the glass before Matt and filling it with the amber liquid.

There was something in Fitzhugh's voice that alerted Matt, and he looked closer at the man, taking note of the worried look on his face. "Something botherin' you, Fitzhugh?"

"Aye, that it is," the old man replied. "I canna get the wee lassie out o' my mind. The worryin' is fair drivin' me insane."

"The lassie?" Matt inquired, wondering what the devil Fitzhugh was talking about. He picked up his glass and tossed back a long swallow of the amber liquid, feeling it slide down his throat smoothly. Then, "What wee lassie, Fitzhugh?"

The Scot's eyes narrowed on Matt. "Have you not heard then?"

"Heard what?"

"The lassie's gone."

Suddenly, without warning, Matt felt an icy chill glide down his spine and slowly spread to his extremities. His heart skipped a beat, then began to thud with dread.

"What are you talkin' about, Fitzhugh?" he rasped harshly.

"Jade," Fitzhugh said, confirming Matt's fear. "The lassie's gone."

Matt jerked to his feet, shoving his chair away from the table. "Where did she go?" he asked sharply. "Out with it, man! When did she leave and who did she go with?" Even though he asked the question, he already knew the answer. LeCroix had been to the fort and had abducted her.

"Sit down, Matt," Colonel Atchison commanded. "Finish your drink. The girl's in no danger."

"How do you know that?" Matt asked sharply, eyeing the colonel. "You have no idea what Henri LeCroix is capable of?"

"Henri LeCroix is not responsible for her disappearance," the colonel said gruffly. "The girl was not abducted, Matt. She left under her own steam."

"I don't believe that," Matt said sharply. "She wouldn't have left the protection of the fort. LeCroix must have taken her."

"Them's my thoughts exactly," Fitzhugh said, sending a triumphant look toward the colonel before returning his attention o Matt. "That poor lassie wouldna gone out o' this fort on 'er own. Not without somebody forcing her to do so."

"We've already been over this, Fitzhugh. Nobody made her do anything she didn't want to do."

"Has LeCroix been here?" Matt asked.

"No. He hasn't."

"I saw him, Colonel," Fitzhugh said. "Saw him with my own two eyes. He was here all right, and he had somethin' to do with the lassie leavin' like she did." Shaking his head woefully, he turned to leave them alone.

"You saw LeCroix?" Matt asked sharply, reaching out a hand to stop the man from departing.

"That I did," Fitzhugh said. "He was here all right. 'Twas the day before the lassie disappeared."

"Nobody else seems to have seen him," the colonel said dryly. "Only Fitzhugh."

"What was LeCroix doing when you saw him?" Matt asked.

"He was leavin' the fort," the man replied.

"Alone?"

"Aye," the Scotsman admitted. "That he was. Alone. But he coulda snuck back inside without me knowin'."

"He couldn't have got past the guard," Colonel Atchison said smartly, obviously irritated at the old man's persistence.

"What about the guard at the gate. Matt demanded. He must have seen her leave. What was his explanation?"

"The guard saw her leave, right enough," Fitzhugh said gruffly. "He was the one who opened the gate to let 'er out o' the fort."

"Why in hell did he let her out?" Matt asked. "What reason did he have? He's supposed to be guarding the fort!"

"Calm down, Matt," the colonel said. "You can't blame the guard. He said the girl was bent on gathering a mess of watercress from the stream near the woods. Said she'd promised to bring him some. When she didn't return within the hour, he reported her missing to his superior who sent out a search party. She was nowhere to be found and there was no sign of a struggle."

"What about tracks?"

"Her tracks led to a stream, which she apparently entered and waded upstream. They couldn't find where she left the water."

"And that didn't concern you?"

"No. They reported the banks were littered with rocks. She obviously wanted us to lose her tracks."

"Dammit!" Matt swore. "Didn't any of you find that unusual?"

"Matt," the colonel soothed. "The girl left here on her own and it was obvious she made every attempt to keep us from following her. She lied to the guard at the gate about her reason for leaving the fort."

"How do you know that?"

"Because she didn't go anywhere near the watercress

growing near the edge of the forest. Instead, she entered the forest. On her own. The guard can verify that. Wherever she is, she's there because she wants to be, not because she's being held against her will.''

"What about the note?" Fitzhugh asked.

"What note?" Matt asked.

"One of the guards gave her a note shortly before she left," the colonel said.

"Have you asked the guard who gave it to him?"

"Of course. He said he found it on a table when he went off duty. Since her name was printed on the outside, he took it to her. We figured LeCroix must have left it for her. It's a fact that she went outside immediately after receiving it."

Matt couldn't stem the flood of feelings that swept over him as he admitted to himself that the colonel must be right. Jade hadn't been abducted. She'd gone voluntarily. And apparently to a previously arranged assignation with Henri LeCroix.

Dammit! He'd trusted her. Had believed the lies she'd told him. Had even allowed himself to care about her. How could he have been so foolish? Jade had wormed her way inside his heart and invaded a piece of him that he'd closed off long ago. And he'd allowed it to happen!

His hurt was an angry knot that began in the pit of his stomach and swept upward until it lodged firmly in his throat, constricting his breathing.

It was obvious, she and LeCroix had conspired together. He must've been waiting in the forest for her. Well, she damn well wouldn't get away with it! Jade was his property: Bought and paid for with cold hard cash! There was no way he'd allow her to escape so easily. No! He'd find her somehow, and he'd make her pay dearly for her deceit.

Matt stayed at the fort only long enough to gather some supplies together and have a word with Silas Brown. It was then he discovered Fitzhugh wasn't the only one in disagreement with Atchison.

"I don't believe it," Silas said, shaking his head in denial. "Jade wouldn't have any part in such dealings, Matt."

Matt wanted to believe him, but found he couldn't. Not when there were so many things pointing to her guilt. "She had me fooled, too," he said grimly. "But the guard said she left under her own steam. And LeCroix was here only a short time before she left."

"I don't give a damn about that," Silas said. "She was here with us for three days, Matt. Long enough for us to get to know her pretty well. She nigh wore herself out tryin' to take most of Mary Lou's workload. That little girl cares about people. It showed in ever'thing she did."

Again, Matt wanted desperately to believe him, but how could he? Everyone agreed that Jade had left the fort on the pretense of gathering watercress, and yet she had made no effort to do so. Instead, she had gone into the forest where the guard couldn't see her, and then had disappeared without a trace.

No! It had to be a prearranged meeting. LeCroix had been to the fort and had contacted Jade. The following day she had simply walked out the gate and went into the forest. It was all done under the watchful eyes of the guard . . . until she disappeared among the trees.

How could she be so despicable and look so incredibly innocent? Matt wondered.

"I don't want to believe she's LeCroix's business partner," Matt told his friend. "But the evidence points that way."

"Evidence be damned," Silas said grimly. "If you was to spend any time with her a'tall, you'd know you was wrong. Just keep that in mind when you find her."

"You seem mighty sure I'll do that," Matt said.

"Yeah," Silas said. "I am. I know you, Matt. When you

got somethin' stuck in your craw, you ain't gonna stop till you get it out. You'll find her, right enough. And when you do, just remember what I said. If you find her alive.''

"What do you mean by that?" Matt asked, sucking in a sharp breath as a fierce pain jabbed at his chest.

"Just that somebody's holdin' her against her will. And whoever it is may not be too friendly.''

With those words ringing in his ears, Matt left the fort behind him. He glanced at the sun, measuring the time left before darkness fell, and turned his face to the north. He had no need to search for tracks. He already knew where he'd find Jade. At LeCroix's trading post.

Sunset found him several miles from the fort, yet Matt wasted no time searching for shelter. He had no intention of camping that night. He must hear her explanation for leaving the fort before his heart would accept her betrayal.

His mind was busy as he sped through the thickly growing pines, so involved with his thoughts that he would have missed the moccasin tracks embedded in the muddy bank of a stream had he not stopped for a drink of water.

He sucked up the cool, refreshing liquid, then pushed himself upright. His gaze swept over a deeply embedded moccasin print absently, then, realizing it had been recently made, he bent to examine it.

The print was unmistakable. Wyandotte. But why would Scioto's warriors be hunting in this area when it belonged to the Delaware? He bent closer, looking for answers on the ground. But there were none to be found there.

Proceeding with caution, Matt headed in a northwesterly direction. He'd only gone a few miles when he reached the crest of a low hill. He lifted his gaze to a rock overhang jutting out from a high ridge above.

Although he could easily circle the hill, he considered the advantages of climbing it, knowing it would afford him a good view of the valley below.

That fact alone sent him upward, scrambling over rocky shale until he reached the top of the ridge. The rocky overhang proved better than he'd hoped. He would have a good viewing point where he would remain hidden from eyes that might watch from below.

Lowering himself to his belly, Matt eased outward, crawling slowly to the edge. As he'd expected, he had a good view.

And he didn't like what he saw.

Sitting below him, perhaps twenty feet, were two warriors . . . Wyandotte braves, armed with both arrow and spear and painted for war.

Matt knew the men were lookouts, sent there to keep watch for any enemy that might approach.

But why?

This was not their territory, he reminded himself again. All the land around the area was claimed by the Delaware tribe, yet there stood two Wyandotte warriors.

An icy chill swept over Matt as he remembered the smell of smoke lingering in the clearing where he'd found the burnt-out cabin.

He looked over the men's heads into the forest beyond. To his knowledge there was nothing there. No settlers, no forts. Nothing the Wyandotte might be concerned with. If they were not painted for war, he might have believed they were only hunters who had strayed too far south.

But the warpaint told its own story. The men below were not hunters.

Perhaps their reason for being there had nothing to do with the white man, though. Perhaps there had been a quarrel among the Indian tribes and they were at war.

It might be so, yet he knew he was grasping at straws. The Delaware and Wyandotte Indians had been friendly for many years. Each tribe depended on the other to keep enemy tribes with a greater number of warriors at bay. For that reason he didn't believe the guards had been assigned there to search for Delaware braves.

But what was their purpose? he wondered. Who were they watching for?

His gaze returned to the two men below. They sat with their legs dangling over a precipice in front of them, a dozen or so feet from the valley floor. Matt knew he could kill them where they sat before they could react to his presence, but did not feel inclined to do so. If others should return to look for the guards and find them missing, or perhaps dead, they would be alerted to the presence of an enemy.

No. Better to leave them alone. That way, none would be aware of his presence while he traveled through the forest to look for the reason the Wyandotte had come where they were not supposed to be.

Thoughts of Jade intruded on his consciousness, yet he shoved them aside. He felt certain she was at the trading post with LeCroix. And there, he was just as certain, she would remain until his mission was completed.

Carefully, he backed off the ledge, making no sound as he left the place where the warriors watched for sign of their enemy.

Then, ever alert to his surroundings, Matt continued on his way, intent on learning the reason the Wyandotte warriors had left their own lands behind to stand watch in Delaware territory.

Something awakened Jade from a sound sleep. She lay silent, barely breathing, listening to the silence, trying to pinpoint her unease, yet hearing nothing in the darkness that could have disturbed her rest.

Moments lengthened, then passed. And although the

silence continued, Jade sensed another presence in the room.

Sitting up in the bed, she tried to penetrate the surrounding blackness, but the shadows were too deep, too thick. "Is someone there?" she asked, her voice sounding loud in the stillness.

No answer.

There was nothing, except the sound of her own voice, to penetrate the pervading silence.

Don't be silly, she told herself. *You're not a child who's afraid of the boogeyman.*

Yet, try as she would, she could not convince herself that she was alone. Not with the fine hairs at the nape of her neck reacting to that unseen presence.

Realizing she'd never be able to fall asleep again unless she made certain there was no one else in the room, Jade shoved the covers aside and slid to the edge of the bed, shoving her feet against the cold wooden floor.

She reached for the lamp left on the nightstand and lifted the glass globe with one hand, while the other fumbled for one of the long, sulphur-tipped wood splints left nearby. Before she could light the lamp, however, she heard a whispering sound on the far side of the room.

"Who's there?" she demanded, sucking in a sharp breath of fear.

"Juaheela."

The voice was cold, utterly devoid of emotion, but when the woman moved closer, stepping into the pale moonlight streaming through the window, Jade realized there was bitter hatred in Juaheela's dark, flashing eyes.

Hearing a loud crash, Jade jerked toward the sound, realizing as she saw the broken glass that she'd dropped the lamp globe and that it had shattered on the wooden floor.

"Leave here, white slave!" Juaheela's angry voice drew

Jade's attention from the broken glass. The Indian woman's stance was almost menacing. "Leave here now! I will not have you near my man!"

"I'm not here because I want to be, Juaheela," Jade told the woman, shrinking away from her obvious hatred. "I would gladly leave if I could. But I cannot. Surely you know that. I am a prisoner, kept here, against my will, by your husband."

"If it is your wish to live, then you must find a way to leave," the woman said harshly.

"Help me, Juaheela," Jade pleaded. "Help me to get back to the fort."

No sooner were the words said then Jade saw the knife in Juaheela's hand. Fear sliced through her. "What are y-you doing here?" she asked hoarsely. "Why h-have you come to my r-room?"

"To kill you!" Juaheela stated grimly. "LeCroix is my husband. I will allow no one to take him from me."

"I d-don't want him," Jade stuttered. "I only w-want to leave this place. Juaheela, help me get away from here."

The woman seemed to hesitate. Jade glanced at the hand that gripped the knife. Had the Indian woman's fingers loosened ever so slightly?

"My husband says he needs you," Juaheela said slowly. "You help him buy rifles and tomahawks for my people."

Jade's brain whirled frantically. Should she confirm or deny LeCroix's words? By denying them, she might be condemning herself to death.

"I will not allow you to remain in my husband's house," Juaheela said. "You must leave or die." Jade was chilled by the obvious hatred that radiated from the Indian woman. "You go to his friend, St. Clair. He will allow you to work in his tavern. Wait there for my husband. But never come to this house again. Never! Stay away from here if you value your life!"

"I need your help Juaheela," Jade said pleading. I don't know where to find the tavern. Nor can I leave here when I am kept under lock and key! Will you unlock the doors for me and show me the way to the tavern?"

"You must help yourself, white woman," Juaheela said grimly.

"How, Juaheela? Surely you could at least unlock the doors for me!" Were the doors already unlocked? Jade wondered. The bedroom door must be. Otherwise, Juaheela could not have entered the room. But there was still the downstairs door—and the man who always stood guard at night.

"My husband is leaving tomorrow," Juaheela said slowly. "He will be gone for several days."

"You will help me then?"

"Perhaps."

"When?"

"Tomorrow night. Be prepared, white woman. Wait until the moon is high. The guard will be sleepy then, less alert. I will unlock the doors for you. You must do the rest."

Could she? Jade wondered. Did she have the nerve to leave the dubious safety of this trading post for the dark, terrifying dangers that lurked in the forest?

"What about the tavern, Juaheela?" Jade asked. "Where will I find it?"

"To the north." The woman pointed in that direction. "Go to it. Remain there. St. Clair will see you are not brought here again if you request his help in the matter. He has enough influence with my husband to make him realize he cannot keep you here. Remain there, white woman. You and my husband will be able to conduct your business from there. But heed my warning. LeCroix is mine. Leave him alone!"

Jade knew it would serve no purpose to protest her

innocence. To do so might change the woman's mind about helping her. For that reason, she said, "I understand perfectly, Juaheela, and you have my promise on that."

"It is a promise that must not be broken," the woman said. Then, without another word, she turned and moved swiftly across the room.

The door opened a crack and Juaheela slipped from the room, closing the door firmly behind her. A soft click told Jade she'd been locked in again.

Chapter Eleven

A loud thump woke Jade and she opened sleep-dazed eyes to see a large, disheveled man looming over her. It was Hal, the man who'd served their meal.

"So you finally decided to wake up," he growled.

"What do you want?" she gasped, clutching the bedcovers tightly against her chin.

He grinned at her, his gaze probing the quilt where it outlined her body, then said, "I brought your breakfast tray, missy." He nodded at the laden tray on the bedside table. "LeCroix said you didn't have no dinner last night, so I figgered as how you'd be mighty hungry by now."

"I *am* hungry," she said, wondering if she should thank him for his efforts, then quickly deciding against it. She didn't believe for one moment the man had any consideration for her welfare, not when he was looking at her in such a lustful manner.

"Well, then," he said, his gaze moving upward until he

met her eyes. "Just set yourself up in the bed and enjoy the repast."

She glanced at the door and saw it was closed. A quick thrill of fear streaked through her. They were completely alone, shut away from the other occupants of the trading post. Would he simply go if asked to do so? She thought not. "Thank you for bringing my breakfast," she said. "Now, if you don't mind, I would like to wash up."

"Don't mind nary a bit," he replied gruffly, leaning against the wall as though he planned to stay a while. "They's some water on the stand over yonder." He nodded toward the far wall. "And they's a washpan."

"Yes, I know," she said grimly. "I used them last night. And I would like to do so again, but I prefer washing without anyone watching. If you don't mind."

"Suppose I do?"

Jade swallowed around a lump of fear. She wasn't about to leave her bed until Hal had left the room. Not when her only garment was the flimsy nightgown provided by LeCroix. "In that case I shall remain abed."

The sound of footsteps against wooden boards straightened the man from his position against the wall. He moved away from her just as the door was flung open.

"Hal!" LeCroix said, taking in the scene. "Why are you in Mademoiselle's room?"

Hal's body was tense as he strode across the room and faced LeCroix. "I brung her meal to her," he said. "I was just leaving."

"Mademoiselle's meals are to be served by Morning Dove," LeCroix snapped. "You are never to enter her room again unless ordered to do so. Is that understood?"

"Sure, boss," Hal said, sliding past the Frenchman toward the open door.

LeCroix turned his attention to Jade. *"Bonjour, ma chérie. I trust you slept well."*

"As well as could be expected, considering I was locked in my room."

"Ah, yes," he said, his gaze running over her in much the same manner as Hal's had done. "The locked door. I fear I must continue to lock you in at night. But hopefully, it won't be much longer."

"What do you mean?"

"Skaggs will soon be arriving. And after that, providing all is well, you will no longer be kept under lock and key."

Skaggs. The name meant nothing to her but she dared not allow him to know it. "Why should my freedom hinge on Skaggs's arrival?"

"I feel I need verification of your identity, *ma chérie*. Since Skaggs is your hired man, he can provide that."

Damnation! she cursed inwardly. She must be gone before Skaggs arrived and gave her away. "I see no reason why you should distrust me," she said stiffly.

"Your unwillingness to accompany me here is a good one," he said.

"Then I pray Skaggs will hurry and provide you with the proof you profess to need," she lied. "When did you say he would be arriving?"

"I did not say," LeCroix said. "But it will only be a matter of days. I sent word last week for him to meet me at Fort Kent. Hopefully he will be waiting there for my arrival and we can return here immediately."

"Hopefully," she said, licking lips that had suddenly gone dry.

Jade knew there was no time to waste. She must leave at once, and to do that she would need Juaheela's help, meager though it was. And she could not go to the tavern Juaheela spoke of. If she did so, and the man—St. Clair—was friendly with LeCroix, she would be sure to find herself in the Frenchman's hands again.

No. She would have to find Fort Sheldon. And it would

take pure luck to do so because she had no idea where it was located. But only there could she find a truly safe haven.

"You are quiet this morning, *ma chérie,*" LeCroix said. "Are you troubled by something?"

"Would you not be troubled if you were held prisoner?" she asked, unable to keep the sarcasm from her voice.

"You are not a prisoner, *mon coeur,*" he said smoothly. "The guards you see are only there for your protection."

She remained silent, unwilling to debate the point, knowing there was no way she could win. LeCroix would never allow her to roam free when he was so uncertain of her identity.

"You did not tell me you were married," she said, her gaze probing his.

"De peu d'importance," he said smoothly. "It is of no consequence, merely a convenience, made to benefit both myself and the Wyandotte Indians. Juaheela's father, Scioto, considers me a blood brother. For that reason I am able to travel through Indian lands without fear of danger. It is the reason we are able to sell weapons to them, *ma chérie.*"

His explanation was not the same as Juaheela's. Jade knew the Indian woman loved LeCroix, knew that Juaheela didn't view herself as a bridge between the Frenchman and her people. Juaheela most certainly wouldn't have threatened Jade if that had been so. But she *had* threatened her, believing Jade to be a rival for the Frenchman's affections.

"Are you sure Juaheela feels the same way?" Jade asked, even as she wondered why she persisted.

"Do not trouble yourself about my wife," LeCroix replied. "She has left the trading post and, will trouble us no more."

Little did he know. Jade kept that thought to herself, knowing he must not learn of his wife's intentions.

She heaved a long sigh. "I am famished, Henri. But I need to wash first. Would you mind . . ." She allowed her voice to trail off.

"*Oui, ma chérie.* I do mind. But, regretfully, I must not delay my journey." He moved closer to her, taking her hand in his. "Will you miss me while I am gone?"

She controlled an inward shudder at his touch. "Perhaps," she said with a small smile. "I don't suppose you would consider taking me with you?"

"*Non!*" he said forcefully. "You must remain here while I am gone. But you will not be alone, *ma chérie*. Have no fear of that. You will be well protected here. My men will see to that."

She had no doubt of that. She would be well guarded, unable to leave the trading post. Her only hope lay with Juaheela.

God! Jade silently prayed. *Please let Juaheela keep her word!* Only Juaheela could release Jade from her prison. And the Indian woman must do it while her husband was gone.

Curling her stiff lips into a smile, Jade said, "Then it is good-bye for now, Monsieur LeCroix." She forced herself to hold his probing gaze. "Give my regards to your brother when you reach the fort."

His smile widened and his eyes twinkled lightly. "I think not at the moment, mademoiselle. My half-brother is unaware of your presence here and I intend to keep matters that way for the moment." He bent to kiss the back of her hand. "*Adieu, ma chérie.* Think of me while I am gone."

Without another word he left her alone.

The auction was over, but the crowd had not yet dispersed, a fact that made the sweltering heat seem even more humid. Sweat-dampened bodies pressed close around Jewel Crawford and the man to whom she'd been sold.

Her anger was a tangible thing as she fought to stay upright amid the churning crush of people. Where in hell was her business partner? Although she'd not heard the name of the man who'd purchased her, he most certainly wasn't the one she'd expected. She'd been told the Frenchman, Henri LeCroix, was a tall man with dark hair, but the man who'd bought her was short and fat, with a bulbous red nose. And from the first moment he'd narrowed his gray eyes on her, Jewel knew exactly what her position in his household was going to be. Not that she was a virginal prude. Far from it. But Jewel had always been careful with her favors, bestowing them where they could do her the most good. The Englishman had nothing she wanted.

Nothing, that is, except her papers.

Why in hell hadn't LeCroix come for her?

Was it possible she'd been given the wrong information about him? Instead of squandering his share of the profits as she'd been told, had LeCroix, in reality, allowed his profits to accumulate?

If that were so, he might have decided to rid himself of her, to continue operations alone. Dammit! She wouldn't allow such a thing to happen! Somehow she'd get herself out of this mess and then she'd find LeCroix, confront him and demand his continued cooperation.

Jewel had no fear of the fat Englishman who'd bought her. He was a stupid pig who carried his brains in his breeches. It would take no effort on her part to outwit him.

His obvious desire for her body didn't concern her one whit. Quite the contrary, for she'd learned long ago how easy it was to trade her body for favors. She'd been able to manipulate men before she'd reached her teens. She'd had a good teacher, Jewel thought bitterly. She'd learned all the tricks of the trade from her mother, who'd been a prostitute until death claimed her at the age of thirty-three.

Jewel prided herself with more brains than her mother ever possessed. Her mother needn't have stayed in the slums. She'd been a beautiful woman and, had she chosen her lovers carefully, she could've become the mistress of an important man.

But she had not. Instead, she'd stayed in the slums, remained there until, ravaged by disease, she'd finally drawn her last breath.

Jewel had been eleven years old then. And, as she'd knelt by her mother's side that fateful day, she'd known what she must do. She'd become a prostitute, too. But her clientele would be carefully chosen. She had kept that vow, and before a fortnight had passed, she'd left the slums, moving to a small cottage owned by her wealthy lover. Before that association ended, she'd caught the eyes of a man more important than the first one. In that way Jewel had climbed the ladder until, finally, she'd had occasion to meet the Duke of Wellingford.

She'd learned her trade well, Jewel thought, as she followed the Englishman who'd bought her. And she'd damn well use that knowledge! The fat pig who'd bought her would be unable to resist. She'd soon gain her freedom. Even if it meant the death of the Englishman.

The day seemed endless, increasing Jade's frustration with her confinement. It would have been easier, she knew, if she'd had something to occupy her time. Even needlework—a pastime that she usually loathed—would have been welcomed. At least, she told herself, her fingers would have been kept busy.

The sun was high overhead when Jade heard a loud

grating at the door. She sucked in a sharp breath and watched the doorknob. Had Hal returned to torment her?

Fearing it was so, she moved across the room, putting as much distance as possible between herself and whoever was in the hallway. Her gaze never wavered from the door.

It opened suddenly, swinging inward with enough force to slap it against the wall with a sharp crack. Fear surged through her as she realized her worst fears had not been imagined.

Hal stood in the doorway.

"Why have you come?" she demanded.

"Brung you something to eat!" He stepped aside to allow the woman who had been hidden from view to pass.

Jade felt a momentary relief when she realized he hadn't come alone. That relief intensified when he remained in the doorway.

"Hurry up, Morning Dove!" Hal snarled. "I ain't got all day to hang around here."

Obviously intimidated by the man, the Indian woman pushed the tray toward the bedside table, then scurried quickly out of the room. Hal shut the door with unnecessary force.

Jade waited until she heard the key grate in the lock again before leaving her position against the far wall. A curt examination of the tray proved disappointing. It contained a bowl of stew, a glass of ale, and a wooden spoon. There was nothing there she could save for her journey.

Scooping up the wooden spoon, she tasted the stew. Heavily seasoned, it was not to her taste. But knowing she needed nourishment to fuel her body, she consumed the stew and drank the ale.

The afternoon passed as slowly as had the morning, but finally, night descended around the trading post, cloaking the forest in shadowy darkness.

Although she'd been waiting impatiently for Juaheela

to come, pacing from door to window, pausing momentarily to search the shadows below, before resuming her pacing again, she still missed the event, and was totally unaware of the Indian woman's return until her door was abruptly shoved open and Juaheela stepped inside the room.

"Juaheela!" Jade exclaimed, keeping her voice low so it would not carry beyond the room. "I thought you'd never come."

The Indian woman's look was disdainful. "Here is food and water." Juaheela shoved two hide skins toward Jade. "The door will be unlocked. Now, keep your promise, white woman, and go! Leave my husband's house before he returns here!" With eyes glaring her hatred, Juaheela spun on her heels and left the room.

"Wait, Juaheela! What about the guards?" Jade hurried through the doorway. But she was too late. The hallway was empty. The Indian woman had disappeared as quickly as she had come.

The sound of voices coming from below tugged at Jade, beckoning her. She crept slowly down the stairs, apprehension gnawing at the edge of her resolve.

Suppose Juaheela had laid a trap for her? Suppose the two men downstairs were only waiting until she left her room before they attacked her?

Poppycock! an inner voice said. *Why would they do that? If they wanted to attack her, all they had to do was unlock her door themselves!*

Besides, she must go through with her plan. The only alternative was do nothing, to wait for LeCroix's return and be found out.

Reaching the bottom step, she peeked around the edge of the stairwell, searching the room for the two men whose voices she'd heard.

They were seated at a small table beneath a lantern that

hung from the ceiling joist. The flickering light made them appear even more sinister than before.

The two men appeared unaware of her presence. Hal bent over a deck of cards, intent on shuffling them, while his companion busied himself with filling their glasses from the bottle on the table.

Her gaze flitted past the two men, stopping on the front door. It was barred on the inside with a heavy wooden plank.

Had Juaheela betrayed her? She must have done so, for Jade would never be able to make her escape that way. Any attempt to open the door would surely be heard.

She pressed her hands tightly together in an effort to ease the trembling that had possessed her.

"Dammit!" Jade gave a start of fear at the exclamation of Hal's companion, jerking her head back, feeling certain she'd been discovered until the man added. "The bottle's empty, Hal! How in hell did that happen?"

"Reckon we must've drunk it all," Hal said with a short laugh.

"LeCroix ain't gonna like us drinkin' so much."

"How in hell is he gonna know? He don't count his bottles, does he?"

"Wouldn't be surprised if he did."

Jade heard the scrape of wood as a chair was shoved back. She remained frozen in place, unable to move until she realized the shuffle of footsteps were moving away from her. She heard the tinkle of glass, then footsteps coming closer this time.

"Deal the cards!" Hal's companion ordered.

Her breath was caught in her throat and her heart beat a chaotic rhythm as she waited on the steps. Was she mad, thinking to escape into the forest and find her way back to civilization? There was no way around those men . . .

even if the door had been left open as Juaheela had claimed.

Shaking away her fear, Jade gathered her courage around her and gave another peep around the stairwell.

Both men were at the table again, but now the cards were in their hands. Her gaze skittered farther, searching the room desperately until she saw a small door that was barely four feet high, set into the wall farthest from the table where the two men were seated. And, amazing though it seemed, the padlock that was obviously used to secure the door hung free.

"You know, Slick . . ." The voice broke the silence, startling Jade. "I been thinkin' real hard about that wench upstairs."

"Sometimes it don't pay to think." The voice—obviously belonging to the man called Slade—was matter-of-fact.

"Hell, don't tell me you ain't been thinkin' about her, too!"

"I ain't paid to think about her."

"A man's got a right to his own thoughts, Slick. No way LeCroix can buy those." There was a moment of silence, then Hal went on. "He wouldn't know if'n we was to go up there and get our ashes hauled."

"I wouldn't bet on it."

"He wouldn't have no way of knowin'."

"Forget it!" Slick snarled. "I got enough trouble without borrowin' some more. Forget about the girl and deal the cards!"

Jade heard a sharp slapping sound and realized Hal must have taken his companion's advice. Suddenly, she heard wood scraping against wood, then the sound of Slick's voice again.

"Gotta take a leak." He stomped his way to the front door.

"You go ahead," Hal said, "I'll get another bottle."

"We ain't finished the last one yet," Slick protested. "What do we need with another one?"

"I intend to get good and drunk!" Hal snapped. "I keep thinkin' about that little chippy upstairs, and I figger if'n I drink enough, it won't bother me so much."

"Then, go ahead!" Slick said grimly. "But don't blame me if the boss comes back early and finds out what you been doin'."

Jade heard the heavy wooden slab being lifted from the slot, then the door grating across the floor as it swung inward.

"Close the damn thing!" Hal ordered. "There ain't no use in lettin' all the cold air inside."

The door slammed shut, and for a moment there was a long silence. Then, suddenly, Jade heard Hal's chair being pushed back. Her blood thundered in her veins. What was his intention?

Heavy footsteps came toward her and she jerked to her feet, hurrying up the staircase and squeezing through the door into the room where she'd been confined.

Then, pressing her ear tightly against the door, she listened to the thud of heavy footsteps climbing the stairs.

Hal was coming after her!

Her gaze flickered wildly, skittering across the room as she searched for something that might be used as a weapon.

The lamp?

It wasn't heavy enough.

The water pitcher?

Perhaps. She snatched it up, mentally judging its weight and decided it, too, wasn't heavy enough for her purpose.

The footsteps were coming closer, stopping just outside the room. A moment longer and the door would open.

Panic-stricken, she snatched up the pewter wash pan

and hurried back to the door, standing where she'd be hidden when the door opened.

A key rasped in the lock, then Jade heard a loud click. Hal had locked the door again! Her heart beat like a triphammer as she heard him grunt with the effort to open it. When it refused to yield, he muttered, "Damn lock must be rusty." Another click sounded, then the door slowly opened.

Jade's muscles tensed, sending a shiver of fear and apprehension sweeping through her. Her fingers tightened on the wash pan.

"Girlie?" Hal whispered. "Where are you, girlie? Ol' Hal's got somethin' for you!"

He took another step into the room, his gaze swinging back and forth, searching the shadows for her, and without allowing herself to consider the consequences, Jade lifted the wash pan and slammed it down hard against the man's skull.

"Unghhh!" he grunted, pitching heavily forward and striking the wide plank floor with a hard crack.

Jade stared at him with widened eyes.

Had she killed him? she wondered.

Was she responsible for taking another man's life?

Leaning closer, she pressed her fingers against his neck and felt the pulse of life flickering there.

"Thank God!" she muttered softly, wondering even as she did why it mattered to her that he was still alive.

Realizing she must move quickly lest the other man return and surprise her, Jade snatched up the two hide bags and hurried down the stairs again, alert for the slightest sound of danger.

To her great relief, all remained silent.

How long would it take Hal to regain consciousness? How long before Slick wondered at his absence and searched for him? She guessed it wouldn't be long, and that thought sent her scurrying toward the small door.

A moment later, she slid through the opening into a vine-covered arbor and closed the door softly.

Despite the coolness of the night, sweat beaded her forehead. She could hear her heart pounding with fear, a fear that steadily intensified as the night closed in around her, enveloping her in a blanket of darkness.

Creeping across the arbor, she peeked around a leafy vine and saw a man standing near the edge of the forest, his back to her.

She sighed with relief when she recognized Slick, realizing there might yet be time to escape before he discovered her flight.

Watching him carefully, Jade slid around the edge of the arbor, hurrying toward the back of the trading post.

A quick run of a hundred yards found her in the depths of the forest, hidden from view.

She paused for a moment, intent on catching her breath and allowing her heartbeat to slow.

A furtive rustling jerked her head around and sent her gaze sliding through the darkness, searching for whatever had made the sound. She heard a faint twittering sound, then a thump, just before a rabbit darted from beneath a bush and dashed into the dense undergrowth.

Her heartbeat had picked up speed again, beating so violently inside her chest that she thought it would surely break through her rib cage. But she must go on, she realized. Must hurry before Slick discovered her absence.

With her breath coming in raspy gasps, Jade moved farther into the forest. The woods were alive with nightsounds. She listened closely to them, identifying the swish of an owl's wing, followed almost immediately by the alarmed squeak of a wood mouse.

With her heart thudding with fear of the unknown, she

crept away on silent feet, moving carefully while her mind urged her to run as fast as she could, knowing that should she give in to that urge, she would likely make enough noise to alert the enemy of her escape.

Time passed . . . and each minute seemed hours, each hour an eon as she made her way slowly through the darkened shadows, stumbling over unseen obstacles, yet knowing she must continue on her way.

Finally, deciding she was far enough away from the trading post so the occupants could not hear her, Jade increased her speed, racing through the forest with only the pale light of the moon to guide her, feeling an urgency to put as much distance between herself and the trading post as she could while enough darkness remained to cover her flight.

Chapter Twelve

Jade ran and ran, with her pulse throbbing in her ears, stumbling occasionally, sometimes falling, then picking herself up to run again.

At times the forest became so dense with growth that a canopy of green completely blocked the moonlight. Even then, though, Jade continued her flight.

Finally, breathless and weary to a state of exhaustion, her leg muscles refused to respond to her brain's command. Her knees buckled and she crumpled to the ground.

Get up! her mind screamed. *Escape while you can!*

But Jade couldn't heed the silent warning, knew she must have rest. Her exhaustion had left her totally helpless, prey to the dangers of the forest, whether it be from man or beast.

"Rest," she muttered, closing her eyes and curling herself into a fall. "Must have rest."

Moments later, she was fast asleep.

Jade had no idea how long she slept, only knew that when

she awakened, the shadows of the night were dissipating, chased away by the graying light of a new day.

Breathing in the heavy scent of pine that surrounded her, Jade shivered and looked up at the storm clouds that were gathering in the sky. They were dark and foreboding, making it apparent that rain was imminent. And, although the resulting downpour should hide her tracks from those who might be following her, she was hardly dressed for such weather.

Jade decided she must find shelter, and she must find it soon.

Her stomach rumbled as she pushed herself to her feet, making her aware of her need for food.

The hide pouches! she thought. Where were the pouches that contained her supplies?

Her gaze slid across the ground, stopping near a flowering bush. There! One of them . . . No! *Both* of them were there, only a few feet apart from each other.

Crawling to the first pouch, she opened the top and dug her fingers inside. Although the food she extracted was unfamiliar to her, it appeared to be some kind of meat mixture, combined with ground berries.

Jade was lifting the food to her mouth, when suddenly a jagged flash of lightning streaked across the sky, followed by the deafening, crackling sound of thunder.

Jade shrank against the trunk of the nearest pine, her fingers clenching the meat patty so tightly that her knuckles whitened from the strain.

She knew she must find shelter as soon as possible. She snatched up the hide waterbag and hurried through the forest, her gaze scooting around the thick woods, seeking something . . . someplace to shelter her from the storm.

The wind that only moments before had been a slight breeze picked up, building in intensity until it was howling around her, whipping her midnight-dark hair into her eyes and flattening her long skirt against her legs.

And then Jade felt the first chilling drops of rain. It pelted her with brutal force, forcing her toward the dubious cover of a huge tree with spreading branches. Even as Jade sought protection there, her mind uttered a protest, for she knew that lightning had a curious way of striking the tallest object around.

It seemed hours before the storm passed over, leaving Jade chilled to the bone, wishing she could build a fire and dry out her clothing, yet knowing even if she had the wherewithal to start a fire, she dare not do so lest others see it.

Remembering what Matt had said about Fort Pitt being located at the apex of two rivers, Jade took note of her position and headed in a northwesterly direction.

How far was it to the fort, she wondered. Hours? Days? Perhaps even weeks? She shuddered to think it might take that long to reach it. Would she be able to hold out that long? The food in the leather pouch would only last a matter of days.

Realizing she had no choice, that she would have to make the attempt, Jade began her trek toward, she hoped, the nearest river.

Two hours of walking found her near the foothills of a high mountain. She was considering the climb when she heard a scuffling noise in the brush behind her.

Spinning on her heels, Jade searched the bushes for whatever—or whoever—had made the sound, but the forest appeared empty save her own presence.

* * *

The sound sent new fear surging forth. There was definitely something—or someone—there—hidden from her view by the heavy shrubbery.

Unwilling to be caught in the open, Jade dashed behind the nearest tree.

Snap, crash, crackle!

Jade forced herself to look around the tree, then sucked in a sharp breath, gut-sapping fear sweeping over her as she saw a huge black bear bursting from the bushes.

Catching sight of her, the animal reared up on its hind legs and uttered a fearful roar, swiping the air with its front paws as it lumbered toward her.

Climb the tree! Jade's mind screamed, and her fingers, obeying the command, clawed at the tree trunk.

No, no! a silent voice protested. *The tree is too small to offer shelter. The bear would snap it in half.*

God! What could she do?

Jade's fear acted for her. Mindlessly, she turned and ran, racing along a narrow deer trail as fast as her legs would carry her, circling around saplings that were in the way and searching frantically for anything that might offer her even the slightest haven of safety.

But there was nothing.

Crash, snap, crackle! The bear was closer! Closer! Even now she could feel its hot breath on her neck.

The bear's roar came savage, angry, as the beast ran on all fours, determined to catch the prey that thought to elude it.

Realizing the heavy thudding was only feet away and that she probably had only moments to live, Jade dodged sideways, throwing herself into the heavy brush that grew beside the trail. Her breath left her in an explosion of pain as she slammed into the dusty ground.

The bear roared out its rage and slashed at the bushes, ripping whole branches aside in its efforts to reach her.

Jade dug her elbows frantically into the dirt, trying to scramble farther into the thicket while the bear continued to roar out its rage and mangle the brush around her.

Her death was almost a fact. She had to do something, but what?

Grasping the root of the bush, Jade tried to pull herself into a small ball, hoping the beast would think her gone and go away itself. But the black bear would not so easily be deterred. It continued to rake the brush again and again as it continued to search out its prey while Jade lay there, eyes closed tightly, nothing more than a quivering mass of fear and pain.

Suddenly, as quickly as it had begun, the beast stopped its frenzied attack. Hardly daring to breathe, Jade opened her eyes and struggled up on one elbow, peering out through a tangle of leaves and gnarled branches.

The animal stood staring at the brush for a long moment, then, amazing though it seemed, it turned its head and lumbered away.

Jade was unable to move for long moments, afraid to leave her hiding place lest the animal reappear. Finally, though, realizing the need to continue her journey, she crawled from beneath the bushes and rose shakily to her feet.

Moments later, she left the place behind and began the long climb up the mountain.

It was almost noon when Jade saw the smoke curling skyward in the distance. She felt an instant chill of dread, remembering the day she and Matt had found Jedediah Collins's burnt-out cabin. It seemed so long ago, but in reality could not have been more than a week.

Quelling her fears, Jade told herself she was foolish, that the chances of happening on another such incident were slim.

She couldn't allow her fears to dictate her movements,

couldn't turn aside from the first sign of civilization she'd seen. No! She mustn't fear what lay ahead. She would surely find safety there.

Jade moved forward on reluctant feet, approaching the clearing slowly, her heart thundering like wild hoofbeats, her throat locked in a vicious spasm.

The fear was almost unbearable . . . the waiting even worse.

A knot in her throat constricted her breathing as the growth of trees thinned, then stopped completely.

Before her was a small clearing dappled with sunlight.

Jade's eyes widened with horror as she realized her worst fears.

There was a cabin. Another burnt-out cabin! Only the chimney remained standing.

She closed her eyes against the horror, swallowing down the taste of bile that rose in her throat.

Silently cursing herself for being a coward, Jade focused her attention on the area around the burnt-out cabin, then felt her stomach turn over as nausea threatened to overwhelm her again.

A man lay there . . . near the corner of what was left of the cabin. And the arrows protruding from his chest left no question about his fate.

A few feet past him lay a woman, her clothing ripped and torn, her bloody skirt bunched around her waist. It was obvious she'd been badly misused before her death.

"Oh, God!" Jade cried, turning away from the sight, forced to expel the contents of her stomach.

When she had done so, she turned back toward the forest, knowing there was nothing she could do for the couple. She'd only taken a few steps when she heard a loud thump. It was followed by another, then another, and another.

She whirled around, fear spreading anew, certain the

savages who were responsible for the nightmarish scene had returned for her.

But there was nobody . . . nothing within her view that could have made the sound.

Thump, thump, thump.

There it was again!

Tilting her head, Jade tried to locate the source of the sound. It sounded as if it was coming from behind the chimney.

Could it be a trap? Something to lure her there?

"Don't be stupid," she muttered aloud, taking a small measure of comfort from the sound of her own voice. There would be no need for such a thing. If anyone wanted to kill her, they could easily do so without luring her behind the fireplace.

Another thought occurred. Suppose there had been someone left alive at the site. Hurt, but alive.

Cautiously, she made her way behind the fireplace. What little color she'd managed to retain drained away.

An old man, wearing a tattered red uniform, lay amid the debris. Although he looked dead, his foot moved slowly, thumping on an old wooden bucket next to him.

She hurried forward and knelt beside his bruised, battered body. The left side of his head was crushed, his eye disappearing in a tangle of flesh and blood. He gave every appearance of being dead.

Even as the thought occurred, his foot moved again, thumping against the bucket, once, twice, three times.

She bent closer to him, her eyes averted from the crushed side of his head, looking at the right eye that was closed.

"Are—are you alive?" she whispered huskily.

The words had barely left her mouth when his right eyelid popped up and he stared balefully at her with the faded-blue orb. His mouth opened and closed, but no sound came forth.

Licking dry, cracked lips, he tried again. "Took you . . . long enough. Thought I'd be dead afore . . . anybody found me." His breath came in harsh, wheezing gasps, as though his lungs had collapsed. "You might . . . near waited too long . . . to come."

"Let me help you," she said, sliding a gentle arm beneath his shoulder. "I have some water here and—"

"No use," he rasped, blood trickling from his mouth, his one eye piercing her, while his gnarled fingers clutched at her sleeve. "I'm . . . done. Only kept myself alive this long so's I could . . . tell somebody what happened."

"You'll be all right," she murmured, her eyes filling with tears of sympathy as she spoke the lie. "You're not alone now. I'll take care of you."

"Listen to me," he groaned, his voice hoarse, filled with a terrible urgency. "I ain't got much time left. Gotta . . . tell somebody what happened. I . . . come all the way from Fort Adams. But them . . . Injuns come after me. Thought they'd stopped me good but . . . I fooled 'em." He coughed and brought up blood. "I fooled 'em all right. Kept myself alive so's I could tell . . . somebody."

"What is it you need to say?" she asked, feeling an icy chill spread through her.

"Gotta tell what Scioto done." He coughed again, and his foul breath assailed her as he brought up more blood. The stench of death was coming out of him. "That Injun . . . an' his bunch . . . attacked Fort Adams. They kept us fightin' for three days and three nights. And when our spirits was at the lowest point, he come in . . . there carryin' a white flag." His fingers tightened on her, digging into her flesh. "He told us we could all . . . go free if we'd lay down our weapons and leave the fort. He said, 'Take your people and your cattle and . . . go. All we want is our land.'

That's what he said . . . but when we left the fort they was waitin' for us. They attacked us and that white flag of truce we carried run red with . . . our blood. Nobody left but me. An' I was bad hurt.'' His nails dug into her arms. "Go warn the other forts,'' the old soldier muttered, his one good eye dimming. "Tell 'em what happened at Fort Adams. Tell 'em if Scioto comes . . . don't believe 'is lies. If they leave under a flag of truce they'll all be killed . . . like we was.'' His body convulsed. "Go,'' he commanded. Then, uttering a gurgling sigh, the life went out of him.

Jade felt frozen to the spot. She couldn't move, couldn't take her eye off the old man's good eye that continued to stare at her.

She uttered a moan of horror. *Go*, the old man had said. *Warn the other forts.*

But where were they? How could she find them? Even one of them?

Forcing her frozen limbs to move, Jade rose to her feet and left the scene of horror, hurrying quickly toward the forest, feeling a small measure of relief as she entered the dense growth of verdant trees. If any of the savages returned—for whatever reason—at least the trees offered some cover.

No sooner had the thought occurred than she heard a noise ahead of her, as though someone—or something—had stepped on a twig.

The sound sent a new surge of fear shivering over her. She searched frantically for the source of the sound and saw a glint of coppery skin as a bare-chested man emerged from behind a large pine.

Chapter Thirteen

Oh, God! The Indians had returned!

Cold black fear, almost suffocating in its intensity, swamped Jade as she stood there, afraid to move one step lest that step proved to be her last.

Although it seemed an eternity of time that she hesitated, it could only have been a mere moment before she forced her frozen limbs to move and slid behind the nearest tree. Her heart pounded beneath her rib cage, sending blood pulsing through her veins, pounding in her temples, as she waited for the shout that would mean she'd been seen.

But it did not come. Instead, no matter how she strained her ears, she heard nothing but the thumping of her pulse, beating in her ears.

Had the Indian been so intent on his own thoughts that he'd failed to see her?

Let it be so! she silently prayed.

Crunch, snap!

The sound that she'd been listening for came abruptly

and her heart gave a fearful jerk. The Indian was approaching her hiding place. Soon she would be discovered.

Her fear was almost overpowering now as she turned to flee . . . and ran into a hard wall of flesh.

She screamed as thick, muscled arms wrapped around her, enclosing her within a cage of steel.

Fighting desperately to free herself, Jade struggled with her captor, beating at him with clenched hands, knowing all the time her efforts were useless. He was too strong . . . too powerful.

He spoke to her then, his voice harsh and commanding, words that she could not understand, words that were—

English! Her captor spoke English.

She stopped struggling, listening to the words he was saying.

"Calm down, Jade," the man said harshly. "You're safe now. There's nobody here but us. Nothing to cause you any harm."

Tilting her chin, she stared up at the man whose hands gripped her so tightly. Her eyes widened with recognition. "Matthew?" she whispered shakily. "Is it really you?"

"Of course it's me."

Sliding her arms around him, she pressed her face tightly against his chest. "I can't believe it's really you," she whispered. The tears she'd been holding at bay welled over, sliding down her cheeks. "I didn't think I'd ever see you again!" She brushed at the tears with the back of her hand. "I thought—thought you were one of those horrible . . . I thought you'd come b-back to kill me, too!"

"You really are glad to see me, aren't you?" He seemed, somehow, puzzled by that fact.

"Yes. Of course I'm glad." She wondered why he would think otherwise.

He continued to study her intently, his gaze probing as though searching her innermost thoughts.

Realizing suddenly that she was still clinging to him, she dropped her arms and took a backward step. "I must apologize for throwing myself at you. I didn't mean to be such a—"

"What's happened to you?" he interrupted. "You have scratches all over your face and arms, and your gown is ripped in several places. Who did this to you? Was it LeCroix?"

"No. I guess it happened while I was running. I was so afraid."

"Of LeCroix? Where is he?"

"I don't know. I haven't seen him since I ran away from his trading post." Remembering what she'd seen such a short time ago, she gripped his forearm tightly. "We have to get out of here, Matt. It's not safe."

"Not safe? Why?"

"The Indians were here. They burned the cabin and—" She broke off, unable to describe the horror of what she'd seen. "It's just like before, Matt. They've been killed. All of them are dead."

"Who's dead?'

"All of them." Her voice trembled with remembered fear. "They're dead. The man and woman who lived in the cabin. And the old soldier, too. It was awful, Matt. Terrible! How could any human being be so cruel? How could they do such a thing?"

Although she was babbling, Matt seemed to understand what she was trying to say.

"It's all right," he soothed, looking over her head as though trying to penetrate the trees blocking his view of the clearing. "I didn't know there were any settlers around here. Where is the cabin, Jade?"

"No cabin," she said, an icy chill sliding over her again.

"It's gone. Burnt to the ground by those savages. I thought you were one of them, Matt. I thought they had come back for me."

"Shh. It's all right. They're gone now. Can you take me there?"

"I don't want to go back."

"Then wait for me here."

"No, Matt!" she said quickly. "Don't leave me alone."

He sighed heavily. "I have to look, Jade. You might've been mistaken about the settlers. They may not be dead."

"Yes. They are."

"I have to make sure."

Realizing he was determined to go, Jade ceased her protestations and led the way to the clearing. She hung back as he examined the bodies, keeping her attention focused on the thick growth of trees edging the clearing. Her ears strained for any sound out of the ordinary, but all she could hear was a faint swish, easily identified as a bird in flight, and the squeak of a woodmouse searching for food in the long grass. Even so, she expected, at any given moment, to see painted warriors erupt from the cover of the trees.

But that did not happen. All remained quiet until Matt rejoined her. "The woman was Bertha McCallister," he said gruffly. "I heard she was getting married the last time I stopped by her folks' cabin. It's gonna be mighty hard on her ma and pa when they hear what happened to her."

Jade felt a momentary relief that she wouldn't be the one taking the news to them. "Are we going to bury them?"

"We don't have time."

Although she wanted badly to leave, she wondered at his reasons. As though she'd spoken aloud, he said, "We have to warn the forts. One burnt-out cabin might've been the work of renegades. Even two is possible."

"But you don't think so?"

"No. There's too many Indians prowling the forest. And they're not after game, either. At least not the four-legged kind. There's something going on out there. Something big. And the settlers need to be made aware of that fact."

There's something big going on out there. The words reminded Jade of the old soldier. "Matt?" He looked at her. "The old soldier . . . I forgot about him."

"What old soldier?"

"Over there." She pointed to the chimney. "He's behind there, Matt. He—" She broke off, swallowing hard as Matt strode swiftly toward the blackened chimney. He disappeared from view, then, moments later, returned. "He's dead, too. I wonder what he was doing here."

"He was trying to warn the forts what happened at Fort Adams."

His gaze narrowed as his fingers curled tightly around her forearms. "He was alive when you found him? Think hard, Jade. Tell me what he said. Everything you can remember."

She told him everything that had taken place since she'd found the old man, ending with, "He was barely alive, Matt. If he hadn't been so determined to tell others what had happened, I'm sure he could never have lasted as long as he did."

"So I was right." He sighed heavily. "The Indian tribes *are* banding together, more than likely planning to attack every fort west of the Alleghenies."

"But it won't do them any good, will it?" she asked. "The forts are strong. The soldiers will protect the settlers, won't they, Matt?"

"The forts are all undermanned, Jade. If enough of the Indians band together and attack one fort, they could stop the flow of badly needed supplies. Without food . . . guns and ammunition, the forts would be lost."

"We must warn them."

He nodded his dark head. "I know. And we'll have to travel fast, Jade. They attacked Fort Adams. Now they'll most likely hit the closest fort to that, which is Fort Sandusky. And since Ensign Paully has never had trouble with the Indians around there, he most certainly won't be expecting any."

"We're going there?"

"We have no choice." He gripped her arm tighter. "Come on, Jade. There's no time to lose."

They traveled for hours, stopping only when Jade became too exhausted to go any farther. But even at those times, Matt would only allow her a few moments' rest. They continued in that manner—moving swiftly for a time, then pausing for mere moments—long after darkness covered the land.

Finally, though, Jade could walk no more. She curled her fingers around a slender pine and leaned her head against it. "Please, Matt,' she mumbled. "We have to stop and rest. I just can't go any farther tonight."

"I'm sorry, Jade. I didn't realize I was pushing you so hard. Sit down for a minute. Rest a while."

"A minute won't be enough." She slid down the bole of the tree until she was sitting on the ground, then leaned against it and closed her eyes. "I'm so darn tired. I feel like I've been walking for weeks."

He squatted beside her. "I know I've been pushing you. But we can't stop yet. Not here. It's too open."

"Too open?"

"We're not far from the trails the Indians use." His voice was gruff, but she could hear the underlying anxiety.

The explanation sent an icy chill slithering over her.

"Is there any place in this forest that's safe?" He didn't answer and that fact served to increase her fear. "My legs feel like rubber, Matt. I don't think I can take another step."

"You can," he insisted. "Just another mile or so. That's as far as you need go. Another mile. The river is close now. And there's a cave by it. I'm not sure how deep it is, but it will be safer than this place. We could spend the night there."

"A mile." She sighed heavily. "All right, Matt. We'll go another mile."

Somehow, she found the strength needed to continue the journey. And, an hour later, they took shelter within the cave.

"I don't think I've ever been so tired in my whole life," Jade muttered, sinking down on the rocky floor. With a heavy sigh, she closed her eyes and slept.

Jade woke abruptly to the sound of falling rocks. She jerked upright, fear shuddering through her, chilling her veins as thoroughly as if she'd plunged into an icy river.

Her gaze swept around the cavern, noting the small fire some feet away. Its flames dispelled the darkness nearby, but beyond its glow there was only blackness, a tenebrous gloom too deep to be penetrated.

"Matt?" she whispered shakily, noting movement in the shadows. "Is that you, Matt?"

He stepped from the darkness and knelt beside Jade. "I didn't mean to wake you."

Noticing his skin gleamed wetly, she asked, "Have you been swimming?"

"Yes."

"Why?"

"Just wanted to see what was on the other side of the river," he said cryptically.

"Did you see anyone?"

"No. We're safe enough here." He reached for his buck-

skin shirt and pulled it over his head. Then he stretched
out beside her.

"Have you had any sleep?" she asked softly.

"Not yet," he replied. "I'm too wound up to sleep."

"The Indians?"

"That, and other things, too." There was silence for
a long moment, then, "Jade. You mentioned LeCroix's
trading post. Did you go there with him?"

"Yes," she replied, her voice revealing her anger. "But
of course you couldn't have known that, could you? He
tricked me, Matt. Then he forced me to go with him to
his trading post."

"Tricked you?"

"Yes. He sent me a note by one of the guards . . . a note
that he'd signed with your name. I thought you sent it,
that for some reason, you couldn't come inside the fort."

"Damn his soul!" Matt leaned up on one elbow. "I
should've known he'd be up to something like that. So
you went outside and found him waiting for you."

She nodded her head. "I was so frightened. *And* angry.
But there wasn't anything I could do about it. He saw to
that when he locked me in one of the rooms upstairs."

"LeCroix will be called to accounts one day, Jade. You
can bet on it. . . . How did you get away?"

"Juaheela helped me."

"Juaheela. Why should she help you? She's LeCroix's
wife."

"I know that. She made that clear. Said she was helping
because she wanted me to leave the trading post. She
seemed to think I was a threat to her marriage. When she
came into my room that night I thought she meant to kill
me. I think, really, that was her intention, but I managed
to convince her that LeCroix meant nothing to me. Still,
it might not have worked if she hadn't thought I was
financing his gun-running business. She told me to go to

another trading post and wait there for LeCroix to contact me. She seemed to think the owner of the trading post would convince her husband to keep our relationship strictly business.''

"What trading post, Jade?"

"I don't remember. Saint something or other.''

"Clair?" he asked quickly. "Was it St. Clair's trading post?"

"That's it!"

"Dammit! I wondered if he was involved! I should've known. The little bastard. And all the while he's been lying, saying how terrible it was that someone was supplying the Indians with weapons.''

"You know him?"

"Yeah. I know him." He was silent for a long moment, then, "So Lecroix still thinks you're the woman who's been financing his business?''

"Yes," she admitted. "I thought it prudent for him to remain unaware of my identity. At least while I was still his prisoner.''

"Very wise of you."

The silence stretched out between them, but, to Jade, it was a comforting silence, made so, she knew, by his presence, by the safety he represented.

"Are you sleepy?" he asked after a while.

"Not now." Her heartbeat picked up speed, began to pound heavily against her rib cage, and she wondered what caused it to react in such a manner. "You must be sleepy, though.''

"For some reason I'm not. More'n likely because I'm still cold. The water in the river is near freezing this time of year.''

"I forgot you were swimming." She ran her palm across his cheek, and his flesh felt cold to the touch. "Maybe we should build the fire up.''

"Better not," he said huskily, placing his hand over hers as though to hold it in place. "The glow from a small fire can't be seen from outside, but a larger one might be spotted."

She hesitated momentarily, wondering if he would consider her forward if she tried to warm him. "It—it might help if you moved closer to me. My body is warm and . . ." Her voice trailed away as a blush crept up her neck to stain her cheeks.

"You don't mind?" he questioned huskily.

Her breath caught in her throat and remained trapped there. "I—I don't mind."

He moved closer to her, close enough so she could feel his body heat. "I'm still cold, Jade. It would prob'ly help if I put my arms around your shoulders."

"Do you think so?" Her heart began to race madly. "I guess—guess you should do it then."

Immediately, he slid an arm around her waist and pulled her closer to him. She closed her eyes, breathing in the musky scent of his body. Her nipples became taut, erect, and her loins tightened. She found herself wondering how his naked flesh would feel against her own.

Unconsciously, she moved her cheek against the buckskin that covered his chest. His hand tangled in her hair and tugged gently. Closing her eyes, Jade tilted her head ever so slightly. Her breath quickened as she waited for what was to come, and, to her supreme delight, she felt the brush of his mouth against hers.

"Jade," he whispered against her lips. "I've wanted to do that for a long time."

"Matt—"

"No," he interrupted. "Don't say anything."

His mouth came down, molding her lips beneath his. Jade felt an uncontrollable shudder of desire as his fingers brushed across her cheek, then moved downward, leaving a trail of fire behind.

He caressed her neck, her shoulder, then the swell of her breast, and her heart raced frantically as his lips left hers and sought the delicate pulse at her throat.

"Matt," she groaned, feeling almost overwhelmed by his touch. "W-What are you doing, Matt?"

"I'm making love to you," he said, raising his head momentarily to look into her eyes. "Do you have any objections?"

"N-no." God, what was she saying? Had she lost her senses? "Uh . . . yes." She felt mesmerized by the heat of his gaze. "We shouldn't do this, Matt. It—it isn't right."

"It feels right to me." He traced the outline of her mouth with his tongue, and the heat of his touch sent shivers through her body.

"B-but we can't," she moaned.

As his fingers worked at the buttons on her gown, Jade caught at them. She couldn't allow him to proceed, no matter how much she ached for his touch. She must not allow him to take such liberties, lest he take her for a wanton woman.

Even as that thought occurred, he pushed the neckline of her gown aside, making her realize that, while she had been holding the one hand, the other had been busy unfastening her gown.

"Matt! You must not—"

She broke off, uttering a moan as his lips fastened on the nipple of her right breast. Incredible heat washed over her, and she shuddered as unfamiliar sensation flooded her senses.

An avalanche of longings, totally unknown to her before, engulfed her, stoking a fire that threatened to engulf her in its flames.

She could feel Matt's lower body grow taut, could feel

it pressing firmly against her thighs, making her even more aware of his maleness. She moaned again as he suckled at first one nipple, then the other.

Then, suddenly, Matt pushed her away from him, struggling with her gown for a moment. She felt something give, then it slipped down, gliding across her flat stomach to her hips.

Cold air struck her flesh as though she'd been doused with ice water and it brought her to her senses. She pushed frantically at him, her eyes filled with horror.

What was he doing? What must he be thinking of her?

Matt released her and she tugged at her gown, moaning softly as she scooted across the floor, putting distance between herself and the man she wanted so badly.

She lowered her lashes, unable to meet his gaze, afraid of what she would see in his eyes. Silence stretched out between them. She knew he was watching her, could feel his gaze on her.

Then, suddenly, he jerked to his feet and strode quickly from the cave, leaving her to wonder if he'd decided to abandon her.

Matt strode through the forest, sucking in deep breaths of cold air, trying to regain control of his feelings. His blood boiled with excitement, pulsing through his veins and throbbing in his temples. He wanted to retrace his steps, wanted to return to her, to take her in his arms and crush her against his aching body.

But he could not. Not with the memory of her white face and shivering body hunched against the farthest wall of the cavern.

Dammit!

He'd let his feelings for her overcome his good sense and literally frightened the wits out of her.

She'd been afraid of him. Of him! His mouth felt dry at the thought and he raked a trembling hand through his dark hair. He'd never forget the way she'd looked at him, so pale and stunned, her fingers clutching her gown against her trembling body, her eyes wide and fearful.

Dammit, why had she been so afraid? Was it because she was a virgin and he had frightened her with his passion? He'd never have gone so far if he hadn't felt her response.

And she *had* responded.

Just the memory of that response, her lips clinging to his, her firm breasts pressed tightly against him, her nipples swollen, taut with desire, caused his lower body to harden again.

Why couldn't he have left her alone? What in hell was wrong with him anyway? He'd had plenty of women in his life—more than his share. But all of them had one thing in common—they were experienced in the ways of the world.

Never—not once in his life—had he ever made love to a virgin.

But he'd damn near done it tonight.

How low could a man sink?

He continued to rail silently, calling himself every name he could think of while shoving through the thick growth of trees. He was so wrapped up in his thoughts, unable to get past the sight of wide eyes staring at him with horror from across the cavern floor, that if a horde of howling Indians dropped from the trees around him, they would have caught him unawares.

Chapter Fourteen

Jade watched miserably as Matt strode from the cavern. His body was rigid, every line stiff with disapproval. She swallowed around an obstruction in her throat, felt unbidden tears flood her eyes and blinked rapidly to dry them.

He was angry with her, absolutely furious.

But then, he should be.

She had led him on, making him believe . . . what? That she was willing, even eager for his lovemaking?

You were! her heart cried. *Eager and more than willing. But when cold reality slapped you in the face you backed away.*

Her face flushed with heat when she remembered the way she'd responded.

His lips had felt so good against her breast! And his flesh, the sweet salty taste of it was something she would not soon forget. Even the memory caused a burning heat in her loins.

She'd never thought it was possible to feel this way. She wanted him even now, had all but begged him to make love to her. And then, when he had done so, she'd rebuffed him, had flung herself away like some fearful child.

She had been afraid, she silently admitted. But not of Matt. She'd been more afraid of the feelings he had aroused in her, feelings that she had never known before, never even dreamed existed. But more than that, she had been afraid of what he would think of her if she gave in to those feelings.

Had she worried unnecessarily? she wondered.

Matt's face had been expressionless when she'd pushed him away. But, like her, he'd been breathing heavily as though he'd just run several miles.

Suppose she hadn't stopped him. What would've happened then?

Oh, God! She wished she *hadn't* stopped him. If only she had it all to do over again. If only she could relive those moments of time. But she could not. They were only a memory now.

Closing her eyes, Jade lost herself in the memory of his touch. She imagined she could feel his hard, muscled body against hers again, could feel his fingers pushing through her hair, holding her head still while he ravaged her mouth.

Why had she run away like a foolish child? The next time—if fate allowed her a next time—she would stay in his arms, would know the completeness of his passion.

She didn't know how long she sat there, engrossed in her thoughts, before she heard his footsteps again echoing through the passage leading to the small cave. Her heart gave a quick leap of hope, then beat fast with anticipation. Matt was returning. Perhaps she would be able to make up for her foolishness.

He emerged from the darkness, but his expression, seen by the flickering firelight, was uncompromising.

Without even a glance in her direction, he stretched out

on the rocky floor, his back to her, and cradled his head on his arms.

"Matt?" she whispered.

"Go to sleep, Jade," he growled. "We've got a long way to go tomorrow."

A quick stab of hurt sliced through Jade and a suffocating sensation tightened her throat. Tears filled her eyes and rained down her cheeks. She knuckled them away quickly, afraid he might turn and see her distress.

She couldn't blame him for his anger, she told herself again. She had been a silly goose . . . a stupid, feather-brained dunce, impetuous and imprudent. A thoughtless, weak-minded child.

Her heartbeat was heavy, her blood pounding furiously as she called herself every name she could think of. Her face was hot with humiliation, and she was glad of the shadows that hid the flush in her cheeks. How could he ever forgive her? she wondered, the pain in her heart a sick, fiery gnawing. She had shown herself eager for his touch, yet when it came down to giving herself to him completely, she'd backed away.

The endless night stretched out before her.

Realizing she needed sleep, yet feeling that her restless thoughts would surely keep her awake, she stretched out on the hard rock floor and closed her eyes.

Moments later she was fast asleep.

Jade woke to a feeling of delicious warmth. Her eyelashes flickered, then lifted and she gazed, incomprehensively, at the cream-colored ceiling. It resembled rock more than anything else.

That realization was quickly followed by another. Her bed was incredibly hard, making her painfully aware of the bruises and scrapes that covered her body.

Feeling a stirring beside her, she turned her head and the cobwebs of sleep dispersed as she saw the man who shared her bed of stone.

Matthew Hunter!

Jade sucked in a sharp breath. He was wide awake, his gaze fastened on her. How long had he been watching her? she wondered.

Remembering the previous night, a flush of embarrassment crept up her neck to stain her cheeks.

Darn it! Why did she have to blush so easily?

Reminding herself she had plenty to blush about, she considered apologizing to him. But what could she say that wouldn't sound foolish? Better that she remain silent and hope a time would come when her actions would speak for her.

His lips twitched suddenly, his eyes crinkling at the corners as though he guessed her thoughts and was amused by her discomfiture. "Good morning," he said huskily. "Did you sleep well?"

"Yes," she murmured, lowering her lashes to shield her gaze. She wished he wouldn't stare at her with such intensity.

"I want to apologize for last night." His dark eyes could have melted butter. She was on the verge of telling him there was no need to apologize, that she'd wanted him as much as he'd seemed to want her, when he spoke again. "I wasn't thinking straight. Blame it on the fact that I was tired . . . and too long without a woman."

Too long without a woman?

She felt as though he'd thrown a bucket of ice water over her.

Last night had meant nothing to him at all. She just happened to be there . . . the only woman within a hundred miles . . . convenient when he needed one.

And she'd thought he wanted *her! Her,* Jade Carrington! What a fool she'd been. What a silly, damned fool!

"It's already forgotten," she said abruptly, rolling quickly away from him. She felt proud of the fact that although she thought her heart must surely break, she'd somehow managed to keep her voice even, distant.

Straightening to her full height, Jade shook her long hair back, then smoothed down her torn, stained skirt. She could feel the acid sting of tears in her eyes, but her voice, when she spoke, gave no sign of her distress.

"How much farther do we have to go?"

"Barring trouble, we should be there before nightfall."

Jade uttered a silent prayer that they *would* reach the fort. Otherwise she would be forced to spend another night alone with Matt. If that happened, she might weaken and reveal her feelings for him. She couldn't allow that to happen. Not now, when he'd as much as told her she meant nothing to him.

Her stomach rumbled suddenly, making her aware of her growing hunger. "Is there any more jerked meat, Matt?" She felt proud that her voice showed no sign of emotion.

"Should be enough for a few more meals. Oughta last until we reach Fort Sandusky."

Striding across the cavern, he scooped up the hide pouch containing the jerky and the water canteen. Loosening the drawstring on the hide bag, he extracted two pieces of dried venison, handed one to Jade, then settled back on his heels to eat.

Jade chewed silently for a moment, her thoughts turning to the journey before them. What would they find when they reached the fort? "Will we get there in time to warn them, Matt?"

"The fort?" At her nod, he said, "I hope so." He chewed his jerky for a while, seeming to be lost in thought.

"What will we do if the Indians have already been there?" she asked.

"We'll cross that bridge when we come to it."

"I hope we're not too late."

"Don't worry about it. Scioto will prob'ly go back to his village first. It's usual to have a victory celebration after a battle. He'll want to brag about his conquests to his people, to tell them how brave he was."

"Brave?" She stared up at him with huge, indignant eyes. "I fail to see anything courageous about a band of savage warriors attacking three defenseless people."

"The Indians see it different, Jade. They believe each enemy they kill brings honor to them."

"Even women?"

"Even women," he agreed. "To their way of thinking, those women, if left alive, would bear children who would eventually take up arms against them. That's why they destroy the babies, too."

"Babies?" She felt horror rising in her throat. "Oh, Matt, how horrible!"

"Don't think about it," he advised. "I only told you to make you understand how desperate our situation is, how we dare not delay reaching the fort."

"Do you really think we'll get there in time, or are you just saying that."

"I really believe it, Jade. And you must hold on to that belief."

She nodded her head. Yes, she'd have to do that. She'd cling to that thought.

Reaching for the canteen, he offered it to her. When she shook her head, he lifted it to his mouth and swallowed several times, then straightened his long legs and pushed himself upright.

"I'm going outside to have a look around. You stay here

and wait for me." Without waiting for a reply, he entered the tunnel and quickly disappeared from view.

When Jade finished her strip of jerked meat and washed it down with water, she reached for her shoes and pulled them on. After she'd laced them tightly, she dropped the canteen beside the leather bag containing their meager supplies, then settled back to wait.

It seemed an eternity before she heard Matt's footsteps in the passage. "Is everything all right?" she asked anxiously.

"Yes." His voice was gruff. "No sign of anyone out there. It should be safe enough to leave now."

Scooping up their supplies, he fastened the leather bag and canteen to his belt, then turned to her. "Ready?"

She nodded her head and followed him out of the cave.

Pontiac stood on the riverbank and gazed across the river at Fort Detroit.

The fort was a considerable structure, with twenty-foot upright poles enclosing an area more than twelve hundred yards in circumference. It was built on a slope rising from the shore which made it easy for him to see most of the interior.

His gaze narrowed on the barracks and storehouses. Although there was movement there, none of the people he could see appeared agitated or fearful of the Indians who stood across the river.

But then, why should they be fearful? he silently asked himself. The occupants of the fort were used to seeing Indians about, as were the French residents who lived outside the fort.

Pontiac had no idea how many permanent residents lived outside the fort, but he did know there were several hundred more of the whitewashed, picket-fenced farmhouses built along the river above and below the fort than the eighty houses that had been built inside the walls.

The Frenchmen who occupied the farmhouses raised produce for sale, formerly to the traders and now also to the garrison.

He ignored the farmhouses and their occupants, knowing there'd be no trouble from that quarter. Not when they were comprised mostly of Frenchmen who had no love for the English dogs who'd so recently conquered them.

No. Pontiac did not expect any trouble from the French. And, because of that, he'd given orders they should be left strictly alone unless they interfered with his plan for taking the fort.

As he would, he silently vowed as his men gathered around him, ready to be told of the next stage in their attack.

Sweat beaded Jade's brow and her leg muscles ached with strain as she glanced at the sun, which resembled a blazing red fireball, hovering above the mountainpeaks in the west.

Sucking air into lungs that burned with the strain of trying to keep up with Matt's long strides, Jade fought against the dizziness that threatened to overcome her.

God, she was so tired, both mentally and physically. Her every ounce of energy was completely spent.

Her knees felt weak, rubbery, and she sagged against a lodgepole pine to keep herself upright. She looked up the trail at Matt, who seemed completely unaware of her predicament.

"Matt!" she called, but her voice was weak, strained. It couldn't have penetrated the distance that separated them, she realized, and it was a distance that was growing longer with each passing moment as his swift strides carried him farther and farther away from her.

She licked her dry lips and tried again. "Matt, please wait. I can't—"

Even though her voice was no louder, something—some sixth sense perhaps—caused him to turn.

He stiffened immediately, then hurried back the way he had come.

"What's wrong, Jade?" he asked gruffly.

"I need to rest."

Her aching legs suddenly collapsed beneath her weight and she slid slowly to the ground. Matt's expression was anxious as he bent over, his face only inches above hers. "Dammit, woman," he growled. "Have you no sense at all? You should have said something. Do you want some water?" Even as he asked the question, he was already unfastening the canteen.

Weak tears stung her eyes but she quickly blinked them away. She took the canteen from him and gulped the tepid water that, at that moment, tasted like ambrosia.

"Easy," Matt said quietly. "Too much at once will make you sick." He studied her face. "Why didn't you tell me you were so thirsty?"

"I-I didn't know at first . . . and then you were going so fast it was hard to catch up."

"Dammit, Jade! Speak up next time."

"I'm sorry," she muttered, lowering her thick lashes to escape his eyes.

She silently cursed herself for being such a coward. She should've had more fortitude, especially now, when there were so many lives at stake.

He lifted her chin and forced her to look at him. "We'll rest here a while, give you time to catch your breath. Do you want something to eat?"

She shook her head.

Reaching out, he took her hand in his and stroked it gently. "I'm sorry I shouted at you. You've been a real trooper through this whole thing."

"No. I haven't. I've been holding you back."

"That's not your fault. Your legs are shorter than mine. It's been hard on you, but you've never once complained."

She laughed shakily. "Don't give me too much credit, Matt. I would've complained, loud and long, if I'd thought it would alter our circumstances."

"So would I," he said softly, his eyes never leaving hers.

Those eyes were darker than she'd ever seen them, mesmerizing, hypnotizing. Her breath caught in her throat and her whole being seemed to be waiting. She remembered how he'd touched her the night before, how his lips had covered hers in that all-consuming kiss.

"It wouldn't help, though," he said huskily, his breath feathering across her lips.

"What wouldn't help?" she asked, caught in the heart-rending tenderness of his gaze.

His lips twitched as though he were amused. "Complaining. It wouldn't alter our circumstances." His head lowered even more, his lips hovering just a breath away, and she stared at him, her body tense with longing.

As she watched, his expression changed. His eyes began to smolder. His gaze slid downward, slowly, seductively, and his look was enough to melt ice.

Her heart jolted and her pulse pounded as she tried to throttle the dizzying current racing through her, fight the overwhelming need to get closer to him, to lose herself in his embrace.

His mouth began to lower until it covered her own in a hard, passionate kiss. But before she could respond, it was over. His head lifted and he set her aside.

"Later," he said gruffly, straightening his big body and pulling her up with him. "Are you ready to go on now?"

Finding herself unable to speak again, Jade nodded her head.

But she wasn't, her heart cried. She wasn't ready at all. Even so, when he strode forward, she followed after him as meekly as a hound dog following its master's command.

Chapter Fifteen

Built in 1761, Fort Sandusky stood on the inlet of the Sandusky River, straddling the main route from Detroit to Delaware country on the Muskingum. Not far from the fort was a Wyandotte village that housed more than a hundred warriors who often came to the fort, sometimes wanting rum, or a gun repaired, or to offer the services of a wife or daughter.

The fort's commander, Ensign Christopher Paully, saw nothing wrong in any of those visits. If truth be known, he had come to look forward to those encounters. In this wilderness they would, at times, go months on end without meeting another living soul, except for their Indian neighbors. And, during the fort's two years of existence, there had never been any trouble at all with them. He certainly had no reason to suspect today would be any different from all the days that had gone before.

He was striding across the parade ground, headed for the sutler's store when the sentry, who stood at his post on the scaffold built near the top of the outer wall, suddenly shouted, "Hey, Chris! Looks like we got company comin'."

Ensign Paully didn't even consider rebuking the young sentry for his familiarity. It was hard to remain formal in such a situation as theirs, but he knew, if the occasion demanded it, the twenty-year-old soldier could be depended upon to address his superior in the manner he'd been taught during his training.

"Who is it, Henry?" he asked, his voice pitched just high enough for the sentry to hear.

"Indians. Looks like Red Cloud in front," the sentry replied, peering closer. "An' I think that's Running Wolf behind him. I wonder if he brought his daughter along with him." Although he spoke the last words in a musing tone, Ensign Paully heard them and was amused by the direction the young sentry's thoughts had taken.

"Well?" Paully inquired, lifting an eyebrow.

"Well what?" the sentry asked, looking down at his commanding officer.

"Did Running Wolf bring his daughter?'

The sentry laughed. "Don't look like it. Leastways I don't see her yet."

Believing the Indians had come to trade, Ensign Paully saw nothing wrong with allowing them inside the fort. However, he was a soldier, and that was reflected in his voice when he said, "How many Indians are out there, Henry?"

The young man looked over the wall again. "Looks like there's five of 'em, Chris. No, wait! There's two more comin' outta the forest now. But that looks like it." He turned to look down at Ensign Paully again. "There's seven of 'em."

Ensign Paully nodded his head and turned to the sentry posted at the gate who'd been listening to the exchange with a great deal of interest. "Open the gate, Charles. Let 'em inside."

Wood grated against wood as the heavy log that secured the gates was pushed aside. Then the guard swung the gate inward to allow the Indians passage.

Ensign Paully strode forward to greet the Indians whose hands were folded inside the brightly colored blankets wrapped around their shoulders.

He was vaguely aware of the sentry beside the gate who continued to watch them, and he made a mental note to reproach him after the Indians had departed for his lack of attention. At the moment, though, he was intent on greeting his Indian visitors.

His attention was diverted, however, when Henry shouted a warning. "Chris! Indians! A whole bunch of 'em headed this away!"

Ensign Paully jerked his head around. "Charles!" he snapped. "The gate!"

"What?" The young man gaped at him.

"Shut the damn gate!"

The words were no sooner out of his mouth than Red Cloud pulled a tomahawk from beneath his blanket and lunged toward the sentry, dealing him a blow that cleaved through his skull.

Ensign Paully reacted swiftly, pulling his saber from its sheath and turning to face the enemy.

"Look out, Chris!" Henry shouted, jumping from the scaffold to come to his aid.

The young man was immediately cut down by a short, squat warrior. He was dead before he hit the ground.

Ensign Paully swung his saber wildly, keeping the Indians at bay momentarily, yet knowing the fight would prove useless in the end. There could be only one conclusion: the fort would be overcome.

The end was more immediate than he suspected. Running Wolf had managed to get behind him during the fight. He waited for an opportune moment, then, with careless ease, swung his rifle around, delivering a hard blow across the back of Ensign Paully's head.

As a red haze began to form around his vision, Ensign Christopher Paully thought about the men who'd been off duty, who lay on their cots fast asleep. If only they could have been warned, some of them might have managed to escape. It was the last thought he had before he slumped on the ground, unconscious.

Jade's heart beat with exertion as she hurried to keep up with Matt. He had increased his pace during the last fifteen minutes, pushing effortlessly through the pine branches, brushing them away as easily as he would have brushed away a fly.

Suddenly, one of the branches whipped back and lashed Jade's cheek. "Oh!" she cried out, unable to stop the cry of pain.

Matt paused momentarily, swiveling his head to look at her appraisingly. "What happened?"

"Nothing," she replied. "The tree branch lashed back and took me by surprise."

"Sure you're not hurt?"

"I'm certain." She pushed back a lock of tangled, damp hair and smiled at him, feeling warmed by his concern. "Is it much farther, Matt?"

"No." He turned his attention to the dense forest around them. "I'd guess we're about a mile from the river now. When we reach it we'll turn north—the fort's about two miles upstream."

She probed the forest ahead, but the trees grew so close together that she was unable to penetrate the verdant thickets. "It won't be easy going through there."

"No. Not easy. But we'll manage." He smiled at her. "Just think about sinking your teeth into a hunk of fried venison, Jade. That'll help keep you on your feet for the next hour."

She tilted her head back and closed her eyes as she envisioned a huge venison steak smothered with hot cream gravy. "That sounds absolutely delicious."

Opening her eyes again, she looked at the treetops ahead, thinking of the fort that lay hidden beneath the canopy of green. "Have you eaten there before, Matt. Is the cook—"

She broke off, frowning at the wispy gray circles drifting skyward. They were strange-looking clouds, almost resembling smoke.

The memory of the burnt-out cabin intruded suddenly, but she tried to push it aside. The clouds couldn't be smoke. They must be rain clouds.

She narrowed her eyes, regarding the clouds intently. They didn't act like rain clouds. Or any other clouds she'd ever seen before. When clouds moved, they floated across the sky, not upward, as those were doing. She tried to tell herself she was imagining things, even tried blinking her eyes to see if they would disappear, but when she opened them again, they were still there.

"What's wrong, Jade?" Matt asked sharply.

"It's—I don't know, Matt." She pointed toward the wispy clouds, still rising skyward.

He uttered a quick curse. "Dammit! We may be too late. You stay here, Jade. Hide in the bushes while I—No, wait. It's prob'ly not safe to leave you here alone. You'll have to come with me, but keep close behind."

"You think it's the Indians?" She could hear the fear in her voice.

"It might be."

"But if that's smoke, it's not much," she argued, unwilling to believe anything else. "It's not like at the cabin, Matt. The smoke may be coming from somebody's cookstove."

"No. It would have dispersed before reaching that height. The fire that made that smoke isn't coming from a chimney. It's much bigger than that."

Fear was Jade's constant companion as she followed along behind Matt. What were they running into? she asked herself. What lay ahead of them? Perhaps they'd be wiser to circle the fort and go elsewhere. She didn't voice that thought before, for she realized immediately that such an act would brand her a coward.

She looked skyward again, hoping the smoke had disappeared, but, if anything, it was heavier than before. And now it was darker, curling upward in thick, black swirls.

"Matt," she said, her breath coming in quick gasps from the pace he was setting. "Look at the smoke. That must be a big blaze."

"It is," Matt said, his expression grim. "And there's no doubt now that it's the fort burning." He gripped her forearm with fingers of steel. "I'm going ahead, Jade. And I want you to wait here for me."

"Here? Alone?" Her breath caught in her throat. "Matt! Don't leave me alone. Please!"

"I have to, Jade. You'll slow me down too much."

"No. I won't!" she denied. "I'll stay up with you." She couldn't be left alone in this wilderness. Not again!

His mouth twisted impatiently. "All right, then. But you'll have to keep up." Without another word, he turned and hurried up the trail.

They'd only gone a short way when they heard a sound that curdled her blood. "My God!" Jade cried, clasping a hand to her breast. "What's that, Matt?"

"Indians," Matt said grimly.

Even though they'd been almost certain what lay ahead, the reality sent terror shuddering through Jade.

Suddenly, a piercing scream rent the air, tortured, wounded, and Jade covered her ears with her hands. She felt nausea welling into her throat and she forced it back. "What can we do, Matt? How can we help them?"

"I'm afraid it's too late to save them," he said grimly. They were close enough now to see the flames that billowed over the treetops. "The Indians have torched the fort. That means it's already over, Jade. Everyone there is either dead or a prisoner of the Indians. Come on. They'll be headed this way soon. And if they see us we'll fare no better than the soldiers in the garrison."

She shivered with fear. "What can we do, Matt? Where can we hide where they won't find us?"

"I think I know a place that'll be safe enough," he said, pulling her behind him.

When they reached the river, Matt pushed her toward a tall, flat rock that leaned over the water. "Crawl under there. As far as you can go. And for God's sake, don't make a sound!"

"What are you going to do?" she asked in a small frightened voice.

Before he could answer, they heard the sound of voices. Her stomach clenched with apprehension, and she fought to keep her fragile control from slipping as Matt pushed her deeper into the shadows.

She began to shake as fearful images built in her mind. "Matt," she whispered. "I can't—"

"Shush!" His mouth pressed against her ear so his words could not be heard by anyone who might approach their hiding place. "You can't make a sound, Jade. They'll be passing by here any minute now."

He was right, she realized as the voices became louder and the footsteps even more distinct. God, how many were there? she wondered. She was aware of Matt's hard muscles holding her still and found a small measure of comfort from his strength.

She squeezed her eyes shut tight, willing her mind to leave this place, to hide in a dark, safe place until this horror was over, but it refused to obey. She was all too aware of the approaching Indians trodding through the forest floor matted with pine needles.

A shrill cry split the air and Jade jerked, imagining they had been discovered. Her scream was smothered by Matt's hand covering her mouth. She swallowed hard, willing her trembling body to subside, straining her ears for another sound—the rustle of bushes that would signal the rapid approach of others, but her fearful, cowardly heart was the only thing she could hear, pounding, beating, thundering in her chest, pushing the chilled blood through her veins to pulse madly in her eardrums.

Would this nightmare never end?

Suddenly, Jade saw them. Indians . . . coming out of the forest toward the river . . . warriors—some of them wearing red and black and yellow paint in bright zigzags across their foreheads and cheeks—clad only in moccasins and loincloths and armed heavily with rifles, bows and arrows, and knives.

Her eyes widened with horror. If the Indians entered the river beside the leaning rock, at least one of them would surely discover the two people hiding beneath it.

She held her breath, waiting, watching, afraid to look away from the Indians who walked two abreast, fearing if she did, that would be the moment they would be discovered. The first man reached the riverside, standing a mere five feet from where Jade and Matt were hiding. He looked across the river for a few moments, then spoke to the man who joined him in that guttural language that was so strange to Jade's ears. Then, amazing though it seemed, the two men turned north, striding up the narrow trail beside the river.

Jade looked at Matt then, her gaze questioning, but his attention was still on the Indians who made their way up the trail worn smooth by countless animals over the years.

Although Jade felt danger had been averted when the Indians took the trail instead of entering the river, she could tell by Matt's tense body that he was still worried. The crack at the back of the leaning rock was large enough for her to see the Indians as they strode quickly by, but it was situated in such a way that the pair beneath the rock could not easily be seen.

She couldn't look away from the long line of Indians— or from the man limping along with them—a man wearing the distinctive red-and-gold uniform of the British soldier. Or what was left of a uniform, for it was ripped, hanging in tatters on his bleeding, mutilated body. It was obvious he'd been treated badly, so badly that Jade wondered how he could remain on his feet.

Even as she watched, though, he stumbled and sprawled headlong on the ground. As though becoming impatient with the prisoner's weakness, the nearest Indian—a thin, wiry warrior wearing yellow and black zigzag across his forehead—struck the captive with the heavy club he carried.

A grunt whooshed out of the hapless soldier. The Indian delivered another blow, then another, while the captive tried to regain his feet.

Jade squeezed her eyes shut, closing them against the brutality and swallowed back the bile that threatened to erupt from her throat. Her horror was so great that she pushed with her feet, trying to move away from the narrow crack.

A fistsize rock slid beneath her foot and she froze instantly. But it was too late. The damage had been done.

She saw the nearest Indian stop short and turn toward the leaning rock, his eyes narrowed searchingly, his rifle poised and ready as he advanced toward them.

"Dammit," Matt cursed. "They know we're here. I'm going to try to create a diversion. You wait until he chases me, then crawl out of here. Run down the river into the forest. Hide in the trees until you judge it's safe to come out."

Jade wanted to protest, to tell him that she didn't want to leave him, but the words died on her lips. Matt knew what he was doing. If they stayed where they were, they would both be captured. But if they separated, perhaps one could go free and bring help.

Matt released her and crept toward the narrow crack, squeezing his body into the opening. She wouldn't allow herself to think what would happen if he became stuck, couldn't allow herself to consider such a possibility. Instead, she concentrated on moving as silently as possible toward the river.

"Aaiiiiieee!" A horrible cry sounded behind her and she knew, instinctively, that it was made by Matt. He meant to claim the Indians' attention, thereby allowing her to escape.

Sliding out from beneath the rock, she sprang to all fours and prepared to run . . . and found herself face-to-face with one of the dreaded enemy. He had been lagging behind the others just far enough to see her leave the shelter of the leaning rock.

She jerked to her feet, dodging around him, intent on racing into the shelter of the verdant thicket so near the river, but he reached out and grabbed her hair and jerked hard, effectively stopping her in her tracks.

Pain streaked through Jade's head and neck, but she tried to ignore it, lashing out with her fists and connecting with his chest. He ignored her efforts, slamming his palm against the side of her head as though she were nothing more than a meddlesome mosquito buzzing around him.

A red haze clouded her vision and she was almost certain she was about to lose consciousness. *Hold on,* her mind screamed. And, somehow, she did, even though it would have been easier to give in, to allow her mind to drift into oblivion.

The Indian shoved his paint-streaked face close to hers, and fear seemed to sharpen her senses. She was acutely aware of him, of his coppery skin, his flattened nose that looked as though it had been broken at one time.

He released her hair, gripping her upper arms instead, his fingers digging into her flesh. She was acutely aware of the musky scent of his body, of the strength of him as he lifted her off her feet, then slammed her hard against the leaning rock.

Stunned, almost immobilized by pain and shock, Jade found the strength to kick out. She connected—by accident she was certain—with the softness between his thighs.

He released her, uttering a strangled sound as he covered his injured manhood with both hands.

Summoning every ounce of energy she possessed, Jade pushed herself upright, trying to lock her knees in place. But she could not. Her legs seemed to have no more substance than a strip of rubber. They crumpled beneath her.

Get away. Flee! her mind screamed. *Leave this place while you can!*

Jade heard the silent warning, but she couldn't heed it. Not with her legs refusing to cooperate.

Crawl! the silent voice commanded. *Crawl away and hide. Do something while the Indian is still dazed.*

She tried. Oh, God, how she tried. Desperately. Using her arms to propel herself along the ground, trying to put more distance between herself and the warrior. But she gained little ground, putting only mere feet between them, and all the while she cursed her useless legs for betraying her.

Still, she went forward, squirming, crab-like, across the ground, all the time wiggling her toes, trying to instill some feeling in them. And suddenly, she did. It was only a curious tingling, but it was there.

Elation swept over her as she realized the feeling was coming back to them. It wouldn't be long now before she could use her legs again . . . before she could get on her feet and run, could race away from this place, from the horrible sounds that were, even now, filling the air—those hideous, ringing cries that were savage, yet pain-filled, leaving her to wonder whether they came from the Indians or the white man who'd been so cruelly treated . . . or perhaps even from Matt who could very well be a prisoner of the Indians by now.

She told herself not to think that way. Matt had escaped into the forest . . . as she would soon. Any moment now she could run. Any moment now she would—

Something wrapped around her ankle hard, bringing her to an abrupt halt.

Chapter Sixteen

Fear was a tangible thing, thundering through Matt's veins as he wedged his large body in the narrow crack and forced it forward. The apprehension was not for himself, however, but for Jade. If he didn't time his attack just right, he knew, there would be no chance the Indians would miss Jade when she tried to escape.

The Wyandotte warrior who advanced on their hiding place, although wary, had yet to see them and Matt knew that, if he could claim the Indian's full attention, Jade had a good chance of escaping notice.

With that in mind, he pushed his wide shoulders through the narrow crevice, feeling the rough surface pull at his skin in places. He ignored the pain, but welcomed the warm flow of blood, knowing it would help ease him through the split.

The Wyandotte warrior eased closer, his gaze flickering back and forth, watchful, wary. Behind him, beneath the rock at the other end, he heard the soft, shuffle of Jade's passage, knew that she must be nearing the entrance.

Matt's fingers tightened on his rifle. It was now or never.

Mustering every ounce of strength he possessed, Matt exited the crevice smoothly, springing forward with the speed of a mountain cat, launching himself straight toward his enemy.

A mighty roar issued from his throat, a scream of defiance, of challenge. "Aaiiiieeee!"

The warrior gave a startled jerk, his gaze fastening on the buckskin-clad man who sprang from the ground at his feet, fringe flying, hair wild, about a face filled with blood lust. It was a sight to raise goosebumps on his flesh, to strike fear in his heart.

He tried to swing his rifle around, to bring it to bear on the wild man, but knew it was already too late . . . even before a shot was fired the warrior started singing his death chant.

Matt's rifle discharged, the musket ball striking his enemy, driving a hole through the middle of his chest.

The warrior stood there for a moment, staring at Matt with glazed eyes. His mouth went slack and his knees buckled. He sprawled facedown on the ground, his voice forever silenced.

The other warriors had been alerted to the presence of an enemy. Three sprang forward, expecting Matt to take flight in the opposite direction. Instead, he ran toward them, laughing loudly, swinging his rifle in a circle above his head as though taunting them, daring them to approach.

His actions slowed them, made them wary, wondering if he was a madman. But their hesitation was only a momentary thing, gone before he could take advantage of it. The nearest warrior—a tall, muscled man—tossed his rifle away and yanked his tomahawk from a thong circling his waist, obviously planning on counting coup.

Matt grinned as the warrior drew nearer, raising his rifle high in the air, then contemptuously tossing it on the ground. He knew his actions were foolhardy. But they were designed to give Jade more time to escape. If he could keep the warriors interested long enough, they'd never realize he hadn't been alone beneath the rock.

Pulling his knife from the sheath at his waist, Matt waited for the warrior to advance. They were almost equal in strength, but Matt had faith in his own ability. The warrior bent slightly as he shuffled forward, his greased hair glistening beneath the sun. Matt stood his ground, watching the warrior move closer until only three feet separated them.

Watching his opponent's eyes, Matt saw the merest flicker and knew the warrior was at the point of attack. As the Indian lunged forward, Matt sidestepped, shoving out his foot to trip his enemy. He could've slain him then, would have done so except for the fact that he'd surely have died with the Indian.

Instead, he took a chance.

With his gaze pinned on his enemy, he smiled widely, then dropped the knife at his feet and stood waiting.

For a moment there was dead silence.

Then, howling with jubilation, his enemies swarmed over him, whooping and howling, striking him blow after blow, driving him to the ground where they continued to beat him. Even so, none of the blows rendered him unconscious . . . they were well placed, painful in the extreme, yet not designed to kill.

Matt had no illusions about his future, though. He knew the ways of the Indians. He was most certainly a doomed man, but they would surely take their time killing him.

The warriors continued to pound him, striking him with fists, kicking him with their feet until his body was a mass of bruises. But finally they ceased the beating, obviously garnering no satisfaction from abusing a man who would not cry out, who gave no sign at all of the pain he must be feeling.

One by one they rose from the ground and joined the others until only one was left standing over him.

Matt was allowed no time to recover from the blows. The warrior reached down and pulled him to his feet, holding him there while the world spun crazily around him, indiscriminately blending green forest and blue sky together in a dizzying, whirling kaleidoscope of colors.

Sucking in a deep breath, Matt winced inwardly at the pain around his ribs and wondered, fleetingly, if the Indians had managed to break some of them.

He closed his swollen eyes for the briefest moment, gathering what was left of his strength about him. He knew the Indians admired courage even in their enemies, knew also that those who exhibited that emotion usually fared better at their hands than those who showed weakness and begged for mercy.

Opening his eyes to a mere slit, Matt searched the clearing for Jade. There was no sign of her, nor of the man the Indians had previously captured.

Relief swept through Matt as he realized that at least part of his plan had worked. He had managed to distract the Indians long enough to allow Jade to escape, and he'd managed to live through it.

Prodded by the nearest warrior, Matt began the long journey that would take him to the Indian village where he—and most likely the other captive—would surely meet their fate.

Jewel Crawford's face was expressionless as she studied the naked man who lay beside her, limp and obviously exhausted from their recent coupling. She was good at hiding her feelings, had perfected that art many years before. Percy Kilbride had not been allowed to see the disgust she'd felt upon arriving at his house—little more than a large cabin really—in the wilderness. Nor would he.

As though realizing he was being watched, Kilbride turned his head and grinned weakly at her. "There's more life in the old fellow than most would suspect," he joked.

Keeping her face expressionless lest he guess her real feelings, Jewel smiled and gave him a sly wink. "More than your wife would suspect anyway. By the way, where did she go?"

His eyes narrowed and his mouth drew into a thin straight line. "To Mabel Dearing's place. The women are trying to organize some kind of ladies' group—a quilting club or a needlework something or other. She said they needed something to do with themselves. My mother found plenty to do without such goings-on." His face had screwed up in displeasure and a vein throbbed at his temple. "My mother would have—"

"Don't get yourself worked up, Percy dear," she said, reaching out and smoothing the pulsing vein. She wouldn't have bothered but for the fact that she needed him. If the old goat suffered a stroke now, she'd be left at the mercy of his wife. And that old bag wasn't known for her gentle nature.

Giving him a long, sultry look, she murmured, "Luck must have been with me the day you bought me, Percy. Just think, I could have wound up with some despicable man who might have taken advantage of my innocence and given me nothing in return."

Kilbride's mood changed instantly. His eyes twinkled and he grinned at her. "You don't expect me to believe you were a virgin, do you, dear girl? During these many years past I've had occasion to make love to more virgins than I could count on both hands ... most certainly enough to know I wasn't your first lover.''

"Oh, but you were, Percy," she cooed, proud of the sincerity that rang in her voice. "It is true that I wasn't a virgin, but I *was* innocent. The man who took my virginity was not my lover. He took me by force.''

She gave a delicate shudder and squeezed her eyes shut, hoping he would believe she was shutting out a sight too horrible to endure. Then, just in case he was too stupid to understand her actions, she shuddered again and said, "Even now I can see his face, and the sight of it chills me to the bone.''

Wrapping her pale fingers around his pudgy hand, she pressed it against the fullness of her left breast. "Make the memory go away, dear Percy," she whispered in a little-girl voice. "Make love to me again. Now, Percy. Let me feel the magic of your wonderful body merging with mine.''

"Oh, my dear," he muttered hoarsely, his breath wheezing in and out of his throat as he caressed the swell of her breast. "If only I could. But I swear I am completely undone. I just don't have the energy left.''

She had counted on that fact. "Then let us lie here together," she said softly. "Just the two of us, with you caressing me like this. It will help to rid me of the memory of that evil man's touch.''

She lay back with a sigh, as though she garnered extreme pleasure from his touch, even managing a soft moan as though stirred to a passionate response. Not likely, though, she told herself. How could she welcome his caresses when, during their coupling, he reminded her of the fat, white worms that she'd seen as a child, maggots that wriggled frantically through food that had gone rotten shortly after they'd acquired it.

Never again, she told herself. No matter what the circum-

stances, she'd use her body—or whatever else she possessed—to make her way in the world. All she had at the
moment, though, was Percy Kilbride, the merchant who
had bought her, who now owned her, body and soul.

But not for long, she silently consoled herself. She would
wait, would bide her time and gain his trust, for it was
probable she would need his help to locate the Frenchman
. . . if he failed to come for her.

She had little doubt, though, that the Frenchman would
come. After all, she'd been told by reliable sources that
he needed the funds she supplied to continue his business.
And she'd made certain he knew those funds were still
available even though she was in difficult circumstances.

Yes, the Frenchman would surely come, and together
they would continue the business of supplying the Indians
with English weapons in exchange for the excellent furs
the Indians used for trade.

And, soon, despite her present circumstances, Jewel's
future as a wealthy woman would be assured. And wealth,
she knew, was the key to success. It could buy anything . . .
even her freedom.

She snuggled deeper into the mattress, uttering a sigh
of satisfaction that must have appeared to be a passionate
utterance to the pudgy man beside her, for suddenly he
moved closer, looming above her.

"I believe I feel him stirring to life now," he said. "Brace
yourself, my dear. Here comes Peter."

Controlling a laugh, Jewel Crawford did just that.

Jade's narrowed gaze swept the clearing as she was forc-
ibly dragged toward the small knot of warriors who stood
with the other captive. Matt was nowhere in sight and she
prayed fervently that he had managed to escape.

Turning her attention to her fellow captive, she saw from

the many bruises and cuts that he'd been sorely mistreated. She kept her eyes pinned on his face lest he feel embarrassed about his torn trousers which left large patches of skin exposed on his upper thighs.

"Are you badly hurt," she asked, trying to control her quivering voice.

"I'm still on my feet," he muttered hoarsely. "Just barely, though."

Before he could say more, the warrior beside him prodded him forward and he fell into line, limping toward a dense growth of scrubs.

Jade, urged onward by the paint-streaked warrior nearest her, stumbled over the uneven ground, keeping pace beside him.

"I'm Ensign Paully," the other captive said. "Commander of Fort Sandusky, or what used to be the fort until these red devils attacked and burned it to the ground. Now there's nothing left there."

"They killed everyone?"

"Yes. Everyone."

"Then you're lucky to be alive."

"Not so lucky. The others died quickly. My death will be slow . . . as slow and painful as they can make it."

She shuddered. "Do you think that was the reason they allowed you to live?"

"I know it was."

"Why? Do they have something against you?"

"I was commander of the fort. A man of power, to their way of thinking. That's reason enough to warrant special circumstances. My death will have a more considerable audience than the men under my command. The entire village of Detroit will probably turn out to witness the burning."

"Burning?" she repeated, her voice quavering.

"Yes." His eyes, when they met hers, were bleak with

the knowledge of his own fate. "That's the usual way. They'll burn me at the stake."

Jade shuddered at the thought. Would she suffer the same fate?

"Do they burn all their prisoners?"

"Not all." He looked at her with something like pity. "Perhaps you'll be spared that torture."

Jade's eyes darted around the forest, hoping to find a way out of this situation. "We can't just stay put and allow it to happen."

"We can do nothing else. Have you noticed how many of them are here?"

"Yes. I noticed." She was silent for a long moment, then, "Maybe you're wrong about their intentions. They might have something else in mind for you."

"I think not."

She shuddered again. But at least Matt had been spared.

No sooner did that thought occur to her than she heard a commotion behind them and realized how large the band actually was. At least two dozen Indians fell in line behind her captors and they were shoving a man along between them . . . a buckskin-clad man who somehow managed to stay upright.

She sucked in a sharp breath as she recognized the prisoner as Matt! He hadn't escaped. Instead, like herself and the hapless ensign, he'd been captured.

"Oh, God, no!" she cried.

He saw her in that instant, and, even from the distance separating them, she could see the color drain from his face, leaving it pale and bloodless. His lips moved and she imagined he'd said her name, although she was too far away to hear a sound.

Jade's guard uttered a guttural sound and poked her with the barrel of his muzzle loader, urging her into the dense scrub. Thorny vines and briars scraped her arms as

she was prodded up a rocky defile. Her breath rasped
harshly, her fear slowly eating away at what was left of her
courage.

Matt walked without resistance, without showing any
defiance whatsoever. Yet he was not beaten. Instead, his
mind worked furiously as he tried to find a way out of their
predicament.

The apprehension he felt was not for himself, but rather
for Jade—for what lay ahead of her if he couldn't figure
a way out of their situation.

He should have been more careful, Matt bitterly told
himself. Dammit, he'd known about the Indian uprising,
had suspected it for some time, and yet, despite that knowledge he had brought her into its midst.

Granted, he'd thought at the time that she was deserving
of whatever happened to her because of her involvement
with LeCroix. But in truth she had not been involved with
the man, nor had she provided funds for his illegal business.

How could he have been so wrong about her? Matt
wondered. How could he have, even for the merest instant,
misjudged her so?

He had been so wrong, so blind . . . so utterly stupid.

He looked at her stumbling along so far ahead of him
prodded by the barrel of a rifle when her steps slowed.
He cursed himself bitterly.

He'd seen the gleam in the eyes of the Wyandotte warriors and recognized it for the malicious hatred that it was.
Although Jade had done nothing to warrant their hatred,
she was not excluded. It was enough that she belonged to
the race of British who were, to the Indian's way of thinking, trying to steal their land.

Matt could not really blame the Indians for their anger.

But he had no intention of standing by while they took vengeance on an innocent girl.

Somehow, someway, he would find a way to set her free.

When Major Henry Gladwin heard about the large number of Indians that were gathering outside Fort Detroit, he called a meeting of his officers. They listened silently to what he had to say, and when the silence was finally broken, it was his second in command, Captain Donald Campbell, who spoke.

"Surely they have more sense than that, Major," the captain protested. "They have neither the manpower or the weapons needed to take this fort. Only fools would even consider making the attempt."

"Don't be so sure of that, Captain. I learned a long time ago not to underestimate those red devils." Major Gladwin eyed each man in turn. "They don't fight the way we do. They're a savage bunch who strike swiftly. They like to ambush their enemies. I learned that the hard way. As did Braddock."

Each man there had heard, at one time or another, of the major's exploits when he'd fought with the English commander, Edward Braddock, during the war against the French and their Indian allies.

Even so, Lieutenant George McDougal protested. "The fort is well defended, sir. There's no way the Indians could penetrate our defenses."

"I agree, Lieutenant. But I'm not so sure the Indians have accepted that as fact." He expelled a heavy sigh. "I've always known there would be trouble when they learned the terms of the peace treaty."

"You think that's what's happened then?" asked Captain Campbell. "You believe the Indians have somehow learned the British have been granted all the land east of the Mississippi?''

"Yes, I do believe that," replied the major.

"Even if they have, surely there's no need to worry," the lieutenant said. "We can hold out against them. We have plenty of water and supplies. Plenty of ammunition to hold out for weeks. Long enough to show those red devils their attack is useless. It's a certainty that none of the tribes have enough warriors to defeat us."

"Not alone," the major said softly. "But together, well . . ." He clasped his hands behind his back and began to pace the floor. "If they combine their forces, they just might be able to starve us out."

Captain Campbell uttered a short laugh. "Excuse me for saying so, Major, but none of those redskins have enough power, enough strength of mind, if you will, to bind their forces together."

"Perhaps not. But I wouldn't care to bet on it." The major held his captain's gaze for a long moment. "Would you, sir? Would you care to bet your life . . . all the lives of everyone in this garrison on that belief?"

"No, sir. I guess I wouldn't."

"Neither would I." The major expelled another deep sigh, then leaned heavily on the desk. "Give the order to double the guards, Captain. And have every man remain on the alert, ready to do battle at a moment's notice."

"Yes, sir."

The captain saluted smartly and left the room to issue the command. Then, one by one, the rest of the men filed from the room, leaving the major alone to contemplate his fears.

Chapter Seventeen

The prisoners' hands had been bound so tightly with rawhide that it cut into their wrists, but their feet had to be left unbound. Even so, as the hours passed and the sun began its slow descent in the west, Jade found herself stumbling more often.

Her lungs burned from the pace her captors set, and she felt as though the sun had lodged in her raspy throat. Sweat dripped down her face, trickling in the valley between her breasts, and her leg muscles ached.

Although she couldn't see Matt, she knew he was in the line somewhere behind her and tried to take comfort from that fact.

She swiveled her head, hoping to catch a glimpse of him, but the Indian next to her—apparently assigned to guard her—glared at her with angry eyes and spoke harshly in the guttural language of his people.

Shaking her head, she felt her tangled hair brush against

her face, felt damp strands stick to the sweat that slicked her skin. "I don't understand your language."

His mouth thinned as he spoke again, jabbing his rifle barrel hard into her side as he prodded her forward at a faster pace.

"Don't waste your breath," Ensign Paully muttered beside her. "*They* don't understand what you're saying."

"And you, do you understand their language?"

"Some of it. Enough to trade with them when they come to the fort. Which they've been doing for the past two years . . . as long as Fort Sandusky was standing." His mouth twisted with bitterness. "That's why they were able to catch us unawares. We had no way of knowing today would be any different from any other day. Dammit! We just opened the gate and let 'em through.

She could see he blamed himself for the incident, yet could find no words to console him. "Do you think they'll make camp tonight?"

"Who knows."

Jade didn't know whether to hope for such a circumstance or pray they kept moving.

Although she was weary to the bone, she dreaded to think what would happen when they stopped. So far, the Indians had contented themselves with prodding her along with their rifles. But, she realized, there had been no time for anything else. If that time were allowed them, what would they do to her?

Matt's thoughts were much the same as Jade's. He worried about stopping because the warriors would surely mistreat Jade in the most terrible way. He was prepared to die trying to stop them, yet knew if that came about, his death would be in vain. There was no way he could win a battle against so many warriors. And, from the looks of poor

Ensign Paully, the man could do nothing to help himself, much less Jade.

Dread settled over him like a heavy cloak as the sun sank lower, finally leaving behind only a bright wash of crimson.

The war party gave no sign of stopping, though continuing to move forward. Matt knew their destination wasn't their own village, because it had been hours since they'd passed the trail leading there. Instead, they'd taken the trail leading west.

The Indians pushed the captives hard, forcing them over a narrow path through the forest that had been traveled so many times by countless others. In time, though, they left that path and took another trail that wound in a northerly direction.

Night had long since fallen when they finally stopped to make camp.

Matt's gaze immediately went to the other captives who were gathered fifty feet away from him.

As though completely overcome by weariness, Jade dropped to the ground and her head slumped forward as she rested it against the base of her neck.

She had barely done so though when a wiry warrior locked his fingers through her hair and yanked her upright again.

Immediately, she uttered a terrified scream that pierced through Matt's heart. He lunged toward her, but was pulled up short by two Indians who held him by the upper arms.

Matt struggled to escape, his eyes riveted on Jade who trembled with fear while three warriors circled her.

God! How could he be expected to stand there and do nothing? How could he watch while they ravished her?

He had to do something! But what?

Realizing he must create a diversion, he worked up what mouth juices he had left in his dry mouth and spat full in the face of the nearest warrior. The Indian jerked back in surprise, releasing Matt while he wiped the dripping liquid from his face leaving only one warrior to hold the prisoner.

And that Indian had Matt's full attention now.

Jerking his knee upward, Matt caught the warrior hard between the legs, and when the Indian loosed the captive to clutch at his injured privates, Matt lunged toward Jade and her tormenters.

He managed ten steps before he was brought down.

Heaving with exertion, he lay on the ground, glaring his hatred at the four warriors who pinned him there.

Jade screamed again and the sound pierced Matt with the effectiveness of a knife, slicing into his flesh and ripping away at his heart. "Leave her alone!" he bellowed, struggling furiously to break free from the four warriors who struggled just as furiously to hold him down.

Realizing he was getting nowhere, Matt pinned his gaze on the man on his right who appeared to have some control over the others. "Tell them to leave the woman alone!" he snarled in the guttural language he had learned so long ago when he had many Indian friends.

The Indian ignored his words. "You fight hard, Hunter," he said, his flat black eyes glittering with triumph. "It is as they say. You are a mighty warrior. And it is I, Gray Wolf, who was responsible for your capture."

"And it will be you, Gray Wolf, who will be responsible for my death!" Matt sneered. He waited a moment for his words to sink in, then added, "But there will be few eyes to witness that event. If the woman is harmed, you will be forced to slay me before we reach Detroit."

The warrior's dark eyes studied his prisoner for a long moment. He appeared to be considering the white man's words. Matt held his breath, hoping his plan had worked, all the while trying to close his mind to Jade's terrified screams.

"It is a great victory to capture you, white man," the

Indian finally said. "You are known throughout our land as a man who prowls the forest, yet leaves, like our own warriors, no sign to show you have been there. Hunter, the white-eyes, whose traps take only enough game for his own use, unlike others of your kind. Your name is on the lips of many warriors, Hunter, for it is said your blade never misses its target." His ebony eyes glittered with triumph. "Your prowess and skill are known to warriors throughout our lands and your courage has never been questioned. And I, Gray Wolf—" he stabbed his thumb at his chest, "will become known as the warrior who captured the Great White Hunter."

"But you will never get me to Detroit," Matt repeated, controlling a shudder as Jade uttered another piercing scream.

"I will get you there." He pressed the tip of his knife against Matt's throat and his black eyes glittered with something like humor. "I can do anything I wish with you. You are the one who is a captive . . . the one who lies helpless on the ground."

Holding the other man's gaze, Matt deliberately raised his head just enough to shove the tip of the knife into his flesh. He watched the humor fade from Gray Wolf's eyes. "If my woman is harmed," he said softly, "I will make certain I never reach Detroit."

"You put a high value on your life," Gray Wolf said. "Perhaps too much."

"I think not. I am not a foolish man. I know the Indian nations have combined forces to drive away the English. My death on the stake would be seen as a great Victory to the red man. It would give your warriors courage for many moons to come."

The Indian nodded. "You speak the truth, Hunter. But I have no need to bargain with you. You are already my prisoner."

"But will you be able to keep me alive until we reach Detroit?" Matt deliberately pushed his neck against the knife tip again, felt the quickening flow of his blood. "See how easy it would be . . . how fast I would die. And I will, Gray Wolf. Take my word for it. If my woman is harmed, then I will force you to slay me where you stand. There will be no great victory celebration then."

Gray Wolf sat back on his haunches, studying Matt intently. Another loud scream split the forest, then another and another.

"Dammit," snarled Matt. "Tell them to leave her alone!"

Gray Wolf jerked his head up and snapped out the order that, hopefully, would gain Jade's release. Then he looked at Matt again. "They were right, Hunter, when they spoke of your bravery. You have much courage."

"Do you know the meaning of the word?" Matt asked calmly. "Or is courage only a name on your lips."

"What do you mean? My courage has never been questioned!"

"Nor am I questioning it now. Only that you know its meaning."

"I know the meaning. Courage is strength, bravery."

"And *hope*, Gray Wolf. Hope gives your heart courage and strengthens your body. Without it, there is nothing, no reason to go on. Look at my woman." The man looked across at Jade, lying crumpled on the ground, sobbing. "See how weak she is? If she does not find courage, Gray Wolf, she will need to be carried to Detroit. And that will slow you down considerably."

"We could kill her," Gray Wolf said. "Then she could be left behind."

"And you would lose a valuable captive," Matt hurried to point out.

"You could give her the courage she needs to go on?" Gray Wolf inquired.

"Yes. I could."

"Then go to her, Hunter," he said with no hesitation, "Give her the strength she needs to travel to Detroit."

Matt wasted no time in doing so, and moments later he dropped to his knees beside Jade's quivering body. Her eyes were closed, squeezed tightly together as though she could shut out the horror around her. If only he could take her in his arms, could offer her the comfort of his embrace. But, with his hands bound together, that was impossible.

Settling himself beside her, he whispered her name. "Jade."

"Matt!" Her thick lashes flew up, revealing fear-ridden green eyes. She pushed herself up and leaned against him. "Oh, God! What's going to become of us?"

Swallowing around a lump that was lodged firmly in his throat, he said, "Take heart, little one. These devils haven't got us licked yet. I've still got a trick or two up my sleeve."

Her eyes became round with wonder. "I should have known." Even as he watched, her expression became less apprehensive and he could see that she believed him. "What are you going to do," she whispered eagerly, wiping at her tears with the back of her bound hands.

"I'm still working on the plan," he prevaricated. "Meanwhile, you must do what they tell you. And you must not allow your courage to slip away."

"They . . . they were going to . . . to—" She broke off and wiped her eyes as fresh tears bubbled over.

"I know," he said, smoothing her dark, tangled hair back with his bound hands. "But Gray Wolf managed to stop them."

"Why?"

"Never mind, little one." He turned his attention to

Ensign Paully who leaned against a tree a few feet away with his eyes closed. "How bad are you hurt, Ensign?"

Paully lifted his head slowly and looked at Matt through swollen eyelids. "I'm still conscious, Hunter. But I wish to God I wasn't." His gaze went to Jade. "Sorry I couldn't help you when you needed it, miss. But at least they released you."

"Please don't apologize," she said softly, wiping at her eyes again. "You could have done nothing against so many."

"How did they manage to take the fort, Ensign?" Matt asked.

"It was easy enough since I ordered the sentry to open the gate and let them inside." Ensign Paully's voice was bitter, angry, but Matt knew the anger was directed mostly at himself. "There was only seven of them in sight and they often come to the fort to trade. Today seemed no different from any other day. Not until they were inside. Then they killed everyone else . . . everyone but me."

"Don't blame yourself," Matt said grimly. "You had no way of knowing what they had planned."

"I was the commander, dammit! The men looked to me for leadership. Some leader! I allowed those bastards to walk in and slaughter my men." His one good eye studied Matt intensely. "I heard you tell the young lady you had some kind of plan."

Matt could see Paully wanted to ask if he really had a plan or if he was only trying to reassure Jade with his words. Matt shook his head and Paully turned away, his shoulders slumping even more, seeming to accept that they were thoroughly defeated.

"You were speaking to one of the Indians, weren't you, Matt?" Jade said, her words more a statement than a question.

"Yeah. He was claiming credit for catching me. I've been a thorn in their sides for a long time."

"Ensign Paully thinks they will burn him at the stake when we reach Detroit." Her eyes were wide with fear. "Do you know what they have planned for us?"

He wanted to lie to her, to say they would be allowed to go free, but knew he must not. She had to be aware of their danger. "They will prob'ly put me to the stake, too, Jade. But I can almost swear to you that you won't have to die that way."

Large tears welled over and rolled down her cheeks. "Oh, God, Matt! We've got to get away from them. We can't just allow this to happen."

"Hush! We will get away. Somehow we'll escape from them."

A warrior approached with jerky and a waterskin and the three of them fell silent, attending to the business of filling their empty stomachs. After the meager meal was finished they washed the jerky down with tepid water. Then Jade leaned her head against Matt and closed her eyes. A moment later, her deep breathing told him she was asleep.

"Ensign Paully," Matt whispered.

The ensign raised his head and looked at Matt again.

"I have to get her away from here. I'm afraid Gray Wolf won't be able to control them much longer." Matt knew he was taking a chance that none of the Indians nearby spoke English.

"You *do* have a plan?" Hope appeared in the ensign's eyes.

"Yes. But I'm not sure it will work. Nevertheless, I must make the attempt." He hesitated. "Do you think you can outrun them?"

Paully shook his head slowly. "I couldn't outrun a turtle with this wounded leg. It's hard enough to stay on my feet."

"I don't like leaving you behind," Matt said gruffly. "There's a good chance they might take their anger out on you when they find us missing."

Paully shook his head. "They're aware of the shape I'm in and they're determined to get me to Detroit where everyone can watch me burn." He shuddered. "If there's any chance you can get away from them, you must certainly do so. If you make it, you can alert Fort Detroit. They might be able to save me."

Matt gave a quick nod of his head. "If we get away Detroit will learn of your circumstances. You can be sure of that."

Becoming aware of a warrior whose eyes were pinned on them, Matt settled back against the bole of a pine tree and prepared to sleep. As he did, the guard who'd been watching so steadily approached, knelt down and wound a thin strip of rawhide around Matt's ankles, securing them tightly. When he had finished the task, he bound Ensign Paully's feet as well. Then, with a lustful gaze at the sleeping woman, he left them alone and settled down beside the fire with several other warriors.

Matt closed his eyes then, feigning sleep, hoping the guards would think he was too weary to make an attempt at escape.

The night passed slowly. Several times he was on the verge of sleep but he always managed to catch himself just before dozing off. He knew he must stay awake, that he had to make his move when the chance presented itself. It was almost morning before the last guard fell asleep, apparently confident the prisoners could give them no trouble.

Matt lay still, listening to the warrior's even breathing. It was time, he decided. Time to put his plan in motion.

His lips thinned. The guards had made a bad mistake when they'd left his hands bound before him instead of pulling them behind his back. It was a mistake they would come to regret.

Sliding his long fingers inside his boot, he removed the slender knife he carried there. Then, carefully, he placed a hand over Jade's mouth, stilling her cry when she woke abruptly.

Her eyes were wide with fear until she recognized him, a fear that quickly became hope as she saw the knife in his hand.

She waited silently while he sliced through her bindings. When her hands were free, she used the knife to cut away the bindings on his wrists. Matt took the knife then and sawed at the rawhide that bound his feet, and when the last thong lay on the ground, he pulled her to her feet, silently urging her toward the forest.

Looking back at the ensign, she whispered, "Matt. We can't just leave Ensign Paully. We need to—"

Matt saw the guard, who lay only a few feet away, stir in his sleep and he swore inwardly. Dammit! Jade's voice had obviously disturbed the warrior.

Hurriedly, he snatched up the fellow's rifle, wrapped his arm around Jade's waist and slung her against his hip. With no sound to mark his passing, he loped into the thick forest intent on putting as much distance as possible between them and the Indians before their absence was discovered.

A shout of surprise spurred him onward. It was followed by many voices that were raised in anger. Matt raced on, ignoring the sounds that told him they were being pursued.

Jade could hardly believe what was happening. Matt had snatched her off her feet as though she had no more substance than a turkey feather and pinned her across his hip.

She dared not cry out to protest his actions lest she give away their direction, doubted that she could anyway with Matt shoving his way through the dense thicket of pine trees without a thought of how the branches sprang back, lashing against her flesh with the intensity of a cat-o'-nine-tails being applied with a strong arm.

Matt continued to run through the uneven ground of the forest while Jade's head spun dizzily and her stomach lurched, continually threatening to disgorge its contents.

A heavy draft against her thighs told Jade her skirt must be bunched around her waist, and if it was, then her linen drawers would be exposed. Jade felt the warmth of a flush crawl up her neck at the thought.

Suddenly, their headlong flight ended. Matt stopped beside a sheer rock wall and, with iron-hard hands, shoved her into a dark hole at its base.

"Crawl in there as far as you can go!" he growled.

"Ensign Paully, Matt," she protested. "What about Ensign Paully? We can't just—"

"Enough, Jade!" he snapped. "Don't utter another sound. Not even one. And get in that cave. Crawl all the way to the end and be quick about it!"

The sound of pursuit, of footsteps crashing over fallen limbs, penetrated her brain and made her instantly aware of how perilous their situation really was. She scurried quickly through the dark shadows that filled the small cave, her head spinning dizzily as she fought to regain her equilibrium.

It was deeper than she had imagined, deep enough that, if Matt could hide the entrance, they might just possibly escape being captured again.

When Jade finally reached the end of the small cave, she turned around to face the entrance again. There was only a small pinpoint of light to show where it was.

A soft shivery sound caused goosepimples to erupt on

Jade's arm. Then she realized it was only Matt, moving through the darkness toward her.

"Don't say anything," he warned, sending his voice ahead of him. "Just keep quiet unless you want them to find us."

She nodded her head to show him she understood, then realized he couldn't have seen the nod. She waited there hardly daring to breathe lest that breath be heard by those who searched for them.

The sounds of pursuit became louder, louder. Jade's body trembled with fear, and she tried to control her tremors. She could hear them now, speaking in low tones as they passed by the hole where their quarry huddled. And then, amazing though it seemed, the sounds slowly faded in the distance. The hunters had passed them by.

The silence seemed deafening as Jade waited, and listened, for the hunters to return. Then Matt moved in the darkness, seeming to be searching for something. Finally, he whispered, "There's a split in the rock behind me, Jade. I think it opens into a cavern larger than this one. Go in there and wait for me."

"We're going to stay here?" She could hear the alarm in her voice.

"For a while. They'll soon realize they lost our trail and they'll come back this way! I need to fix it so there'll be no trace of us. Now hurry up. I don't know how much time we have before they return."

Fear forced Jade into the crack she'd found and into the larger area beyond. She waited there, just beyond the split, for Matt to join her again. A moment later, he did, pulling some branches along behind him. Although it was dark, she realized he must be sweeping the area clear of prints. When he'd finished, he entered the larger cave where she waited, then wedged dried branches into the split to hide their passage.

No sooner had he joined he before she asked the question that nagged at her conscience. "Why didn't we bring Ensign Paully with us?" she asked, and knew her voice was accusatory.

"He was in bad shape," Matt said coldly. "He couldn't have made a run for it."

Neither could I, Jade thought, *but you carried me.*

A flush of shame crept up her neck and stained her cheeks. "I'm sorry," she whispered unsteadily. "I should have known there was a reason."

"He knew what I had planned and he was in complete agreement."

"What will they do to him?"

"Nothing they wouldn't have done before we escaped." His voice was stiff. "He was asleep when we left, still bound hand and foot so they'll know he didn't help us."

"Do—do you think they'll find us?"

"Who knows?" She felt, rather than saw him shrug his shoulders. "I took every precaution."

"Are you going to forgive me for thinking you abandoned poor Ensign Paully?"

"There's nothing to forgive."

"Yes, there is," she said in a small voice. "I should have trusted you without question, Matt. I'm sorry I didn't."

He wrapped his arm around her shoulder and pulled her into his embrace. "Don't give it another thought, Jade." He leaned back against the floor, taking her with him. "God, I'm so tired."

"Did you get any sleep at all?"

"No. I didn't dare go to sleep. Afraid I wouldn't wake up until it was too late. I thought sure the guard would doze off long before he did."

"Go to sleep now," she said softly. "I'll stay awake and keep watch."

"All right. But be very quiet, Jade. The Indians will

realize they've lost our trail before much longer. Then they'll be coming back this way.''

"I'll wake you if they come.''

A moment later, she heard his even breathing and realized he was already fast asleep.

Jewel arched her back, stretching aching muscles as she watched Martha Kilbride scrub the root vegetables she was preparing for the evening meal. The woman looked up from her work and frowned at her bond servant. "If you're done scrubbing the floor there's plenty more work to be done."

There was always work to be done, Jewel thought. More than enough for the two of them. She looked beyond the woman to the open window and saw Percy Kilbride returning from his visit to a neighboring farm.

Moments later he entered the kitchen, his face creased with worry. "I have some bad news, my dear," he told his wife. "There's talk of an Indian uprising. We're all going to take refuge at the fort, just in case there's any truth in the matter." He looked at Jewel. "Help my wife gather our belongings."

"An Indian uprising!" The words were a shriek, made by Percy's wife. "God, Percy! We'll all be killed!"

"No we won't, my dear," the man consoled, passing Jewel by to go to the other woman. "We're going to Fort Adams this very day. There's plenty of space in the back room of my store for a bed and everything we'll need for a short sojourn there. Just until the threat of an Indian war is past."

"Then come along, Jewel," Martha Kilbride said, seeming to have been calmed by her husband's words. "Do as Percy instructed and help me gather some things together to take to the fort. I won't be able to rest until we're safe inside its walls.''

Jewel followed meekly behind the woman, never allowing the words of rebellion that sputtered to the surface to be vocalized. But her time would come, she vowed. Soon she would be free of the merchant and his wife. Soon LeCroix would come for her and never again would she wash another dish, nor scrub another floor. When that happened she would be the one in command.

Chapter Eighteen

Jade lay beside Matt, listening to his even breathing, her ears straining for sounds outside the small chamber, but try as she would, she heard nothing unusual, nothing except an occasional flutter of a bird in flight, the squeak of a woodmouse, and the rustle of leaves in the wind.

Time passed. Moments . . . eons . . . she could only guess at how long she waited. Then, finally it came, the sound of voices, barely distinguishable, yet unmistakably human sounds.

Fear slithered an icy path down her spine, tensing her muscles, winding through her stomach and coiling it into a hard, tight knot. Her heartbeat quickened with dread. She tried hard to decipher their words, to find just one that she could understand, knowing that, if she could, it would surely mean the new arrivals would be friendly to the fugitives.

But, try as she would, not one single word the newcomers uttered made sense to her.

Reality struck her like a swift blow as she realized the Indians had returned.

Oh, God! If Matt should awake abruptly, should speak aloud, the Indians would be sure to hear him!

No sooner had that thought occurred before Jade covered his mouth with one hand.

He awakened immediately, wary, his senses completely alert. Jade knew that by the way his muscles tensed, the way his eyes flew open to stare into hers. Seeming to recognize her fear, he reached out and lightly squeezed her shoulder.

The two of them remained motionless, silently waiting, each of them hardly daring to breathe lest they be heard by the hunters.

An eternity of time seemed to pass as Jade listened to the sound of countless moccasins crunching lightly over the forest floor that was matted with pine needles. Finally, though, the sound of her fast-beating heart covered all else and she realized, as she felt Matt's tight muscles slowly relax beneath her palm, that the Indians had passed them by.

"They're gone," Matt's breath whispered against her ear. "We'd best remain here a while, though. Just until we're sure they won't double back again."

The thought of that sent a shudder through her.

"Cold?" Matt pulled her tightly against him.

"Just afraid," she whispered. "Afraid of what they'll do if they catch us again."

He was quiet for a long moment, then, "I'm sorry I got you into this, Jade."

"It's not your fault, Matt."

"I disagree." His voice was harsh, self-condemning. "I didn't do you any favors when I bought you."

"Now I must disagree with *you*. If you hadn't bought me, Henri LeCroix would have."

His expression was troubled. "Maybe you'd have been better off had he done so."

"How can you say that?"

He cupped her face with his palm. "Don't you see that his trading post is the safest place to be now? It's prob'ly the *only* place west of the Alleghenies the Indians won't attack."

"I don't care," she whispered. "Despite everything that's happened, I'd rather be with you than with Henri LeCroix."

His arm tightened around her, pulling her closer to him. Stroking the contour of her cheek with his calloused palm, he whispered unsteadily, "Do you really mean that, Jade? We're in one hell of a mess here. And I can't guarantee it will get any better. In fact, there's a good chance we may not survive."

"I know, Matt. I have no illusions about my future. But that is nothing new. My future has been uncertain since the night I stabbed a soldier from King George's army. I expected to die on the gallows for that misdeed. Do you think I cheated destiny then, Matt. Do you think fate has only just discovered the mistake and is determined to end my life in this manner."

"Don't talk that way, Jade. You're not going to die. I won't allow it to happen. You're too young, too beautiful to die. Somehow we'll get out of this situation. I'll find a way to take you back East where you'll be safe."

"Perhaps." Her voice was wistful. "But I have to be prepared for the worst. And I am. It's just that I wish . . . I wish . . ." She couldn't go on. How could she explain her feelings without sounding like a harlot?

"Wish what?"

"Never mind."

"Tell me," he insisted. "What do you wish?"

"There are so many things I haven't done yet. So many

things I have yet to experience. I just hate that I will n-never experience them now."

"What, Jade? What would you like to experience?"

A hot flush of embarrassment rose up her cheeks and she lowered her lashes.

"Tell me," he urged softly.

She caught her lower lip between her teeth, then, "I-I've never loved before," she admitted unsteadily. "And I wish—I wish I could have done so. I wish I could know—could experience love. That I could—could—" She couldn't go on, could hardly believe she had told him as much as she had, for she'd surely exposed herself to ridicule.

Incredibly, though, he did not laugh. Instead, he drew a long, shaky breath. "I've never loved before either, Jade."

"Truly?"

"Truly . . . until now."

She caught her breath, her eyes becoming round with surprise. What did he mean? she wondered. Did he—could he—might he possibly care for her?

If he did care . . . if that's what he meant, then, when her time came, she could die easier, knowing that someone—Matt—had loved her.

His head moved closer, mere inches, yet enough so that his mouth could cover hers in a hard, possessive kiss that almost stole her breath away.

"Oh, Matt," she breathed, but the sound was smothered beneath his lips.

Her arms slid around his neck, her body trembled with delicious anticipation, remembering the last time he'd held her this way and how gloriously wonderful it had been.

Lifting his head, he gazed long into her eyes and his voice, when he spoke, flowed like hot honey over her. "I've wanted you so much, Jade. Ever since the day I first laid eyes on you.''

"Even then?'' she whispered tremulously.

"Even then. The wanting has been a constant ache, a hunger that continually gnawed at my gut.''

He shifted around until he could lay her against the cool, damp earth. Her breasts rose and fell with her quickened breathing as he began to remove his shirt. Her gaze followed his movements and she was almost mesmerized by his lean, muscled torso.

His buckskin made a soft sound as he cast it aside, then came quickly back to her, his fingers fumbling with the neck of her gown. When the buttons were undone, he pulled the garment over her head and tossed it toward his shirt. His fingers were at the ties of her linen drawers then, pulling at them, tugging in impatience. Then, moments later, the drawers joined the other garments.

Naked and breathless, they came together.

His mouth covered hers again and one calloused palm cupped the fullness of her right breast while his other hand slid slowly down her bare thighs and hips and over the flat planes of her stomach. Seconds turned into minutes and his mouth and hands became bolder, stoking a fire deep inside her body that burned hotter with each passing moment.

She writhed beneath him, needing something more of him than what she was receiving. "Please,'' she murmured unsteadily. "Please, Matt.''

As though he'd only been waiting for that particular moment, Matt moved himself over her, positioning himself between her legs and probing firmly at the apex of her thighs. She felt a sharp pain that was quickly gone, then a fullness like nothing she'd ever known before.

When he began to move, she groaned softly and he immediately stilled.

"No," she muttered frantically. "Don't stop, Matt. Don't ever stop."

He began to move again, slowly at first, than faster and faster, building a rhythm that she tried hard to match, inexperienced though she was.

Their bodies were fused into a hot, throbbing whole as he moved urgently, almost roughly, against her. Her breath came in hot gasps as she was caught in a tailspin of desire that blossomed and spread until finally it burst upon her, sending wave after wave of pleasure so intense that tears stung her eyes and blurred her vision.

Matt gave one last push and then shuddered spasmodically. He crumpled against her and she lay there, clasping him tightly, vowing that this would not be the end of it. She would not give up so easily. Not when she'd just found her love.

Jewel Crawford followed along behind Percy Kilbride and his wife, Martha, as they crossed the parade ground toward the general store he owned. She was enraged at being made to carry Martha's carpetbag while the woman carried nothing. Jewel's head was lowered in her fury and she paid no attention to the people around them . . . not until she heard a familiar voice call out.

"Well, I'll be damned! There she is now! Hey, Jewel! We were just coming to find you!"

Jewel dropped the carpetbag at her feet, the puddle of water going unnoticed as she turned toward the speaker, identifying him as Slick Donahue, the man she'd used as a go-between in her dealings with Henri LeCroix. Beside Slick stood a tall, dark-haired man who looked at her as though she had suddenly sprouted another head.

"This is the woman?" the man demanded, his lips drawn

into a snarl, his dark eyes flashing furiously. "Are you sure, monsieur?"

"Of course I'm sure."

"Jewel!" snapped Martha Kilbride. "Stop dawdling, girl, and come along now!" Sighting her carpetbag in the puddle, she uttered a shriek. "Oh, my God! You stupid girl. Just look at what you've done! Don't you have any sense at all?" She turned to her husband. "Percy! Just look at what she's done! She dropped my carpetbag in the mud! Do something, Percy!"

"Yes, my dear."

Jewel barely heard the woman's enraged squealing, nor her husband's reply. She was still frozen to the spot, staring at Slick and his dark-haired companion. "You wouldn't be Henri LeCroix?" she finally managed in a hopeful voice.

"Indeed I would be, Mademoiselle Crawford. But you are quite a surprise to me." His expression was no longer enraged, instead, it was thoughtful. "It seems a grave mistake has been made."

"You bet there has!" she snapped, her temper surging forth. "Where in hell have you been anyway?"

Percy had taken her arm in a tight grip, but she shook it off, waiting for LeCroix to explain himself.

"What is all this, Jewel?" Percy asked, eyeing the two men coldly. "Who are these gentlemen and what do they want with you?"

"Percy!" His wife's strident voice rang out. "Make that girl pick up my carpetbag and come on. Right now."

Kilbride threw a quick look at his wife. "Just a moment, dear." He tugged at Jewel's arm. "Come along now. Mama's becoming impatient with us."

"Non, monsieur. A moment, please. I am Henri LeCroix." He bowed low at the waist as he introduced himself. "And you, monsieur?"

"Percy!" Martha Kilbride's face was flushed, her foot

tapping the ground steadily. "I refuse to stand here any longer."

"In a minute!" he told his impatient wife, his gaze never leaving LeCroix. "If you're askin' what my name is, then it's Percy Kilbride. I own the general store here. Not that it's any of your business."

"I am a friend of Mademoiselle Crawford. And as such would like to speak privately with you on her behalf. I assure you that you will greatly benefit from the meeting."

"Percy! Now!"

"I'm coming, dear!" Kilbride spoke in a long-suffering voice, then eyed LeCroix with distaste. "Sounded to me like you and Jewel had only just met. And, as you can see, I'm in a great hurry right now. Perhaps, though, there will be time for a conversation later."

"An hour?" LeCroix persisted. "At the saloon? It would be worth your while to come."

"I refuse to stand here any longer, Percy Kilbride! Either come now or suffer the consequences!"

Whatever the consequences of ignoring his wife any longer would be, the mere thought of enduring them was enough to energize the portly fellow. He stooped low enough to scoop the satchel from the ground, then, with Jewel's arm clutched tightly, he scurried after Martha.

Jade awakened as dawn seeped into the small cavern, turning the deep blackness into graying shadows. She arched her back and sighed. She felt marvelous. Absolutely wonderful, totally relaxed. She shifted her legs and a slight soreness of her muscles brought back the memory of their lovemaking. She turned to look at Matt, feeling a delicious tingling in remote parts of her body. His beard was coarse and stubbly, his thick, dark hair disheveled, but it was the most handsome face she'd ever seen in her life.

Remembering how urgently they'd come together, her lips twitched in a smile. She was surprised at the intensity of her own response, had never dreamed such feelings existed. He had awakened after that first loving and made love to her again, exploring her body with his eyes, his hands, and his mouth, raising her to extraordinary heights of passion until she thought she would surely explode. She *did* explode, she reminded herself.

Matt had carried her along to dizzying heights, keeping her there until she could barely contain herself, had bitten her lip to keep from screaming with ecstasy as her body shuddered again and again in an unending series of explosive releases.

Her eyes devoured his face, relaxed in sleep. God, how she loved him. And no matter how many times they made love, Jade felt sure she would never get enough of him. No matter how long they lived.

And they *would* live, she thought fiercely. She would never allow herself to think otherwise. They would go back East and they would live out their lives together.

Jade refused to allow herself to consider anything else.

Even so, the doubts slowly crept in again and her fears returned tenfold. What if they didn't get out of this? Had she only just found love to lose it again? She couldn't stand it if that happened. Perhaps the Indians wouldn't kill her but would keep her for a slave instead. To suffer at the hands of those red devils for years to come was more than her mind could bear.

If they killed Matt, then she'd want to die, too. Nothing, no one, would ever be able to take his place.

Please, God, she silently prayed. *Don't let me lose him now. Not when I've just found him!*

"Jade?" Matt's voice whispered against her ear, making her aware that he had awakened. "We'd best not stay here longer, dear. It should be safe enough to leave now."

"I hate to leave," she sighed, clinging to him.

"So do I." He moved away from her and reached for their clothing.

"Do you think we have a chance of getting away, Matt?"

"There's always a chance." He handed her gown across, picked up his trousers and slid his legs into them. Lifting his hips, he pulled the breeches over them and fastened them at the waist.

Following his example, Jade pulled her gown over her head and threaded her arms through the sleeves, pulling it down across her breasts and hips. When they were both completely dressed, Matt cautioned her to stay in the cave until he'd made sure there was no one about.

She waited tensely until he returned, fearing that at any moment she would hear one of those piercing, undulating cries the warriors used when they attacked.

But it did not come. Instead, the silence continued until, a few short minutes later, Matt entered the cave again and motioned her forward.

They hurried away from their place of refuge, traveling in a northwesterly direction, avoiding the well-traveled path and forcing their way through the thicker growths where the going was rougher. And, of necessity, they traveled at a slower pace.

Even so, when their path began to take them uphill, Jade began to tire.

She appealed to Matt. "Could we stop for a short rest, Matt? I'm so tired. My legs feel like I've been walking forever and I'm almost certain my feet are covered with blisters."

"We'll stop for a few minutes," he said gruffly. "But we dare not delay long. Sit over there. On that rock." He pointed to a slab approximately two feet across. "Let me see your feet." Without waiting for her agreement, he slipped off her right shoe and examined her foot. "The seam is coming loose in this shoe, Jade." He checked the other one and found it in even worse condition. "Your shoes won't last much longer. If I had a piece of hide I could make you a pair of moccasins."

"But you don't have any," she said mournfully, rubbing her swollen foot. "These will have to do." She examined the shoes and frowned at the split seams. "If we had some thread perhaps we could mend them."

"I could slice a strip of leather from the bottom of my shirt, but we'd need some kind of needle." He frowned at her. "Do you think you can make do with them a little while longer?"

She nodded her head. "I don't really have any choice, do I."

"It is imperative that we reach the fort as quickly as possible, dear. But if your feet get any more blisters on them you won't be able to travel."

"Do you know how much farther it is?"

"About twenty miles."

"You seem to know this area well."

He looked around him. "I've trapped these woods for the last ten years." He smiled at her. "Do you think you can go on now?"

"I'll certainly give it my best try." She pushed herself to her feet again. "I can hardly wait until we reach the fort, Matt. I'm going to have a hot bath and soak for a long—"

She broke off suddenly, uttering a terrified shriek as a score of Indians left the cover of the trees and completely surrounded them.

Chapter Nineteen

They didn't have a chance.

The warriors were upon them before Matt could react and, all too soon, they found themselves bound tightly with rawhide strips that cut deeply into the flesh of their wrists.

They traveled hard, the Indians forcing them along the narrow trail leading beside the river. Even so, the day was at its end when they reached the Indian village. The sky gave no hint of that fact, though. The clouds were dark and heavy and, to Jade's mind, seemed to hold a threat of what was to come.

She tried hard to stay beside Matt, but her guards would not allow it. Each time she attempted to move toward him, one of the warriors would prod her with his rifle, forcing her away.

As the village came in sight ice-cold dread washed over her in waves. Fear ran strong, gaining momentum with each beat of her heart, threatening to erupt from her lips in a long, drawn-out scream.

But, somehow, Jade managed to hold it back. Somehow, even though nausea tore at her empty stomach and her teeth chattered violently, she managed to stop the scream from erupting. Only the smallest moan slipped from her lips, not even enough sound for the nearest guard to hear with all the noise going on around her.

With her hands clenched at her sides, forming tight, shaking fists, Jade fought against giving in to the knowledge that hovered at the edge of her mind.

They were going to die!

Horribly, slowly.

And there was nothing . . . no one to save them.

Jade had one small consolation, though, one the Indians could not be aware of. When the end came, she and Matt would be together.

Her eyes sought Matt, knowing his presence would help her bear what was to come.

"No!" she cried, unable to stop the horrified protest when she realized they were being taken in two different directions.

"Matt!" she screamed, hurling herself toward him.

Her passage was immediately blocked by two hefty Indians. She looked past them and saw Matt struggling with his captors, saw the poles standing upright in the middle of the village and realized the man bound to the stake wearing a tattered red uniform was none other than Ensign Paully.

"Matt!" she screamed again, struggling to break through the warriors blocking her way.

His gaze met hers across the distance separating them. "Don't fight them, Jade!" he yelled. "And try not to show any fear. Whatever happens, don't let them know you're afraid."

If their situation hadn't been so dire Jade might have laughed at his words. How could she keep them from knowing she was afraid when her nausea was rising rapidly, threatening to spew from her mouth? She tried to force her mind away from her body, attempted to shut out the cacophony of sound that bombarded her ears.

But she could not. No matter how hard she tried, she could feel the reality of the moment, could feel the hatred and hostility aimed at her from so many different directions. It beat at her in ever-increasing waves, swelling over her, making her head spin wildly until a red haze formed around her vision.

Jade's legs crumpled and she fainted.

Matt grunted as blow after blow rained down on him, robbing him of breath. His lips were clamped tightly together, holding back the sound, for he refused to give voice to his pain.

A quick glance at the man beside him told him that Ensign Paully fared no better. While the women used sticks to beat them, the children gathered firewood and threw it at the feet of both captives.

Matt knew what that meant. Both he and Ensign Paully were going to be burned at the stake. But then, he had known for days that would happen. He knew his fate was well and truly sealed.

Perhaps, though, Jade might survive.

When Jade awakened to find herself sprawled facedown on a hard-packed dirt floor she had no slow awakening, no momentary gap in memory. Instead, she woke immediately to harsh reality knowing that she and Matt were captives, along with poor Ensign Paully.

The thought of Matt jerked her upright. What had they done with him. More to the point, what had they done *to* him?

Using her bound hands for leverage, she pushed herself to her feet and turned her attention to her immediate surroundings. She had been lying with her head away from the entrance, a hide flap that was closed except for a narrow triangle. Through the slit of that small opening light flickered softly as though from many campfires . . . or one big fire.

Oh, God! she thought. Ensign Paully had said the Indians would burn them at the stake.

Had it already happened? Had they burned the two men alive while she lay unconscious, completely unaware of what they were doing?

She had to know, had to see for herself!

With her bound hands impeding her progress, Jade scurried toward the entrance, pushing the hide flap aside to peer outside. But the moment she poked her head through the entrance she felt a heavy blow across her shoulders.

The breath whooshed out of her lungs and she struck the ground hard. She lay there for a moment, her breath rasping harshly, trying to recover her senses. Then, rolling over, she looked up to see a guard standing over her.

Uttering a guttural command, the guard pointed inside the hut. Slowly, she obeyed the command, but not before she had seen the two men tied to the stakes.

"Oh, God! Thank you," she whispered, knowing the moment she saw them, their bodies fully erect, that both Matt and Ensign Paully were alive.

But for how long? she wondered. How much longer did they have before the Indians began their torture? How much longer before the Indians set fire to the wood piled at their feet? How long before she heard their screams, before she smelled their burning flesh? If only there was something she could do, some way she could save them from their fate.

How could she, though? What could she do for them when she was unable to help herself?

She searched the primitive dwelling, hoping to find a solution there, hoping to find a weapon laying discarded and ignored. But there was nothing. Other than a few clay pots and earthenware bowls, the hut was empty.

"Oh, Matt," she whispered despairingly. "Is this the way it ends?"

Only silence greeted her question.

The women finally stopped beating the prisoners and turned their efforts to helping the children gather wood. Because of that, the pile at Matt's feet was steadily growing, reaching up to his knees and moving outward in a two-foot circle.

He tried to ignore the Indians who occasionally paused in their work to jeer at him, tried to think of Jade instead. He'd had a glimpse of her when she'd left the tepee, and although it was only momentary, it was enough for him to see that she was unharmed. He could only pray that she remained that way.

Matt was abruptly brought back to his own plight when a squat heavyset woman stepped behind him and pulled at his dark hair. He ignored her, believing she only meant to torment him until she squeezed his upper arm, obviously testing the muscles there. He looked at her then, saw the gleam in her eyes just before she squatted beside him and felt his muscular thigh.

What in hell was she about? he wondered, watching as she turned to an older man that Matt, judging by the garments he wore, had taken to be chief of the band.

"Loping Wolf," she said, in the harsh, guttural language

of her people. "This woman claims the right to have that man." She pointed at Matt, making certain the chief knew her choice. "He is strong and will replace my slain husband."

"You cannot have him," Loping Wolf replied in the same language. "He is Hunter. His will is too strong for him to remain a captive."

The woman narrowed her gaze on Matt again, then smiled. It was not a nice smile. "He would not be a captive. This woman will take him for a husband."

"No, woman," Loping Wolf said. "If you wish to claim a white-eyes for your husband, then you must settle for the other man."

Her flat black eyes seemed to reflect disappointment as she accepted the fact that Matt was not for her. She turned to the other captive then, her lips curled in contempt as she ran her eyes over his abused body. "He is not as strong as Hunter, but I suppose he will have to do."

Ensign Paully, having dealt with the Indians for the last two years, knew some of their language but not enough to explain their actions when they began slicing through his bindings. "What's happening, Hunter?" he asked. "What are these devils about now?"

"The woman has invoked tribal law," Matt replied, his lip curling in a wry smile. "She has convinced them to free you."

"Free me?" Ensign Paully's eyes showed his great relief. "Then they're not going to burn me?"

"No."

"God, man! What news!" As the bonds parted and fell to the ground, Paully flexed his wrists and feet, trying to renew the circulation in his limbs. "I wonder why she did it?" he mused.

"She wants a husband."

"Husband?" Ensign Paully blinked with surprise. "Well,

I guess that beats dying, doesn't it? And just maybe I'll have a chance to escape and warn the fort what these devils are about.'' He frowned at Matt. ''What about you, Hunter? They're not still going to—''

''Afraid so,'' Matt said tightly. ''But don't worry overmuch about it.''

''Dammit, man! Of course I'll worry about it.''

Matt shrugged his shoulders. ''Worry if you must, then. But either way, it'll do me no good.''

''Maybe one of their women might take you.''

''No. Loping Wolf, the chief of this band, won't allow it. He says I wouldn't be willing to stay with them, that I'm too dangerous to have around.''

''Maybe there's something I can do,'' Ensign Paully said uncertainly.

''Not for me. But maybe for Jade.''

''I'll do my best, Hunter. You can rely on that.''

''That's all I can ask.''

A commotion near the edge of the tepee where Jade was confined caught their attention. Several warriors stood near the entrance, arguing with a crowd of women. As Matt watched, one of the warriors stooped and disappeared into the lodge, exiting a moment later with Jade.

''What're they doing?'' Paully muttered, watching the Indian pull Jade toward them.

Matt was afraid he knew, and that knowledge ripped at the heart of him. He strained at his bonds, even though he was aware they were too tight, the rawhide too strong to be broken with mere muscle.

''What's happening, Matt?'' Jade cried, struggling uselessly against her captor, who slammed her against the post and held her there while another Indian sliced through the bonds at her wrists, yanked her arms behind the stake and bound her wrists tightly with tough rawhide. ''What are they going to do with us?''

"I don't know, Jade." Matt couldn't bring himself to tell the truth as he saw it, couldn't utter the words that would take every remnant of hope from her. "Perhaps this is just their way of keeping us both in sight."

"Whatever their purpose, I must be g-grateful that it brings us together again." There was only a slight quiver in her voice to show her extreme fear.

He managed to summon up a smile for her. His cracked, dry lips reacted immediately, splitting in several more places until he could feel the warmth of his own blood bubbling forth.

"Oh, Matt," she cried. "Your poor lips are bleeding."

"So they are," he agreed. "I'm afraid they're useless for kissing right now."

"How can you joke at a time like this?" she asked, moisture brightening her green eyes. "Our situation is desperate, Matt."

"I know," he said gruffly. "And I've been trying my best to think of a way out of it, Jade. But so far I've come up with nothing."

Her gaze went to Ensign Paully, standing helplessly to one side.

"Yes," Matt answered for the ensign before Jade could ask the question. "He's free."

"How did he manage that?" she asked. "Perhaps we could do whatever it was and—"

"I'm afraid not," Matt replied. "Ensign Paully was claimed by one of the woman to replace her dead husband." His mind had been working frantically, trying to devise a plan to save her from the ordeal the Indians had planned for her. "Listen to me, Jade. That big Indian over there . . . the one wearing a beaded headband. That's Black Crow and he's been looking at you mighty hard since we got here. It should be easy to get him interested in you. All you'd have to do is smile at him and—"

Her eyes became round with surprise, but that emotion was quickly smothered with pure rage. "How can you even suggest such a thing, Matt?"

"Don't look at me like that," Matt rasped hoarsely. "I'd suggest anything that might save your life."

"Perhaps she'd rather be dead," Ensign Paully muttered.

"Nobody would rather be dead," Matt grated. "Even the dumbest animal fights to survive."

"My God, Hunter, they'd ruin her!" Ensign Paully cried. "They would—would—Well, you know well enough what they would do to her."

"I know. And the thought of it pains me like a knife twisting in my gut. But the other thing . . . for her life to end the way those red devils plan would be even worse for me . . . and her."

"I would rather be dead than live without you, Matt!" Jade said through clenched teeth.

"Don't say that," Matt said.

"I mean it." She shuddered. "The thought of one of those savages touching me—f-forcing me to—to—God, just the thought of it turns my stomach."

"You've been sick before," Matt said harshly. "I daresay you'd get over it soon enough."

"I'd never get over it, Matt! I'd carry the memory with me to my dying day!" Her voice lowered suddenly. "Just as I'll carry the memory of yesterday with me." Her eyes had darkened, becoming the color of a stormy sea. "We'll get out of this!" she said fiercely. "I just know we will."

Even as she spoke, an Indian woman walked up and dumped another armload of wood at Matt's feet. She was followed closely by a boy of eight or nine who carried another load which he dumped on top of the ever-increasing pile.

"Hunter," Ensign Paully said in a choked voice. "I wish

to God there was something **I could do**. But **against** so
many . . . well, it would be impossible."

"Please don't blame yourself, Ensign Paully," Jade said
in a trembling voice. "You could do nothing to save us.
Why should you die as well?"

The woman who had rescued Ensign Paully suddenly
became impatient to leave. She struck him sharply across
the shoulders with a heavy club, uttered a harsh command
and curled her gnarled fingers around his forearm to urge
him away from his companions.

He looked back at them, his expression one of mute
wretchedness, then stumbled along with the woman who
now owned him.

Jade's throat ached with defeat as she watched the pile
of wood around Matt continue to grow.

"Don't look," Matt said. "And take hope, dear sweetheart. They haven't put any wood at your feet. Maybe they
have other plans for you. Perhaps they only mean to make
you watch me die."

"God, Matt! Do you think that makes me less terrified?
I would rather lose my own life than watch you suffer such
a death! There's nothing left for me without you. They
might as well kill me, too, and be done with it."

"Don't say that, Jade! Don't even think it!"

Suddenly the drums began to beat.

"What's happening?" she asked.

A tall, muscular warrior approached them, carrying a
lighted torch. The sight of it caused terror to surge anew.
"Oh, God, no!" she cried, her anguish peaking to shatter
her last threads of control. She turned her face to the sky
and prayed for the courage to bear the ordeal the Indians
had planned for them. It was then she realized the clouds
had become thicker, darker, almost angry-looking.

If only they would open up and send down a torrent of rain. If only they would—

As though her wish had made it a reality, a loud clap of thunder sounded, reverberating through the sky. It was followed by a jagged streak of lightning that ripped through the graying light, stretching toward the ground as though intent on splitting the earth asunder. Then the heavens opened up and the rain came down.

"Aaiieee!"

The cry was long, undulating, and it was quickly followed by others. As the rain fell in torrents, the Indians milled around, seeming uncertain of their movements.

Thunder rumbled again, quickly followed by another streak of lightning that reached down with jagged fingers. It split a tall oak tree as neatly as though it had been cleaved by an ax. The crowd had obviously had enough. The Indians raced toward their dwellings, leaving the captives to face the elements.

Rain slashed at Jade's head and ran in cold, gushing streaks down her face. The endless hammering thunk of each droplet echoed the pounding of her heart. Thunder sounded again, booming across the sky, and again, it was followed by a streak of lightning. She ducked her head, trying to escape the punishing water before it invaded her nostrils and drowned her.

Feeling a tug on her wrists, Jade's heart jerked with fear. She swiveled her head, trying to see who was pulling at her bonds, but the rain was pouring down so hard that her vision was limited. She could see nothing but a bulky shape bent low near the back of the post. She felt another tug on her wrists, and then the rawhide bindings dropped away. A quick slash set her feet free as well, and then the man who'd freed her straightened, revealing his weathered, leathery face.

Badger! Somehow, the old man had learned of their plight and had come to save them.

He gave her no time to utter her heartfelt thanks, for he turned to Matt and quickly sliced through his bonds.

"Come on!" Matt shouted, his voice competing with the thunder that continued to reverberate around them. "There's no time to lose!"

Realizing he was right, because at any time the rain might stop and the Indians take up where they'd left off, Jade raced away with them, hurrying toward the cover of the forest. But the lashing rain made traveling hard, for their vision was limited to only a few feet. She stumbled continually until, finally, Matt picked her up and slung her across his shoulders.

Jade didn't know how long they traveled, only knew that it seemed like hours before they reached the river's edge. Then Matt slid her from his shoulder and stood her on her feet and whispered against her ear.

"We're going to be passing through enemy lines, Jade. Don't make any noise and, for God's sake, hold on to my shoulders."

She nodded, shivering with cold as well as fear since her garments were soaked through. They entered the water then and began to swim slowly through it. They'd only gone a short way when Jade saw a wooden fortress looming directly ahead of them, its outlines indistinct in the rain that continued to fall in lashing torrents. Amazing though it seemed, the fortress had a gate that reached out into the water.

"Let's just hope the sentry hears us before the Indians do," Matt said, making a fist and banging on the gate.

Immediately, a voice on the other side challenged them. "Who goes there?"

"Matthew Hunter!" Matt identified himself. "Let me in! I have to see Major Gladwin right away."

There was a loud scraping, then the gate was opened a mere crack. Just enough to allow them through. Matt pulled Jade inside quickly, and after Badger had passed through the sentry, quickly closed the gate again.

"What're you doing here, Hunter?" the sentry asked, obviously well acquainted with Matt. "Don't you know there's Indians out there?"

"That's why we're here, Muldoon," Matt replied. "We know what those devils have planned. We got ourselves in a mess trying to come here and apprise Major Gladwin of the situation. If Badger hadn't happened along just at the right time—" He broke off abruptly, his gaze going to Jade. "You'll hear all about it later, Muldoon. Right now someone needs to take Miss Carrington to the Hartford cabin."

"I'd rather stay with you," Jade said quickly.

"You need to get out of those wet clothes," Matt told her. "Sally would skin me alive if I didn't send you straight to her."

"Private Brown," Muldoon snapped. "Show the young lady where the Hartfords live."

The young soldier who had stood silently by suddenly snapped to attention. "Yes, sir!" He saluted smartly and spun on his heels, waiting for Jade to follow him.

"What about you, Matt?" she asked, unwilling to be separated from him. "Will you be coming later?"

"I'll be there just as soon as I've spoken with the major." He brushed his hand across her cheek. "Don't worry, Jade. The Hartfords are good friends of mine. Sally will be glad to have you there."

Since there was nothing else she could do, Jade followed the sentry.

* * *

Badger walked with Matt as far as the sutler's store, then expressed an extreme desire for a glass of whiskey. They separated and Matt went on his way.

Major Gladwin expressed surprise when he recognized Matt. "I didn't expect to see you here," he said gruffly, pointing to a chair a few feet from his own. "I thought you went back East. Somebody said to Charleston."

"I'd better stand," Matt said, pushing wet strands of hair back behind his ears. "As it is, I'm dripping water all over your floor."

"Don't worry about the damn furniture," Gladwin said. "You look like you've been run through the mill."

"Feel like it, too," Matt said, slumping down in the chair and heaving a sigh of relief. "Damn, I'm tired."

"Cigar?" Major Gladwin asked, pushing a box toward Matt.

Matt nodded and reached for one. "I guess you know you have other visitors, too." He eyed the major. "Outside the walls."

"I know. Their leader, Pontiac, sent word they wanted to have a Calumet dance inside the fort. Said he wanted to cement our friendship. Sounded like a good idea to me."

"I'd reconsider if I were you."

"Why?"

"I don't know this Pontiac fellow, but I do know he's lying through his teeth. He has every intention of taking the fort." He told of the plan and the taking of the other forts, of the burnt-out cabins and the bodies he'd found near them.

"I should've suspected something was afoot," Major Gladwin said. "So he's expecting to gain entrance by trickery and take the fort." He frowned thoughtfully. "I'm told there's been several Indians inside the fort today, each of them requesting the loan of files."

"To shorten their rifle barrels no doubt," Matt said grimly. "They're probably planning on concealing them beneath their blankets tomorrow."

"Forewarned is forearmed." The major bit the end off a cigar and stuck it in his mouth. "We'll be waiting for those red devils when they come inside. And we'll see who gets the biggest surprise."

Chapter Twenty

Jade shivered with cold as she followed the sentry to a row of cabins built along the farthest wall of the fort. She waited beneath the sheltering eaves while the young sentry rapped sharply on the door. It was opened abruptly by a small, dark-haired woman wearing a blue linen gown beneath a crisply starched white apron.

"Why, Joey," she said, a smile spreading across her face. "How nice of you to call. Where have you been keeping yourself these last few days? Come on in, boy. Come on in. I'm afraid Virgie Lee's not here, though. She went over to the Lester cabin to visit Mary Helen."

His face flushed with embarrassment. "This here's an official visit, ma'am. The lady over yonder just come to the fort, an' since she don't have no place to stay, they sent her over here."

"And quite rightly, too," Sally Hartford said, looking past his shoulder to where Jade stood. "I'm sorry, dear. I didn't see you in the shadows. Come on in out of the weather. You, too, Joey. If you can spare the time.''

"I can't, ma'am," the young sentry replied regretfully. "I'm on guard duty now. But maybe later . . . if Virgie Lee's home, then I could stop a while.''

"She won't be home tonight, Joey. She's stayin' the night with Mary Helen," the woman said with a smile. "Mrs. Lester has been savin' some dried apples and the girls are plannin' on bakin' pies. You could drop by there if you've a mind, but—''

"Uh . . . no, ma'am. I guess I'll just wait until Virgie Lee gets home again.''

He backed quickly away from them, stumbling in his haste to depart now that he'd learned the object of his affection was not around.

Immediately, Sally Hartford turned her attention to Jade. "Joey forgot to introduce us, dear, but I guess you already know my name is Sally Hartford.''

"Yes. I heard them say. My name is Jade. Jade Carrington." She looked ruefully at her sodden garments. "I'm afraid I'm dripping wet.''

"Don't worry about that," Sally said quickly. "Come on in and let me find you something dry to wear.''

"I hope I'm not putting you out.''

"Goodness no, child. Not at all. I'm always glad for company. We don't get many new faces around here." She led the way to a small bedroom, took a gray dress from a wardrobe and added some undergarments, laying them across the neatly made bed. "You're about the same size as Virgie Lee. Her things should fit nicely.''

"Will she mind my borrowing them?''

"Not the least little bit. Virgie—her name is really Virginia—has a heart as big as gold. She'd be delighted to think she could be of help. Now you put those dry clothes on while I put the kettle on to boil.''

The moment the door closed behind the woman, Jade stripped away her sodden garments and donned dry, clean clothes. Then, gathering up the wet clothing, she joined Sally in the kitchen.

"Just on time. The kettle is on the boil." The woman moved briskly around the room, placing two cups on the table and adding tea leaves to each cup. "Set yourself down and rest a while." She poured steaming water over the tea leaves, then returned the kettle to the stove. "We'll have tea and biscuits while we're waiting for something more substantial. It won't be much longer. Maybe an hour before the beans will be done."

"Tea is fine," Jade said, accepting a cup gratefully and sipping at the hot liquid. She felt the effects almost immediately, felt the cold slowly seeping away.

Sally Hartford sat across the table from Jade, sipping the hot tea from her own cup, her gaze traveling over her guest, taking note of the scratches and bruises on the exposed flesh of the young woman's face and arms. "Do you feel like talking, Jade?" she asked softly. "Do you want to tell me how you come to be here in this condition?"

Jade frowned and put down her cup. Sally, misinterpreting her actions, said quickly, "Don't feel like you have to tell me anything, dear. I don't intend to be nosy, but you looked like you'd seen a good bit of trouble lately."

Jade uttered a small laugh. "A good bit of trouble hardly describes what I've been through lately."

Sally reached across the table and covered Jade's hand with her own. "Do you want to tell me about it?"

Jade did.

And she found Sally so concerned, so sympathetic, that, before Jade knew what she was doing, she had told the woman everything that had happened to her, beginning on the night she'd slain one of the king's men.

"You poor thing," Sally said, patting her hand.

Jade flushed with embarrassment. "I didn't mean to bother you with my troubles. It's just . . . well, once the words started coming, there didn't seem anyplace to stop. Not until I reached the end."

"I seem to have that effect on people."

Jade laughed. "Yes. You do."

Sally looked uneasily out the window. "You said Matt Hunter is with Major Gladwin right now?"

"Yes."

"What about Badger. Where did he go?"

"He said something about going to the sutler's store."

Sally's eyes twinkled. "He'll be after a jug of whiskey."

"He deserves one . . . and more." She shuddered. "Both Matt and I would be dead if Badger hadn't found us. If I had the funds I would keep him in jugs for the rest of his life."

"I imagine you would, dear. I imagine you would." Sally pushed back her chair and crossed to the window, peering out into the darkness. "I don't like having Virginia away from home at a time like this. I think it would be better if we keep the family together for a while. Just until this thing with the Indians is settled."

Jade controlled a tremor of fear. "The walls are high, Sally, too high to be climbed, and the gates are secured by guards. You don't really believe the Indians could force their way in here. Do you? Not since the fort has been alerted?"

"No, no," Sally said, turning back to give Jade a quick smile. "We're perfectly safe here. It's just me, you know. When there's danger anywhere about, I feel better having my family around me."

A brisk knock sounded on the front door and Sally hurried to open it. "Matthew Hunter!" she exclaimed, stepping back to allow him entry. "You get in this house right now. Imagine! Waiting so long to come see me, and when you do, it's with news like this.''

It was obvious to Jade that they knew each other well.

"Dammit, Sally! You could at least say hello before you start yellin' at me!'' Matt picked up the woman and kissed her soundly before setting her on her feet again.

"Who's yellin'?'' she asked, frowning severely at him. "If anybody's voice was raised it sure wasn't mine.''

"Like hell it—''

"Stop your fussing and set down over there by Jade while I pour you some tea. Unless you want something stronger. I think there's some whiskey left in the cupboard.''

"Tea is fine.''

The little woman bustled about, setting out another cup, and adding tea and pouring water over it. "Supper will be awhile, Matt. But not too much longer. And Calvin should be gettin' off duty any minute now.''

"He may be late, Sally,'' Matt said, pulling out a chair and seating himself beside Jade. "Major Gladwin scheduled a meeting with his officers.''

"Only natural that he would. But we won't wait supper on him. I'll keep his warming on the stove.''

Matt covered Jade's hand with his own. "Are you all right?'' he asked softly.

She nodded her head.

"What does the major plan to do about Ensign Paully?'' Sally asked, reaching for a large stirring spoon that hung from a nail behind the stove to stir the briskly boiling beans. "Is he gathering troops for the rescue?''

"I see Jade's already told you what happened.''

"Yes. She told me. Does the major already have a plan to rescue the poor boy?''

Matt shook his head. "Ensign Paully is in no immediate danger, Sally. An attempt to rescue him at this time would surely fail and would leave the fort seriously understaffed.

Anyway, there's too many Indians prowling around outside. Our troops wouldn't be able to leave the fort even if we tried.''

"But what about Ensign Paully? Surely you're not going to just leave him there?''

"For the moment we can do nothing else.''

"Matt's right about there being no immediate danger to him,'' Jade put in, trying to make the woman feel better about circumstances that could not yet be changed. "I'm sure, since the woman who claimed him wanted him for a husband that he'll be treated well.''

"I know Ensign Paully well,'' Matt said. "He won't be there long. He'll go along with them until he makes them think he won't try to escape, and then he'll leave.''

"It just seems so cruel,'' Sally muttered. "He's one of the king's men and we know he's a captive. We should at least make an attempt at rescue.''

"That would give away our advantage, Sally. You must see that.''

"What do you mean, Matt?''

"The Indians don't know we're here. They think they'll take the fort unawares. But Major Gladwin will be ready for them. Perhaps they'll take it as a bad sign.''

"A bad sign?''

"Yes. You know the Indians are a superstitious lot. They couldn't know how we learned about their plans. If we're lucky they may believe we can read their minds. Or were told of their plans by someone in the spirit world. They wouldn't dare rise against the British if they were helped by spirits.''

"Do you really think they might believe such nonsense?'' Sally asked.

"Maybe. And maybe not.''

Sally gazed into her teacup as though searching for

answers there. Finally, she uttered a heavy sigh. "I just feel like we're deserting poor Ensign Paully."

"I know. But believe me, Sally. He would understand . . . and he would be in complete agreement with the major's actions."

"I guess we'll have to leave the poor man's fate to the Lord," Sally said, pushing herself away from the table. "It's a fact that it was *His* hand that brought you to us, Matthew Hunter." She gave a delicate shudder. "If you hadn't come, those red devils might have carried out their evil plan." She pushed her chair away from the table and rose to her feet. "I hope you two don't mind if I leave you alone for a while. I feel right afraid for Virgie Lee, and I know I won't rest easy until she's home again."

"You go ahead and don't worry about us," Matt said.

"I hope you're plannin' on staying, Matt." Sally pulled a slicker off a hook and pushed her arms into it. "There's always room on the settee if you've a mind to stop a while with us."

"I'll bunk down in the barracks," he said quickly. "I told the major to look for me there if he needed me."

"As he surely will. There's none around here that know them Indians like you, Matt." She reached for the door handle, paused, then looked back at Jade. "You just make yourself at home, Jade. I'll be back real soon."

Jade waited until the door closed behind the woman, then turned her attention to Matt. "I know you didn't want to upset her, Matt. That's why I waited until she left. But I really need to know if the Indians present a danger to us here?"

"I can't deny there's danger," he replied gruffly. "But the major has been warned now. He knows what to expect and he'll be ready for them when they make their move."

"Did he—the major—have any suspicion that anything was wrong?"

"He had suspicions." He explained quickly what he'd learned from Gladwin, ending with, "He thinks the attack will come when the Indians come for the Calumet dance. Before he allows them inside he'll send all the women and children to the supply building. It has thick rock walls and there's no way the Indians could get inside. Neither will they be able to burn it."

"I'm frightened, Matt."

"I know." He pulled her into his embrace. "You've been through so much already, my love. But you'll come through this, too." He tilted her chin and gave her a long, hard kiss. Then, putting her aside, he rose to his feet.

"Matt," she protested quickly. "You're not going, are you?"

"I wouldn't if it weren't necessary, Jade. But I need to find Badger while he's still sober enough to hear what I'm saying."

"When will I see you again?"

"I don't know." He caressed the contour of her cheek. "I might be tied up for a while. Just stay with Sally and Virgie Lee and you'll be safe enough."

"But will *you* be safe, Matt?"

"I'll be fine, sweetheart." He opened the door and looked back at her. "Don't worry. This will all be over soon."

"What then, Matt?" she asked softly. "When this is over, what then?"

"Then our future will begin, Jade. We'll have the rest of our lives."

She'd wanted to hear him say that. Needed badly to hear those words. And now that she had, she felt a deep satisfaction fill her being. Even though they were under threat of attack from the Indians, even though they might die tomorrow, Matt loved her. And that knowledge was enough to help her through whatever might be waiting ahead for them.

With her own love for him shining from her expressive green eyes, Jade stood on the tips of her toes and covered Matt's lips with her own in an endearingly sweet kiss. When it was over, she watched him leave the house.

Everything would be all right, her heart sang.

This infernal Indian war would soon be over and, when it was, she and Matt would find the happiness that both of them had so long been denied.

All she had to do was wait a little longer.

Chapter Twenty-One

Matt had only been gone a few moments when Sally Hartford entered the cabin followed by a young woman whose features resembled the elder woman's enough for anyone with a discerning eye to know their relationship was that of mother and daughter.

"Where's Matt?" the young woman asked, her blue eyes glowing eagerly.

Releasing the handful of blue gown that had kept her skirt out of the mud in her wild dash across the parade ground, she smoothed out the wrinkles, trying to tidy herself while waiting for an answer to her question.

"Virgie Lee!" Sally admonished. "Is that any way to greet a guest . . . without even sayin' your howdys?"

"I'm sorry," Virgie Lee said quickly, pushing at a few strands of long blond hair that had escaped the ribbon confining the rest of the curling mass at the nape of her neck. "Howdy." She stepped forward and stuck out her hand. "My name is Virgie Lee. And I guess you're Jade."

"Yes. And I'm pleased to meet you, Virgie Lee." Noticing the way the young woman's eyes kept sliding around the room as though she expected to find Matt hiding somewhere, she took pity on her. "As for Matt, he's already gone."

"Gone? Oh, Ma!" She turned her attention to her mother. "Didn't you tell him he could stay here with us?"

"I told him, Virginia," her mother said sternly. "But when there's men's business afoot they all like to keep together." Sally moved to the cookstove, opened the grate and pushed several pieces of wood onto the smoldering fire.

"Horsefeathers!" Virgie Lee said with disgust, pulling out a chair and plopping herself into it with a flounce of petticoats and blue skirt.

Jade felt herself envying the girl who could only be a few years younger than herself. It was obvious Virgina Lee had never been alone, that she had never known what it meant to be without the loving protection of her parents. Unlike Jade, who'd spent the last few years fending for herself.

"Ma said Matt brought you here," Virgie Lee said, eyeing Jade curiously. "Are you his—"

"Virginia Lee!" Sally's scandalized voice interrupted. "Don't you dare ask such personal questions." She thumped the young woman on the head several times to punctuate the command.

"Ma!" Virgie Lee whined, rolling her eyes at her mother. "I hate it when you do that."

"Well, don't make me do it!" her mother snapped.

"All right," the girl said, her lips already curling into a smile. "Do you need any help with supper, Ma?"

"No, Virgie Lee. I only have the cornbread to make before it's done. Why don't you show Jade that sampler you're working on?"

Virgie Lee agreed, rising quickly from her chair. "Come. It's in my room."

"I haven't thanked you for the loan of your dress," Jade said, following after the girl. "I hope you don't think me presumptuous for accepting your mother's offer without first waiting for your permission."

"Of course not. Ma said you were soaking wet." She pushed open the door to her room and stood back so Jade could enter, then quickly closed the door.

"The sampler isn't anything special," she said, hurrying to the chest in the corner and pulling out a small square of white linen and holding it out for Jade to see.

"It's lovely," Jade said, reaching out to trace the small flowers and leaves with the tip of her right forefinger.

"It's nothing special," Virgie Lee said dismissively.

She tossed it carelessly into the trunk and closed the lid again, then crawled onto the bed and crossed her legs beneath her. "Sit down," she ordered, patting a spot beside her. "And let's talk."

A smile twitched at Jade's lips. It was obvious that Virgie Lee hadn't the least interest in showing her the sampler, had only agreed to do so because it would mean leaving the room where her mother worked. Now that they were alone, Virgie Lee meant to get answers to her questions.

"What do you want to talk about?" Jade asked, taking delight in tormenting the girl.

"Matt, of course." Virgie Lee's eyes twinkled with humor as she leaned toward Jade. "Every female in this fort, starting at the age of twelve and leaving off at sixty will want to know what you were doing traveling through the forest alone with Matthew Hunter. Were you captured by renegades and he rode up on his white charger and carried you away?"

"Something like that," Jade replied.

"Really?" Virgie Lee squealed. "Oh, gosh, you don't know how much I'd like to have been in your shoes. To be rescued by Matt . . ." She uttered a long sigh and shivered dramatically. "Mary Helen will just about die. She's sweet on him, you know. So is Carol Ann and Hannah and Cynthia Elizabeth. They're all going to be so envious. I am, too, of course, but Matt never looks at me like he does Mary Helen and Cynthia Elizabeth." She wrinkled her nose. "He still thinks I'm too young, but fourteen's not all that young, is it? Lots of girls get married at fourteen. Thelma Sue did."

The girl continued to ramble, the words bubbling out of her like water from a spring. And since answers didn't seem to be required, Jade allowed her thoughts to drift, allowed herself to wonder about all the young females who'd been named as ardent admirers of Matt.

"Don't you think so, Jade?"

Having been pulled back to reality by a question, Jade said, "I'm sorry, Virgie Lee, my mind was wandering. What did you say?"

"I asked you if you didn't think Matt was the handsomest man you'd ever met."

"Oh, yes. He's undoubtedly that. But please don't tell him I said so."

"Oh, I wouldn't. I'm not a featherbrain like Olivia. Don't ever tell her anything you don't want the whole fort to know."

"I won't."

"Sooo." Virgie Lee drawled the word out. "Are you or not?"

Jade blinked in confusion. "Am I what?"

"In love with Matt?"

Suddenly, the door was pushed open and Sally stuck her head inside. "Supper's on the table," she said.

Jade slid off the bed, taking advantage of the woman's presence to escape the questions.

"Is Daddy home?" Virgie asked, following them to the kitchen.

"No. He sent word he'd be eating with the major tonight."

"Oh, horsefeathers! I wanted to ask him about the doll head he's carving for Mary Helen's baby sister. Her mother already has the body made and they're just waiting for Daddy to finish the head."

"Don't bother your father about things like wooden doll heads, Virgie Lee," her mother said. "He's got more important things on his mind right now."

"I know. And I won't say anything yet. But maybe tomorrow—"

"Not tomorrow, either."

"How long must I wait then? Her birthday is next week and her mother needs time to attach the head and—"

"Virginia!" Sally said sharply. "Let it alone."

"Yes, ma'am." Virgie ducked her head slightly. "I'm sorry, Mama. Of course there's more important things. Are we in very much danger from the Indians?"

"Oh, honey," Sally sighed, wrapping an arm around her daughter's shoulder. "You know whatever danger exists, your daddy and the other soldiers will handle. And I didn't mean to be sharp with you, it's just that sometimes you don't seem to know the meaning of danger. Go on now, set yourself down and let's eat before it gets cold." She pointed at the chair Jade had occupied before. "You sit over there, Jade. Virgie Lee, pass her the cornbread."

Although they spoke no more about the danger posed by the Indians, Jade knew the subject must be uppermost in their minds . . . as it was in hers.

But it did little good to worry about it. At least the fort afforded them safety. And, although the Indians were most certainly a threat, as long as they remained inside the fort they were safe from immediate danger. And they would remain safe, as long as their food supplies and ammunition held out.

After the meal was over and the kitchen had been cleaned Jade retired for the night. Only then did her exhaustion claim her. She was fast asleep only moments after stretching out on the large feather mattress.

It was late when she awoke the next morning.

Hearing the sound of voices through the thin walls, Jade scurried from the bed, hurrying toward the washstand in the corner. Could Matt's voice be one of those she was hearing? she wondered. She hurried with her morning ablutions, splashing her face with water before donning the borrowed dress. After pulling on her shoes and fastening them, she ran a comb through her hair to eliminate the tangles and hurried to the parlor.

Hiding her disappointment that only mother and daughter were there, Jade greeted them with a smile. "I apologize for sleeping in," she said.

"There's no need, dear," Sally said, putting aside the fabric she'd been busily embroidering and moving toward the kitchen. "We waited breakfast for you."

"You shouldn't have done that!" Jade protested. "I don't want to be any trouble."

"Pshaw!" the little woman said. "You're no trouble at all, Jade. You just put such thoughts out of your head. Neither of us were hungry yet anyway."

"What about your husband?"

"Daddy didn't come home last night. He stayed with the other soldiers," Virgie announced, pulling out a chair and seating herself at the table. "You sit over there, Jade, where you did last night. No, you can't help Mama. Everything's done already. See! Your cup has tea leaves in the bottom. And the gravy and biscuits are already done, just kept warming on the stove."

"I see you have everything in hand," Jade conceded, sinking down in the chair. "But I feel selfish, foisting myself on you this way and then not helping out with the work."

"You can help with the washing up," Sally said briskly. "I'm in the middle of embroidering a bodice for Virgie Lee's new dress and I could use the extra time to work on it."

The conversation continued in that vein. Virgie Lee described the dress Mary Helen's mother was designing for her to wear at her upcoming birthday party. "Mary Helen's hoping Matt will still be here. That dress of hers will make the men's eyes pop. With the new corset her mother ordered under the dress, Mary Helen's breasts are swelled out like cow udders just before milking time."

"Virginia Lee Hartford!" Sally snapped. "Young ladies do not speak of breasts . . . nor do they liken them to swollen cow udders."

"Mother!" Virgie Lee's voice exactly copied the tone of her mother. "How can Jade know how Mary Helen's breasts look if I don't mention them?"

"I'm sure Jade could care less about Mary Helen. Or any portion of her body. Now close your mouth, child, and eat your breakfast."

"Listen to her," Virgie Lee said, her eyes twinkling at Jade. "Did you ever hear anything so ridiculous. How can I eat my breakfast with my mouth closed?"

"That'll be enough of your smart mouth, young lady!"

"Yes, ma'am." Although the girl lowered her head and turned her attention to her breakfast, Jade knew the chastisement had left her completely unaffected.

She was proven right when, only moments later, Virgie Lee brought up the subject of the upcoming party again.

"I do hope Matt will be there. You'll come won't you, Jade?"

"I don't know if we'll still be here then," Jade replied. "Anyway, I haven't been invited."

"Horsefeathers! You don't need an invitation to a party in this fort. Everyone here goes. There will be singing and dancing and—" She broke off and looked at her mother. "You said Joey was here last night, Mama. Did he mention the party? He hasn't said anything about taking me yet. And if he doesn't speak up soon I may not be available."

She continued to prattle on and on about the upcoming party, speaking of this one and that one and the dresses that were being made for friends. Jade was grateful for the friendly chatter that helped pass the morning. Without it, she knew, her mind would have been constantly absorbed with Matt's continued absence.

Even so, her eyes wandered often between the window and the door, the latter remaining firmly closed throughout the morning.

Finally, around noon, the door was flung open and a tall, dark-haired soldier wearing the insignia of a captain stepped into the parlor. With barely a nod to acknowledge their guest, he turned his attention on his wife.

"The women and children are gathering in the supply house, Sally. Major Gladwin issued orders for everyone to be there within the hour."

"Do you think there's much danger, Calvin?" Sally asked, clutching his sleeve tightly.

"No, dear," he said gruffly, patting her shoulder awkwardly. "You're in no danger whatsoever. We're only doing this as a precaution. We don't want the lot of you in the way if things get out of hand. Don't you fret over it."

"Do you think things might get out of hand, Daddy?" Virgie Lee asked, her blue eyes round with fear.

"No, child, I don't," Captain Hartford said. "But we

don't intend to take chances. Not with our families." He smiled at her to show her there was no reason to be afraid. "This will be over soon and I'll be able to finish whittling out that doll head of yours. You go with Mama to the supply house and stay there until you're told to leave. And, Virgie Lee, don't do anything foolish."

"Papa! I don't have feathers for a brain!"

"I hope not. But there was that time when Joey went hunting outside the fort and you wanted to prove that you were as good with a musket as he was so you—"

"I know," she said mournfully. "But that was last year. I was only thirteen then."

"And now you're fourteen," he teased lightly. "A grown-up young lady with beaux who come calling."

"Joey couldn't really be called a beau," she muttered, her cheeks flushing.

Jade stood apart from the others feeling like an intruder standing outside a lighted window watching and yearning to be part of the family. She couldn't leave the room though, not when there was a chance Captain Hartford might mention Matt's name. Matt might even have sent her a message.

But it seemed he had not, for Captain Hartford left without having delivered one. Perhaps, though, she consoled herself, Matt had been kept so busy there was no time for other things, no time to even consider the woman he'd brought with him to the fort.

But that consolation proved to be of short duration, because the three of them had barely entered the supply house when a slender, fiery-haired young woman hurried across to greet Virgie Lee.

"I saw him, Virgie!" the young woman exclaimed. "And I asked him right out and the answer was yes!" Her whiskey-colored eyes glowed with excitement. "Just think of it. I'll be the envy of every woman there, dancing every single waltz with Matthew Hunter."

"Not every single dance, Mary Helen! Matt wouldn't do that."

"Yes he would too." Mary Helen's lips pouted. "You just wait and see if he doesn't." She whirled around the room; her skirts flying around her. "You should have seen the way he looked at me. I swear, he seemed to be mesmerized, as though he couldn't believe how I'd blossomed out."

Jade felt as though she'd been plunged into a bucket of ice water. She hated the little twit who seemed to think Matt was her personal property. Jade had the urge to wind her fingers through that fiery swatch of curls and pull every strand of hair out. But somehow, she controlled the urge.

Keeping her feelings under tight control, she joined the older women who spoke of other things besides parties and dancing and new gowns. But, even though she listened to the flow of voices around her, she couldn't get Matt out of her mind. Nor could she forget the fact that, even though he'd had no time to visit her, he'd obviously found the time to visit Mary Helen.

Matt wondered if they were making a mistake by allowing the Indians into the fort. He stood in the shadows of the scaffolding that was designed as a watchtower for the guards observing as the gate slid open.

Immediately, Pontiac and perhaps fifty other warriors filed through the entrance. Matt kept a watchful eye on the man who'd designated himself the leader, for he knew the situation was definitely volatile. There was no way they could be sure their plan would work. Pontiac was unknown to them, as was his way of fighting. If he was a braggart, thinking only of conquest, he might order an attack even

in the face of so many odds. And if he did, many lives
would be lost—some of them belonging to the soldiers
who occupied the fort.

Matt's eyes slid to Major Gladwin who turned at that
moment to motion Matt forward. A few quick strides later
saw Matt beside the officers who made their life work that
of guarding the fort.

"Pontiac," Major Gladwin said formally. "This man is
my friend, Matthew Hunter. He intends to watch your
Calumet dance. As do my soldiers."

The Indian grunted. "I know of Hunter."

Matt nodded, his gaze never leaving the other man's,
his body coiled, his senses wary. "I am known by many red
men, Pontiac. And all who know me are aware that my
word is good. They know that when I pledge friendship
my word is to be honored."

Something flickered in the Indian's flat black eyes. His
body tensed and his gaze left Matt's to slide along the
soldiers who were lined up on the parade grounds, their
muskets held loosely with their fingers firmly on the trig-
gers.

"You have many soldiers here, white man," Pontiac commented, his eyes returning to the major. "I do not consider
that as an act of friendship."

"My soldiers are here to view the Calumet dance," the
major said calmly. "If we are to be friends, Pontiac, then
they must also be included."

"We cannot perform the dance with so many soldiers
watching." Pontiac turned to his warriors and motioned
them back toward the gates. "We will leave the fort now."

"Open the gates, Private!" the major ordered.

The gates were flung open and one by one the Indians
filed out of the fort.

"He knew we'd been alerted," Major Gladwin said. "The
moment he saw you, he knew."

"Yeah. He knew," Matt agreed. "He prob'ly heard about me escaping, but he sure didn't expect to find me here. Wasn't too pleased about it, either."

"You're right about that." The major bit off the end of a cigar and stuck it in his mouth. "We did manage to surprise the wily rascal." His lips curled around the cigar. "Did you see how fast he moved them Indians outta here?"

"Yeah. I saw it." He looked toward the storehouse. "Think it'd be okay for the women and children to leave the storehouse now?"

"I don't see any reason to keep them there. Do you?"

At that moment they heard a loud, undulating warcry and Matt spun quickly around . . . just in time to see a flaming arrow fly over the wall and bury itself on the nearest roof.

"Put that fire out!" the major roared.

Other yells and other arrows followed the first one. Then a bucket brigade was started, the men hurrying to put out the fires before they could take hold and burn the houses down.

Gunfire sounded.

Bullets whizzed past the soldiers manning the scaffolding and the sentries returned the fire.

Suddenly, a scream from inside the fort walls told Matt one of the guards had been struck.

"Get more men on the walls!" the major roared, running to the north wall which was under the heaviest attack. "Double the guards over here."

Matt ran up the steps to the scaffolding and knelt behind the wall, aiming his rifle at an Indian fitting another arrow into his bow. Taking careful aim, Matt squeezed the trigger and watched the Indian drop. Immediately, though, another warrior took the place of his fallen comrade.

Where had they all come from? Matt wondered, reloading his rifle and squeezing off another shot. He'd never seen so many Indians together before. It was obvious the nations had banded together to stage this attack, equally obvious that the fort was in trouble. He sent a silent prayer toward the heavens that they could hold out until reinforcements arrived.

Chapter Twenty-Two

Jade tried to ignore the booming sounds that penetrated even the thick walls of the storehouse as she dampened her cloth in the bucket beside the bed and wrung it out. Then, slowly and carefully, she bathed seargeant Dobbs's face and neck and the part of his chest that wasn't covered by the bloody red bandage in her effort to cool his heated, feverish flesh.

But it was hard to ignore the sound of battle, hard to forget that Matt was somewhere out there, probably exposed to both arrows and musket balls. And the more time that passed, the harder it became.

"You look worn out, Jade." Jade recognized the soft voice as Sally Hartford's. "I don't think you've had much rest since this whole thing started."

"How long has it been now?" Jade asked, looking up at the dark-haired woman whose face—that had been so young-appearing before—was now lined with fatigue.

"The battle will be going on two weeks tomorrow," Sally

muttered. "And they've been the longest and hardest two weeks I've ever spent."

"Only two weeks?" It seemed forever.

Sally moved closer, bending over the bed and lifting the edge of the wounded man's bandage. "Looks like the bleeding's stopped now."

"I noticed that when I last checked," Jade said, rising unsteadily from the chair. "Are you sure you don't need a break, too, Sally?"

"Don't worry about me, dear. I've just had a cup of hot tea," the older woman said. "You go on now and rest easy about your patient. I'll take good care of Seargeant Dobbs while you're gone."

"The doctor was here a little while ago," Jade said. "He told me Dobbs wouldn't make it if the fever didn't break soon."

"I know. But with all the washing down he's been getting, the fever won't have no chance."

Jade hoped Sally was right. The Seargeant was a good man. She'd hate to see anything happen to him.

Uttering a heavy sigh, she arched her aching back muscles as she glanced down the long row of cots where the soldiers who'd been wounded lay. "How many of them are there now, Sally? How many wounded and dead?"

"Four dead and twelve wounded." Sally dipped the cloth in the bucket of water beside the bed, then wrung the excess water out of the cloth before reapplying it to the Seargeant's feverish skin.

"But most of the wounds suffered were at the beginning of the battle," Sally said huskily. "It's been several days since they brought any new ones to us. Now try to put it out of your mind and go get something to eat."

Put it out of her mind?

Jade felt hysterical laughter rising at that thought, but managed to hold it back. How could she possibly put it out of her mind when Matt was out there somewhere in the middle of the battle?

Where would it all end? she wondered, looking at the boxes and barrels of supplies that had been pushed against the walls to make room for them. Each day that passed saw those supplies dwindling more and more.

What would they do when the ammunition ran out? And the foodstuffs . . . how long could a soldier fight without food in his belly?

She didn't know the answer. And, although it was a question that continually plagued her, she wouldn't allow herself to ask one of the other women.

Moving down the row of wounded, she stopped beside the cot where Virginia Lee was tending a young soldier whose arm had been shattered by a musket ball.

Virginia had, of necessity, matured greatly during the last two weeks. She was no longer Virgie, the young girl whose thoughts revolved totally around boys and the latest fashions. Instead, she was Virginia, the young woman who worked countless hours beside the older women, attending the soldiers who'd been wounded in battle.

"How is Joey?" Jade asked softly.

Virginia looked up at her with moist eyes. "He's not doing well at all, Jade. The doctor said there's a good chance he'll lose his arm."

"No!"

The protest was uttered weakly, but it was enough to make them aware that Joey had finally regained consciousness.

"Don't let him take my arm, Virgie," he muttered, gripping her forearm. "Promise me. Don't let the doc cut it off."

His eyes flowed with a fierce light as he tried to extract the promise from her. He tried to push himself to one elbow, tried to swing his legs over the side of the cot, but he was too weak. Virginia easily pushed him back onto the mattress again.

"Don't fret, Joey," she soothed, smoothing his hair back from his forehead.

"You gotta promise me," he muttered, closing his eyes tightly. "You gotta do it, Virgie."

"Joey, please listen to me. Nobody's going to take your arm unless its absolutely necessary. But if it means your life . . ."

"No!" His eyes snapped open again. "Not even then! I'd rather be dead, Virgie! I wouldn't be no good to you with only one arm! Promise me you won't let 'em take my arm!"

Tears rolled down her cheeks and Jade could feel Virginia's anguish as she conceded to Joey's request. "I promise," she whispered. "You can rest easy, Joey. No matter what happens, I won't let the doctor take your arm."

Swallowing the lump in her throat, Jade watched the girl bending over Joey, wondering if Virginia could keep the promise she'd just made. If the doctor found it necessary to remove the young man's arm, could Virginia really stop him?

"Would you like something to drink, Virginia?" she asked softly. "Maybe a cup of tea?"

"No," the young woman replied. "Not now. But maybe later."

Jade left Virginia and strode briskly across the room to the stove. For weeks now the kettle had never been allowed to become empty, and the water was always on the verge of steaming.

After making herself a cup of tea, Jade glanced toward the door that was kept barred from the inside. A woman leaned against the wall there, her shoulders slumping with weariness. Jade wondered how long she'd remained in that same position, waiting beside the door in case one of the soldiers needed to enter, either to bring a wounded man or to carry more supplies and ammunition away.

Jade strode quickly to the door. "Would you like me to relieve you for a while?" she asked. "You look completely worn out."

"I am, my dear," the woman said, rising immediately from the chair. "You wouldn't think sitting beside a door could be so wearing."

"It's the strain of waiting," Jade sympathized. "The not knowing what's going on out there, wondering how much longer we'll be in here and—"

She broke off as several hard raps were delivered on the thick wooden door. Opening the tiny porthole, she peered outside and saw one eye set in a mass of leather wrinkles staring back at her. "It's Badger," she said, fumbling with the heavy bar that fastened the door.

When the door was finally released, she pushed it open eagerly, hoping the old man brought good news.

"Badger!" she exclaimed, barely allowing him through the door before she curled her fingers around his forearm. "It's so good to see you! You don't know how worried I've been!"

"Not about me, I warrant."

"Of course I was worried about you."

She uttered the lie with careless ease. There was no reason for him to know that she'd forgotten about him completely until now.

"Have you seen Matt?" she asked eagerly. "Is he all right? Are the Indians gone yet?" A ridiculous question, she realized, almost the moment she asked it. If the Indians were gone, there would be no sound of battle. "Is Matt all right?" she asked again. "He hasn't been wounded, has he?"

"Slow down, gal," he said gruffly. "Give me time to answer one question afore you ask another one."

"I'm sorry, Badger. But I've been so worried about Matt. And you, of course."

"Course," he said, his lips twitching.

"Badger, please!"

"Matt's doin' fine, I reckon," the old man growled. "Leastways the last time I seen him he was. He ain't here no more."

"What do you mean?" she whispered. "If he's not here, then where is he?"

"Left on the *Michigan* early this morning. Sent out by the major along with several of the soldiers. If they can run the blockade they'll be bringin' back troops and supplies." His faded eyes went to the boxes and barrels left in the storehouse. "Hope we got enough left to last until they get back."

"If they can run the blockade?" Those words, spoken by the old man in a matter-of-fact voice, were the cause of the fear that suddenly blossomed through Jade. "What does that mean, Badger? What blockade must they run?"

"The Injuns ain't gonna let a schooner leave here if'n they can help it," Badger replied, prying her fingers loose from his forearm. "Now leave me alone, young'n. I gotta get some ammunition out to the wall afore the men fightin' there run out."

Jade felt numb as she watched the old man stride toward the boxes of ammunition. He counted the boxes that were left, frowning all the while, then picked up a box and strode toward the door again.

"Leave the door open!" he growled. "I'll be back."

She took advantage of the open door to step outside and breathe the fresh air, becoming aware immediately of the acrid smell of sulfur.

She became aware, too, of the sudden silence. Not a sound could be heard in or around the fort.

Her heart gave a jerk of hope. Was it over? Had the

Indians given up and retreated? Oh, God, let it be true! Let the battle be over!

Her gaze narrowed on the scaffolding built high on the wall and she saw a young soldier raise himself from a squatting position until his back was bent just enough to allow him to remain unseen from those who might be lurking outside.

The silence continued. Moments passed. Long, silent moments that stretched out slowly. A smile began to form on Jade's lips and, even from this distance, she could see the young soldier gradually relax. He straightened to his full height and leaned over the wall, apparently to better view the area below.

"It's over," Jade whispered. "The Indians have finally gone." She turned to inform the other women, and as she did a musket boomed outside the fort. The sound jerked her around . . . just in time to see the young soldier's head explode.

Horrorstruck, Jade stumbled backward, would have fallen if the warehouse wall hadn't been directly behind her.

Tasting the bile that rose in her throat, she fought to control it.

"Go back inside, young'n," a voice said gruffly.

Realizing that Badger had returned unnoticed, Jade looked at him with glazed eyes. "His h-head exploded, Badger. One minute it was there and the next it just . . . exploded."

"Come on," he said gently, curling gnarled fingers around her forearm and pulling her inside with him. "There ain't no use thinkin' on it no more. Nothin' anybody can do for 'im."

"He's out there now," she whispered. "Outside the wall where *they* are. Those savages have him now and they can do anything they want with him." Matt, too, she realized suddenly. Matt was out there among those bloodthirsty Indians. Did they already have him? Had the Indians exploded his head, too?

"Matt," she whispered, fighting against the darkness that threatened.

"Matt's just fine. That boy can take care of his ownself!" Jade could barely hear Badger's voice breaking through her fear. "Miz Hartford! Come over here an' see to this young'n."

"I don't need . . ." Jade's voice faded away as she gave in to the threatening darkness.

On the deck of the schooner *Michigan* Matt sighted his rifle on the big Indian in the nearest canoe, the same Indian who had, just moments ago, downed Seargeant Morris.

Matt had no need to look. He already knew Morris was dead, had heard the death rattle in his throat that was followed immediately by silence.

But now the Indian would pay for what he'd done. Matt would make certain of that.

Taking careful aim, Matt tightened his finger, slowly squeezing the trigger. The man uttered a piercing scream, then pitched headlong into the water.

Matt turned his sights on the next man in the canoe. He had no need to choose his target now, knowing all the occupants were enemies. Any one of whom could, if left alive, take the lives of the soldiers who manned the schooner.

Matt was determined to hold the Indians away from the *Michigan*, knowing that so much depended on him doing so. If those in the fort were to survive, the schooner must break through the Indian blockade.

And they *would* survive, Matt thought fiercely, carefully

squeezing off another shot and finding immense satisfaction in the fact that another Indian had toppled, lifeless, into the water.

A musket ball zoomed past his cheek, so close to his flesh that he could actually feel the air displaced by its passing.

Matt jerked back involuntarily, his reddened eyes searching for the man who'd fired at him.

Spotting the offender, Matt brought his rifle up and returned the Indian's fire. He heard a loud cry just before the warrior toppled into the river.

The battle raged on, none of them knew exactly how long, while the sail that was supposed to push them through the water hung limp. The men at the oars strained their muscles, trying their best to push the boat past the blockade.

A movement above him jerked Matt's eyes overhead. As he watched, the sail billowed and the boat glided faster through the water.

"Look!" a man shouted. "The wind's rising! We're gonna do it, boys! The wind's gonna help us go through!"

"Hooray, hooray!" the shouts rang out, echoing over the schooner as the boat moved faster and faster.

Matt sank onto the deck, reaching for his rifles to ready them for another attack. But before he'd finished loading them, the schooner had sailed out of range.

They had done it.

The schooner *Michigan* had successfully run the Indian blockade.

Chapter Twenty-Three

Jade gripped the bucket handle tightly as she hurried across the parade ground. A musket sounded, booming loudly outside the fort walls.

Having become accustomed to the sound of battle, she didn't even break stride. Instead, she continued on her way, carrying the water to the mess hall where the doctor now tended the wounded.

Her gaze was narrowed, continually alert for anything out of the ordinary. And for that reason she spotted the soldier, slumped on the ground beside one of the cabins, his head dipped forward, his chin resting against the base of his neck.

Her footsteps quickened as she changed directions. Water sloshed from the bucket, soaking the bottom of her skirt, but she paid no heed to it.

Setting her bucket on the ground, she leaned over the soldier, placing a hand on his shoulder. "Are you all right?" she asked quietly.

He raised his head, looking at her from glazed brown eyes. "I don't rightly know, ma'am."

"Would you like some water?"

He nodded slowly, the movement seeming almost to take more effort than he had left.

Unhooking a tin cup from her belt, she dipped it full of water and held it to his lips. He drank slowly at first, but after he'd swallowed a few mouthfuls, he took the cup and eagerly consumed the water.

"How long has it been since you've eaten?" she asked, her eyes searching his body for any sign of wounds. There were none that she could see.

"I don't know," he said. "I been on the back wall for two nights and the food never seemed to make it back that far. I ain't really had much time to think on it, though. Been too busy loadin' my musket and shootin' at the shadows out there. Just the damn shadows . . . don't think I hit none of them redskins. Just shootin' at the leaves movin' in the wind."

"You need something to eat," Jade said. "And a place to rest out of the sun."

"Seargeant said to go to the barracks and sleep, but I couldn't seem to make it there."

"Let me help you," she said, slipping her arms beneath his. "We'll take you to the barracks, get some food in your stomach, then you can sleep."

He stood unsteadily and took a wobbling step with her help. "Don't know why we just don't give up," the soldier said. "Maybe if we was to surrender the Injuns would let us leave."

"No they wouldn't," Jade said quickly. "We can't believe anything they tell us. But it's all right. Matt Hunter has gone for help. He'll be back soon with reinforcements."

"He's been gone for three weeks now," the soldier said.

"It shouldn't've taken them that long. I don't think we can count on them no more."

"We can count on them, soldier. Matt won't let us down. He'll be back."

He turned his head to stare at her with eyes that were suddenly bright with hope. "You really believe that, ma'am? Really and truly?"

"Really and truly. Nothing will stop Matt from returning. And he'll have plenty of men and supplies with him when he does. They'll drive those Indians away from here. They'll run away like whipped dogs with their tails between their legs."

Somehow, those words of Jade's made the rounds in the days to come and they became a battle cry used by the men to keep their mood high.

Jade's firm belief that Matt would return, that he would bring the badly needed supplies and enough troops to relieve the soldiers who fought so valiantly to defend the fort from its attackers, made her popular with the women who tended the wounded as well as the men who defended them.

Despite her busy days, she managed a smile and a few words of encouragement for those who crossed her path. Many of them, those whose spirits were at a low ebb, deliberately sought her out, to gain courage from her firm belief that rescue was near. But they didn't know how hard it was for her to keep her own spirits elevated as each passing day brought no sign of the *Michigan,* nor its crew. Nor would they know, she quietly determined.

She would keep her growing unease to herself. One day, the schooner *would* return. And when that day came she would be reunited with Matt. She would not allow herself to believe otherwise.

* * *

Jewel Crawford descended the stairs to the large room on the bottom floor of the trading post. Ignoring Hal, who had stationed himself behind the bar, she poured herself a glass of whiskey and joined LeCroix at a nearby table. "Henri," she said, sliding into the chair across from him. "I'm bored." She allowed her gaze to travel over the primitive room before returning to him. "I thought this was a trading post, but other than a few trappers and that Indian wife of yours, nobody's been around here."

He threw her a quick look, then returned to perusing the bottle before him. "It is because of the war, *ma chérie*. When it is over the people will come again."

"Meanwhile, I rattle around this place with nothing to do. With no female companionship whatsoever."

"You would have had female companionship had my men not been so lax in their duties and allowed Mademoiselle Jade to leave." He shot a heated look at the man behind the bar. Jewel could see he was still enraged at the girl's escape.

"She did leave," Jewel pointed out. "And I'm not so sure we would have got along anyway."

"I think not." His look was cold. "The two of you would not have been compatible."

She leaned toward him. "Why don't we go east until this war is over, Henri?"

"No. If it is the company of other females you wish, then I will send for Juaheela."

"I have no interest in your wife, Henri. In fact, she gives me the shivers."

Frowning, Jewel recalled meeting his Indian wife. There was something about the woman—the way Juaheela looked at her—that made her afraid for her life.

And Henri's assurances did little to relieve her fears.

Henri himself was enough, at times, to put the fear of God into her. She'd never—not seen a man so angry as Henri LeCroix when he'd arrived at the trading post and discovered the little bird—the one he'd mistake for his business partner—had flown the coop. Because of that, Jewel had wondered at his relationship with the woman.

How could he have made such a mistake? Jewel wondered, tucking a strand of long dark hair into the fashionable mass of curls that crowned her head.

Whatever the reason, he'd certainly paid dearly for the mistake. The merchant hadn't wanted to lose his prize and he'd made the Frenchman cough up a goodly sum before handing her papers over.

God! Those papers. They were all that was keeping her here in this godforsaken land. If she had her papers again, she would take the next ship back to England, would forget about the business she had going with LeCroix. After all, she'd already gone from the wharves to a mansion, using nothing but her body and her wits. She could do it again if it became necessary.

Yes. If it became necessary. As it seemed it might.

Matt stood at the bow of the schooner *Michigan* and scanned the trees lining the banks of the river ahead. Any one of those trees could hide the enemy, but if they were to reach Fort Detroit they had no recourse except to go by way of the river.

"Guess it won't be much longer now, Hunter."

Matt had no need to turn his head to identify the man who had spoken. He had come to know him well. He was Major Robert Rogers, commander of the American Rangers.

"If the wind stays favorable, we should make it before nightfall," Matt said brusquely.

"I doubt it will be easy," Rogers answered gruffly. "Those red devils won't let us through without a fight. They're sure to be waiting in ambush at the river's narrowest point."

"I know," Matt agreed. "But they won't stop us. We got through them when we left Fort Detroit and we'll do it again to return."

"No." Rogers's keen eyes studied the left bank. "They won't stop us. We'll be ready for 'em when they make their move."

Matt threw a quick look at Rogers. The grin on his lips told how eager he was to face the coming battle. Matt felt grateful the man had come, and that he'd brought along twenty of his famous Rangers. Each and every man of them had proven themselves capable many times in the past. They were as much at home in the wilderness as the Indians who lived there. Good men to have in a battle.

"The river narrows just around the next bend," Matt said abruptly.

"Guess I'd better alert the others." Rogers left Matt and joined Captain James Dalyell, aide-de-camp to Lord Jeffrey Amherst who was commander-in-chief of all the British forces in North America. Dalyell had brought along a detachment of two hundred and sixty men.

Matt was anxious to see the fort. How had it fared while he was gone? How had Jade fared? It had been so long! More than a month since he'd set out to find reinforcements. A lot could have happened in that time. The Indians could have overrun it weeks ago.

But no, Matt silently chided himself. He couldn't allow himself to even consider such a thing. The fort was strong. Jade, and the others who occupied the fort, had remained safe within its walls.

Matt looked up at the billowing sail. It wouldn't be much

longer before he saw her, either. If the wind held, they would arrive before another two hours were gone.

Even as the thought was born, the sail became limp.

Others had noticed the sail, too. Rogers strode forward to stand beside him. "Looks like that's it, Hunter. The wind has failed us. We'll have to anchor in the middle of the river now. The Indians will have to use canoes, which will give us the advantage when they attack tonight."

Not one man among them disputed the likelihood of attack. Each of them knew it was a certainty.

But when the Indians did attack, the men aboard the *Michigan* were ready for them.

That night, the silence of the forest was broken by the reverberating roar of broadsides from the guns of the warship.

The men worked swiftly, dumping black powder into cannons, stuffing them with wadding, then loading them with grape. The gunners put the torch to the fuse and the cannon exploded, belching forth nails and chains and fire, ripping the frail bark canoes to shreds.

The Indians scattered like a covey of quail disturbed by hunters, withdrawing to solid ground and taking cover in the forest. And then they hammered the schooner with bullets from hundreds of rifles until the *Michigan* pulled anchor and drifted downstream out of range.

"The *Michigan* has come!"

"The *Michigan* is back!"

Jade was crossing the parade ground when she heard the cries and she stopped dead in her tracks, staring up at the sentries who had uttered them.

Could it be true? she silently questioned, her heart leaping with hope. Had Matt, after more than a month away, finally returned?

She hurried toward the scaffold and climbed the steps, intent on seeing for herself. Her presence went unnoticed by the soldiers who lined the scaffolding, their eyes glued to one particular spot on the river.

And then she saw it.

The brisk wind pushed the schooner swiftly through the water. It sailed upstream, undeterred by rifle fire from the shore-bound Indians.

Suddenly, a cannon boomed on the schooner's deck, spewing forth both shot and flame toward the east bank where the Wyandotte town was located. The sound was quickly repeated, over and over again, as the *Michigan* continued to bombard the Indian town.

A lump lodged firmly in Jade's throat as she watched the schooner come to anchor before the water gate. She uttered a heartfelt prayer, then hurried down the steps again, intent on being near the gate whenever Matt came through.

She waited among the crowd of cheering people, watching anxiously as troops disembarked, her gaze searching for one particular man among them.

And then she saw him.

Matt strode swiftly through the crowd, his gaze searching left and right. Jade knew the exact moment when he saw her . . . when his lips spread in a wide smile.

She wanted to run to him, to throw herself into his arms and yet she could not. Major Gladwin had already claimed his attention. Soon, though, she promised herself. He would come to her when there was time. Until then, she must content herself that he'd returned safely.

"It's hard to believe they really made it."

Jade turned to see Sally Hartford at her elbow. "I knew they would," she said softly. "I knew Matt wouldn't let us down."

"I know. And your faith in Matt kept the rest of us sane through this nightmare."

"Do you think it's over now, Sally?"

"Not over yet," Sally replied. "But it soon will be. They've brought enough men to rout those red devils, to make them know what they're up against when they fight the British." She looked at Matt again, then turned her attention back to Jade. "He'll be looking for you as soon as he's done. Why don't you wait for him at the cabin. That will give the two of you a chance to be alone."

"Do you think anyone would mind?"

"There's not a soul in this fort would mind, my dear. You've worked hard for nigh on to two months now, doing everything you could for those that needed it. Now you go on and clean yourself up so's you'll be looking fresh and pretty when the major finishes with Matt."

Needing no further urging, Jade headed toward the Hartford cabin, intent on freshening up before Matt's arrival.

Matt stood beside Badger, one part of his mind listening to the conversation around him while the other part thought about Jade. She'd appeared well enough, he mused, but he'd only seen her at a distance. He wanted nothing more at the moment than to go to her, to take her in his arms and draw her into his embrace—

Becoming aware there was an argument going on, he turned his attention to what the men's words was.

"The supplies we brought won't last more than a few weeks, Major Gladwin," Rogers was saying. "And that's not near long enough. I doubt Pontiac will be retreating anytime soon. He's got you pinned down in here. And from what I've heard about him, he's prepared to stay however long it takes. Did you know he's got warriors digging trenches around the fort?''

"I know," Gladwin said. "He's tried to breach the walls by pushing carts loaded with burning logs against them. I don't know how many times we've had to form water brigades to put the fire out. Damn his soul. He's seen to it that we haven't had one night of peaceful sleep since he first attacked.''

"Well, we've two hundred eighty more men to add to the defenses now," Dalyell said grimly. "That should be enough to rout the devils.''

Matt permitted himself a withering stare. "What do you propose, Dalyell? Is it your intent to walk out there with your two hundred and eighty men and scare the breechcloths off Pontiac and his warriors?''

"I'll do more than scare them, Hunter," the man said shortly. "I'll do what should have been done in the beginning. The only way to handle the Indians is to shove the war down their throats. Major Gladwin has only prolonged the siege by remaining on the defensive inside these walls. I propose to launch a daybreak assault on Pontiac's Ottawa town.''

"I think that would be a grim mistake," Gladwin said.

"As do I," Rogers said.

"Your propose to sit here then?" Dalyell asked. "Is it your intention to do nothing more than what you've already done, to continue to hide like a rabbit in a hole and use up all the supplies we brought? You better reconsider, Major. Amherst expects more than that from us.''

Although Major Gladwin was technically Dalyell's superior, Dalyell was fresh from headquarters and was a favorite of Amherst. It was for that reason alone he decided to yield to Dalyell.

"Very well," he conceded. "We'll do it your way.''

Matt spoke out then. "You're makin' a big mistake,

Major Gladwin. If you send troops out there, a lot of good men are going to die."

"I believe that, too," Major Gladwin said in a low voice. "But Dalyell is a favorite of Amherst. And he's fresh from headquarters, bound to know what Amherst would want done."

"Just because Amherst wants it done don't make it the right thing to do," Matt said shortly. "I learned several things while I was gone, Major. Most of the forts along the thousand-mile frontier are under attack. Only Detroit, Niagara, and Pitt are holding out. That's enough to make me believe you've been doing the right thing by just holding out."

"How long can we continue to do that, though?" Major Gladwin asked. "Before long, the supplies you brought will run out and we'll be in the same position as before."

"Maybe not. I heard Colonel Henry Bouquet is gathering every able-bodied man he can find to go to the aid of Fort Pitt," Matt said. "You know the way the forts are situated, Major. If Pitt can be saved and Indians driven back, then there'll be aid for Niagara and Detroit."

"Makes sense," the major agreed thoughtfully. "Does Bouquet know how badly we need troops here?"

"I don't think so," Matt replied. "Which means someone will have to apprise him of the situation."

"You mean send out a messenger?"

"Yeah."

"Do you have any idea how many Indians are out there? A man would be a fool to try to get through them."

"Maybe."

"If a man *was* sent, he'd have to be a man used to the wilderness." The major's eyes were penetrating. "He'd have to be a man like you, Matt."

"I know. And I'll be ready to leave when Dalyell does. His troops should be able to create enough diversion out front so the Indians won't be giving the water gate much attention."

Major Gladwin nodded. "A lone man just might be able to slip through without notice." He clapped Matt's shoulder and squeezed it lightly. "If you're going, Hunter, may God go with you."

"I expect *He* will be along with me ... if I make it through them," Matt said.

He left the major then to search for the woman who had occupied so much of his thoughts during the past month. She flung the cabin door wide and threw herself into his arms, twining her fingers through his hair and lifting her face for his kiss.

Jade clung tightly to Matt, hardly daring to believe that he was really there.

"Oh, God, Matt!" she murmured, gazing up at him through moist green eyes. "It seems like years since you held me like this." Putting her hands to his unshaven cheek, she ran her palm across his whiskers.

"Do you want me to shave before we make love?" he asked gruffly.

"Are you going to make love to me?" she whispered, gazing up into his soft eyes.

"You bet I am," he muttered, pulling her lower body hard against his own. "Either before or after."

"Before, please."

Pushing her into the cabin, he kicked the door shut with his boot. "Where?" he growled, scooping her into his arms.

"Virgie Lee's room," she replied.

He strode quickly to the room, tossed her onto the mattress, then quickly closed the bedroom door.

He strode toward her then, stripping his garments away

as he did and tossing them carelessly aside. Jade watched
his buckskin shirt land against the far wall and her eyes
went to his chest, became riveted on the corded muscles
there. The mattress sagged beneath his weight and he bent
to removed his boots.

Breathlessly, Jade began to unbutton the bodice of her
gown, but before she'd finished, Matt was beside her.

"Slowpoke," he muttered, finishing the task for her and
pulling the unwanted garment over her head. He quickly
removed the rest of her clothing and smoothed his palm
over the gentle flare of her hips.

"Oh, Matt," she breathed, her pulse thundering
through her veins. "I love you so much! I was afraid I
would never see you again."

"Shush," he muttered, lowering his head to cover her
mouth with his.

His tongue slipped between her lips and gently, eroti-
cally, he moved it in and out while at the same time pulling
her closer against his lower body, close enough for her to
feel the hard strength of him. She moaned low in her
throat as his fingers began to stroke her nipples.

She moaned again, pushing herself against the
throbbing hardness that pulsed against her thigh.

His mouth lifted then, sliding languidly across her face.
His tongue caressed her earlobe, then swept down her
jawline, across her shoulders, traced a moist path down
her flesh until his mouth found the taut nipple on her
right breast. She moved restlessly beneath him, her breath
coming in harsh gasps as he suckled first one breast and
then the other.

Seeming to sense her great need, he left her breasts,
moving over her stomach with his hot tongue, tracing a
moist path around her navel.

She twitched beneath his ministrations, barely able to

endure the exquisite torture. "Matt, please," she muttered huskily. "Please, Matt."

He lifted his head and stared down at her. "Please what, Jade? What do you want?"

"I want you to make love to me," she whispered, barely able to hear her own voice above the pounding of her heart. "Now, Matt! Right now."

As though he'd only been waiting for those particular words, Matt positioned himself above her body. He entered quickly, burying himself in her flesh.

Stifling a scream of ecstasy, Jade arched her body against him, forcing the strength of him deeper into her body. She clung to him then as his hips rocked back and forth, each rhythmic stroke propelling her higher and higher, stoking the flames of desire until she had reached the peak. Her eyelids fluttered as she exploded, her whole being consumed with ecstasy. Then, as though he had been waiting for that particular moment, Matt uttered a hoarse cry and his whole body tensed. A moment later, he collapsed against her and they lay there, replete in the aftermath of their loving.

Chapter Twenty-Four

Matt was leaving at dawn!

Jade could hardly believe her ears when he'd told her he was going. She'd tried to plead with him, reminding him that he'd only just returned to the fort, that it wouldn't be cowardly for him to stay and allow someone else to go search for Colonel Bouquet.

But he had been deaf to her pleas. Nothing she said had swayed him. Nothing she *did*—neither her tears nor her kisses—had changed his mind. He was mule-headed stubborn, determined to place himself in danger again. And this time he would go alone.

The cabin door had barely closed behind him before Jade went to search for Virginia Lee. The girl would understand her feelings and she would surely be able to help. But even Virgie, young as she was, had expressed horror when she'd learned what Jade intended. Jade was as determined as Matt, though, and nothing anyone could say would change her mind.

Finally, realizing Jade could not be swayed from her decision, Virginia Lee agreed to help her.

Jade was waiting when Matt arrived at the cabin at first light. She opened the cabin door before he could knock and watched silently as he pulled her into his arms.

"I don't want you to worry about me," he said gruffly, tilting her chin to gaze into her moist green eyes. "I'll be back before you even know I'm gone."

She swallowed around the lump in her throat. "I can't talk you out of leaving?"

"No. This is something I've gotta do."

"Then go," she whispered, turning her face away, afraid her expression would betray her. "Just go on, Matt."

Gripping her chin tightly, he forced her to look at him. "I don't like leaving you this way."

"Then don't."

"I have to go," he whispered. "Smile for me before I leave. Let me take that with me."

"I don't feel like smiling."

He dipped his head then, covering her mouth with his. The kiss was long and passionate. When it was over, he quickly put her away from him. "I'll be back," he said gruffly. Then he strode quickly away from the cabin, going across the parade ground toward the water gate.

She knew it was his intention to wait for the troopers to march through the front gate, then leave while the Indians' attention was diverted from the gate.

Knowing she had little time to waste, Jade hurried to the room she shared with Virgie Lee and snatched up the uniform the girl had stolen from the laundry and pulled it on. After sliding her arms into the shirtsleeves, she pushed her hair beneath the collar, then buttoned the shirt.

With boots on her feet and a tricorn hat clamped firmly on her head, Jade felt secure in her masquerade.

* * *

"Some kinda fog out there." The young sentry who stepped out of the shadows couldn't have been more than fifteen years old. "Sure glad I ain't the one goin' out in it. No tellin' how many Injuns is waitin' out there. You sure as shootin' won't see 'em, neither. Not until they're right on top of you."

Matt was inclined to agree with the young sentry, but the fog could work for him as well. He looked toward the front gate, watching the troops who stood at the ready, waiting for the signal to leave the fort. And, briefly, his thoughts turned to those last few moments with Jade. He hated to leave her like that, but knew he could do nothing else. When she had time to think it over, she would be able to see that he had no recourse except to go.

He was brought back to the present by a loud squeaking and knew the front gates were being opened. The Indians would know it, too. His muscles tensed. "Ready when you are," he told the sentry, who unlatched the water gate and swung it open the merest crack. Matt squinted into the fog that moved like gray ooze across the water, then, winking at the young man, he slid into the water and passed through the gate.

Having completed her disguise, Jade left the cabin just in time to see the water gate swing shut behind Matt.

Striding swiftly across the parade ground, Jade wondered if she could get away with her masquerade.

"Halt! Who goes there?" The young sentry's voice cracked as he tried to sound commanding. In his hands he carried a Kentucky long rifle.

"Open the gate, Private," Jade said, keeping her voice

as low as possible. "I've got orders to go with Matthew Hunter."

The young soldier didn't even question her right to go. "You'd better hurry then," he said, pushing the water gate open again. "Matt Hunter wasn't lettin' no grass grow under his feet when he left here."

He opened the gate a narrow slit and she slid through, holding her rifle up as she'd seen Matt do. When the gate slid shut behind her, she looked around to find Matt . . . and saw instead a dark wall of fog that was too deep to penetrate.

Matt held his rifle and ammunition pouch above the waterline, treading water as he moved closer to the tree-lined bank. In the distance he could hear the sound of battle and knew that the Indians were not allowing the troops to leave the fort without a fight.

Drawing closer to the riverbank, Matt slid smoothly among a blanket of deep green lily pads that floated on the river water.

Then, quietly, he made his way along the willows lining the bank, keeping beneath the cover of the overhanging branches. The guttural, undulating cries behind him, still distant, told him the Indians had not yet taken up pursuit. Still, he could not afford even a moment's delay.

A movement in his peripheral vision caught his attention and he quickly focused on the spot, probing the water for any sign of movement.

There. Only a short distance away, emerging from the fogbank, was a rifle held high, in the same manner that he had held his own. One man? he wondered. An Indian, perhaps, left to guard the watergate?

He hid among the trees, waiting for his pursuer to come closer. There was something about him that nagged at

Matt. Then he realized what it was. The man was wearing a tricorn hat. Could the major have sent a man after him for some reason?

Matt waited silently as the man came closer . . . waited . . . waited.

Suddenly, a glint of sunlight broke through the fog, glancing off the rifle barrel and striking the soldier's face. The sunlight was gone as quickly as it had come, but it left Matt wide-eyed, blinking in astounded surprise.

Damn! It wasn't a man who approached. It was a woman . . . the last person he would have expected to see.

What in tarnation was Jade doing . . . following after him this way, dressed in a soldiers uniform?

A snap behind him jerked his head around. He probed the dense green thicket, saw a quick movement that was quickly followed by another.

Warriors!

Guards, more than likely.

Matt had to think fast! Jade was headed that way, unable to see them. But they damn sure wouldn't miss her! Not if she left the river there.

"Indians, Jade!" he shouted, wading into the water swiftly. "Dive under the water!"

Realizing that he'd called attention to his own position by uttering the warning, he sucked in a large draft of air, then dove quickly beneath the water himself as several shots rang out.

He felt the water displaced around him as lead missiles sliced through the surface. But he ignored them, swimming toward Jade whose body was little more than a blur in the muddy river.

Reaching out with one hand, he pulled her deeper into the river, hoping to escape the bullets that were peppering the water with such speed.

He stayed there for long moments, his rifle between his

teeth, pulling with all his strength as he sought to put as much distance as possible between them and the warriors.

Even though his lungs began to burn, screaming out, agonizing for air and his ribs ached from holding that last breath, he continued to swim, his legs kicking out, his arms pulling at the water until he was almost dizzy from the effort.

Finally, Matt realized he could go no farther. He would either have to surface or drown. Since dying was not in his plans, he swam quickly toward the surface. His head broke into the open air and he gasped, sucking in deep breaths of life-giving air while his frantic gaze searched the surrounding area for signs of danger.

All around them was silence. Nothing to be heard except the gentle lap of the water against the riverbank.

Putting his mouth against Jade's ear so the sound would not carry, he whispered, "Don't make any noise. Not a single sound. Just follow me to the riverbank. And if you hear anything, Jade, anything at all, dive deep."

She nodded to show she understood, then, cautiously, they made their way to the east and pulled themselves out of the river, over some mossy rocks and to a hidden ledge.

And there they stayed, facedown, totally exhausted until Matt's heartbeat finally slowed. Only then did he raise his head to look at her.

"What the bloody hell do you mean coming out here?" Although the words were spoken in a whisper, they were nonetheless angry.

"I wanted to go with you."

"And because of that . . . because of what you *wanted*, you've put both our lives in danger. Bloody hell, woman! Don't you have any sense at all? It's not enough that I've got to keep myself alive. Now I've got to worry about you too!"

Jade choked back her tears and remained silent. How

could she possibly defend herself when she could see now that Matt was right. She had placed her own wishes above her good sense.

"I could go back." Her voice was small, ashamed, her words squeezed out past the lump in her throat.

"Dammit, woman!" Matt snarled. "Don't you have any sense at all? You can't go back! The Indians are thicker than flies around the water gate. They'll have sounded the alarm by now."

He swore bitterly, his dark eyes glaring furiously at her.

"I—I'm sorry, Matt."

"Sorry's not enough," he gritted. "But there's not a damn thing we can do about it now. Not a damn thing. You'll just have to go with me!"

Chapter Twenty-Five

Matt moved soundlessly as he worked his way through the dense forest intent on covering as much distance as possible before dark. He was aware of Jade trudging along behind him, weary, yet uttering no word of complaint.

Knowing how deeply she regretted the strained silence between them, Matt had been tempted to accept her muttered apologies and allow his heart to soften toward her. Yet the temptation was only a momentary thing, gone almost as quickly as it had come.

It was imperative, he knew, that Jade be made aware of the consequences of disobedience.

Since she was unskilled in the ways of the forest, Matt must, of necessity, go at a slower rate of speed to accommodate her shorter legs. And that meant he could cover less ground. It meant it would take longer for him to reach Bouquet. And it meant that help would be longer reaching the fort. Her actions could have many repercussions, some that might lead to the loss of many lives.

No. He couldn't allow himself to soften. She must be made aware of the foolishness of her actions.

The forest was growing thin, the trees more widely spaced. A short distance away from them was a little glade filled with sunlight.

Gripping Jade's forearm to stop her forward movement, Matt paused momentarily to make certain there was nothing to indicate the presence of others.

His narrowed gaze scanned the trees around them.

Finding nothing out of the ordinary, he entered the glade and motioned her forward.

When her breeches snagged against a thorny bush and ripped, leaving a piece about an inch square behind, Jade reached for it automatically, pulling it free, and tucking the small scrap of fabric deep into her pocket.

Despite himself, Matt felt a quick stab of pride. Jade had the makings of a good woodsman. She had already learned not to leave anything behind, even a piece of cloth, lest it reveal their presence to the enemy.

As they crossed the glade, Matt was aware of every sound around him, aware of the pine needles crackling underfoot, of the rustle of leaves as the wind soughed through the trees.

His nostrils twitched with every scent carried on the wind, of the flowering bush in the sunlit glade, of the damp, dead smell of the pine needles that littered the forest floor nearby.

A twig cracked behind them and he froze, holding his breath as he swiveled his head to meet whatever lay behind them.

A shadow flicked quickly in his peripheral vision and he turned slightly, then breathed a sigh of relief as he realized it was only a squirrel racing toward a large tree with a pine nut in its mouth.

But his relief was only short-lived.

Something whizzed toward him and he jerked aside, feeling the wind of its passing as it came close to his upper body.

"Indians!" he said harshly, curling his fingers around Jade's upper arm and urging her quickly across the glade.

His mind was already absorbing the fact that the missile had been an arrow and, had it struck him, he would surely have died on the spot.

"Crouch low and run toward that thicket ahead," he commanded.

He could see the fear in her eyes, but despite that, she acted without hesitation, racing toward the dense growth of trees.

Matt ran beside her, knowing the enemy was close, knowing as well that, if he weren't careful, they'd soon be taken prisoner or lying dead on the ground.

And he had no intention of allowing that to happen.

Nothing must be allowed to stop him from reaching Colonel Henry Bouquet. Nothing.

Jade hitched up her overlong breeches and ran toward the thick growth of trees as fast as her legs would carry her. She knew she had made a muddle of things when she had followed Matt away from the fort. And she was determined to remedy her mistake.

Her heart thumped with the effort she expended, yet she paid it no mind, determined to reach the grove of trees that Matt had pointed out. She was aware of him running beside her as they entered the dense thicket, then raced along a heavily beaten path.

Jade ran until her breath gave out, continued to run another few feet until her legs suddenly gave way and buckled beneath her.

But before she struck the ground, Matt swooped her up

and clamped her against his side and continued to race through the forest, pushing through branches with one arm while the other held Jade firmly against him.

She allowed him to carry her until she got her second wind, then muttered a protest. When he continued to run at breakneck speed and her stomach contents were threatening to erupt, she raised her voice to make herself heard.

"I—I'm all r-right, Matt." The words were jerky, managed somehow between bone-jarring strides. "You—you can put me d-down now."

He set her on her feet with hardly a break in stride, then wrapped his fingers around her forearm and pulled her along with him for another mile or so.

Although they'd obviously left their pursuers behind them they continued in that vein, traveling swiftly through the forest, pushing past limbs and through tangled vines for days on end until they finally came to a rough road that had been carved into the wilderness.

"Forbes Road," Matt explained when she asked how it came to be there. "General John Forbes cleared the way five years ago when he marched to wrest the Ohio from the French."

It was easy to see the road had never been more than a wagon track and it was already being reclaimed by the forest and weather.

"It's the way Major Bouquet will come," Matt explained gruffly. "We'll keep to the cover of the forest, but we'll travel near the road. That way we won't pass them without knowing."

They continued to travel as they had done before they reached the road, stopping to rest only when they could go no farther. And always, Jade was made aware of their great need to hurry, to send help to the fort before it fell beneath the Indians.

Jade couldn't let her mind dwell on such an event, though, for to do so would make her lose her senses. Nor could she allow herself to consider their own capture. The thought of being subjected to the savages again was almost more than she could bear.

She was tired to the point of exhaustion when, one day, as darkness settled over the land, they came upon a clearing where soldiers were bivouacked.

Jade sucked in a sharp breath and turned to look at Matt. "Is—is it them, Matt?" she asked.

"Yes. It must be. Colonel Henry Bouquet and his men." He clutched her forearm and they moved forward out of the shadowy forest.

A young sentry jerked toward them, musket held at the ready. "Who goes there?"

Matt froze instantly, his gaze on the rifle. "Matthew Hunter," he replied gruffly.

"Come on in," the sentry said. "But don't make any sudden moves. And put your rifle over your head."

Matt complied with the order, raising his rifle over his head with both arms and walking slowly toward the sentry.

"You too!" the sentry snarled, his rifle moving to cover Jade.

"Me?" she squeaked, flinching closer to Matt, her rifle still dangling loosely at her side.

"Do it!" Matt muttered. "He believes you're a man, Jade."

She raised her hands quickly, only then remembering the uniform she wore.

"Hell's fire!" the sentry exclaimed as they drew nearer. "Is that a woman with you?" His gaze swept the length of Jade's long ebony hair.

"Yeah," Matt replied.

"You can put your hands down, ma'am," the sentry said. "Sorry about that. Didn't know you was a woman." He turned his attention to Matt again. "Hand your rifle over and state your business."

"I've come from Fort Detroit to find Colonel Bouquet, Private. Send word to him that Matt Hunter's here to see him."

"Send word to the colonel that we got company," the private told a soldier standing nearby.

Matt eyed the tents spread out in the clearing. It was a pitiful-looking army at best. Its members looked weary to the point of exhaustion. "How many men you got here, Private?" he asked.

"Colonel Bouquet will tell you anything he wants you to know."

The soldier sent to deliver the message to Colonel Bouquet entered a tent. A moment later, another man emerged. "Who you got there, Private?"

"Says his name is Hunter, sir. I don't know who the lady is."

"Hunter?" Bouquet thundered. "Matthew Hunter?"

"The same," Matt said. "And if it's all the same to you, I'd like to put my hands down now."

"Hell, yes!" the colonel said. "What're you doin' out here anyway? Where did you come from, man?" Bouquet's long strides carried him forward at a swift pace.

"Fort Detroit," Matt said. "You're badly needed there, Colonel. They're low on supplies and there's more than a thousand Indians surrounding the fort."

Bouquet nodded. "I'm not surprised. That Pontiac must be quite a leader. I've been told this whole thing was his plan. And it was a brilliant one, too. Already, most of the forts along a thousand miles of frontier have fallen to the Indians. From what I've heard, only Forts Pitt, Niagara, and Detroit are holding out."

"You heard right, Colonel. I don't know about Niagara and Pitt, but Fort Detroit is in a bad way. I'm not sure how much longer they can hold out without troops to relieve them." Matt looked toward the corral. "I hope you have a spare horse I can ride."

"We've spare horses enough. But I'm afraid Detroit will have to wait for a while. Just until we've routed the Indians surrounding Fort Pitt."

Matt could see the sense of that, since the regiment was marching in a direct line with Fort Pitt.

"Who's that with you?" Bouquet asked, his attention turning to Jade. Immediately, his eyes widened with surprise. "Tarnation, man!" he exclaimed. "Is that a woman with you?"

"I'm afraid it is," Matt replied ruefully. "And I'm afraid she's going to drop where she stands if she doesn't get some rest soon."

"Private," the colonel snapped. "Walk the young lady to my tent and get her some food!"

"I couldn't possibly take your tent," Jade protested, smoothing back her tangled hair. "If you have an extra blanket, then I could just curl up on the ground anywhere and—"

"Nonsense!" the colonel said. "Let a lady sleep on the ground when I've got a perfectly good bed? I wouldn't hear of it! I'll be up most of the night anyway, so you take my bed with good conscience."

Tired as she was, Jade ceased her protestations. She followed the trooper to the tent and lay down on the cot. And before the private returned with a tray of food, she was fast asleep.

Chapter Twenty-Six

A soldier approached Matt with a plate of food. "The lady fell asleep before she ate," he said, handing Matt the plate.

"She needed sleep more than food," Matt replied, squatting beneath a large tree and scooping up a spoonful of beans. "We've been traveling fast since we left Detroit last week and she hasn't had much rest."

"Not much food, either, I would imagine," the colonel said, seating himself on a large flat rock.

Another soldier approached with two cups of hot coffee, handing one to the colonel and the other to Matt.

"Has the lady been with you since you left Detroit?" Colonel Bouquet asked, studying Matt over the rim of his cup.

Matt gave an abrupt nod. "She'd already left the fort before I knew what she was about. There was no way of getting her inside again." He spooned another bite of beans into his mouth. After he'd swallowed them, he said,

"We've had nothing but jerky and a few berries for the past week. And very little of that."

"We'll see the lady has a good meal when she wakes up."

"I'd appreciate that." Matt took a hefty swallow of coffee that had a distinctive flavor. Chicory had probably been added to the coffee to make it last longer.

"You said Detroit's in bad trouble. How many men are there with Major Gladwin now?" the colonel asked.

Matt told him about Dalyell and Rogers and the men under their command.

"Major Rogers is a good man," Colonel Bouquet mused. "He's an experienced Indian fighter. So are those Rangers of his. They should be able to hold out until aid reaches them."

"Under ordinary circumstances I would agree, Colonel," Matt said gruffly. "But Major Gladwin has allowed Dalyell to assume command and he doesn't know those Indians. He's under the impression that a bold attack will scatter them."

"A bold attack!" the colonel exclaimed. "Does he mean to leave the fort then?"

"Yeah. He was ready to march on Pontiac's town when I left the fort," Matt said. "He was taking two hundred and eighty-seven men along the river road. His plans were to use the bridge at Parent Creek."

"A bridge?" Bouquet frowned heavily. "Good Lord, man! What can he be thinking of? If the Indians catch them on the bridge they'll be annihilated. How could Rogers go along with such a plan?"

"Rogers didn't have any say in the matter."

"Why not? He and his Rangers are the only experienced Indian fighters among the bunch. Where did Dalyell position them?"

"In the middle," Matt said wryly.

"They'd have been more useful on the vanguard."

"Rogers pointed that out to Dalyell, but he disagreed. And since Dalyell was in command, Rogers had no recourse except to go along with his plans."

"And you have no notion about the outcome of the battle?" the colonel asked.

"I have a notion all right. But no real knowledge. I have a feeling the plan went wrong."

"So do I. It would've taken more than two hundred and eighty-seven men to scatter those Indians. And Pontiac has more than a thousand warriors with him. Pontiac is a crafty fellow," he mused. "I went up against him when I was with Braddock. The man's a natural born leader. If you look at his side of this war, you'll realize the full magnitude of what he's undertaken. Somehow, he's banded Indian tribes together that usually fight each other. The man has some kind of charisma, otherwise he couldn't hold them all together long enough to say Jack Sprat! I heard the Iroquois, Wyandotte, Mingo, Delaware, and Shawnee are banded together in the east. And even the Cherokee and Creek who usually keep to the south are part of this thing."

"As well as the Ottawa, Potowatomi, and Kickapoo on Lake Huron," Matt said grimly. "And the Chippewa, Menominee, Winnebago, Sauk, and Fox on Lake Michigan. Hellfire, man! He's got every tribe in the Indian nations under his damn spell."

"The scope of this thing is unbelievable," Bouquet mused, idly swirling the coffee in his cup. "Absolutely unbelievable. It won't be easy breaking his hold on so many warriors."

"No," Matt agreed. "Not easy at all."

"Amherst would do well not to underestimate Pontiac . . . or the power behind him."

Matt's forehead creased with frown lines as he looked

around the clearing where the soldiers were bivouacked. "How many troopers do you have here, Colonel?"

The colonel's gaze swept the area as though he were counting them, which was an impossibility, Matt knew. "I have two hundred and fourteen men from the forty-second regiment, Hunter. And one hundred thirteen from the seventy-seventh. Along with one hundred and thirteen of my own Royal Americans." The colonel's expression was solemn. "When you add them up, they total four hundred and sixty men."

As Matt watched a soldier who tended the horses, the man seemed to stumble. It was only a momentary thing, for the soldier quickly recovered but it was enough to worry Matt. "Some of them don't appear in the best of health," he commented.

"Some of them aren't," Colonel Bouquet replied. "In fact, sixty of the men from the seventy-seventh regiment are weak from tropical diseases . . . a souvenir from the battle over Havana last year. They're being carried forward on litters."

Matt stared at the colonel with surprise. "You're actually carryin' men on litters into a battle with the Indians?"

"They're Scotsmen, Hunter," the colonel replied, as though that explained everything.

And it did. "Then they'll do in a pinch."

"You'll be traveling with us to Fort Pitt?" Colonel Bouquet inquired.

"Yeah. If you can provide an escort to Fort Ligonier for Miss Carrington."

"As you can see, we're short of men, Hunter." Colonel Bouquet was thoughtful for a long moment, then, "But I suppose an escort, unencumbered with cattle, could make good time. I could have Seargeant Donovan take her to the fort. He could be with us again before we could possibly reach Fort Pitt." He nodded. "Yes. I suppose an escort could be provided."

"Then I'll be going with you."

"Good, good." The colonel pushed away from the table and stretched his lanky frame. "It's getting late, Hunter. I know you must be tired. What do you say we turn in now?"

"Sounds good to me." Matt replied, knowing that dawn would come all too soon.

After excusing himself, Matt found an extra blanket, wrapped it around his shoulders and stretched out in the colonel's tent near the cot where Jade slept. Moments later, he was fast asleep.

He awakened at first light and, after a quick look at Jade who was still sleeping, hurried to help the men break camp. Before the hour was out, the army was ready to leave. Every tent had been dismantled and packed away except for the one Jade occupied. And that, Matt knew, would be taken down by Seargeant Donovan and the two men assigned to escort Jade to Fort Ligonier.

When the order was given to pull out, Matt realized the moment he'd been dreading had come.

Keeping in mind the fact that Jade had already put herself in extreme danger by following him from Fort Detroit, he was determined to prevent such an event from happening again.

That set the tone for their final conversation.

He leaned over her, drinking in the sight of her, with her long silky hair spread out in a dark cloud around her. God, she was so beautiful! It tore at his heart to leave her, yet he must.

As though his thoughts had reached into her sleep, she opened her eyes and smiled up at him. "Matt?" Her voice was a soft whisper. "Is it time to leave?"

"Yes. It's time. And I didn't want to leave without saying

good-bye.'' He forced a smile to his lips and swallowed around the lump that had suddenly lodged in his throat, but when he spoke again his voice gave no sign of his distress. Instead, it was light, friendly. "You have a safe trip, Jade, and take good care of yourself.''

"But—but where—'' Her thick dark lashes blinked at him in surprise. "What do you mean, Matt? You're not leaving without me . . . are you?''

For an instant everything inside him went still. He shifted his gaze to the canvas behind her, carefully avoiding her eyes. "I can hardly take you into battle with me,'' he said gruffly. "Of course I'm leaving you.''

"Out here?'' she whispered. "Alone? But what shall I do?''

"You won't be alone,'' he said, meeting her eyes again and trying to ignore the hurt he saw there. "The colonel's sending an escort to take you back to Fort Ligonier. You should be safe enough there.''

"But Matt—''

His lips tightened and he glared at her impatiently. He didn't like what he was doing, but he had no choice. Jade had to go. He must convince her of that. He could not take the chance that she would follow him. "Jade!'' he said sharply. "I don't want a repeat of what happened at Detroit! You are *not* to leave your escort. Not for *any* reason. Do you hear me?''

"I hear you,'' she whispered. Tears welled in her eyes like soft green pools and she blinked rapidly as though she wished to conceal her weakness from him. "I wouldn't be so foolish again, Matt. I realize I put many lives in danger by following you.'' She clasped her hands together tightly, studying them for a long moment. "Will you b-be coming to the fort for me l-later.'' Her voice had suddenly developed a quiver. "I mean, if—if you make it through the coming b-battle.''

He couldn't allow her even that one small hope, he knew. He dared not do so. If she decided the danger he faced was too overwhelming, she might break her promise and follow him.

"No." It was a wonder the lie didn't choke him. "I have my doubts that we will ever meet again. But you're not to worry about anything," he assured her quickly. "I left your papers with Silas, along with some instructions, before I left Fort Sheldon. Just send word to him that you're needing them now. He will take care of everything. No cause to worry, Jade. You'll be just fine."

She blinked back tears and turned her head abruptly. He couldn't stand to see her in pain, yet he could do nothing to alleviate it.

With his heart a huge ache inside his chest, his hand moved of its own accord, reaching out to her. The move was never completed, for he exerted every ounce of strength he possessed to stop its progress.

"Well, Jade," he said, clearing his throat. "I guess this is good-bye. You take care of yourself." Before his heart could betray him, he turned to leave.

"Matt!" Her hand snagged his forearm.

He looked back at her, his muscles tense, his stomach coiled into a hard knot. "Yes?" he inquired, managing to lift a casual eyebrow.

"Are you leaving without kissing me good-bye?" Her voice was small, uncertain.

Try as he would, he couldn't make himself leave the tent. He wanted to kiss her, wanted to feel her lips beneath his own, but he dared not do so. Yet neither could he leave without touching her again. His expression became guarded as he leaned over her, intending to place a light kiss on her forehead.

But it didn't work that way. Jade had other ideas.

Her arms crept around his neck and she lifted her face,

her luminous green eyes shimmering brightly. His gaze caught on her perfectly formed mouth and his eyes narrowed.

With her mouth close to his, she brushed her lips lightly over his and his body reacted immediately, becoming tense with longing.

He told himself to move away, to break the spell he was under, but his damned body refused to obey the command.

The kiss that had been intended as a light touch of friendship ignited suddenly into a raging inferno as he forcefully jerked her slender form tightly against his hardened body.

A small whimper escaped her lips as he hungrily devoured the sweet moistness of her mouth.

The sound brought him to his senses and he broke away. He stood there for a long moment, his breath rasping harshly, his heart thundering like a herd of wild horses beneath his rib cage.

He wanted to take her in his arms again, to hold her close and never leave her, but the sound of hooves beating against the hard ground made him aware of his responsibilities, succeeded in clearing his head.

"Good-bye, Jade," he rasped harshly. "Take good care of yourself."

Hurrying out of the tent, he mounted his horse and rode away, and not once did he allow himself to look back.

Jade stood in the tent, fighting tears and railing at her helplessness. Matt had left her. As casually as though they'd been nothing to each other . . . nothing more than friends.

And not once had he looked back. She knew because, painful though it was, she had watched him leave.

A faint movement intruded on her misery and she

turned to see a burly seargeant approaching from her left. She lowered her eyes to hide her abject misery from him.

"Ma'am?"

She threw him a quick glance and realized he was staring at her with something like pity in his expressive brown eyes.

Well, she didn't want his pity! Her chin snapped up and she fixed her gaze on the billowy white clouds overhead. "Yes?" she inquired in an even tone of voice.

"We need to be on the move, ma'am. There's food on the table over yonder." He pointed toward a table under the spreading branches of a large oak tree. "You can eat while we finish breaking camp. If we hurry we can make it back to Fort Ligonier by nightfall. Colonel Bouquet said we was to take you there, then rejoin the regiment."

"Thank you, Seargeant," she said. "I'm not really very hungry this morning."

"I know," he said gruffly. "But you need to eat to keep up your strength."

"I won't hold you back," she said, then strode quickly toward the table to partake of the food that she really didn't want.

Chapter Twenty-Seven

Jade's shoulders slumped wearily as she gazed at the fort a short distance away. Although firmly intact, its walls showed some sign of recent damage, which led her to believe that, at one time or another, it had been under attack by the Indians.

"Are you all right, ma'am?"

The voice belonged to the man who rode beside her, the big, burly seargeant who had obviously appointed himself her temporary guardian.

"Yes. I'm all right, Seargeant Donovan," she replied.

As right as anyone could be, she told herself, when they've just left behind the only person in the world who really matters to them.

The seargeant seemed to guess her unspoken thoughts. "There ain't no need for you to be frettin' yourself about Matt Hunter, ma'am," he said gruffly. "From what I've heard about the man he'll give a good accounting of himself when he goes up against the Injuns."

She looked at him from beneath her thick lashes. Was she so transparent that everyone knew how much she loved Matt?

"We ain't far from Fort Ligonier now, ma'am," the young private who rode on her left said. "Won't be long now before you'll be able to get some rest." His gaze was admiring. "I heard tell you walked more'n a week with nary a complaint. Reckon your feet's got blisters on 'em."

"My feet has blisters on top of blisters," Jade said wryly.

"That's a long way for a woman to walk," Donovan said gruffly. " 'Specially a little bit of a thing like you. I'm surprised Hunter didn't leave you behind."

"He tried," Jade admitted quietly. "But I wouldn't stay behind."

The seargeant cleared his throat as though he were suddenly embarrassed. "The folks in the fort are a friendly bunch of people," he said gruffly. "I know most of 'em fairly well since Ligonier was my first post after I joined up. They'll take good care of you here."

"I wouldn't want to put anyone out."

"Now, ma'am," he chided gently. "Nobody's gonna feel they're bein' put out. They're gonna be battlin' over which one of 'em is gonna have the pleasure of helpin' you out of your troubles."

Jade managed to summon up a smile for the burly seargeant who had gone out of his way to make the trip as comfortable as possible for her. He was a kind man indeed, had tried hard to cheer her up.

But nothing could make her feel cheerful in the circumstances. She still felt the pain of Matt's good-bye. He had refused to allow her even the tiniest hope that he would come to her after the battle was over.

The sun was an orange ball hovering over the western horizon when they reached the fort. And their arrival created a minor flurry.

It seemed everyone in the fort was interested in the newcomers. Jade found out why after the churned-up dust on the parade ground had finally settled back onto the hard ground.

"What are you doing back so soon, Donovan?" a man called out. "I thought you was bent on beatin' hell outta them Injuns! You ain't gonna tell us you're all that's left outta the whole regiment, are you?"

"If I did tell you that, Otis Tanner, then I'd surely be lyin'," the burly seargeant said gruffly, reining up his horse beside the command post. "Fact is, we ain't seen nary a one of them Injuns yet." He dismounted and crossed to Jade's horse.

"Nary a one?" The man scratched his head. "Then why in hell are you back here? Thought you was bent on savin' Fort Pitt from those redskins?"

Reaching up to Jade, seargeant Donovan lifted her from the saddle. When she was firmly on her feet, he turned to answer the fellow's question. "We got orders from Colonel Bouquet to escort this young lady here."

"Lady?" The man bent slightly to peer beneath the tricorn hat that shaded Jade's face. "Well, damn me for a fool! It *is* a lady, ain't it. An' from the looks of her, she's a mighty weary one, too."

"Where'd you find 'er, Donovan?" another voice called out.

"What's goin' on, Donovan?" said yet another voice as the curious crowd surged closer around them.

"Ever'body's gonna know ever'thing that I do soon's we get this little lady settled," the gruff seargeant said, curling his fingers around Jade's arm and urging her toward the command post.

Jade's head was a dizzy whirl now and she fought against the encroaching darkness. She didn't know whether it was caused by too much sun or the confusion around her. She stumbled, then, with the seargeant's help, managed to right herself.

"You men don't have the brains God gave a jackass!" a woman's voice suddenly cried out. "Seargeant Donovan! That girl is plumb tuckered out. She's gonna drop in her tracks if you don't do somethin' about it right now."

Jade knew the woman was right, for her knees seemed to have no more substance than rubber. She stumbled again, then tried to lock her knees in place, unwilling to make a fool of herself in front of the crowd. But she felt dizzy suddenly. Blackness swirled around her, eddying, trying to pull her deeper into the thick darkness.

"Bring her to my cabin," a soft voice said.

And then Jade knew no more.

Despite his best efforts, Matt couldn't get Jade out of his mind. He went over their last moments together and wondered if he'd been unnecessarily harsh with her. Perhaps he'd handled things the wrong way. Maybe there had been no need in making her believe he cared nothing for her.

Damn! Why hadn't he just tried to make her realize how much danger she'd be in if she tried to follow him again?

Yes, he decided, he *had* been unnecessarily cruel. He hoped, when this was all over that she could find it in her heart to forgive him.

Matt tried to put thoughts of Jade aside, knowing he couldn't allow himself to become distracted while scouting for the regiment. He rode from one end of the column to the other, his narrowed gaze constantly on the trees that fringed the rough wagon road.

The ox wagons had been left at Fort Ligonier to free the troops of their slow pace, but the small herd of beef cattle and the three hundred and fifty packhorses churned up as much dust as the wheels on the wagons would have done. It wasn't long before Matt felt as though he'd been eating and breathing dust for days.

The forest remained silent as the day wore through, and with Fort Pitt only twenty miles away now, the tension increased with each passing mile. If the Indians were going to make an attempt to stop them from reaching the fort, they'd damn well have to do it soon.

As the vanguard neared the little stream of Bushy Run Matt's vigilance increased. The forest on either side of the road had become unnaturally silent. The birds were no longer flittering from branch to branch, the squirrels had disappeared from view.

Matt's grip on the reins tightened and he edged around the column of soldiers to take up position beside Colonel Bouquet.

"Seems unnaturally quiet, don't it, Hunter?" the colonel muttered.

"Yeah," Matt agreed quietly. "They're out there, Colonel."

A movement flickered at the corner of his eyes and Matt swung his gaze around quickly, catching a glimpse of a naked form before it disappeared again. Although the glimpse was only fleeting, it had been enough to see the slashes of red and black paint on the body, the grotesque white and green that encircled the mouth and eyes.

"Get ready," Matt warned under his breath.

The attack came with stunning abruptness. Two companies charged with fixed bayonets to clear the road and the Indians fell back before them. But even as they did, muskets sounded from the forests on both sides of the road. Many soldiers fell where they stood, caught in a crossfire in the middle of the road.

"Pull back!" Colonel Bouquet shouted, seeming to realize that was the only way of saving his convoy.

A short distance behind them the road ran over the shoulder of a low hill. The horses and cattle were left on the upper slopes, the wounded carried to a slight depression on the top where they could be sheltered by a wall of grain bags. When that was done, Colonel Bouquet arranged his men in a perimeter about the lower slopes of the hill. Each man was now facing outward from the circle toward the enemy.

The Indians pressed their attack, confident the battle was almost won.

But they were mistaken. The soldiers, who'd seemed no more than a ragtag regiment, were in their element now, doing what they were trained to do. They refused to be beaten by the savages.

The battle raged on . . . throughout the night and into the next day. The sun was hot overhead and the troops were thirsty, but there was no water available to alleviate their suffering.

The Indians kept them under fire constantly, and although the troops suffered heavy losses, Bouquet's influence over his men never wavered. They looked only to him, merely waiting for him to determine their actions.

It was noon of the second day when Bouquet made his move. It was a simple maneuver. He feigned a retreat.

The Indians were startled when the men on the south slope rose from their positions and began to run. Then the men on the north flank followed suit. The Indians— overconfident and expecting to see panic among their enemies—rushed forward, intent on slaying them before they could escape.

It was then the company on the west slope—a regiment of Highlanders who had been hidden from view—charged the mass of Indians.

Before the Indians could react, a company on the east

slope, who'd also been hidden from view, surprised them from the other side.

It was more than the Indians could handle. They scattered like a covey of quail disturbed by a hungry fox, not even stopping when they reached the cover of the dense forest.

Matt watched gleefully as the Indians fled before the jubilant Highlanders, knowing the battle was one that would always be remembered.

Bouquet had taught the Indians a valuable lesson. They had learned the English soldiers, even while fighting in a place the Indians had chosen, could still win the battle.

It was a lesson they wouldn't soon forget, and perhaps it would make the Indians less eager to wage war on the English.

Matt watched Colonel Bouquet striding among his troops, estimating the damage wrought by the Indians while praising the efforts of his men. It had been a long day and everyone was bone-weary, yet when the order was given to resume their march to the aid of Fort Pitt, not one man raised a voice in protest.

The victory at Bushy Run had more effect on the war than Bouquet could even imagine. The Indian commanders had been Custaloga, head of the Delaware's Wolf clan, and a Seneca warrior named Guyasuta, who had at one time been Washington's guide. But there was another leader among them, too. One who had joined his small band with theirs for the purpose of battle. That leader was Scioto.

The English victory had its effect on the Indian morale, since they had lost some of their assurance they could defeat the enemy. But it had a greater effect on Scioto. He was completely demoralized by the outcome of the battle. He had lost many men of his band and he blamed those losses on the fact that their weapons were poorly constructed.

And it was his daughter's husband who had supplied those weapons . . . for a great cost to the Indians.

Remembering the promise he'd made to his daughter some time ago, Scioto gathered what was left of his band together and took the path leading to the trading post.

They traveled throughout the night and well into the next day, and all the time Scioto burned for revenge against the English for what they had done. It was growing dark when they finally arrived at the trading post. They didn't bother knocking. The lower floor was empty, so Scioto mounted the stairs. His daughter had said the white woman's room was at the top of the stairs.

He kicked the door open, staring into the room at the couple who lay entwined on the bed.

"Scioto!" the Frenchman gasped, pushing aside the bed-covers and scrambling off the bed. "I was not expecting you!"

Scioto's face, which was usually impassive, broke into a wide smile as he stared at his daughter's husband, who had obviously been coupling with the woman. The moment he entered the room, he'd known what must be done.

And it wasn't like he was depriving his daughter. There were many brave warriors who would be seeking her as a wife.

He raised his hatchet, preparing to make her a widow.

As Jade swept the cabin floor, she watched the little blond-haired girl skipping across the floor, remembering the first time she'd seen her.

It had been several weeks ago and Millie had been bending over her when she'd woke shortly after fainting on the parade ground.

She smiled as her mind traveled back to that moment in time when she had opened her eyes to see the little girl with blond hair leaning over her. "Are you sick?" the child had asked curiously.

"Millie!" a woman's voice had scolded. "You get off that bed and leave the lady alone. Right now!"

Approaching footsteps had jerked Jade's head around and she'd seen Clara Tucker, the dark-haired woman who'd scolded the burly Sergeant Donovan. The woman was most obviously pregnant, her stomach protruding outward.

"How are you feeling, dear?" she had asked, and Jade knew right then that the two of them were going to become friends.

And they had. During the past weeks Jade had made herself indispensable to Clara, taking much of the work off the little woman who would be ready to deliver her babe in another month.

Millie, tired of being cooped up in the cabin, sidled up to Jade and extended the puppy she held toward her.

"Don't you think my puppy is pretty?" the little girl asked, smiling up at Jade. "It's a boy doggie and Mama says I have to be careful with it because it's just a baby. Look at its eyes, Jade. They ain't open yet. I didn't know babies was born with their eyes closed? Did you, Jade?" Her own blue eyes were wide as she waited for an answer, then when it wasn't quickly forthcoming, she said, "Huh, Jade? Did you know it?"

"All babies aren't born with their eyes closed, Millie," Jade said. "Human babies already have their eyes open when they come into this world."

"They do?" The girl stuck her thumb in her mouth. "I didn't know that?" She looked down at the puppy clutched tightly to her chest with her other hand. "Mabel Brown's baby didn't come with teeth, but my puppy has teeth. Do you wanta see its teeth, Jade? I could show you. I could hold its mouth open till you—"

"No, honey, that's all right," Jade quickly assured the little girl. "I've seen baby puppies before."

The puppy began to squirm, trying to escape from the little girl's clutches. "Keep still, puppy," Millie ordered sharply. "He does that sometimes," she told Jade. "He don't know that he could fall and hurt himself."

"Maybe you'd better take the puppy back to its mama now," Jade suggested. "I think it may be getting hungry."

"Maybe it is." The little girl frowned down at the puppy. "Are you hungry, puppy," she inquired. "Do you want your dinner?" She looked up at Jade again. "I think it *is* hungry, but Mama told me to stay in the cabin with you. How is my puppy goin' to eat if I can't take it back to its mother. Do you think it might like a biscuit?"

"No, Millie," Jade said. "But just let me get the floor swept and I'll go to the stables with you so the puppy can be with its mama."

"Okay." The little girl plopped herself down in a chair and continued to deluge Jade with questions.

And so it had been for the past three days. Looking after the children left little time for Jade to worry about Matt, and for that she was grateful. The nights were the hardest, after the work was done and she was lying on the narrow cot, her thoughts would drift to him and the way she'd felt with her flesh against his flesh.

"Are you nearly finished now," Millie asked, jerking Jade's thoughts to the present again.

"Just nearly."

The door opened abruptly and Clara entered the cabin followed by Betsy, her eldest daughter. Immediately, Millie leaped toward her sister. "Will you go with me to the stables, Betsy? My puppy's hungry. It needs its mama."

"Go on with her, Betsy," Clara said, sinking heavily onto

the wooden rocker her husband had made her two years before. Picking up the basket of needlework always left beside it, she began to thread a needle with yarn.

When the door had closed behind the two girls, Clara said, "I hope Betsy entertains Millie for a while. That child drives me crazy with all those questions of hers." Tears suddenly misted her eyes. "I don't like being this way. I don't know what's the matter with me lately."

"Of course you know," Jade contradicted. "A woman in your condition always gets nervous when their time is as close as yours."

"I shouldn't be so nervous, though. I've already had two young'ns, Jade. You'd think havin' a babe would be natural to me by now."

"I don't think birthing the babe is what's making you nervous," Jade said softly. "I think it's waiting for the event to happen."

Clara smiled at her. "You're right, of course. You've been a godsend, Jade. You can't possibly know how much we appreciate you being here with us. Especially Bill and me. We owe you a lot."

"If a debt is owed, it is surely mine," Jade replied quickly. "I don't know what I would've done if you hadn't taken me in when you did."

"Horsefeathers!" Clara said. "You don't owe us nothing, and I don't want to hear no more of that nonsense." She frowned at Jade. "You been worryin' nights over that man of yours, haven't you, Jade?"

Jade didn't bother explaining that Matt wasn't her man, nor would he ever be. "I can't help but worry about him, Clara. It's been over a month now and I've not heard a word from him." Not that she had expected to hear, not directly anyway, but she *had* hoped to catch a word of Matt when the messenger arrived from Fort Pitt, which had been relieved by Colonel Bouquet. But there had been nothing, not one word spoken about Matt.

Jade had no way of knowing if he had survived the battle at Bushy Run. The thought that he might be dead tore at her heart.

The messenger had held them enthralled with tales of the battle that had taken place at Bushy Run. They had suffered heavy losses that day. It was said that one hundred fifteen English had either been killed or wounded, which would have been a quarter of their number. Nobody knew how many Indians had lost their lives that day, but the guess was that they'd suffered as many losses . . . or more.

The regiments had suffered no further losses when they rescued Fort Pitt. In fact, there had been no battle. The Indians had fled as they approached. It was said that Bouquet had won a great victory, that his efforts had changed the course of the war. If he had lost the battle, then Pittsburgh would soon have fallen and the war greatly prolonged. But by winning the battle, they had proven the might of the English forces. The next time Bouquet marched into the wilderness, the Indians would not be so willing to attack.

Jade continued to hunger, in vain for news of Matt. It was said there had been a few days' lull after the battle at Bushy Run before the Indians resumed their devastation along the frontier. But when they did renew the attack, they resumed with even greater savagery than before.

The Pennsylvania-Virginia frontier was experiencing a devastation worse than any suffered before, even during the French War, which had lasted for seven years.

It was said that even the New York frontier was gripped by fear.

And that fear, in the wilderness, was reflected daily in the faces of those people who took refuge behind the walls of Fort Ligonier. Even though they felt the Indian threat, life went on. Clara had her baby, another girl, and Jade delighted in bathing the babe. Even so, most of her thoughts were filled with the man she loved.

Matt, knowing Bouquet couldn't be relied on to relieve Fort Detroit, realized he must take the message to Major Gladwin.

He had been on the trail leading to Fort Detroit for one day and one night when he heard the sound of approaching footsteps and quickly took cover behind a flowering bush.

A moment later, a small band of Indians came into view.

Matt remained hidden as they approached, his gaze narrowing on the Indian who led the group. It was Scioto, LeCroix's father-in-law.

Even as he watched, the band of Indians stopped to drink from their waterskins.

The warrior nearest Scioto reached out a hand toward the chief's rifle. It was then Matt saw the long black hair dangling from the rifle barrel.

Matt sucked in a sharp breath, his gaze riveted to the scalplock. The hair looked to be at least three feet in length. His heart jerked with fear, but he told himself what he was thinking was impossible. The hair couldn't be Jade's. It had come from another head, not hers.

Sergeant Donovan never returned, an inner voice reminded. *Nor did any of the men who escorted Jade to Fort Ligonier.*

No! his heart screamed. It couldn't be true. Jade was at Fort Ligonier, safe behind its walls.

Then who does the hair belong to? the inner voice asked. *How many women have you ever seen with hair that long?*

Matt knelt there, refusing to acknowledge what he knew must be true, listening as Scioto's companion said, "You are to be envied, Scioto. The scalp is a good trophy."

He fingered the bloodied scalp on his own rifle. "Your daughter may not be happy that I have taken her husband's scalp."

Matt eyed the dark scalp on the man's rifle. He felt a great sense of satisfaction to know that Henri LeCroix was dead.

The warrior with LeCroix's scalp continued. "I will trade my scalp for yours, Scioto. The Frenchman's scalp for his woman's."

The Frenchman's woman! Matt's gaze went to the long, shiny black hair again, unable to accept what he knew must be so. Somehow, LeCroix had gotten to Jade again, had taken her back to his trading post.

No! Matt cried inwardly, refusing to accept what he was hearing, what his eyes were telling him. God, he couldn't accept such a thing! Never! He swallowed back the bile that threatened.

"My daughter should have killed the woman instead of helping her leave the trading post," Scioto said, and each word stabbed brutally into Matt's heart. "Juaheela should have known her husband would go after the woman and take her back again."

Matt squeezed his eyes shut tight, fighting back the bile that was surging upward.

"Why did Juaheela help the woman run away?" the warrior asked.

"She was afraid her husband would be angry with her if she killed the woman," Scioto replied gruffly.

His companion laughed and looked at the scalp dangling from his rifle. "She need worry no more about her husband," the warrior said.

"Nor the woman." Scioto ran his hand down the length of the long, silky hair that would have reached down to a woman's hips.

"Eeeeaaaaahhhh!" Matt's pain erupted in a terrible roar

as his hand reached for his knife. Jerking it from its sheath, he charged forward, burying the blade in Scioto's chest before the Indian had a chance to react.

As the blade struck, Scioto staggered, glaring at Matt with surprised fury. Matt twisted the blade then, making certain the man suffered before he died. And he did suffer, Matt knew. As Scioto's knees gave way beneath him, his companion leaped toward the man who'd killed his chief.

Matt lashed out with his foot, catching the man's knife hand with an uppercut. The Indian howled with pain and staggered backward. Wrenching the rifle out of Scioto's hand, Matt raced away through the forest before the other warriors could gather their wits enough to take up pursuit.

He ran then, with his heart thundering through his chest, Matt raced through the forest and along the river-bank.

Almost immediately he heard the sound of pursuit. Realizing he'd be overwhelmed by sheer numbers if they caught him, Matt headed for the river located less than a mile away. When he reached it, he wasted no time.

Sliding both rifle straps across his shoulder, he waded into the water until it swirled around his hips, then dove into its depths and swam beneath the surface as long as he could hold his breath.

When he was sure he'd lost the Indians, he swam ashore and gently removed the long ebony hair from the rifle. He buried his face in the silky locks. And then, for the first time since he was a boy of five, Matt cried.

Deep, heartrending sobs shook his entire frame as tears rolled down his cheeks, and all the while he murmured her name over and over again.

Chapter Twenty-Eight

Four months passed and, with winter dogging his heels, Pontiac lifted the siege on Fort Detroit realizing his warriors must hunt for food if their families were to survive the winter.

It was November when Matt and Badger reached the Forbes road on their way to Fort Ligonier. And several innocent-looking clouds covered the noonday sun.

Both men had been silent for some time, each busy with their own thoughts. And the only sound to mark their passing came from the horses they rode; the occasional jingle of a bridle and the clip-clop of hooves against hard ground.

As they approached the clearing where Matt and Jade had said their last good-byes, Matt's body became tense with strain.

Badger noticed the difference immediately. He glanced toward Matt's hand, the one clutching the reins, and saw the whitened knuckles. As he watched, Matt's long fingers slipped between the buttons of his buckskin shirt as they had done so many times during the past four months.

Memories of Jade filled Matt's mind as he rode past the clearing and he caressed the skein of long silky hair that lay against his heart.

Suddenly Badger swore. "Dammit, boy! You oughta bury that thing."

Matt's heart gave a sudden jerk, then picked up speed. He had no need to question Badger's words. They'd had this conversation before. "You know I can't," he rasped harshly.

And Badger *did* know. Matt couldn't bear to let go of the scalp since it was all he had left of Jade.

"It don't seem decent," Badger grumbled.

Matt didn't bother to reply.

The first snowflakes of the year began to drift lazily down and, although they melted as soon as they touched the ground, the two men hurried their pace, intent on reaching the fort quickly in case the weather changed and they found themselves caught in the middle of a full-blown blizzard.

The snow continued to fall, but in the same gentle manner and there was still no accumulation by the time they entered the fort. They had been traveling for weeks and both men were bone-weary, but, knowing how much the people inside the fort hungered for news of the war, they ignored their weariness long enough to satisfy the crowd that had gathered around them.

"Pontiac has withdrawn his warriors," Matt said, mounting the steps beside the sutler's store and taking a seat on the bench kept on the boardwalk there.

"Is it over then, Matt?" Max Wheeler asked, reaching inside his shirt pocket for the makings of a smoke.

Matt had known Max for years. He had a wife and son to worry about. "I don't think so, Max. I believe, come spring, Pontiac will renew the siege. But we've been given a reprieve. At least through the winter. Maybe Amherst can convince Parliament to send more troops before then."

"Damn Injuns," muttered a man on Matt's left. "Amherst oughta send troops to their towns and destroy ever last one of 'em. That'd show 'em a thing or two."

"Dalyell tried that. It didn't work."

"Heard Dalyell was dead," Max Wheeler said.

"He is," Badger growled. "And he took a lot of good men with him. I was with 'em that day and barely escaped with my hair."

As Badger continued his version of the battle, Matt leaned wearily against the outer wall of the store and allowed his thoughts to drift. It was a beautiful time of year, the snow drifting lazily down. Although they'd never spoken of it, Matt felt certain Jade would have loved the snow.

His gaze skimmed across the parade ground to the fort laundry as the door opened and a woman stepped out carrying a laundry basket. She stopped abruptly, obviously curious about the crowd that had gathered outside the sutler's store.

Jade.

The name drifted across his mind and Matt straightened himself, feeling a tightening in his gut. He stared at the woman who reminded him of his lost love, then silently cursed himself for doing so.

Jade.

Would he ever be able to accept her loss? he wondered. He prayed that he could, but feared he could not. If only she hadn't died in such a horrible manner, if only—

Suddenly becoming aware of the silence, Matt jerked his attention back to the present and realized everyone was staring at him expectantly.

"Your mind must be somewhere else, son," Badger told

him. "Else you'd be mighty quick to say 'thankee kindly' to Max Wheeler's invite to supper."

Matt summoned up a smile. "Guess my mind *was* wandering," he admitted. "I sure wouldn't want to pass up one of Maggie's meals."

"Then we'll look for the two of you around five," Max said with a smile. "I guess I better go tell her to set two more plates on the table."

Max left them then, obviously eager to reach his wife with the news they would be having guests for the evening meal, and when Matt looked toward the laundry again, the woman who had reminded him of Jade was no longer there.

Jade hurried into the Tucker cabin, her heart thundering loudly in her chest. It was hard to believe that after all this time Matt had finally returned.

But he had! She had seen him with her own two eyes.

Matt was alive! And, despite the words he had spoken when they parted, Matt loved her. She was certain of it. As certain of that fact as she was that, as soon as he'd briefed the fort commander on the latest news from Fort Detroit, he would seek her out.

She set the basket full of laundry in the parlor and pressed her palms against her flushed cheeks.

She would have to hurry. He would come to her soon and she wanted to look her best. She practically ran to the bedroom she shared with the girls. She had to tidy herself quickly, couldn't let him see her this way, with strands of hair escaping from the knot she'd fashioned at the nape of her neck.

How should she fix it? she wondered, seating herself before the vanity and unfastening her hair. And, God, what should she wear?

She wanted to look her best for him. Perhaps the green gown with the bodice that Clara had embroidered with green threads. The color matched her eyes exactly. She frowned at her reflection. Maybe that would be too obvious, though. Perhaps if she just brushed her hair and powdered her nose . . . No! It was a special occasion and she would treat it as such. She would wear the green gown.

She ran the brush over her hair quickly, then pulled her hair atop her head and began to arrange it in loose curls. She'd only pinned the first curl in place when she heard the front door open.

Her heart gave a sudden jerk. Could it be Matt?

Unable to stop herself, she ran into the parlor. Clara stood just inside the door, her babe clutched to her breasts, her eyes glittering.

"You already know," she accused.

Jade didn't bother being evasive. "Yes. I know." Unable to contain her excitement, she clutched her hands over her breasts and swung around and around amidst a swirl of skirts. "I can't believe it, Clara," she cried. "He's alive and he's here!"

"And you're obviously not ready to see him," Clara chided gently. "Not with your hair looking like that. And that dress. I do declare—It's the old blue one I gave you when you first come to stay with us."

"I was going to wear the green one," Jade admitted. "But I wanted to put my hair up first."

"Leave it loose," Clara advised, bending to put the babe in her cradle. Men usually like to see a woman's hair long and hanging down her back."

"He does like it loose," Jade admitted. "I just thought since this was a special occasion . . ."

"Leave it loose," Clara advised.

"Do you think I should go to him or wait for him to come here?" Jade mused. A sudden thought occurred and she pressed her hands against her flushed cheeks. "Maybe he doesn't know where I'm staying!"

"If he doesn't already know, he can find out soon enough. The fort's not that big, Jade. And no, I wouldn't go to him," Clara said, answering Jade's question. "It wouldn't be seemly. He's the man. He should come here to see you. That's the proper way of it."

Jade didn't care about the proper way. She just wanted to see Matt as quickly as possible. It had been so long since they'd been together. Months. And during that time she didn't know whether he was alive or dead.

But the waiting was over now! It was finally over. Hurrying back to the bedroom, Jade slipped out of the worn gown and into the new green one. Then, after brushing her hair and tying it back with a green ribbon that exactly matched her gown, she settled down by the window to wait.

Matt ate the last bite of his pumpkin pie before refusing another piece. "I'm gonna have to say no, Maggie, bad as I hate to do it. My stomach has been empty so long, it's objecting to so much food at once."

"Mine is, too, but I ain't gonna listen," Badger said gruffly, holding out his plate for another piece of pie. "No tellin' when I'll have another chance like this. Pumpkin' pies ain't easy to find where I'm goin'."

"You're not leaving so soon?" Maggie inquired quickly. "You two just got here. I thought sure you'd stay around for a while. At least a few days."

"Not me," Badger said. "I got my traps to run whilst the Injuns is busy feedin' their families. Reckon I can have a load of beaver pelts back East afore spring comes."

"What about you, Matt?" Max asked. "Are you moving on with Badger?"

"I'll be moving on," Matt admitted, idly twirling the spoon beside his plate. "But we're going different directions."

"You're going east then?"

"Yeah," Matt said. "It's been a long time since I left home. More'n a year now. And the cabin my folks built is sure to be needing some work done on it."

"Has it been settin' empty all this time?" Maggie asked.

"Yeah. A neighbor's been keeping an eye on the place, but he don't have the time to continue doing it. Sure would hate for the roof to fall through." Yeah. He would hate that. The old homeplace was all that was left of his parents. His fingers slid between the buttons on his shirt and caressed the silky hair that had been Jade's.

It's important to have something left. a silent voice said.

Matt was conscious of Badger's frowning disapproval as he continued to caress the ebony locks that curled over his heart. He was used to the old man's looks and paid no attention to him.

Realizing Badger had finished his pie, Matt pushed his chair back from the table. And, after complimenting his hostess on the excellent meal she had provided and promising to return the next evening, he excused himself and followed Badger across the parade ground to the barracks where the men slept.

Jade lay abed and stared at the ceiling. Her heart felt like a shriveled knot inside her chest. It was past midnight now, and although she had waited and waited, Matt hadn't come to her.

Instead, he had taken supper in the Wheelers' cabin.

Even after she'd been told he'd gone there, Jade continued to wait. He would come, she told herself. He must!

But he had not.

She had seen the two men leave the cabin, had watched from the window as they had crossed the parade ground to the barracks. Even then she had waited, sitting there watching for hours until finally she realized he wouldn't be coming.

It was then she accepted the fact that whatever feeling Matt might have once had for her was completely gone. There was nothing left between them.

Only her love had endured the separation.

The next few days were hard for Jade. She went about her work with a quiet despondency. When Clara tried to cheer her up, she would deny her feelings. "I'm perfectly all right, Clara. Don't worry so much about me."

But she wasn't all right. At night she would use her pillow to muffle her sobs.

Her misery was so complete that, ever since the day Matt arrived, she hadn't wandered far from the cabin. Instead, she busied herself with inside chores, looking after the baby and ironing, mending everything that had the slightest tear in it.

That was her occupation the day the door suddenly burst open. Jerking to her feet, Jade saw Matt standing in the doorway, staring at her as though she had suddenly grown two heads.

She dropped the sock she was mending and backed away, suddenly afraid of him. "What do you want?" she gasped.

Every muscle in his body was tense and he was leaner than she remembered.

"What do I want?" he bellowed, his eyes glittering wildly. "What in hell do you think I want, Jade?"

"I don't know," she said meekly.

"When I think of all the months I suffered. All the *hell* I endured because of because of . . . My God! And you stand there calmly and ask me what I want!" He kicked the door shut and moved toward her, his gaze never once leaving hers.

"You—you're not making sense," she said, stepping back uncertainly.

"I'm not making sense." He shot her a look of pure disgust. "Dammit, woman! *You're* the one who's not making sense."

Jade stood trembling before him, wondering what had made him so hysterical. When he took more steps toward her, she moved back again, trying to keep some distance between them.

"What are you so upset about?" she asked.

"Upset?" he sneered sarcastically. "Who's upset?"

"You seem to be."

"I've been here for days, Jade!" he reminded grimly. "Four of them. And you haven't once been near me."

"You haven't been near me, either."

His long fingers slid between the buttons of his shirt and pulled out a hank of long black hair. She stared at it, wondering what it was. *"This* is the reason I didn't come to you, Jade. Now what in hell was *your* reason."

He threw the hank of hair at her and it struck her in the middle of the chest. Horror surged forth then and Jade screamed, jerking backward while she stared at the grisly thing that had fallen to the floor at her feet.

"Wh-what is it?" she whispered unsteadily, her gaze riveted to the long black locks clinging to the piece of scalp.

He gritted the ugly answer between clenched teeth.

Matt began to pace the floor like a caged animal, stopping occasionally to throw a stony look in her direction.

"W-Whose s-scalp is it?" she stammered meekly, knowing it must have some kind of significance.

"I don't know!" he roared, his eyes locking onto hers again. "But, dammit all, Jade! I've thought for months that it was yours."

"Mine?" Her heart picked up speed and her pulse began to pound heavily through her veins. "You thought that was mine? That it had been taken from my—my—"

"Yes." He stopped pacing and pulled her against him. There was a harshness in his grip that spoke of feelings he was trying hard to suppress. With her head resting against his chest, she could hear the heavy pounding of his heart. "Thank God I was wrong, Jade. Thank God that damned thing wasn't yours!"

She could feel him shudder against her. And, although she didn't really understand what was going on, Jade knew she was where she wanted to be, held firmly in his embrace with the sweet musky scent of him filling her nostrils.

Closing her eyes, Jade lifted her face and felt his lips covering hers in a kiss so hungry that it took her breath away.

When he raised his head, she opened her eyes to find him staring down at her with such an agonized expression that she was compelled to cup his face between her palms.

"Oh, God, Jade," he whispered unsteadily. "I can't believe you're here. I can't believe that you're really alive." He clutched her shoulders and pushed her slightly apart from him. His eyes began to glitter again. "Why in hell didn't you let me know you were here?"

"But you knew, Matt. You saw me the day you arrived. I had just left the laundry and you looked straight at me."

"It *was* you."

"Yes. And it wouldn't have been proper for me to go to you," she said quietly. "I waited a long time that night. But when you didn't come . . . and then the days dragged on and you still—" She broke off, staring at him with hurt eyes. "Why didn't you come, Matt? Why did you wait so long?"

"Because I didn't know you were here. I thought you

were dead, Jade. Dammit, I thought that scalp belonged to you!"

"Me!" she squeaked, looking at the hank of black hair laying on the floor. "You thought *that* was mine, and you carried it around with you? Like some kind of trophy?"

"I thought it was all I had left of you." He shuddered against her. "I wanted to die."

Large tears gathered in Jade's eyes and fell slowly down her cheeks. Matt kissed her again, kissed her neck, her eyes, her nose, then his lips returned to her mouth as he pressed moist kisses anywhere he could reach.

She began to sob then, great tearing sobs that shook her body like a reed in the wind and he stood there, holding her tightly.

"Ah, little one, please don't cry," he whispered huskily.

But Jade couldn't stop crying. No matter how hard she tried to control herself. When her sobbing finally ceased, she looked up at him, examining every inch of his dear, beloved face. "Are you all right, Matt?" she asked shakily. "Are you really and truly all right?"

"Yes. Now that you're in my arms, I'm really and truly all right. Everything is fine again."

"Oh, Matt, I'm so sorry. I know you were angry with me before and you had every right to be." She knew she was babbling but couldn't stop herself. "I couldn't stand it when you left me like that. Just rode away and never once looked back at me. It's been horrible, Matt. Horrible. I didn't know if you were dead or alive and when I thought about—"

"Shhh." He put a finger across her lips to stop the flow of words. "Don't talk, little one. Just let me look at you. Do you know how very much I love you, Jade?"

"You do?" she cried, her eyes shining with wonder. "I was afraid you had come to hate me."

"Never, sweetheart. I knew, from the first moment we met. I knew."

"Knew what?" she asked softly.

"That you were my destiny."

"And you mine, Matt."

Resting her head down against Matt's chest, she uttered a silent prayer that God had seen fit to send her to these distant shores. He must have known she would find contentment in her savage destiny.

Author's Note

Pontiac's warriors were scattered beyond the reach of his influence that winter of 1763. And, during that time the Lake Indians had time to reflect on their situation. Since they inhabited the richest fur-bearing lands, they would be the ones to suffer more if they were successful in driving the English away. If the English were gone, then how could they trade for the coveted goods only the white man could provide?

A peace faction began to form among them, arguing the merits of coming to terms with the English. The Seneca were among that group. They were the tribe most exposed to English attack.

Meanwhile, Pontiac appealed to the French for help in defeating the English. They turned him away. Although they had needed Indian help in their war against the English, they had been bitterly defeated and had no intention of going to war again.

In the spring of 1764, Pontiac renewed the attack on

Fort Detroit, but with fewer warriors behind him. Even so, Detroit was firmly cut off from the rest of the world as the second year of Pontiac's war began.

Colonel Henry Bouquet returned east and began to gather another army, designed to end the siege at Detroit. But it wasn't until October 3, 1764, that his preparations were sufficient to justify the risk of advancing into the center of Indian territory.

His army of five hundred regulars were flanked by hundreds of frontiersmen, all skilled in woods fighting. They marched at a deliberate pace, averaging eight or nine miles a day, they advanced inexorably toward the towns of the Shawnee, Delaware, and Mingo. Those tribes became more apprehensive each day, knowing they could expect no help from Pontiac, who continued his siege at Detroit.

The army continued their advance, crossing the Muskingum. In late November they were only a few miles from the Indian's principal towns. The Indians realized they must either leave their homes and the supplies they had set by for the coming winter . . . or they must negotiate peace.

They chose the latter.

Bouquet demanded the return of all white prisoners. The Indians protested, but in the end gave way.

Bouquet returned to Pittsburgh on November 28. He had not fought a battle but he had subjected himself to every risk of battle and had won a solid victory.

On December 5, Governor Penn proclaimed the end of the war.

But he was wrong. It was not until late August of 1765 that Pontiac agreed to a peace treaty. Only then was the siege at Detroit lifted and the war with Pontiac—which lasted two and a half years—finally came to an end.

* * *

If you would like a bookmark please send a self-addressed, stamped envelope to BETTY BROOKS c/o Kensington Publishing, 850 Third Avenue. New York, N.Y. 10022.

ROMANCE FROM JO BEVERLY

DANGEROUS JOY	(0-8217-5129-8, $5.99)
FORBIDDEN	(0-8217-4488-7, $4.99)
THE SHATTERED ROSE	(0-8217-5310-X, $5.99)
TEMPTING FORTUNE	(0-8217-4858-0, $4.99)

Available wherever paperbacks are sold, or order direct from the Publisher. Send cover price plus 50¢ per copy for mailing and handling to Penguin USA, P.O. Box 999, c/o Dept. 17109, Bergenfield, NJ 07621. Residents of New York and Tennessee must include sales tax. DO NOT SEND CASH.

ROMANCE FROM FERN MICHAELS

DEAR EMILY   (0-8217-4952-8, $5.99)

WISH LIST   (0-8217-5228-6, $6.99)

AND IN HARDCOVER:

VEGAS RICH   (1-57566-057-1, $25.00)

WATCH FOR THESE REGENCY ROMANCES

BREACH OF HONOR   (0-8217-5111-5, $4.50)
by Phylis Warady

DeLACEY'S ANGEL   (0-8217-4978-1, $3.99)
by Monique Ellis

A DECEPTIVE BEQUEST   (0-8217-5380-0, $4.50)
by Olivia Sumner

A RAKE'S FOLLY   (0-8217-5007-0, $3.99)
by Claudette Williams

AN INDEPENDENT LADY   (0-8217-3347-8, $3.95)
by Lois Stewart